THE JEWELLED HAND

THE JEWELLED HAND

and Other Tales of Mystery and the Macabre

Lionel Sparrow

Edited and with an introduction by
JAMES DOIG

VALANCOURT BOOKS

CONTENTS

INTRODUCTION

Lionel Sparrow was an Australian journalist and newspaper proprietor who wrote more than two dozen horror and crime short stories for the national periodical, *The Australian Journal*, and for local newspapers in Victoria. Never well known even during his lifetime, Sparrow deserves recognition as one of the first Australian writers who wrote mainly in the Gothic mode, and more generally as a significant writer of tales of horror and the macabre—his stories are often set in exotic locations and his plots are over-wrought, dripping with atmosphere.

Lionel Sparrow was born in 1867 in the small Murray River town of Wahgunyah, situated about 300 kilometres north-east of Melbourne, and was the eldest of six children, one of whom died in infancy. His father, Isaac, was American, born in Minerva, Essex County, New York. On 6 October 1866 at the House of William Otter in Rutherglen, Victoria, Isaac, 37 years old and a miner by trade, married Louisa Helena Brown, who was born in London and 25 years old. He died in Wallsend, NSW, 1894, and Louisa died in Melbourne. She was described a "dressmaker" and is buried in a pauper's grave at St. Kilda Cemetery. Lionel seems to have been living with her at St. Kilda when she died.

Sparrow began his long association with newspapers in Newcastle, where he started an apprenticeship at the age of 14, and worked in Sydney, Melbourne, and Sunbury. In 1911, after working on the *Riponshire Advocate* for six years, he moved to Linton, a Victorian mining town about 150 kilometres east of Melbourne, where he lived for the remainder of his life. He bought the local newspaper, the *Grenville Standard*, and retained it until his death. He married Alice Eliza Miller in 1904, and they had three children, two daughters, Mamie and Una, and a son, Geoffrey, who followed his father into journalism and became federal president of the Australian Journalists Association.

From all accounts, Lionel was a quiet, self-effacing man, small in stature (about 5'4"), but generous and well regarded. He was very involved in the life of Linton as, among other things, a vestryman and church warden at St. Paul's Anglican Church, a founding member and president of the Linton Dramatic Club, and a founding member of the Old Lintonians Association, which first met on 9 October 1913.

At the time of his death on 9 April 1936, he was described by one of the locals in the *Grenville Standard* as a "go ahead little man" always in the vanguard of progress. A notice in the *Grenville Standard* following his death tells us something of Sparrow's interests and character:

> Had Lionel Sparrow's ambition matched his intellect, he would have won lasting fame in the field of literature. But his soul was too big to desire worldly greatness and the envy it provokes. He was content, after providing for the needs of those dependent upon him and his own wants, to enjoy the works of his favourite authors rather than seek to emulate them.
>
> With kindred spirits he was always ready to discuss what he considered 'worth-while' subjects, and rarely failed to impress them with the breadth of his knowledge and the length of his mental vision. He possessed a fund of quiet, but genuine humor, which harmed none and entertained many.
>
> Had Mr Sparrow chosen to widen his sphere, he could, on several occasions, have sold the *Standard* and gone where his talents would have been more widely appreciated; but he preferred to remain at Linton. As he often remarked to the writer of this tribute to his merits, the place suited him, and he liked the people—so why change? He made many friends and had no enemies.

He had literary aspirations, and apart from the stories he wrote for *The Australian Journal*, he also published poems in the celebrated Australian literary journal *The Bulletin*, twenty-four of which were collected into a slim volume, *Poems*, under the byline "Ignotus." During the 1890s Lionel Sparrow also wrote stories and serials for the *Sunbury News and Bulla and Melton Advertiser*. Some of these were reprints from stories published in the *Australian Journal* with slightly altered titles, such as "The Wrestler of Tokio" and "The

Mystery of Mervale," but others appear to be first and only publications, such as the serials, "The Tragedy at Waritungah" and "The Loss of the 'Black Swan.'"

The stories he wrote for *The Australian Journal* were clearly influenced by the "sensational" type of fiction that was popular at the time, in Australia represented in particular by Marcus Clarke, whose *Sensational Tales* was published in 1886. However, the writer whose work most directly inspired his own was Edgar Allan Poe. Sparrow clearly delighted in tales of mystery and the macabre and he showed unusual inventiveness in his grisly and morbid plots. A typical example is the "The Jewelled Hand," which appeared in the August 1887 issue of *The Australian Journal*, when Sparrow was nineteen. This story is a grand guignol Gothic horror story featuring an ingenious decapitation machine that would not look out of place in a Roger Corman film. Set in Spain, the tale features a narrator who reveals his increasing obsession with decapitation and whether or not will remains in the mind after severance. This leads him to construct a machine for decapitating human beings, which he uses to murder his closest friend, Don Alvaro, a man of great mind and willpower, who proves the theory by obtaining posthumous revenge.

A series of gothic melodramas followed, which were published in quick succession in 1888. It seems reasonable to assume that Sparrow wrote the stories as a group and then sought publication—certainly they are very similar in theme and style. In "The Torture of the Clock," set in underground vaults, presumably in Europe, the narrator is cruelly tortured by the evil Zaroni who is himself destroyed by the fate prepared for his victim. "The Tenant of the Third Cell" is about a father's thirst for vengeance against the rejected suitor who poisoned his daughter and nephew the week before their wedding. When he catches up with the murderer he is more than satisfied to discover him hideously deformed by leprosy. What is particularly striking about these stories is their excessiveness—we have violent murder, mutilation, disfiguring disease, and torture (both physical and psychological). Take for example, the following description of a sword fight in "In the North Wing," which occurs after the mad Sir Phillip Margrave has plucked out the eyes of Lady Alice Tremaine:

It was not a duel which ensued. It was a fight of madmen—a mutual butchery. There was no attempt at defence on either side. Each struck blindly at the other, and every blow, every thrust, took effect. In a few seconds both combatants, pierced in twenty places and bathed in blood, rolled on the marble floor. Sir Phillip Margrave, as he fell, breathed his last. But Cyril Vere-hurst lived some moments; that is to say, long enough to feel the embrace of the Lady Alice, who had seized the Damascus sword which her hand, groping about, had touched, and had plunged it into her breast. And then, falling upon the body of her lover, she mingled her last sigh with his.

Others may have been influenced by the decadent literature of the day. Consider the following paragraph from "Irene":

I looked upon her as she lay, still, and white, and cold. Her beauty had always been great, but now there seemed in it a very pronounced, though indefinable, weirdness that rendered it almost superhuman to my eyes, and I shuddered as I thought how soon would this matchless handicraft of nature be the food of the worm. For many minutes I stood gazing at the motionless face, the closed lids, the heavy raven hair, the slender but exquisitely moulded arms, the delicately perfect outlines of the bosom. I had been suffering acutely, and my nerves were highly strung by excessive draughts of laudanum. It may be that I uttered some wild words, for I have an indistinct remembrance of an agitation of some sort within the room; however, I was led away, and found myself next morning in my own chamber.

Another *fin de siècle* tale is "Seagram's Manuscript," published in October 1895, which is an opium tale. In the story the narrator obtains a manuscript from a former friend within a few weeks of his death in an opium den. It reveals his intense depression after his sister's death and the terrible dreams haunting him in which he murders his closest friend, who was his sister's fiancé. In an obsessed dreamlike state he kills him and for a time finds relief because the dreams stop. However, he is soon haunted by guilt—opium gives him ease and the sleep which he once again craves.

Sparrow published stories regularly throughout the early 1890s, but after 1895 his output slowed considerably as his life became centred on his journalism and newspaper work. However, he did publish the occasional tale, such as "The Lady with the Veil," which appeared in *The Australian Journal* in June 1903. This is a bizarre revenge story in which the narrator, a wealthy man, has a hereditary disease that manifests itself in an abhorrence of perfumes, particularly patchouli.

Almost from the start of his writing career Sparrow mixed his Gothic stories with adventure and crime tales, some of which had an Australian setting. The first of these was "The Glass Dagger," a crime romance about a woman who falls in love with the brother of a convicted forger who is transported to Australia. Some of these stories, like the Gothic tales, have exotic locations—"A Tale of Tokio," for example, is a strange story about a failed Japanese wrestler's obsessive hatred of the narrator, a westerner, who only manages to escape his murderous intentions through the intervention of an earthquake. "The Purple Death," published in August 1906, is set in Melbourne and is an unusual melodrama. The narrator makes the acquaintance of the brilliant and saturnine Dr Wainwright, a scientist and rival for the affections of Marie Seymour. Wainwright kidnaps him and attempts to drive him insane through an experiment where he is locked in a room and continually exposed to the color purple.

His later stories were published at irregular intervals in *The Australian Journal*. He abandoned the excessive Gothic trappings of his earlier tales and introduced occult/psychic elements from Eastern religions, perhaps influenced by Theosophy.

His last horror story, "The Vengeance of the Dead," is a vampire story set in Melbourne, which again has a strong flavour of Eastern mysticism. Martin Calthorpe, an occultist, dies mysteriously as does his wife soon afterwards of a wasting disease. Before long, the narrator's sister, Winnie, falls ill and dies, and his other sister, Connie, starts to decline. The narrator and Connie's fiancé, Harry Thornton, an adept in the mystical arts, seek the help of Ravanna Dâs, a Hindu Brahman, who reveals that Calthorpe was a black magician whose spirit left its physical remains to pray on the living for sustenance.

How were Sparrow's Gothic stories received by their readers? That the stories continued to be published suggests they were well received and that there was a demand for them. Nevertheless, at least one of the stories prompted a critical letter to the editor. The editor, William Smith Mitchell, responded to the reader's comment on "The Torture of the Clock" as follows:

> We regret that you [W. Neale] could discover neither "sense nor meaning" in the story "The Torture of the Clock," of a recent issue of the journal. The tale appeared to us as complete, to thoroughly explain itself, and to be of a highly interesting character. The abrupt commencement to which you probably refer—where the incident is at once related without introduction—appears to be a characteristic of the author. It is suggested that you have not read the tale with care, especially as regards the opening.

Mitchell was the editor of *The Australian Journal* throughout Sparrow's literary career, and it is certainly conceivable that he encouraged Sparrow's writing and directed him into other genres, styles and plots. Sparrow's work as proprietor of the *Grenville Standard* prevented him from developing as a writer of sensational fiction. This is to be regretted as his tales are a cut above the standard popular fiction of the time, both in terms of the quality of his prose and in the often exotic and bizarre nature of his plots.

The obituary and notices that appeared in the *Grenville Standard* after Sparrow's death do not mention Sparrow's Gothic stories at all, rather they focus on his journalism and his verse, and his great contribution to the community in which he lived. Perhaps they were considered too grisly or horrific to mention; certainly, they would have appeared out of character for the mild-mannered little man of "quiet and friendly disposition" and "high literary and musical tastes." The stories reveal a creative and passionate imagination and they should be more widely known.

JAMES DOIG
Australian Capital Territory, 2025

THE JEWELLED HAND

B ut I swear to you, señors, that you are mistaken—utterly mistaken—in your conviction of my insanity. If I have spoken no word throughout this long tribunal—if I have remained insensible to the questions and demands of you, my judges—it has been solely from horror of my terrible crime, or rather of the appalling circumstances attending the commission and the concealment of that crime. You think I am mad; you cannot conceive, you cannot realise that anyone in the possession of reason could be so utterly lost as to commit such a deed as mine. You search in vain for a motive—for even a *possible* motive and, finding none, imagining none, you say that I must be mad, and, being mad, you would suffer me to live. But I tell you, señors, life to me now is a horror—death means rest. I prefer death. Therefore I will relate to you, in so succinct and so precise a manner, all the details of my fearful crime that you will assuredly end by pronouncing me sane and fit to undergo the direct penalty of the tribunal.

You know that the unfortunate Don Alvaro was my friend—my companion. You know that he was dear to me as a brother—and perhaps dearer than a brother. Yet bear in mind, señors, that I did not *love* him as a brother; for I have never loved a human being. I respected Don Alvaro—respected and admired him—chiefly for the grand, the matchless power of his great mind—and also for the immense knowledge and the wonderful memory he possessed. But that wonderful mind, that resistless will, endeared him to me most. It was but seldom that I saw the full force of this will displayed; it may be—indeed, I believe—that its *full force* was never displayed until——

But you are impatient, señors; I must speak plainly and precisely, as I promised. Yet, it will be necessary for me to impress upon your mind the vast difference that existed between Don Alvaro and myself. His great power of will rendered all objects easy of attainment; there was nothing he could desire which his will was inadequate to reach; but his desires were few and simple, because his mind was so high and great and powerful—because he used his iron will to govern, not others, but himself. My own character was of a different order; my mind, though intellectual, possessed no force—though it could concentrate itself at times;—it was excessively imaginative, and the gift of a true imagination confers a pleasure which is perennial and exhaustless. This I know, by the memory of my youthful existence. But, many years ago, I experienced an adventure of such a fearful nature—I suffered the torture of such appalling moral horrors—that my nerves were unstrung for ever; and that vivid imagination which had once been a pleasure to me was now twisted and warped out of all semblance to its former self, and I became a prey to the most morbid fancies—I became slave to the most terrible nervous horrors, frightful conjurings of a diseased imagination. This pitiable state of my mind, increasing with each new day, would, beyond a doubt, have been fatal to my reason, had it not been for the restraining and soothing influence of my friend's society. With this being near me, life became a possibility, and at times even tolerable: I was saved by him from becoming a maniac. Don Alvaro himself, I believe, never suspected the real extent of my nervous malady; my horrible imaginings were unknown to him, as to others. The sensitive soul within me shrank from the thought of another knowing the dread secrets of my wild and perverted imagination. Don Alvaro merely thought that my nerves were weak and easily irritated; his knowledge extended no further than that—so assiduously (though how painfully) did I conceal from him my true state.

Doubtless, señors, you find me circumlocutory and tiring; yet bear with me, for now that I have explained, or tried to explain to you my mental condition, I shall be more able to proceed with my narration of the remarkable circumstances attending my crime and self-conviction.

Once, at night, I was engaged in conversation with my friend. Then it was that the first link of a fatal chain of events was forged.

Don Alvaro was showing me a curious antique vase of glass when suddenly—perhaps on account of some sudden change in the atmosphere—it snapped at its slenderest part, and the upper portion fell to the floor.

"How strange!" exclaimed my friend, "did you not notice, José, how singularly the top parted from the rest—cleft, as it seemed, by some invisible blow."

"Yes," I replied, my morbid imagination conjuring up a weird simile. "It fell as falls the head of the criminal when severed from the body by the axe of the executioner."

"Ah!" said my friend, "that is a singular way of illustrating the breaking of a vase. But," he added after a long pause, "your metaphor has brought before my mind something I must have read many years ago, for I remember it but dimly—and yet it would doubtless interest you, who revel in the science of physiology."

I listened eagerly, with an intense interest not to be accounted for even by the fact that it was my own especial and favourite study which was concerned in what my friend was about to disclose. I held my breath as Alvaro continued:—

"It was a discussion—an argument—between two notable physicians; and the question was whether for a moment after the head is entirely separated from the body, the faculties of the mind do or do not retain their seat—whether the brain ceases its functions immediately the blow has been struck which severs the neck. One of the disputants, I think, maintained that, so far from any doubt existing, it is impossible for the brain to cease its working *immediately*, unless the executioner blunders in his task. But the other learned man ridiculed the theory, averring that, even if the *brain* did live for a second or two after the neck was severed (which, however, he by no means admitted), most certainly the *consciousness of the mind* could never exist for the merest fraction of a second. Now, my own opinion, José, is that this moment of consciousness after decapitation must necessarily depend on the vitality of the victim, his strength of mind, and the facility with which the headsman accomplishes the work. But I see you are distressed by this frightful reasoning, this terrible speculation. Let us dismiss the subject."

And the subject was dismissed—from *his* mind; from my own it could never—never be driven. There were two reasons why the question should impress my mind so deeply. The first was that my imagination, as you know, had become diseased, perverted, warped, so that such a weird subject could not fail to retain a place within it; the second reason was that the study of physiology, which had in earlier years formed my chief intellectual pleasure, had now grown into a morbid passion—almost a monomania. In my researches—remember this, señors—I spared nothing to ensure success. Hitherto, by wealth, assiduity, daring, and perchance a superior science, I had overcome all difficulties. No means did I consider unscrupulous to attain my end, for that attainment was in me a passion, which I had no will to curb, nor even desire to resist. Doubtless you know, or you have heard of, the great physiological discoveries that I have made. Well, there are others, in the darker and more unknown shades of the science, stupendous, incredible, which I have not ventured to give to an unbelieving world, but which will be found in my cabinet when I am dead.

Señors, I feared, with a deadly fear, the idea which Don Alvaro had promulgated in my mind. I tried to loathe it as horrible, and I tried to ridicule it as absurd, and not worthy of solution. I feared the idea, on account of a terrible, yet indefinable, foreboding of evil which filled my soul. But all my efforts to forget it were futile—and they were worse, in that they increased the horrible suggestiveness of the thought—the irresistible, and at first undefined, *longing* that seized upon my disordered mind—the gloom of the vistas of terrible speculation through which my sere imagination, delighting in the pursuit of unknown horrors, wandered slowly.

And at length I could deceive myself no longer. No longer could I disguise the fact that what I desired with so ardent, so nervous a desire, was, in dread truth, the solution of that hideous mystery involved in the question which my friend had propagated. I longed with a frenzied, resistless longing that I had never yet known, to satisfy myself whether the power of thought could live, even for one second, after decapitation. Day after day, night after night, this terrible longing burnt within me, torturing me like glowing fires.

And now, impelled by the desire, I began gradually to reflect, to plot, to *prepare*.

I started by persuading myself that the thing was impossible, that the end to which my infamously audacious desire urged me was unattainable. And I said—"I will, however, imagine it to be really possible, and I will make the preparations I would make were it possible. It will amuse me, and, perchance, even appease my longing."

And I set about the task.

I procured a long, straight, finely-tempered sword. I rendered the blade, by constant sharpening, keen as the finest razor. Then I enclosed it in a velvet sheath, through which the air could not penetrate, and locked it securely in a strong bureau. This done I searched among my art-possessions, and found an ebony casket, upon which a great painter had set the seal of his genius. I stood this box against the wall, and measured its height. Half an inch below its summit I made a hole in the wainscoting, in which I fixed a knob, very small, which projected a quarter of an inch, and which the lid of the box, when raised, would press inwards. I now removed two or three planks of the oaken wainscot, disclosing a space sufficient for my purpose. Then—but there is no need to detail so minutely all my proceedings. Suffice it to say that after many days—for I prolonged my task as much as possible—there was in the wall, about eighteen inches above the box, a long, narrow, horizontal slit, concealed by a thin strip of paper, coloured like the oak. And in this narrow aperture, ready to flash forth, the sword was hidden. I had contrived that it should revolve upon a pivot at the hilt, with which was connected a most powerful steel spring. The point of the blade was held in its place by a strong lever, the withdrawal of which would release the spring, and the keen blade would describe a half-circle with resistless force just above the casket. The heavy tapestry of the apartment I had here drawn aside, just sufficiently to be clear of the circuit of the sword. And round about the box were scattered soft cushions, which had all the appearance of having been thrown there carelessly.

All was now prepared.

For what?

Many—many hours I passed in contemplating the deadly engine I had constructed; I pondered long upon my work. The "preparations" which I had said would amuse me and appease my ghastly longing, were now completed, and what was the result? You may guess, señors, I longed more intensely than ever. There was nothing now to do but lure the victim to that chamber of death, induce him to kneel before the casket, and to raise the lid, and so spring the hellish machine. The keen blade would dart forth, describe its flashing circle, and the head would roll softly among the cushions placed there for the purpose of breaking or annulling the force of its fall. I would be present—I would be standing quite close—I would watch the head as it fell—I would fix my eyes upon those of the head, and from their expression I would be able to divine if thought yet reigned within.

And now came the important question of the victim—who was to be the victim?

I swear to you, señors, that at that moment the thought of sacrificing my dearest friend was as far from my mind as it had been a month—a year before. Then whom did I condemn to be the victim of the experiment? I will tell you—and believe me, señors—it was *myself*. Many times before had I contemplated suicide, and now, as I pondered over my plan, it seemed to me that to die for science was glorious—heroic. I had almost decided—would to heaven I *had* decided!—when two difficulties, till then unthought of, presented themselves to my mind, and both were insurmountable. In the first place, unless a witness were present (which was not to be thought of), it would be obviously impossible to leave any record by which science could be apprised of the results. The second difficulty was even more important:—How could I be at all certain, that my power of will was such as to render the theory even possible, if I put that theory into practice by sacrificing myself? I felt that my mind would succumb more easily than that of any average individual. This thought was suggested by the words of Don Alvaro himself:—"I think that this moment of consciousness after decapitation must necessarily depend upon the vitality of the victim, his strength of mind, and the facility with which the headsman accomplishes the work."

Now, among all my acquaintance who possessed the greatest vitality—the greatest will?

Don Alvaro.

I shuddered at the obvious reply.

Yet it was so. It could not be gainsaid. If Don Alvaro became the victim the result of the experiment might be considered as decisive. If *his* mind were extinguished by the stroke of the sword—if *his* will did not survive decapitation—then the theory fell to the ground. The thing was impossible.

In fact, if the experiment was to be made it must be made upon my dearest friend—a man who trusted, and perhaps even loved me. I felt fear and abhorrence at the thought; yet it was not the idea of punishment in this world or another that made me pause. I could avoid earthly retribution, and in the Christians' hereafter I had no belief. But to lure to his death a man who had been my only friend for many years—who could not think ill of me—whose trust in me was unbounded, to do this clashed with the instincts of old-time chivalry that was in me. Had I been able to procure another victim in the same degree fitted for the experiment, would I then have hesitated an instant? No.

But I swore that Don Alvaro should *not* be sacrificed. Yet how could I prevent it? I could not warn him against myself, and put him on his guard, because I could not confess to him the base treachery to which I had been tempted.

At length I said:—"I will end all. I will seek that rest for which I have so long sighed—I will die. This deadly machine will suffice to accomplish the act."

And with this intention I advanced towards the box, knelt before it, and placed my hands firmly on the lid.

As I was about to raise it a footfall sounded on the threshold. It was a step that I knew.

I sprang up quickly, and confronted Don Alvaro himself, who had entered the room, followed by his little pet monkey, Juan. I had not seen him for a few days, and he greeted me with heartiness, embracing me affectionately, as was his wont. But I could not return that warm embrace.

He was in high spirits, and talked gaily and loud, not noting my own coldness and painful abstraction.

A few minutes after his entrance his glance fell upon the cushions on the floor, and he spoke jestingly of my carelessness. Then, for the first time, he noticed the box, and the painting on the lid struck his artistic eye. He began to admire it.

"Ha!" he exclaimed, "whose work is that? I must know the artist. I seem to recognise the genius of the design." And then he advanced towards the casket. A cold sweat stood on my brow.

"That," I stammered in a choking voice, intending now to warn him of the true character of the casket, "that is—it is—I have been merely amusing myself—the lid—do not——"

"What!" cried Don Alvaro, "did you paint that? Oh, come, José, do not tell me that it is your own work?"

And he sprang forward, fell lightly on his knee before the casket, and looked closely at the painting. And now all things reeled around me. I could not move—still less could I speak. I was conscious that Don Alvaro was saying something, but I heard not his words—only a confused murmur, as of many distant voices. But I could see, and, oh, with what distinctness! My eyes devoured his every movement. I followed his hands as they wandered over the lid, doubtless, in explanation of whatever words he was speaking. I saw them at length rest upon the side of the lid.

And then, of a sudden, there came over me that hellish desire—that ghastly longing. It came with a rush, and I waited—it seemed for hours—waited the *solution of the problem!* Ah, the anguish of suspense! My heart forbore to beat, my eyes almost started from their sockets.

The hands of Don Alvaro began to raise the lid. I suffered a concentrated agony. I wished to cry out to him in warning; I wished to rush forward and drag him from that fatal box; but I could do neither, for the whole action of my being seemed suddenly suspended. And now higher and higher rose the lid—higher, and *still higher!* Great God! would the stroke never come?

There came at length a sound—a sound that I *felt* rather than heard—a horrible thrilling *whur-r-s-sh*. It was the rush of the sword in its lightning circuit.

I sprang forward. I saw the head sink to the cushions. The eyes were turned towards me, like the dying eyes of a Cæsar. I fixed my own upon them, and I knew by a single glance that in that ghastly object—that in that gory trunkless head—there lived a mind, a will, a thought.

The eyes, at first, had an inquiring light in their gleaming depths. But in a second that had vanished; doubtless the expression of my own made it vanish.

And then their gaze concentrated itself; they burned—they flashed—they dilated; they pierced my inmost soul with their mute but deadly reproach.

And now a most appalling thing happened.

After decapitation, the body had sunk down on the cushions, turning half round with the force of the fell blow, and leaning against the box, almost in a sitting posture.

The eyes of the head, after bending their fierce light upon me for perhaps a second, now seemed, if possible, to flash with a brilliancy yet more intense, as they turned their glance away from my own eyes, and fixed it upon the body.

I followed that deadly glance, and shuddered with a horror for which the world has no name as I beheld what followed.

The right hand of the headless body began to rise!

My limbs tottered—I sank to my knees—but my eyes never left the hand; and it continued to rise, slowly and steadily.

And as it rose—that long white hand, upon which gleamed an opal ring, surrounded with brilliants—as it slowly rose, the fore-finger as slowly extended itself, and pointed—pointed straight at my shuddering form.

The headless body pointed at its destroyer!

How long the hand remained uplifted, rigid, motionless, menac-ing, denouncing, I know not—it seemed for ages.

I could not move—I was transfixed—I was turned to stone, and when at length the hand lost its rigidity gradually, and sank slowly to the side of the headless corpse, I experienced a feeling, not of relief merely, but of a most intense—a most supreme happiness.

The falling of the hand broke the charm that compelled my glance to fix itself upon it, and, looking a last time at the eyes of the head, I saw that they were dark with the shadow of death. That awful will was dead. Only a skull now remained.

A moment after the hand of the headless trunk had ceased to point. I sank into a long and deathlike swoon.

And when consciousness returned, the first faint streaks of dawn were stealing through the lattice of my window.

I sprang to my feet as memory called up the events of the preced-ing night, and looked round to assure myself that it had not been a hideous nightmare. The objects lying on the cushions told of its appalling reality.

I sank into a couch, and, calm in my despair, I reflected.

The question (in which I now felt no interest) was decided. The will and the mind could not only live after decapitation, but could exert such a power over the body from which it had been separated, as to bring about the terrible result I had witnessed.

The thing had been done, and could not be undone; it only now remained to remove all traces of the body, and to divert suspicion.

I had long since prepared for this exigency. I had the means of so utterly destroying the corpse, that not the faintest trace of it would remain. By a chemical process, known to few, I could consume the body without fuel, without fire, and leave not even the ashes to betray me.

I prepared the acids, etc., which were to be used for this purpose, and subduing as best I could the horror and loathing that could not be suppressed, I set about my fearful task.

To destroy the cushions upon which blood had fallen I used fire. I carefully burnt every ensanguined fragment.

It was necessary that I should divide the body into small fragments, so as to leave no ashes. The head could, however, be consumed whole, and the action of the acids accomplished this in a few minutes. When nothing of it remained I felt intense relief. It is the *face* of the dead that most agitates the murderer, the mere trunk had no horrors for me compared with the head.

I then began with the body by severing the right hand. This done, I was about to submit it to the acids, when I suddenly remembered that the garments must be destroyed. The fire was expiring; there must be no delay. I stripped the body and burned every thread of the garments. This work lasted longer than I had calculated on account of the fire being so low, and the absence of fuel wherewith to replenish it. But at last the smallest fragment disappeared, and once more, nervous, agitated, and horribly fatigued, I turned to the body. My mind was becoming more and more confused, but rallying my faculties, I looked round for the hand. I could not see it. Where had I left it? Had I destroyed it? I could not remember. Yet it must be so since the hand was no longer there. I turned to the body.

But I will not weary—I will not disgust you, señors, with the details of my frightful work. At length all was accomplished. There now remained not a trace of that valiant gentleman who a few hours before had been instinct with virile life—not a trace, I thought, with a wild exultation.

With what delight did I throw open the door! With what exhilaration did I feel the cool air fan my feverish brow, and saw the sun shining on the calm and silent river!

But as I opened the door yet wider, something passed me with a rush!

It was an animal;—it was in truth the little monkey, Juan, which had always evinced a most intense and unaccountable fear of myself. His presence throughout the enactment of that hideous drama I had been unaware of, or had forgotten. Juan, apparently fearing me now more than ever, darted from the door, and flew like lightning from my sight, in the direction of his dead master's mansion.

Señors, I need tell you no more. You already know the rest. You know how, tortured by remorse and fearing solitude, I sought society. You know how, on that fatal night, when I and some friends were discussing the strange disappearance of Don Alvaro—you know how the accursed ape, suddenly appearing in our midst, sprang upon a table, and, with a horrible grin, held before my eyes a ghastly object, at sight of which all were horrified—but none felt a tithe of my own supreme horror.

For, as you know, the hideous thing that the ape held up—the sight of which forced from me that terrible self-conviction—this ghastly object was the hand—the jewelled hand—of Don Alvaro!

And now have I not related all the details of my crime? Have I not accounted for everything?

You are stricken dumb with horror—but do you still think that I am mad? You reply not—you shrink—you shudder—you cannot look upon me! Yet say—do I not merit death?

THE MASTERPIECE OF GERALD WAYNE

In the year 1865 I was part owner of what was generally known as "Gray's Station." There were four of us. We were all young Englishmen, who, "in search of El Dorado," had left the land of our birth for that of the Antipodes. We tried our luck first of all on the diggings. We were tolerably successful. But we soon came to the conclusion that the goldfields were by far too hard and rough a school for English gentlemen to learn "colonial experience" in. We looked round for an easier life. That of the squatter took our fancy. We had money, and bought Gray's Station outright.

There were, as I have said, four of us. Two were brothers; their name was Wayne. The third was a cousin of the brothers, and bore the same name. The fourth was myself, their old school-fellow.

George, the eldest of the brothers, was a tall, dark, fine-looking fellow, who bore much resemblance to the younger in point of personal appearance, but who, in character, differed from him to a remarkable extent. He was intensely passionate and self-willed on occasions, but a good fellow enough in ordinary life. He was somewhat taciturn, and was, therefore, not a very cheerful companion. His brother Frank was altogether different. A more light-hearted, joyous youth never lived; he seemed created for no other purpose than to reap all the enjoyment that life has to give, without experiencing an iota of its sorrow. Everyone liked him. Gerald Wayne, the cousin, I can only describe as, simply, a genius. He was a painter. His very soul was in his art. An intense lover of the ideal—detesting, abjuring all that was not of the very highest order of the beautiful and poetical in painting—his pictures were not appreciated by any except the few who possessed a sufficiently elevated sense of true art to comprehend the peculiarity of the genius with which they were so strongly impregnated. They did not sell, but this was a drawback of which Gerald took little heed. Painting was with him a passion; he had a lofty ideal of his own creation, and he never even thought of descending from it to please the popular taste. He made no "potboilers."

Between the two brothers there was much affection, though they differed so greatly in character. Gerald Wayne was well liked by them both. He himself loved George, who had once, at the risk of his own life, saved that of Gerald. The artist never forgot his debt, as will be shown hereafter.

As regards birth and education we all considered ourselves above the middle class of English society. The brothers Wayne were the younger sons of a baronet of a good old family, and Gerald was the son of this baronet's brother. My father was a naval officer, who died in indifferent circumstances. I had, in coming to the colonies, left at home my mother and sister. Now, however, being part possessor of a large station, I considered myself sufficiently established, as it were, to invite my relations to join me. I was, moreover, urged to do so by my three friends. I decided, and in due time my mother and sister arrived at their new Australian home.

For three years I had not beheld them, and our meeting was a happy event. My mother looked, if anything, younger; the sea voyage had invigorated her. My sister, the sweet little Evelyn of fifteen I had left in England, had grown into a tall, graceful, lovely girl of eighteen.

Everything was made as comfortable as possible for the ladies, who, as they became more and more accustomed to it, grew to like an Australian life.

The intrusion of a beautiful girl into our home had a very visible effect upon my three friends. They had become, as the natural consequence of living out of society, somewhat careless of their appearance and a little roughened in manners, but now, in the presence of the refined young lady, they were, in all respects, English gentlemen once more. They became Evelyn's knights, each vying with his companion in amusing her and preventing her from growing weary. This chivalrous attention was carried to an extreme which appeared to me (the brother) almost ridiculous, and I often laughed over it with them.

Nearly a year passed away—and passed monotonously, as those acquainted with ordinary station life will not deny; that is to say, it was monotonous for me. I cannot tell how the time passed with the others; perhaps it was different with them.

During this time there occurred an incident which caused me to feel some apprehension and uneasiness. It was this.

Two or three miles away a river flowed. In the spring of the year boating excursions on the river were a delight, and constituted Evelyn's chief out-door pleasure. One morning the joyous, the handsome, the ever-laughing Frank Wayne took possession of the beauty and carried her off in a boat. They were away the best part of the day.

There was a rough wooden pier on the river-bank, which was very high—some twenty feet or so above the water, except in the rainy season. Steps led down to the boat from the end of this pier.

I happened to be riding that way, and thought I would wait awhile for them. I left my horse on the bank, and walked nearly to the end of the pier. I looked around. The boat was not to be seen, but there being a bend in the river close to the pier I reasoned that it might be quite alone, without being visible. I sat down on the edge of the pier, intending to wait a little while.

But scarcely had I seated myself when I was startled by the sound of voices. I looked round. The boat was not to be seen. However, the truth soon became apparent to me. The young people had returned and were landing at the steps, hidden from my view. I advanced to the edge of the pier and looked down; it was so. Frank and Evelyn were standing on the bottom step. They did not perceive me, because they were looking in the opposite direction. They did not hear me, for a reason which shall be made apparent. Frank had Evelyn's hands within his own. Her head was bowed over them. Something, I know not what, impelled me to watch and listen.

"You love me then, dear Evelyn?" said Frank.

"Yes," murmured my sister, almost inaudibly.

"Better than anything else in the world?"

"Yes."

"And you will marry me?"

"Yes."

He kissed her. They turned to ascend the steps. I stepped back. I jostled against a man. It was George Wayne. I looked at him in surprise. He was very pale, and evidently much disturbed in mind, but he rapidly recovered his composure, and by the time the young lovers had arrived at the top of the pier, none could have suspected him of any mental discomposure whatever. Yet I felt that he had heard all I myself had heard, and I was intuitively disturbed by the conviction.

"Ah, truants," cried George, in a hearty tone, rather unusual with him, "where have you been? Why have you deserted us in such a way?" And he rattled on merrily, much to my surprise, for George was, as I have before said, rather taciturn.

As for the affianced lovers, they seemed not to notice the change in George's manner, absorbed, as no doubt they were, in their own new-found happiness.

From that day I kept my eyes open. George was unmistakably in love with Evelyn, whose heart was given to his brother. Frank, who had always been a happy fellow, now seemed to have reached the highest pinnacle of human joy. I myself envied him; what, then, must have been the sentiments of George? From my heart I pitied the brother whose love, though unrequited, was yet so deep and passionate. I once made an attempt to gain his confidence, but he repulsed my advances in a courteous yet very decided manner. He shunned the society of us all, Evelyn's the most of any. He began to take an increased interest in the business and management of the station, and soon affected some radical changes which benefited us considerably. All this I knew was but a mode of preventing his mind from being occupied too much by the thought of his hopeless attachment.

George's zeal for the prosperity of the station increased daily; at the same time his love grew stronger and stronger from the very efforts he made to extinguish it. It must be remembered that I alone perceived this. The others, indeed, wondered at the change wrought in his character, but he concealed the real cause so well that no one, so far as I know, entertained the slightest suspicion of it.

George often took trips to Melbourne on business. In fact, he spent all the time he could away from the station. It was just after he had departed on one of these trips that a terrible event happened—a mysterious event.

George always rode a great part of his way on horseback. There was a bridge spanning the river. It was about a mile higher up from the rough pier I have already mentioned. On the present occasion George took this route, as usual. We were all at the station at the time; it was not less than four hours after the departure of George that any separation took place among the rest of us.

George left in the morning.

In the afternoon Frank took a horse, and went for a ride. A solitary excursion on horseback was by no means unusual with him. He loved to wander about the bush, and along the banks of the river.

We expected him to return at six o'clock, or seven at the latest. He did not come.

At about eight o'clock his horse, with empty saddle, and bridle hanging loosely from his neck, was caught near the station.

This looked ominous. We were alarmed.

Gerald Wayne and I, accompanied by two or three of the station hands, immediately set off in search of the missing man. We passed the night in following the tracks of the horse, which led us through the bush, in a circuitous route, to the pier, then to the bridge, back again to the pier, and then to where the horse was caught. But nothing could be ascertained as to the whereabouts of Frank Wayne. We returned, inexpressibly wearied and disheartened. My poor sister was in utter despair.

The next morning a black-tracker was procured, and the search resumed. But the tracker's instinct was at fault. It had rained heavily in the interval, and he could discern very few traces of the missing youth. It appeared that Frank had dismounted both at the pier and at the bridge. The tracker was of opinion that the horse had come away from the bridge, leaving Frank there, but of this he was not sure; it might have been at the pier that Frank had dismounted last. One thing was certain—the horse had left Frank either at the pier or at the bridge. The tracker's task was a very difficult one, from the fact of there being other traces besides those of the young man, from which he had to separate them.

The day passed, and nothing transpired. But the next morning our worst fears were realised. A shepherd had found the body of the unhappy young man several miles down the river, caught in the boughs of a tree which overhung the water.

He was conveyed to the station, a doctor procured, and it was ascertained that he had been dead since about eight o'clock on the night of his disappearance; that he had been drowned; not the slightest indication of violence was found upon his person; death was caused simply by drowning. It was known that he could not swim; evidently he had fallen into the river.

An inquest was held, and a verdict returned "in accordance with the evidence."

George Wayne was telegraphed for from the nearest town, and arrived in the greatest haste and agitation.

There had been a moment—it was but a moment—when I connected Frank's death with the rivalry between him and George, which none but I and George knew of. This terrible thought lasted, I say, but the briefest instant; then the utter wildness and absurdity of such a theory struck me, and I despised and hated myself for the thought. The thing was utterly impossible, either reasonably or morally. Frank's death had occurred many hours *after* the departure of George; and a brother—oh, it was impossible.

If there were anything needed to utterly dispel the wild thought I had harboured, the sight of the terrible grief depicted on the white face of George Wayne more than supplied it. Grief is too weak a term; it should be called despair. I pitied him intensely, as much almost as I pitied my sister.

Evelyn had sunk into a sort of stupor—she was stunned by the blow. But I felt instinctively that the brother's sorrow was far more poignant than the lover's.

George Wayne went away. He must, he told me, have complete change of scene if he would recover from the fearful blow of his brother's death. He departed.

It was a year before we saw him again. Evelyn's grief subsided into a settled gloom. She appeared to take no interest in anything. For many months she never smiled, and seldom spoke. However, this did not last. Time gradually converted her great grief into a tender memory. She began slowly to recover health and spirits. And when George Wayne returned to the station, he found her a sad-eyed, reserved, and serious girl, not bright and vivacious as she had once been, and yet not so melancholy but that she could smile and converse with a pleasant and charming demeanour. And I saw that he yet loved her passionately as heretofore.

*   *   *   *   *

It is now time that Gerald Wayne should be brought a little more prominently forward. Hitherto I have written little of him, principally because he played so small a part in the events I have described. Gerald Wayne was one of those men who, while they escape notice, are much more worth studying than others who thrust themselves more into the light. He had ever lived in a sort of perpetual retirement—in a world of his own—like many true geniuses. But, since the death of Frank, I could not help noticing that he became, if possible, more retired than ever, and that an unusual gloom seemed to have fallen upon him. He avoided everyone, but especially George, whose departure soon after the terrible event seemed to give him great relief, and whose return seemed to disturb him intensely. Impossible as it was for me to guess at the real cause, I could only assign one reason, which had in it, perhaps, some particle of truth. I had come to the conclusion that the cousin, in common with the brothers, had fallen in love with my charming sister. In this supposition I was correct, but why such a circumstance should cause him to avoid George so much I could not comprehend, unless it was an over-sensitive desire to shun any untoward collision with one whom he knew to be a rival; and this theory, weak as it may appear on paper, yet had to one who understood thoroughly the character of the artist no little force.

But let me hurry on to the end, for I have no wish to withhold any longer the revealment of the true sense of Gerald's mysterious gloom, and of the mystery attending the death of poor Frank.

Gerald had his own quarters at the station, which were held sacred by everyone as the sanctum of a genius. I, who, as one of the few who truly appreciated his peculiar works, was allowed (and even invited) to intrude upon him at any hour. I had the "run" of his quarters, and was in the habit of spending much of my time there.

A little after the return of George it became suddenly apparent to me that Gerald Wayne had, as far as I knew, ceased to paint. He would arrange his canvas and his colours, sit at his easel, brush in hand, but the brush never touched the canvas. He would sit perfectly still for hours in a deep reverie, while his eyes, fixed upon vacancy, would often light up with a strange light, by which I, who alone saw it, was unpleasantly affected, and grew at length, in a vague manner, to dread. Without assigning to myself any reason therefor—but, rather, urged by a sort of instinct—I kept a strict watch upon the artist. But watching elicited nothing, although I felt intuitively that there was something which certainly *could* be elicited.

Now, just above the artist's studio there was a sort of loft, in which were stowed old pictures, half-finished paintings of his own, and other artists' lumber. A kind of half-stair, half-ladder, led to this loft. The loft itself was partitioned into two rooms, one of which was secured from entrance by a strong door. I know not what had been its former use, but it now contained nothing but an old easel, some paints and brushes, &c. One day, long before the precise period of which I am now writing (a few months after the return of George Wayne), the artist had locked the door of this room and lost the key. As the room contained nothing that he required, he had not taken the trouble of procuring another or having the lock picked.

One night I lay awake for some hours after retiring, and as, at little past midnight, I was at length sinking into sleep, I heard distinctly the sound of soft footfalls outside the door of my apartment. Grasping a pistol which lay ever ready to my hand, I cautiously opened my door, and as cautiously peered forth into the darkness.

The owner of the footfalls had passed the door, and was walking slowly and with regular step along the corridor. The figure bore a taper, and was enveloped in a long dressing gown. In an instant I recognised the gait of Gerald Wayne, the artist. Impelled by an irresistible impulse of a something more than mere curiosity, I followed silently in his footsteps.

He had evidently just come from his bedroom, and was taking the way that led to his studio. I followed him there. To my surprise he did not pause an instant, but began to ascend the ladder stair with the same regularity of progress which had characterised his movements hitherto. I followed as noiselessly as possible. All this time I did not see his face.

We arrived at the loft. I wondered what would now transpire, for here, I thought, the mystery of his midnight wandering must reveal itself. But I was mistaken. To my intense astonishment he slowly took from the pocket of his dressing gown a key, evidently that which had been lost, and proceeded to open the door of the second apartment which I have said the loft contained. The door swung open, and the artist entered. I was afraid he would close it after him, but he never even turned round, and I followed him in. The door slowly closed, too, of its own accord.

All this time I had been chilled, yet all the more interested, by the strange and weird solemnity which seemed to cling to the artist's movements, and I felt by a sort of instinct that they were prompted by no natural cause, but rather by some vagary of an over-wrought brain. The truth, simple as it was, had never occurred to me.

The painter placed the candle on a shelf at the wall, and then turned around and faced me.

That is to say, I saw his countenance, but in an instant I became aware that I was by him unperceived; and in an instant the real truth flashed through my mind. The expression of his face, or rather its absence of expression, told me in a moment that he was in that strange state called somnambulism. In common parlance, the artist was a sleep-walker. This discovery increased my curiosity tenfold.

I looked round the room. In the centre, placed so as the light of the candle would fall upon it, was a scarcely more than half painted picture, set upon an easel. The appliances of an artist were close at hand.

The artist seated himself at the easel and took up his brush and palette.

I sat down on an old chair just behind him, and, looking over his shoulder, began to study the half-finished picture.

Never shall I forget the strange, shuddering thrill of horror that ran through my veins and congealed the blood therein as I looked upon the canvas.

The painting, as I have said, was little more than half finished; but, nevertheless, in an instant I caught a vague idea of the terrible tale which was written upon it, though not yet completed.

It was a beautiful scene, and one that I knew well. It was the representation of a bridge, under which rolled the dark waters of a river—the bridge, in fact, which I have mentioned in connection with Frank's death.

If confined to a mere landscape painting, the picture was complete. Everything inanimate had been executed on the canvas; but on the bridge there was a scene from life.

In the foreground a horse, startled, was in the act of galloping away; in the background, standing out clear against the silhouette, there was a second horse. These figures were completed. The artist, I thought, must have wrought at his midnight task many times ere this present one.

The rest of the picture was yet unpainted. The artist began his task. He painted with that superhuman rapidity which could only come from the peculiar power of somnambulism. In less than an hour the outlines of two more figures showed themselves. Both were human forms.

The one was leaning backwards over the railing of the bridge. He was being forced over by a hand which grasped his throat. The hand belonged to a figure that stood over him. The rapid brush still plied at its weird task. A few swift touches, and a likeness—a faithful portrait—seemed actually to flash into sight.

It was the likeness of the dead Frank Wayne, and rested upon the features of the form which was being forced over the railing of the bridge.

It was the likeness of Frank indeed; but how changed—how utterly transformed! I had read somewhere that countenances which express fear and horror most vividly are those whose ordinary and usual expression is one of joy, but I never appreciated the remark till now. The face I saw was frightful in the intensity of its agony of terror and despair.

No less terrible was the one which soon appeared above it, wrought by the painter's superhumanly rapid hand. It expressed in their extremes demoniac rage and the madness of an intense passion. It was the countenance of George Wayne.

The strangely weird and horrible power of the picture thrilled me so that for many minutes calm reflection was denied me.

When at last I recovered my faculties sufficiently to reflect, the whole truth—the terrible truth—which had for some time been struggling to free itself from the chaos of bewilderment in my mind, now burst upon me with a breathless suddenness and force. Frank Wayne had fallen by his brother's hand! George Wayne was a fratricide!

The picture was finished. The artist rose, seemed to contemplate it for a moment, then took a gauze veil from the shelf, and with it enveloped his weird work.

Then, taking up the taper, which had burned very low, he turned and opened the door.

Fearful that he might lock me in, I darted past him into the other room. As before, he appeared not to see me, and, locking the door, he descended the steps. I followed. He returned the way he had come, and I noticed a thing which, had I been in an ordinary frame of mind, I would have greatly wondered at. The artist suddenly paused, and, stooping, placed the key in a crevice in the wall close to the floor, where, doubtless, it had been lost. I followed him to his room, saw him extinguish the taper and get into bed, and then I returned to my own couch; but, as may readily be supposed, not to sleep.

The rest is soon told. Space will not permit me to describe it in elaborate detail.

The next day, having formed my plan of action, I led the artist and George Wayne to the room in the loft, where I unveiled the picture, to the astounded gaze of one—to the horrified vision of the other.

I turned towards the fratricide. But on the very first sight of the awful picture he had sunk to the floor, and was already expiring from a fit of apoplexy.

The artist himself swooned. Of course, in his waking hours, he had not the slightest knowledge that he was painting, perhaps, the most powerful picture that ever man executed. The picture is still there on the easel veiled. The door of the room is always locked.

In due time Gerald Wayne told me how, being near the fatal bridge, he witnessed the terrible scene he afterwards depicted on his canvas. How, for many minutes, he remained paralysed in his covert; how he could attempt no rescue, not being able to swim; and of the thoughts that occupied his mind as he returned home to the station, which he reached a little before the horse was caught. At first it had been his intention to reveal all; then the thought of the great debt he owed to George Wayne, who had saved his life, occurred to him, and he felt it was impossible for him to betray the man who had preserved him from death. He had then kept silent. But heaven, in its just anger, decreed otherwise, and the picture was painted which revealed the ghastly secret.

We never knew what actually led to the murder—or how it came to pass that George Wayne was at the bridge at a time when, by the laws of probability, he should have been many miles away. Gerald saw only what he represented in his picture.

The artist at length became the husband of Evelyn, who knows nothing of the terrible drama connected with the death of her first lover, and of the existence of that wild and weird picture which I feel that I can justly designate as the Masterpiece of Gerald Wayne.

THE GLASS DAGGER

It had been raining heavily all the evening, but the clouds were breaking now, and already a few stars were twinkling through the rents. The flaring gaslight glimmered on the wet pavements almost cheerily, as if promising a complete clearing up of the unpleasant weather. In the street there was a great clatter—vehicles of all kinds were speeding swiftly to their various destinations. The opera was just over, and those people who were fortunate enough to possess a sufficiency of this world's wealth availed themselves of hired conveyances, while the comparative few who were cumbered with a superfluity of it entered their own luxurious carriages, and, well protected from the cold and possible rain or sleet, were conveyed to their still more comfortable habitations.

There were, however, two persons who, while having carriages of their own, and money enough to hire half the hansoms in London, preferred to walk and stretch their limbs after three hours of sitting. They never even thought of using other means of locomotion than those with which nature had provided them. Strong and healthy and young, they could have "finished fresh" after a twenty-mile tramp, and would have enjoyed the exertion. And now they were but too glad to feel the cold, keen air in their faces after the heat of the theatre.

One of them was a young lady of eighteen and the other a stalwart youth of not more than twenty-two. Both were tall and handsome. The young man was English—there could be no doubt of it. But the girl, dark-haired, dark-eyed, olive-skinned, carrying her fine head with queenly grace, was unmistakably of foreign extraction. But in fact, although her father was a native of Seville, she was born in England, and had only once or twice seen her father's country. There was nothing foreign in her speech or manners—quite the contrary; and everyone who knew her thought that only in her physical attributes was there anything Spanish, and it was quite natural that they should make this error, for nothing had as yet occurred to arouse her deeper nature. She was English on the surface, and none looked beneath.

The young lady's name was Frances Valentes, and that of her companion was Arthur Grayling. The following conversation will, perhaps, sufficiently explain the relations in which they stood towards each other.

"I say to you again, Frances," the young man said, rather excitedly, "that you should not let this uncle of yours stand in the way of your life's happiness. The thought of that man's prejudices and fads coming between us makes me feel by no means friendly towards him, I can tell you."

"If I did not know that the virtue of patience is almost a stranger to you, Arthur," said the young girl, in a calm tone of voice, "I would counsel you to wait until those prejudices are conquered. My uncle has always been so very kind to me that to act contrary to his wishes would pain me more than you can realise."

"Oh, but they will never be conquered—never!" cried Grayling, energetically. "He is so ambitious in regard to you, that to see you married to me—to the brother of the man whom he sent to Botany Bay by his fatal evidence—to see this would crush him completely, poor fellow."

"Oh, Arthur, don't talk so cynically. Uncle will yield when he at length realises how—how——"

"How much you love me, darling!" said the young man, looking tenderly at her, and modifying his former discontented tone into one as sweet and soft almost as her own. "Well, do you know, I very much fear that the more he realises that fact the sterner will become his objections."

Nothing more was said for a while. Frances was reflecting on the strangeness of the fate that had given her as a devoted lover the very last man her uncle and guardian would have chosen as a husband for her, since Arthur's brother, a reckless reprobate, had been transported for forgery upon his evidence, and he had, besides, been his greatest enemy through life. Arthur's thoughts were very different; he had a project in his mind, the nature of which he had once already hinted to Frances, but she had repulsed it firmly on that occasion, and he hesitated to renew his proposal, which was certainly ill-advised and desperate. It was only when they came to her uncle's door that he made up his mind to speak again.

As he "kissed her good-night," he whispered: "Will you consider again, dearest, what I spoke of a few days ago? Think how we love each other."

She did not reply, but he felt her tremble violently, and, as he walked away, he muttered—"She will consent soon, and then— well, I will have avenged my brother, as well as won my dear little Frances." It is certain that he spoke these words, for they were heard, and remembered.

Mr. Maynard was a banker, but had retired from business, contenting himself with sundry modest speculations on the Stock Exchange. He was, nevertheless, an austere man—a man of the most rigid principle. His conscience was clear; he had never committed a mean or dishonourable act—at least he felt, or tried to feel, that he had not. But there were times when an unpleasant fear would come over him. He would ask himself whether he had not, on a certain occasion, allowed himself to be carried away by a feeling of hatred, and would try in vain to entirely justify himself in the course he had taken. Certainly, the thought that he had possibly been the means of condemning an innocent man to such a terrible fate as "penal servitude for life," must be by no means a pleasant one for the most unscrupulous of men, and though the man's guilt had been so clearly proven that scarcely a doubt could exist, yet Mr. Maynard's mind was tortured often by this one great fear. He had been experiencing one of his dark hours, and was yet suffering, when Frances entered to say good-night, as was her custom.

He turned and glanced towards her with something of a frown on his pale features, and said, as his hand mechanically toyed with the curiously-wrought glass dagger which served him for a paper-knife:

"Ah, Frances, just returned? By the way, have you succeeded in bringing that young Grayling to a sense of his folly yet?"

The girl stopped, and for a moment could not reply. The tone and the words were so unusual, so abrupt, so unexpected.

"What do you mean, sir?" she said, proudly, her face pale, and her dark eyes flashing.

"I mean, my dear," he replied, "that I do not think it advisable that you should be seen so often with a man to whom you are not engaged, or likely to be."

"Oh," said Frances, in a tone that made him start, "then I am not engaged to Mr. Grayling?"

"Certainly not—at least, with my sanction and consent."

"And if I ask your sanction and consent to our engagement you will refuse?"

"I will."

Frances sank slowly into a couch on the other side of the little table at which Mr. Maynard had been writing. Her face was pale, her eyes had a strange light in them, and on her lips a peculiar smile hovered—a smile that somehow made her uncle feel as a man who is menaced with some unknown peril. As she said nothing more, he affected to take no further notice of her, but began writing, as if to intimate that the question was settled for all time, although in his heart there was un undefinable fear of approaching trouble or something worse.

Frances' mind was in a whirl. For some minutes she could not think clearly, and her eyes mechanically followed the quickly-moving pen in her uncle's hand, and, straying thence, fixed themselves upon that strange paper-knife, an object with which she had been familiar from infancy. It was a work of art in its way, fashioned like a Malay's crease. In the centre of the blade, following its undulatory shape, was a thin line of red, such as could be made on paper with a quill pen; it extended from the haft to within a quarter of an inch of the point. The blade was an inch wide, and rather thick in the centre; it was double-edged, rather blunt than sharp, and a little chipped. The handle was stained a purple colour, but the waving blade was perfectly clear and white, save only for the red streak mentioned above.

Frances, half-unconsciously, fell to thinking of this familiar object. It had been used for its present purpose so long—how strange that it had never been broken; so many falls had it had, too. But though the edges certainly were a little chipped, the fine and delicate points had remained as sharp as on the day that it was made. Surely some fate preserved it intact—if so, for what purpose? Was it destined to play a part in anyone's life? Perhaps—but just then it was covered with a newspaper that her uncle pushed aside.

"Well, my dear Frances," he said, in the kindliest tone he could assume, "is it not rather late for you? Those fresh, rosy cheeks——"

She stood up, and flashed a look upon him that checked all further speech. Then, with pale, set face and clenched hands, she left the room ere he could even muster up sufficient presence of mind to say "good-night."

Reaching her own chamber, Frances threw herself upon her bed. Here, strangely enough, as she tried to collect her thoughts, the dim *spectrum* of the glass dagger floated before her vision.

Half an hour afterwards she arose, and—her teeth clenched, her eyes flashing, her whole demeanour revealing a fixed resolve—she muttered fiercely, "I will do it; there is no other course."

On the morning following, the maidservant, whose duty it was to put in order the apartment which was called the study, entered, as usual, with broom and duster, and was very much surprised to find her master sitting in his accustomed chair at the little table. His letters and papers were scattered about, and, although he was leaning back in the chair, apparently asleep, his hand, holding a pen, rested on the edge of a sheet of paper, on which he had written two or three words. The servant, not wishing to incur her master's displeasure should he awake and find himself enveloped in a cloud of dust, discreetly retired, and busied herself in her other duties.

When the bell rang for breakfast, however, Mr. Maynard, usually very punctual at meal times, did not appear; and, strangely enough, Frances, who was wont to be in the breakfast-room some minutes earlier, to see that her uncle's peculiar delicacies had been duly provided, and to welcome him when he appeared, had not yet come down. These things, so very unusual in such a well-regulated house, rather troubled the good old lady, who had been housekeeper for nearly twenty years, and, after waiting a few minutes, she sent up to Miss Valente's apartments; but the servant soon returned with the strange intelligence that neither the young lady nor her maid were in the house. Greatly disturbed, and entertaining fears which she could scarcely have put into words, Mrs. Rushton, after ascertaining that the carriages and horses were all in their accustomed places, and that none of the servants had seen Frances leave the house, resolved to inform Mr. Maynard at once of what had taken place. The maidservant had told her that he was asleep in his study, and she repaired thither, and, emboldened by the urgency of the circumstances, she tapped him on the shoulder and called to him, with no result. As she was about to repeat these efforts she was struck by his extreme stillness and the deadly pallor of his face. Dazed and confused by a terrible fear that sprang up in her mind, she started back, but at the same moment her eyes caught sight of those three or four words that the pen of Mr. Maynard still hovered over. She read them easily enough, but at first they were as meaningless to her as Egyptian hieroglyphics on a sarcophagus would have been, and it was some time ere she fully realised their terrible signification. The words were—

"My murderer is Fran——"

That was all. The last word was unfinished. Death had overtaken the writer and paralysed his hand. Nearly fainting as she was, Mrs. Rushton controlled her emotion and examined her master. For some time she found no wound. Suddenly she stumbled over something on the floor. Picking it up, she found that it was the haft and portion of the blade of the glass dagger which Mr. Maynard had for years used as a paper-knife. It was a familiar object to the housekeeper, and, even in the midst of her intense surprise, she could not help noticing that the red line in the centre of the blade was gone, and a slender hole, such as a fine needle could have been thrust into, was left. But this fact, so significant, suggested nothing to the good Mrs. Rushton, who knew little of poisoned daggers. All she thought of was that the other part of the curious weapon must be buried in Mr. Maynard's body. She found the wound at length— it was in the left side of the chest, near the shoulder. There was no blood on the garments, and, putting aside the coat, she saw the broken piece of glass slightly protruding. Touching it, she found that it could be withdrawn easily, but on attempting to remove it the fact became apparent that it was broken lower down, for only an inch of glass came away, and a little thick blood oozed from the wound. With a slight scream, the poor old lady fell fainting on the floor.

* * * * *

On the patio of their residence in Seville, one bright afternoon, a young, newly-married couple were sitting, enjoying in silence the knowledge that they were near each other, and sharing each other's hopes and fears of what the future might bring forth. Perhaps in the long, sad, wistful smile with which they regarded each other, might be discerned more of fear and foreboding than of hope and joy.

Suddenly their thoughts were disturbed by the entrance of a servant, who bore some papers.

"I have brought you the English files you asked for, señor," he said, addressing the young man, who took them somewhat eagerly from his hands, and dismissed him.

"Now, dear, we will see if anything has been said of our flight," he remarked; and each took one of the papers, and began glancing hurriedly through them.

Suddenly the young man uttered an exclamation, which was quickly repeated by his bride, whose pallor was alarming. They had both seen, apparently, what they had feared to see. The lady's paper, being of later date than that of her husband, had in it a further development of the bad news. The paragraph in question was headed—"The Maynard Murder."

After exchanging an affrighted look, they both began to read. The later paper detailed the inquest on the body of Mr. Maynard, and the following extracts will serve to explain what had occurred after Mrs. Rushton's discovery of the murder:—

"Anne Rushton, recalled, deposed that, to the best of her knowledge and belief, no one had known of the existence of poison in the glass dagger. It was familiar to most of the servants of the house, none of whom could have suspected the true nature of the red streak; could not say whether Miss Valentes was aware of its deadly properties. . . . Did not know who the unfinished name indicated, if not Frances, the Christian name of Miss Valentes; could not tell whether the young lady had left the house on the night of the murder or very early the next morning; from the preparations for departure that had been made, considered that she must have been in the house at the time the crime was committed; knew that Miss Valentes was angered with her uncle for his objections to her engagement with Mr. Arthur Grayling; did not know whether she had had a quarrel with Mr. Maynard on the night of the murder; could not tell how Miss Valentes had procured duplicate keys with which to leave the house secretly; was almost certain that the doors were locked at twelve.

"John Maddox, a coachman, deposed that he knew Mr. Arthur Grayling, having been in his employ. Remembered the night of the murder; was passing Mr. Maynard's house on that night, and saw Mr. Grayling part with a lady at the door; heard him talking to himself a few minutes afterwards; as nearly as he could recollect, the words were: 'She will consent soon, and then my brother will be avenged, and I will have my little Frances.' If those were not the exact words, they were to that effect. Knew that Mr. Grayling's brother had been transported through Mr. Maynard's evidence.

"The jury, after much consideration, returned a verdict of wilful murder against Frances Valentes and Arthur Grayling. The coroner remarked that, strong as the evidence was, it was still circumstantial evidence, and he hoped that there would be further development of this strange affair."

The foregoing is extracted from what the lady read. When she came to the end she uttered a low moan of agony, and fainted. The young man—Arthur Grayling—called to his wife's maid to attend to her, and then, pale as the dead, rushed from the place. When, hours after, he returned, he was informed that his wife was dangerously ill and out of her mind. He hastened to the sick-room, and was distracted at the state of his beautiful bride. She was delirious with fever, and did not recognise him. The faithful maid begged him to leave the room, and, the physicians joining in her entreaties, he suffered himself to be led away.

Grayling passed a night of agony. In the morning he was not allowed to see Frances, whose state had become even worse, though they told him she would soon recover if not disturbed. He, to pass the leaden hours, read in the other papers all that concerned the murder of Mr. Maynard, in which he was accused of being an accessory.

Suddenly he started with surprise, and an emotion of grief, though not unmixed with joy, passed through his heart. This is what he read:—

THE MAYNARD TRAGEDY.—A STRANGE CONFESSION.

"It will be remembered that a few days ago a desperate pair of burglars were captured in *flagrante delicto*. One of these men has confessed himself to be the assassin of the unfortunate Mr. Maynard, and turns out to be the brother of Arthur Grayling, whose disappearance with Miss Valentes caused him to be suspected of complicity in the act. It will be recollected that this brother had, many years ago, been transported for life for the crime of forgery, and that the evidence of Mr. Maynard had been mainly instrumental in procuring him the sentence. This was adduced by the evidence given at the inquest, and is corroborated by the statements of the man Frank Grayling. We append the following as a verbatim report of his strange confession:—

"Hugh Maynard and I had been sworn enemies all through life. I was the black sheep—the reprobate; he the exemplary young man. His life was a success in every way; mine was an utter failure. This did not moderate his hatred, and it intensified my own. At last a trap was laid for me by one of my worthless associates. A cheque was forged, and cashed at Maynard's bank. Circumstances pointed strongly towards me, and the evidence that Maynard gave was so strong that I was convicted, and condemned to penal servitude for life. I swore then that if ever fate permitted me to return to England, I would kill my enemy, and every night, during years of unimaginable misery, I renewed this vow. I resolved that if what is called "good conduct" in convict life could procure me a mitigation of my sentence, I would spare no efforts to obtain favour. And so my days were passed in servile cringing and other baseness, which, to me, rendered the punishment tenfold more arduous. But my purposes were served thereby. After ten years a "ticket-of-leave" was granted to me, and I became a shepherd. I sold my master's sheep to procure money for a passage to England, where I at length arrived. By this time I was fully as depraved and brutal as the average convict, and I was not likely to shrink from the act which I had vowed so many times to perform. I soon found my enemy's house, and learned that my brother Arthur, the only being in the world who never hesitated to take my hand—was in love with Maynard's ward, and that he was against the marriage of his niece with a convict's brother. I smiled as I thought that my revenge would benefit the only man I cared anything about. Well, I need not detail how I procured admission to the room in which the crime was committed. Suffice it for me to say that, with the two hundred pounds which I had left, I bribed the footman, whose duty it was to answer the door bell at night, to smuggle me into the house at some good opportunity, and show me the way to my enemy's room. This he did, and one night, very late, I crept upon him as he sat at a table thinking. I grasped my sharp clasp-knife firmly, intending to end him, if possible, at one stroke. But suddenly my eyes caught sight of a curious glass dagger, fashioned like the crease of the Malay, and an impulse came upon me to use that instead of my knife. It would not betray me, and it looked as if it would serve my purpose just as well. When a few paces from my victim I threw off all restraint, and strode boldly up to where he sat, taking up the glass dagger, and grasping it in my right hand. Giving my enemy time to recognise me, for a wrong is not fully redressed unless the victim perfectly realises how and why he is to be punished, I struck him in the chest with all my strength, and the glass blade snapped off short. He gave a quick gasp, but failed to articulate, though I could see that he was yet conscious. Something prompted me to look at the piece of glass that remained in my hand. I did so, and saw some red fluid issuing from the centre of the blade. I thought at first that it was blood, but the next moment it flashed through my mind that the dagger was poisoned, for I had noticed that it bore a slender line of red in the blade. I now felt certain of his death, and hastened to quit the house. At the door I glanced back, and fancied I saw him move, and in the stillness I heard a sound as of a pen upon paper. But I hurried I away, and was let out by the footman I had bribed. I only wished now to leave the country, and it was to obtain funds for this purpose that I joined in the burglary."

The thoughts of Arthur Grayling on reading the foregoing may as well be left undescribed, for they were in a whirl, and confused at that. Shame and sorrow for his brother's misguided and wasted life mingled with joy at the thought that the horrible charge against his beloved wife would fall to the ground, and, providing that she grew well and strong once more, they would yet be happy in each other's love.

When his mind calmed somewhat, he found a still later paper, which, commenting on the event, gave out that no "extenuating circumstances" existed which could save Frank Grayling from the gallows. "In this case," it concluded, "we have two very strange coincidences—the elopement of Mr. Grayling and Miss Valentes early on the morning following the murder, and the resemblance of the unfinished name which the dying man wrote with that of Miss Valentes'. These circumstances so clearly pointed to that young lady as the murderess of her uncle that the acutest mind would have been deceived."

Gradually the fear abated, and Frances grew well, her recovery being much helped by the glad, and yet sad, tidings.

Neither cared to return to England. They were happy in each other's love, and desired no more. And fair, sunny, golden Seville remained their home.

THE VEILED WOMAN

My situation was now one of extreme peril. I was wounded—desperately, dangerously wounded—and almost fainting from the terrible weakness caused by incessant loss of blood, though there yet remained in me a certain vigour, which sufficed to enable me to retain my seat in the saddle.

The sky was starless, and very dark. I could not see the ground, but knew from the sound of the hoof-strokes thereon that it was a road—possibly a much-travelled road—along which I was being carried. The steed, too, did not seem to be wandering at random, but rather to be traversing a remembered and accustomed path. It was very probable that he, having comprehended the words of his late master, was indeed bearing me to shelter and to succour.

I had no idea or thought of treachery. The Spaniard, dying fast, could not avail himself of his horse, and, in a last act of chivalry and generosity, had bequeathed to his wounded enemy the means of escape from death. Not one of either his or my comrades lived. I alone had survived the carnage of that brief but terrible *mêlée*. I had the despatches still safe at my heart. I might yet be able to carry them through. Perhaps, but for the hope of accomplishing this, my proud spirit might have shrank from accepting life at the hands of the Guerilla chief. None the less, I felt the magnanimity of his action. Now especially, sick and weak unto death as I was from physical exhaustion, my fierce heart so softened towards the dying bandit that he seemed to me grand, and noble, and full of generosity; and his face and form appeared before my faltering vision at irregular intervals—a sombre, yet cheering, apparition gazing at me through the gloom with eyes full of a smiling serenity, belonging rather to the illimitable blue of the heavens than to aught on earth.

This illusion of semi-consciousness faded quickly as I became aware of a change—at first indefinable—in the movements of the horse. At length I perceived that he had left the road, and was now traversing an irregular and rugged path, which, to my great relief, gradually became smoother and straighter as he proceeded, until, through the darkness, as far as the dimness of my sight allowed me to see, there stretched a gloomy vista, with still, ghostly trees and dense undergrowth on either side. It seemed to me that many, many hours elapsed ere this dreary path was ended. I was so exhausted and weak that, had the horse not proceeded at a walk, I must have fallen from the saddle. The motion caused a continuous hemorrhage, and at times a most deadly faintness came upon me, and this was accompanied by a sickness of the heart—a weariness of the soul—a great desire for unconsciousness—for the ending of all things forever—for a cessation of my acute sufferings, in what-ever form. Death had no terrors—life no regret; all I longed for was oblivion—a sweet rest.

At later times I have fancied that these dreamy thoughts were those which presage a swoon—that I was then lapsing into uncon-sciousness; for there have been moments when I have fancied that I could recall a thought—not fully defined, but still a thought—which, resolved into words, would be—"*This*, then, is death!" At that moment all physical volition was departing from me; it was only by a mechanical tenacity of my stiffened limbs that I kept my seat. At length nature was succumbing to the unnatural strain. But at this critical period the horse mounted a slight aclivity, from which my wearied and faded vision perceived an object that staved off, for a time, the impending swoon. A habitation—a chateau, probably—was before me. Joy was kindled in my fainting heart and in my sinking soul. Yet, the next moment a strange—an unearthly thrill ran through me. No doubt, a sensation of nervous terror, on account of the gloomy aspect of the building—so grim, so lonely and silent in the darkness of the night; for how could there come to me a perception of what was to happen therein? Concentrating all my remaining strength, I succeeded in retaining consciousness until the chateau was reached.

The clatter of my horse's shoes on the paved courtyard aroused the inmates of the chateau, and in a moment I was surrounded by men, some of whom bore lanterns. There were many, many faces around me, which the light illumined, but of these I saw only one—pale and menacing. It was that of the Spanish chief, whose horse had brought me there. It was the face of him whom I had left apparently dying on the plain—who bore so close a resemblance to the Guerilla I had killed.

"It is he! It is the accursed Frenchman—the slayer of Pierrez, my brother!"

These words I heard uttered in a deep and thrilling voice, and saw the chief indicate me with a passionate gesture. Then the flickering lights, the fierce faces, and the black sky reeled around me; the last reserve of human vigour was exhausted. I knew no more.

On the return of consciousness I was aware of a clammy coldness, a stifling atmosphere, and an intense darkness. I could not move—not that I was bound, but on account of an extreme stiffness of the limbs and a most terrible weakness. For many minutes I lay still, in a species of apathy or torpor. I knew only that I lived; my mind exerted itself to seek no further knowledge. Thoughts lay dead; mere consciousness of existence alone remained. The return to life from a swoon has this peculiar stage, which, however, lasts but a brief space of time. The brain soon regains its activity. The first *thought* that arose in my mind was that I lay in some place unknown to me—but I could not determine, on account of the intense blackness surrounding me, the nature of the *locale*. Where was I? Where *could* I be? Through long vistas—long and dreamy vistas of speculation—my mind wandered, and for many minutes no apprehensions of danger mingled with my calm and shadowy reflections; but, as my mind grew clearer, an appalling fear suddenly froze my blood, and caused my heart to almost cease its feeble beatings.

This deadly coldness, this stifling air, this impenetrable darkness—what meant these? I had read and heard of living beings buried in mistake, and even by design. Could such be my fate? Until now I had not moved; but, as this unutterable fear came upon me, I scarcely dared to breathe, lest there should be no more air in the grave; and at the thought of making the slightest motion my heart grew sick, in that the dread of touching cold and clammy earth or the sides or top of a coffin was too ghastly even to contemplate.

The mental torture of the fear, and, doubtless, the extreme

weakness of my body, caused me to lose consciousness once more.

The awakening from this second swoon was, compared with the recovery from the first, a joyful one. This time there was no darkness, no coldness, no scarcity of air, and I was not alone.

On opening my eyes I saw that I was in a small apartment, in which a bright fire glowed. The chamber contained no furniture save a table, a shelf, and the bed on which I lay, and there were no windows. The walls, floor, and ceiling were black.

A woman, clad and veiled in black, was standing near the fire, motionless, gazing therein. She was muttering to herself the while, but with an indistinct accentuation, so that I heard only a confused murmur. She was tall and slight, though of exquisitely modelled form, and was strangely clad. Soon she drew back from the fire, as if what she saw in the glowing coals saddened or displeased her, and moved about the apartment, displaying a weary, listless grace in all her motions. She was heavily veiled, and I could see but a hand—white and small, and thin to emaciation, which closed and unclosed occasionally. Suddenly she perceived that I was conscious, and made a hurried movement of surprise, drawing her veil yet closer.

"Oh, señor! has life at last returned to you? How long have you been awake? Did you see my face?"

These strange words were spoken in the purest Castilian, and in a voice full of an extraordinary sweetness, with which mingled an infection of deepest gloom. What made me shudder as I listened? Should I not have thrilled with delight? Why, then, tremble with an undefinable horror? I replied not to her questions, but, though she paused, she seemed to await no answer.

"My face is beautiful," she said.

Then she mixed something in a glass, approached, and bade me drink. I did so and fell into a deep and dreamless slumber.

I awoke greatly refreshed, but it was many minutes ere I remembered the veiled woman, with her strange utterances and stranger actions; for my thoughts flew back to an earlier epoch—that of the terrible *mêlee* in which all but I had fallen—all but I and the Guerrilla chief, whose brother I had, unfortunately for myself, slain in the fight. He was now a deadly foe, at whose mercy I, wounded and helpless, possibly dying, lay. I had heard strange tales of the vengeance of these lawless chiefs—awful tales, to which I had always lent an incredulous ear. Could they have been true? If so, for what fate was I reserved? Death, no doubt—a hard and bitter death. Then, with a rush, the vision of the veiled woman, like that of an angel of mercy, passed before me; but here again a peculiar sensation crept over my heart—the chill of an undefined and reasonless dread. Her words I remembered with clearness—exaggerated clearness. It seemed to me that they had not their real meaning, but a mysterious signification—a gloomy import; or could it be that my extreme weakness caused such shadowy thoughts—originated such gloomy reflections? I know not, but know that the words "my *face* is beautiful," formed themselves in my mind ever and anon like a minor cadence—a subtle undercurrent of melody—in a strain of music; and they were full of many unusual, many peculiar meanings, other than the direct signification of the words themselves.

My wounds had been carefully dressed. I felt an inexpressible relief, though scarcely able to move. The apartment was lighted by the large fire that still glowed therein. As I have said, there were no windows, and the walls, floor, and ceiling were black. By earnest observation I was enabled to perceive that they were all of stone. But what startled me most was the fact that there was no door in the room; and, though the blazing fire illuminated every part, I could discern nothing that seemed to be a means of ingress or egress. Yet there *must*, I thought, be an opening of some kind, else how could I have been placed in the cell? I scrutinised the walls afresh, but could still see no break in the dusky monotony of the ceiling, roof, and floor. The chimney was apparently the only aperture in the cell. Yet, I breathed freely enough, and surely there must be means of supplying air to allow the fire to draw. I know only that I could *see* none. At first I did not realise what this condition of things might mean; no dread came upon me. I lay perfectly still, in a half-dreaming state, merely wondering at what I saw. A feeling of sweet rest pervaded my being. My thoughts were not clear—not defined. I was content. I neither hoped for nor desired any change in my condition, for my mind had not as yet acquired sufficient strength to look beyond the present. But gradually—very gradually—I began to experience a sensation of uneasiness. A dull pain seized upon my limbs. I made efforts to move, which caused some of my wounds to open slightly. I again lapsed into motionlessness, but it was not the pleasant calm of the first moments of my awakening; it was an anxious stillness—a *waiting* for some unknown relief. This state continued for many minutes, during which I tried in vain to concentrate the forces of my weakened intellect upon the condition in which I had found myself. And now, while I thus wearied my brain with earnest but fruitless endeavours to comprehend my real state, there came to my nostrils a very faint and indefinable odour which I had not noticed hitherto, though it appeared to me that it must have been present for many minutes.

Hours seemed to pass—hours of weary and painful thought— and still I could not account for that strange odour. There were times when I no longer smelt it, but it always returned; and at last, just as, with a groan of mental anguish, I was relinquishing all effort and all hope, there came wafted to my nostrils a breath of the odour much stronger than any that had preceded it, and at the same instant the *truth* burst upon me with overwhelming suddenness. What I had smelt was the odour of fresh mortar. The doorway had been filled up with masonry!

I was entombed alive!

Once more I swooned. But at the moment when consciousness left me I heard a strange indistinct sound—a sound of blows being struck—one, two—and then all was dark.

However, this swoon was not of long duration. Perhaps a draught of cold air which fanned me aided materially in restoring consciousness. The air came through an aperture in the wall, caused by the withdrawal of several of those bricks or stones which had been used in filling up the doorway. Someone outside was engaged in removing them. It was clear now that the hideous fate intended for me had been revoked, or that deliverance had come.

There was no sound save that made by some instrument upon the masonry. I waited in great suspense, listening to the monotonous striking of the iron. At first I thought not of the comparative silence, but soon a sense of wonderment began to steal over me. Why did I hear no voices? I observed, too, the uniformity of the sounds. It seemed that but one instrument was used, and the seemingly slow progress confirmed this idea. I came to the conclusion that only one worker was engaged.

Hours seemed to pass, that could have been but minutes, ere the opening was sufficiently large to admit a human form. I waited with breathless expectation to see my rescuer. At last a dark object appeared in the rugged aperture. It was a black veil. The veiled woman was my deliverer.

She approached me with the listless grace that I well remembered. But that grace had in it now a hurried, eager motion. She started at seeing that my eyes were open.

"I have come to save you, señor," she said, in her sweet, murmuring tones; "to save you from the vengeance of the chief. You were walled up by his orders; but I shall assist you in escaping from these dungeons."

Then, with marvellous strength and dexterity, she lifted the mattress and my wounded form from the bedstead to the floor, and dragged me through the opening, proceeding along a corridor many yards in length, until at last she paused from the wearisomeness of her toil before a half-opened doorway. Pushing the door wide open, she drew me into a cell somewhat similar in shape and size to that from which she had rescued me.

I was much shaken by the journey; some of my wounds were bleeding freely. She made me swallow a little wine, and then, murmuring some words, which I did not quite catch, but among which I remember "destroy traces," she left me, closing the door as she went out.

The apartment into which I had been dragged was similar in shape to that which had been intended for my tomb, but was furnished much better and more elegantly, bearing many evidences of a lady's refined taste. It seemed like a reading-room and sleeping-room combined. There was a bed; book-shelves, well stocked, were ranged on the walls, and a table and chairs of antique appearance were scattered about; soft carpet covered the floor, which, I doubted not, was of stone, for had not the veiled woman spoken, of "these dungeons?" The walls were hidden by heavy crimson tapestry, upon which curious, and, in some instances, grotesque, and even horrible, devices ware wrought in gold. As the tapestry swung heavily and slowly to and fro, these strange devices had the effect of changing continually—a weird and terrible sight to nerves shattered like my own. I observed that there were no mirrors in the room, and this caused me to wonder whether the veil ever left that mysterious being's face, if only in order to enable her to see the reflection of her own features, and I now remembered again her strange words—"My face is beautiful." While puzzling over these things a drowsiness came over me, and I fell into a long and heavy sleep.

For days, weeks—it may have been for months—the veiled woman nursed me untiringly, and at last I grew well and strong; my wounds healed slowly, but without ill effects.

The veiled woman spoke little, but there was ever, I thought—and still think—an increased tenderness in her sweet tones each time she addressed me. As I grew better my curiosity became greater, and more difficult of restraint. I felt that her history was strange and unique—that the mystery which surrounded her would be worth unravelling. I began to study deeply her tones and her actions, and in no great length of time I had formed some sort of conclusion. The woman had either been confined in these dungeons on account of symptoms of insanity which may have been perceived in her words or actions; or, she was the victim of some plot, and had been placed here by those who feared to kill her. In either case, madness was in her. Plainly I perceived that her reason had long been shattered. The conviction came upon me stealthily; I found myself regarding her as one would regard a lunatic, even before I had reached the sad conclusion.

Upon what pivot her madness turned I could not know. It would, I thought, be worse than useless to put questions to her that might arouse the most dangerous elements of her malady; yet, on one occasion, I could not restrain myself from saying, observing her to be in a more than usually rational mood:

"But tell me, dear señora, why you wear that horrible veil. When will you afford me one glimpse of that beauty which, I know, is behind it? Can you not see that I am dying to behold your face?"

Immediately the words had left my lips I regretted their utterance. A strange and deadly light gleamed in the eyes of the veiled woman—the dark, dangerous fire of insanity. It, however, subsided soon, and when she spoke her voice was as sweet and as tender as before.

"Have I not told you that my face is beautiful," she said. "But you may not see it yet, on account of a vow I have made. However, I will show you my portrait, painted not more than a year ago by a great Italian artist—or, rather, you may see it by pressing that silver knob yonder."

She pointed out the knob, and I advanced towards it, not failing to perceive, however, that she had turned her eyes in the opposite direction. I pressed the knob, and a panel opened from the wall, disclosing the portrait.

As a work of art, the painting itself was wonderful. But the supreme, the marvellous living beauty of the face! I felt as though I were in the presence of an angel as I contemplated this counte-nance, that far surpassed my most ardent imaginings of the Houris' superhuman loveliness. I seemed to no longer tread the earth. I was uplifted—I was floating, with a seraphic motion, through an ether of supreme delight. Paradise seemed to open itself before me, and an angel with a beauty passing that of the daughters of men seemed to invite me to a heavenly embrace. I had lost all indi-viduality—I was entranced. And hours passed that to me were but seconds of ecstasy. And, at last, the face appeared to recede, and the features grew dim in the distance, but soon I followed, and then we were in the clouds, speeding through azure skies with superhuman swiftness, until lofty gates of crystal appeared before us. The lovely face sped through, and I essayed to follow, but the immense gates swung together, hiding from my view the angel's face, and losing all my serial lightness, came reeling down—down, through endless clouds—down to the black and gloomy earth, and——

Awaking with a start from my marvellous dream-vision I became conscious that the panel was closed, and that two icy hands clasped my brow, while drops of moisture fell on my face. The veiled woman stood over me, weeping. The moisture on my cheeks was her tears.

But the impression wrought on my mind by the superb loveli-ness of the face I had seen was too powerful to be effaced by an emotion which, however poignant, I could imagine no reason for. And so, realising that the picture in the panel was the portrait of her who stood before me—that beneath that hideous black veil was the original of the painting—I, impelled by a desire that I could not repress, attempted to raise the sable folds so that I could gaze upon the living beauty underneath; but she, divining my intention, caught my wrist in a steel-like grasp, and repulsed me with a strength for which I was all unprepared. I could see that her dark eyes blazed with a terrible light, and I became afraid, and implored pardon for the indignity I had been about to inflict. At length she grew calm, and when she spoke it was with that wonderful sweetness of tone which so well harmonised with the great beauty of which I believed her possessed. But now her voice was infinitely more sad and touching in its tenderness than it had ever been since first I heard it.

"Señor," she said, "you must fly without delay. I have provided for your escape. These caverns were constructed for the purposes of the *contrabandistas* of Spain, and have various outlets, one of which is known only to myself; by it you shall escape. A horse, ready saddled, is waiting. First, however, I will explain to you why you must not see my face. I was of one of the oldest families of Spain, but very poor. All its members were scattered or dead, and I, when very young, was left to the care of a distant relation—a miserly villain, who conceived the inhuman idea of selling me to a wealthy, ambitious, intriguing, Roman priest named Leon Navarro. But I succeeded in communicating with a young cavalier who loved me; who, failing in his attempt to carry me off—for I was too closely guarded—waylaid the priest, and, by the aid of friends, forced him to write a confession of the whole plot, and a renunciation of his robe and of his vows. This was done after a long night of the most exquisite tortures, and it was only when the strong determination of Navarro was broken—when his iron will was conquered by supreme bodily anguish; that is to say, when his life was almost spent—it was only then that the confession was obtained. This, signed and witnessed, was sent to the Papal authorities at Rome, and Navarro was excommunicated. My lover was too honourable to take the life of this infamous wretch. Navarro was liberated when the act of excommunication was accomplished. But now he became a demon. With the death of his fierce and lofty ambition all that was human in him also died. You know him. He who left you, wounded and unable to move, in a cell of which the entrance was walled up—left you to gaze at an expiring fire—type of your expiring life—until, slowly and bitterly, death came to end your anguish—he is Navarro!

He devised for you, the slayer of his brother, whom he valued only as an indispensable aid to his projects—for you he devised a fearful death. But for me, the indirect destroyer of his great and passionate ambition, this monster planned a most hellish, a most inhuman revenge—a living death. My lover he killed, but not before he had shown him the living horror into which his demoniac cruelty had transformed me, and then—but hark!"

I could not listen, but she evidently heard faint sounds in the distance, for she instantly caught my arm and dragged me out of the cell, leading me through a maze of passages, up and down steps, through doors, which she locked after we had passed, and round turnings that bewildered me. At last I caught the sounds which had long been apparent to her acute hearing. They seemed very close, and suddenly I was startled by an explosion.

"On—on!" cried the veiled woman; "they are blasting the doors. They will be upon us!"

It was very dark, yet my guide never paused, never hesitated, but led the way with unerring instinct, as it seemed to me.

At last, to my unspeakable relief, a flash of light appeared before us—a kind of light which I had not beheld, it seemed, for years—*sunlight.*

Several more explosions had resounded.

"Oh!" cried the veiled woman, panting for breath, "they will be here! On, señor, for your life—a few more paces!"

But the approaching sounds redoubled.

We were now in a long, straight passage, at the end of which a flight of stone steps could be seen. These evidently led to the outer world, for it was upon them that the sunlight shone.

"Ha! they are here!" cried a powerful voice just behind us—a voice which I too well remembered: it was that of the Guerilla chief, the former priest, Navarro.

We reached the steps just as several shots were fired. I was slightly wounded, but succeeded in springing up a few of the steps. There, stayed by a strange impulse, I paused and glanced back.

Four carbines were covering me from a distance of six paces. The veiled woman was in the act of falling at the foot of the stairs. A gust of wind from the opening above raised the black veil and threw it over her head.

The sunlight streamed full upon her unveiled features.

I sank down upon the masonry, overcome with a deadly terror.

But it was not on account of the levelled carbines or the fierce faces of the Guerillas that such horror overwhelmed me. It was because of a most unearthly—a most appalling hideousness—the work of a supreme cruelty—which I beheld beneath the sable veil of the dead woman.

The Guerillas themselves staggered back, lost in horror. These lawless men, who feared naught in heaven or in hell, paused; nor dared advance a single step nearer to the awful thing that barred their way.

The voice of Navarro at length broke the spell that seemed to hold everyone but he in thrall.

"Fools!" he cried, "fire upon him ere he escapes!"

The Guerillas raised their carbines. But ere they could fire I had sprang up the steps, mounted the horse that was waiting, and rode off at a mad, headlong speed—on, on, until, flaked with foam and falling from fatigue, my courser stopped before the bivouac of Marshal Soult, and I was safe.

THE TENANT OF THE THIRD CELL

There is here no need, clouded and weak as my intellect has of late years become, for laboured efforts of memory; there is no single detail in the events of which I have now to tell you that cannot be at will recalled. Though many—though *very* many years have passed into eternity since then, and though in all other things my faculties are now sadly deficient, the slightest effort confusing them to a pitiable degree, yet the mere utterance of a name evokes from "the grey ruins of memory" a tumultuous rush of thronging recollections; awakes a thousand tragic echoes that seem to be not the mere repetitions of my own voice throughout the lofty room, but rather the dim, far-off echoes of voices that I loved, and of voices that I hated, bringing in their train sad, ghastly visions of the things that happened at that dread period of which I speak—a period full of sorrow, of terror, and of death.

Viola! Beloved name; beautiful child, now, alas! long departed. Gerald! warm-hearted and generous youth, my daughter's betrothed—falling into the cold embrace of the grim angel Azrael, for no greater sin than that of loving her whom another loved, of winning the prize that another had hoped to, but could not, win. These two beings, living pictures of love and innocence, with what intensity of regret are they remembered. With what sad thoughts is the recollection of their sweet manners and their beautiful features ever accompanied. But *Victor Rolaire*—ah! what are these sensations which sweep over me at the sound of *that* name—at its sinister echoes? Why do I close my eyes, fearing to behold in the dark corners and shadowy recesses of the lofty apartment some vision replete with horror—a vision of things which I once saw in dread reality? But let me not attempt the analysis of these feelings, for the mind must be calm—transcendently calm—for such an arduous task. Let me rather, lest I be accused of embellishing a plain statement of facts, pen, as clearly as I can, these recollections of a now far-distant epoch of my life.

Of myself it will be sufficient to say, merely, that my name is Ainsley; that I have abundance of what men call wealth; that I come of a fiery race, in whom the spirit of vengeful retaliation has ever been strong—too strong, alas! in most cases; and, lastly, that, marrying young, I found myself ere I was forty a widower with a lovely daughter of eighteen, in whom all that intense, passionate, and somewhat moody love which I had borne my wife was centred.

In the old and rambling Elizabethan house in which we lived Viola and her cousin Gerald Wendyl grew together. They wandered in childhood over the hills and in the woods and by the river until the time arrived when the necessity of education separated them, and then only at intervals of six months they saw each other. But ere the youth was twenty their troth was plighted. His parents were dead; he was alone, and it was not singular that his former playmate's image should fill his sorrowing and lonely heart with love, nor that she, whose guileless thoughts saw in her boy-lover all the gallant and generous chivalry of romance—all the noble attributes of poetic manhood—should yield her fresh young life to his keeping, and trust him as he, unfortunate youth, deserved to be trusted.

Alas! for the dark and accursed hour that saw the form of Victor Rolaire cross the threshold of our peaceful dwelling. This sinister being, cast athwart our path by some dread fatality, was one of those strange exceptions of human life and character in whom the desire for the attainment of an object becomes, under the slightest restraint, a passion ruthless and irresistible, to which the man himself is the veriest, the most abject of slaves. The life—the habits of Victor Rolaire were not of an evil or a vicious nature; his demoniac attributes were purely latent, and existed, I am willing to believe, entirely unknown to himself. His terrible capacity for crime could not have been suspected from his manners, his countenance, or in even that very peculiar expression which, at rare periods, shone in his dark and gleaming eyes; an expression produced, I think, more by the involuntary contraction of certain adjacent nerves than the dilation of the orbs themselves.

This man's charming gaiety and engaging *insouciance* had won

Gerald's heart at school, where they had first met, and where they had developed a friendship deep enough—on one side at least— to survive temporary separation. Their acquaintance had been renewed, and now, as the nuptials of poor Gerald and Viola were fast approaching, Victor Rolaire was still residing in the locality, ostensibly for the purpose of his vocation as an artist.

From the moment of his first meeting with Viola I could see that he was exercising the full strength of his great fascinations to gain her heart, and to oust therefrom the image of the friend who trusted him so generously and so loyally. But the days passed on, and I *would* not perceive the danger of allowing so passionate a being to indulge in hopes that I well knew would never be realised, for the affections of Viola were too surely and irrevocably given to her cousin Gerald to admit of change, be those fascinations what they may. And one day I saw that Viola was very sad, and much agitated, on account of some deep emotion, which was caused, I doubted not, by something that Rolaire had said; and thenceforth I noted that she cared not to meet him, and even intentionally pre- vented many interviews which would otherwise have come about in the ordinary course of events. I also noted, but with little anx- iety, that Rolaire grew daily more and more gloomy, that his gay *insouciance* had departed, and that the strange expression to which I have before alluded came oftener than at any previous time into his peculiar eyes, and that it deepened perceptibly at sight of the happy Gerald; that moreover, when any of those little ever-recurring evidences of affection common to young lovers made themselves apparent, he turned his face aside, that none should see its white- ness and passion. All this, I say, was apparent to me; but how *could* I know what was passing in the man's passion-distorted mind? How *could* I trace in these circumstances the horrible thoughts that must have filled his distraught brain? And yet how bitterly I have reproached myself for not arriving at the knowledge in time to pre- vent the fearful tragedy that was so soon to be enacted! "Either," said a great American genius, whose own life afforded a gloomy instance of the truth of his aphorism—"either the memory of past bliss is the anguish of to-day, or the agonies which *are* have their origin in the ecstasies which *might have been*." And it is thus with me. Yet, what boots it *now* to tell of the long and weary hours of bitter communion with my soul that I have endured? What avails it *here* to describe the painful thoughts of those nights of agonising regret during which I have waited for the dawn, only then to find that the gay sunlight mocked my anguish—laughed at my gloom? Of these dark portions of my unhappy life I will not speak further, lest I weary you thereby, but will now detail the few events of which my narrative is composed.

One calm, misty afternoon in summer my daughter had gone out riding with her affianced and Victor Rolaire. This day was but seven days distant from that on which the wedding was to take place. Rolaire had apparently regained his former buoyancy of spirits, as though, in relinquishing all hope of winning the heart of Viola, he had banished regret; but I, who observed the expression of his eyes, could not force myself to think that he was entirely reconciled to the union of the two lovers. He knew—he *must* have known—that in the event of the death or the faithlessness of Gerald there would still be as little chance for him as ever; and this is, doubtless, the reason that he did not attempt to remove the youth from his path, or to destroy by wile the implicit faith reposed in each other by the young girl and her betrothed.

The day had been very warm, and the ride long, and I doubt not that it had been designedly selected by Rolaire, who had proposed the excursion. The shadows of the trees were fast lengthening when they returned. I, who had been strolling through the park, as was my daily habit, had paused near the little ivy-covered cottage which Victor Rolaire had selected as a residence and studio. I had entered the little garden, and had seated myself on a rustic bench near a pretty little arbour, through the leaves of which I could see a small round table and some chairs, and in one corner a cask of cider. While I was dreamily gazing at these things the sounds of voices and of horses' hoofs struck upon my ear, and I knew that they were returning; but still I sat on the rustic seat, and did not hasten to meet them, but only waited. They came into view. I saw them dismount at the gate, and fasten their jaded horses to the low, ornamental fence, and then walk along the path, laughing and chatting the while, but in a tired manner. And, as they still approached, and the purport of their talk made itself apparent to me, I understood that Rolaire was pressing them to take some light refreshment ere they left. And now, while I yet sat on the rustic seat, they entered the leafy arbour, and sank, in a sort of happy and contented exhaustion, into the chairs that were round the little table. Then Victor Rolaire gaily entreated them to honour him by tasting his wine; but Viola laughingly protested that she never drank wine, and Gerald declared that the beverage he fancied most then was cider, a cask of which stood in the corner, as I have said.

"Then," exclaimed Rolaire, "cider let it be. I will go to the cottage and get some glasses, for I perceive there are none here."

And as I still sat, dreamily listening and gazing, he procured the glasses, and filled them with the cider from the cask.

"Look!" he cried, suddenly, pointing through the open entrance of the arbour, "the sunset! Let us drink to the glorious sunset!—to those wondrous hues that tinge the hazy sky—to them let us drink; and may the sun go down as beautifully on the seventh day from this—the day of your nuptials, Gerald—the day when your real happiness begins, Miss Viola!"

He spoke in an impassioned tone; and compelled thereby their gaze to the horizon, where the "sunset seemed to beckon far away;" and though I, too, gazed in the same direction, I did not wholly miss observing the actions of Rolaire. A hurried movement of his arm arrested my attention; I caught the gleam of something in his hand—something that might have been a small phial; and—could it be?—his hand paused an instant over Gerald's glass and over Viola's; but in the next moment he spoke again, calling upon them to drink to his toast. They raised their glasses, as did he.

A sensation of uneasiness, quickly merging into one of alarm, came over me. What had happened? What had been done? Surely something terrible—but I could not tell, I could not think *what*— and I trembled violently as I told myself that there was something about to happen that I must prevent, but—these things are not to be explained—I could not rise; I could not speak!

May heaven, in its divine mercy, pardon me that moment of hesitation. Thralled as by a vertigo, I could not move, and still less could I articulate. But suddenly, by a violent effort, I broke the spell that bound me, and rushed through the leaves with a loud cry, intending to dash the glasses from their lips. But it was too late! They had swallowed the deadly draught!

* * * * *

One hideous night of grief and regret I spent, ere the stunning effects of that fearful event wore off; and then the wild spirit of my race—that quenchless thirst for vengeance—asserted itself strongly within my breast; and, as the day dawned, I had written an account of the tragedy, to be laid before the authorities; had directed the oldest and most trusted of my servants what to do; and then I set out in pursuit of the assassin—went forth to take the life of him who had robbed me of all that was left in the world to brighten my days, and assuage the sorrow caused by the death of my wife.

How, for weeks and months, I tracked the fugitive with an accuracy which must have been the result more of intuition or of instinct than that of lucid deliberation; how he escaped again and again, and each time more narrowly than before; how relentlessly and untiringly I kept him in view—all this need not be here detailed. Suffice it to say that I found myself, at the end of a year, in the great city of San Francisco. During this time my steward had corresponded with me as much as the uncertainty of my whereabouts would permit, and from his communications I had gathered that a verdict of murder had been brought in against Victor Rolaire—that a quantity of the same poison as that with which he had done the foul deed had been found among his possessions; also, that there were some people who hinted their belief that my hurried departure had not, perhaps, been caused by a desire for vengeance—that, in fact, I was an accomplice in the murder of my own child; that I had favoured the suit of Rolaire, and had aided him in his revenge! This dastardly calumny, he considered, was merely propagated by the police in order to cause my return. If so, nothing could have been more ill-advised. It had the effect, instead, of intensifying, if possible, my deadly thirst for vengeance; I would prove my innocence of all participation in the crime otherwise than by returning. I would never relinquish my efforts until either I or my enemy was dead.

In San Francisco, then, at the end of a year, I found myself, having tracked him thither. But here, as elsewhere, he succeeded in eluding my pursuit. Several times I had come within an ace of running him to earth, but on each occasion he had contrived to escape. On the last he sought concealment in the Chinese quarter, and although I employed a man who knew every corner of that mysterious place, I lost sight of Rolaire, who seemed to disappear as utterly as if the earth had engulfed him for ever. But I did not relax my exertions, and be sure that I spared neither money nor labour to attain my end. With each new failure the desire to triumph became more intense within me. He had not left the city—that I knew; my spies watched every outlet; but to find him within passed my powers for the time. Where could he be hiding? Under what disguise could he be concealed? *Was* he within the city? Had any of my spies blundered? These were some of the questions that vexed me night and day. In the meantime I had made a new enemy. One of the men whom I had employed on first arriving at San Francisco had proved false. He had betrayed me into an ambush, from which only my own nerve, resolution, and unusual physical powers had saved me. My first act, on seeing that I had been betrayed, had been to shoot down the traitor. In the *mêlée* that ensued I was myself desperately wounded. A month elapsed ere I recovered, and then it was more by exertion of the will than otherwise that I regained strength and energy.

Scarcely had I arisen from my bed of sickness than the same false spy who had betrayed me presented himself before me—like myself, he had recovered from his wound. I need not recount this wretch's servile protestations of remorse and anxiety to atone for his vile act. He came, he said, to inform me as to the true whereabouts of my enemy. Little as I believed him, I could not afford to despise the slightest chance of finding Rolaire. I told him, therefore, to explain his words. He began by asking me did I not know a house on the outskirts of the city—a house rented, but not occupied, by a Dr. Fayle.

I knew the house; I had also heard of Dr. Fayle as an experimentalist and specialist in certain deadly diseases, and I understood that he experimented in this house on patients who seldom left the gloomy tenement except on their way to the grave. Therein, asserted the spy, was Victor Rolaire; but he, the hardy, the more than robust, was not there as patient. He was not there for a specialist to practise upon; he was there simply to avoid my vengeance.

How unlikely that I should look for him in such a place—that I should seek *him* in a house whose tenants had so little hope of life left that they were glad of extreme experiments being tried in which there could be only the remotest chance of success! He had bribed the doctor to allow him to hide there until I should weary of my search. He would live there for a year, for two, for ten years, were it necessary, so that in the end he escaped. The spy told me these things in such a manner that I could doubt no more; besides, the tale was plausible enough. *If* it was true, it was now impossible for Rolaire to elude me. I would buy the house, the land, the patients for ten times their value if nothing else availed. I may remark, in parenthesis, that the spy, although in the chief particulars he spoke truth, had planned for me, in revenge for his wound, a fate far worse than death, which will be presently made apparent, and it was only by the divine mercy of heaven that his demoniac scheme did not succeed.

I determined, then, to trust the wretch once more, but to be very wary. Therefore, I arranged with certain men that they should be in concealment when I arrived with the spy, who had consented to lead me to the door of the room in which I would find Victor Rolaire. A prearranged signal would bring them to my assistance in a few seconds.

Accompanied by the spy, therefore, I set out. Arriving at the place, the man asked for Dr. Fayle, begging permission to show a visitor over the house. I was now too excited to be surprised at anything, otherwise the ready acquiescence with which the doctor (who was then engaged on an unusually serious case and could not appear personally) complied with the wishes of the spy would have astonished me. I afterwards discovered that my conductor was the doctor's confidant; that he provided him with *cases*; that horrors were enacted in that house which will never see the light of day.

We entered the house. I was armed with a derringer and a keen bowie-knife; it was with the latter that I intended Rolaire should die. A death by the bullet is almost painless; that which is caused by the thrust of steel is *felt*, and leaves the mortal agony plainly written on the distorted features of the victim.

We passed through several rooms; my companion was recognised by the attendants or servants—this I could not help observing, even in my greatly excited state. At length we came to a flight of stone steps, which led to a cell underground. A man stood on the top step, with whom my conductor exchanged some few words, which did not then attract my attention, but which have often occurred to me since with a horrible significance.

"Stop! where are you going?" said the man.

"It is I—Vargrave. Let us pass," said the spy; "we are going to the cells."

"To the cells!—are you mad?—do you know that in the third cell——"

"Hush, fool! Who should know, if not I?"

The man drew back, and we descended the dark, stone stairs.

I had not hesitated, nor felt any desire to pause, as yet; and even here, on the steps which led to these living tombs, my nerves were firm, and I even thought, scornfully, what a coward the wretch must be, after all—what a craven soul must be his—that he could conceal himself *here* from his foe; that he could prefer existing in such a place as *this* to periling his life by meeting a single man. But in no epoch of his career had I known him to display even animal courage, and therefore I marvelled little at his desperate course.

We descended the damp and foul-smelling stone steps, and passed along a passage, pausing at the third door from the entrance. Here my conductor paused.

"This," said he, "is the cell occupied by our enemy. The door is locked, but your strength will amply suffice to break it down."

I turned round to reply, but the man had disappeared. A dreary chill passed through my heart as I noted this circumstance.

But, recovering my nerve, I placed myself against the wall of the narrow passage, and then, with one spurn of my foot, I burst through the only barrier that stood between me and my foe.

I endeavoured, but for some time in vain, to pierce the semi-darkness which the hate that blinded me rendered as black as Erebus. There was a subtle, sickly, mysterious odour in the air, and a heavy stillness; these filled my soul with horror, and I trembled as one ever trembles on the threshold of the Unknown. But I grasped my dagger firmly, and strove earnestly to see through the dense gloom, which the very dim, flickering light, of an oil lamp in the passage failed to dissipate. Some minutes elapsed, and at length my eyes became accustomed to the darkness. The damp, sickening effluvia seemed rather to increase than to diminish. The den was quite destitute of furniture.

At the farthest end, enveloped in moist, filthy rags, lay a human form. I recognised it not, but I *felt* that it *must* be that of Victor Rolaire, my hated and long-pursued enemy. I had run him to earth at last.

But here I paused—I know not why—and the dagger fell from my grasp. At the noise it made in striking on the moist stone floor the prostrate inmate of the cell turned slowly and laboriously, and looked in the direction of the sound. And as he did so most of the rags fell from his unsightly form, and I saw that his only clothing consisted of these damp fragments.

I stood still, transfixed by the hideous spectacle that met my dazed vision. A sickness for which mortal language has no expression came upon me, as I slowly realised the appalling truth.

For then I knew that my vengeance—the weak, hasty vengeance of man—had been forestalled by the dread wrath of heaven; and I shuddered, lost in horror, at the effect of that mighty anger portrayed in the living, breathing thing which lay before me. Of what avail were earthly vengeance *now*? Did the shades of Viola and her unfortunate betrothed *still* cry out for vengeance? On whom, then—on *what*—should justice be visited? Not, surely, on *that* which was before me. Impossible! Oh, heaven, vengeance is indeed thine—is thine alone.

All that now remained of Victor Rolaire, the young, the handsome, the robust, was that huge, bloated, swollen, nearly senseless being, in whom all human passions, sentiments, and enjoyments are merged into one inordinate and ghastly craving—a craving for *moisture*, for dampness and darkness. All that was now left of the man whom I had sworn to slay was that hideous, crawling, less than human thing, described by the terrible word—A Leper!

THE TORTURE OF THE CLOCK

We had now reached the nethermost of the vaults, but this we did not enter, for my captor, impelled by some mysterious influence, recoiled from the threshold as though an unseen hand had thrust him back. I noted also that he made a gesture of horror or fear, or was it merely the irritation of the mind on account of the failure of the will to overcome certain nervous sensations common to all who thus leave the habitations of men to encounter the shadowy horrors of the Unknown, with which the imagination filled these silent catacombs? No doubt his mind pictured the dead of past centuries wandering through the great gloomy vaults—their last earthly home. But was it not more probable that the sudden recollection of a former crime froze this man's heart with horror?—this man, who, till now, had strode through the maze of galleries and corridors with firm and stately tread, never pausing once, even at the ghastliest of those mysterious sights which had confronted us so many times on our subterranean journey.

Although I was cognisant of the fact that my hereditary enemy held my life in the very hollow of his hand—and also that his purpose was to crush that life by means of unheard-of tortures—though most fully aware of this, hope did not for one moment desert me. No; amidst the sharpening of those bodily agonies and privations with which Zaroni had sought to unstring my nerves and weaken my intellect—hope had been ever with me. For, while the power of *thought* lives in the breast of him who is menaced with death, hope does not, and cannot, utterly depart. The more terrible the death that threatens, the stronger is the desire for life, and while that desire remains, however supine, hope triumphs! That which we call despair is the surrender of the desire to live—is the death of thought; so long as the mind lives, hope cannot die.

Since my entrapment into the catacombs I had exchanged no word with Zaroni. When he considered me sufficiently weakened, morally and physically, he had come to the cell in which he had placed me, bound my arms, and then caused me to precede him, while he pushed me with his unsheathed rapier to the right or left whenever we turned into a new passage. But now, halting before the entrance to the last and deepest of the vaults, he, for the first time, broke the long silence he had maintained.

"Oh!" said he, while his fierce, black, solitary eye gleamed through his mask like a glowing coal in the gloom, "Oh! that you had a brother, a sister, a wife, a mistress, a child—anyone whom you loved better than yourself—that I might mete out to you the same punishment your parents suffered."

From the moment that the closed door of the vault had met my vision it had inspired in my heart a mystic sensation, not of dread nor of horror, but of something perhaps more terrible than either and when Zaroni's glance, as he spoke those words, also fell significantly on the massive door, I shuddered; for instinct told me that *there* stood the barrier which alone separated me from the long sought remains of my father and of my mother. From this moment my eyes never left the door, and that mystical emotion of which I have spoken gradually grew more and more defined as Zaroni proceeded, until at length I knew that it was a desire—a frantic longing to be within that vault—though I felt also that it was there the most terrible of deaths awaited me. Zaroni continued:

"Until the day when, in your demoniac cruelty, you inflicted on me a punishment which, but for my hope of revenge, would be worse—far worse than death—when you branded my face with that most frightful device which now distorts it, and which I must always hide, even from myself—until that day I wished no more than to behold you dying in bodily anguish—until then I had intended for you a death of mere physical torture, which would have more than satisfied a vengeance that was not mine, but my father's. Now, however, I have devised a death of which the physical agony, though sufficiently fearful, will be as nothing compared with the *moral* horrors attending it."

He paused again, and, seeing that I yet gazed steadfastly at the door of the vault, he placed himself between me and the closed entrance, so as to be able to look into my eyes. His movement did not for a second divert my gaze, and I was only dimly conscious of the black mask which shrouded what once had been a face, and of the fierce eye that glared into my own.

Then this man, to whom vengeance was the sole object in life, told me the tale of my parents' death—the manner, the place, and the date of which had hitherto been unknown to me. You, who so well know the pride of my race—even you, must marvel that I did not quail before this fearful recital—that my countenance preserved its serenity of expression throughout all that diabolical narrative.

Amid the silence of the catacombs—in a hush which was that of death itself—the voice of Zaroni seemed to whirl around me like the moaning current of some fathomless gulf, wherein the spirit of Crime has found a home.

"Beyond that door at which you gaze the remains of your parents are lying. In that vault they lived for many months, while you—you, Ventronio, their child, played, laughed, prattled, above them; your voice came to their ears by means of tubes in the walls, but they could not utter a sound in reply, for they no longer possessed the power of speech. With his own hands my father had wrenched away their tongues. This act served more than one purpose. The vault yonder opens into another, similar in form and size. Your parents were not together; a door like this separated them. They could neither see nor speak to each other, yet both knew that the other was near. Your father knew that his bride was separated from him by a door—a door which the shortness of his chain would not allow him to touch. He knew this, but could not know that his wife was aware of *his* proximity. 'She knows that you are in my power,' said my father to him, 'but she is kept in ignorance of your fate, and suspense is fast destroying both her mind and her vital forces.' These words he also said to your mother; he made their great love the means of their terrible chastisement. You, I know, can well imagine the anguish of both—each aware of the other's proximity, yet ever doubtful if the other possessed the same knowledge; and both hearing, at intervals, the prattling of that loved child, whom they despaired of again beholding, and whose probable fate they shuddered to contemplate. You, who gaze so steadfastly at that door, may well imagine all this."

Zaroni here paused, so that he might gauge by the effect of

what he had uttered the probable effect of that which was still to come. But I remained impassible, though I was sick at heart—oh! unspeakably sick at heart!—from hearing of the sufferings of my parents, told by such lips. And of what Zaroni said further there are many things which I cannot repeat to you, though my memory will retain them for ever. He spoke of atrocities so heavy in horror, so ferocious, so really fearful, that—but, oh! to think of them brings to my mind visions that appal me—that turn my blood one moment to seething lava, the next to ice. Let not, then, my mind wander amidst these horrors—horrors which will not suffer themselves to be revealed. Oh! Giulio, if you knew all you would not marvel that I have often wished I had never recovered from that trance in which you found me—that my memory of those things was forever swallowed up in Lethe's wave.

Zaroni taunted and tortured me with long recitals of these horrors, seeking to provoke a revealment of the terrible rage and pain which surged within me. Several times I almost fainted from the severity of the struggle to keep my fury under restraint. But my determination and pride, and also that strange feeling—a mingling of desire and expectation, which the sight of the door of the vault inspired within me—enabled me to subjugate my emotions, and keep myself from succumbing to this species of mental anguish. And in the midst of that anguish, mingled with the peculiar desire to behold my parents' remains—you are aware that I have no recollection of ever seeing them in the flesh; I was separated from them at too early an age—a longing to know the *manner of their death* pervaded my thoughts. And this I will relate to you, in the words of Zaroni:

"Tiring at length of these tortures of the body, my father resolved, by a supreme blow, to break the proud, and, till then, invincible spirit of his captives.

"They one day fell into a long and death-like trance, awakening from which they found that the little light they had hitherto been accustomed to had completely vanished; they were now enveloped in absolute darkness—not the darkness of night, but rather that of some fathomless pit. The walls of the vault (they were both in the same one now, though they knew it not) had been rendered even blacker than before, as also had the few objects therein. Their bodies and their garments were black. They could not behold their outstretched hands, which were neither lighter nor darker than the darkness itself. The conviction that their sight had been destroyed, though by what means they could not divine, gradually came upon them. Such darkness as they existed in must have been, indeed, terrible; but was rendered a hundred-fold more appalling by the absence of all sound. The silence was almost as absolute as the darkness. It was a torture so hideous in moral horror that the first day had scarce passed ere they were using their utmost exertions to produce sound. They leapt and stamped upon the floor—the soft piled carpets emitted no appreciable sound. They would have shaken their chains—glad even of that melancholy clangour—but these had been removed, and silken cords now bound them, each to the opposite wall. Their hands were bound close together, or they would have clapped them. Their voices did not avail them; they could not articulate, and the sounds they emitted from their throats so horrified them that they preferred even the silence. At length, as a last resource, they cast their fleshless bodies against the massive walls; their bones produced a dull, dead, vibrationless sound, which was gone the instant it had been made, and left no echo. Yet, slight as these sounds were, they sufficed to make known their presence to each other, and my father—on visiting them— found that they had begun to gnaw the cords that prevented them from enjoying the solace of being together. They could not speak to each other—they could not see each other; they could not, had they been free, have embraced, for their hands were firmly bound. Yet the gnawing of the ropes revealed the fact that, even in this dire extremity, hope had not fled from their souls. But this fact made my father's vengeance the keener and more complete.

"And now, knowing that their reason must soon succumb and relieve them of their misery, my father resolved to end all by one great and terrible blow. He would let them *see each other!*

"You must pause and reflect, Ventronio, ere you can fully appreciate the grotesquerie—the appalling cruelty of this most horrible plan. You must reflect—you must picture to yourself what must have been their sensations, dragging out a hideous existence amidst darkness and silence like those of a tomb. You must remember the bodily tortures I have told you of—how they were deformed—even more than you have deformed *me*. They were black and hideous—they no longer bore the slightest resemblance to the lowest of humanity. Their aspect was that of the monsters sometimes seen in antique arabesques, but even more appalling. Earth possesses no reptile to which I can compare their hideousness.

"When reason was trembling in the balance, sinking hope was revived in their breasts by the sight of a spark of fire in the centre of the vault. It illumined not an inch of the intense darkness. But with each succeeding hour this spark grew brighter, and the captives, who had at first believed it to be but a phantasy of their imagination, at length became convinced that blindness had not after all, been part of their thousand miseries. Hour by hour the spark grew in volume and radiance, and increased its feeble circle of light, and at length it grew so large that the captives could perceive the dim, very dim, outlines of their forms. Then their cords were so lengthened that only a few paces separated them.

"The light had been lowered during this lengthening of the cords. But of a sudden its full radiance shone out, and the captives beheld the other. ('Think, Ventronio!' said Zaroni, dusky fire glowing in the tragic depths of his solitary eye—'think! they beheld in each other the horrible metamorphosis of their former selves!')

"For an instant, as though petrified by the sight of their frightful aspects—their mutual hideousness—they stood still, each staring at the other's black and distorted visage, no doubt wondering what had so transformed them into fiends. And then, impelled by one common impulse—possessed with one common horror, the fearful realisation of the dire fate which had befallen them—they recoiled from each other; they sank noiselessly to the soft carpets of the vault; they uttered a ghastly, gurgling, inarticulate cry, which welled up from their hearts, shattered by that terrible blow, and in that cry their life went out! That supreme anguish, born of their love, which no individual suffering could have called forth, crushed even their proud spirits, and, after enduring a moment of moral torture—to which a lifetime of the direst physical agony was as nothing—they died.

"Such, Ventronio, was your parents' end. And yonder vault saw their death. Yonder vault holds that ghastly secret!"

★　★　★　★　★

The torch had seemed to die away slowly, swallowed up in a gloom deeper than its feeble light could illumine. The tall figure of Zaroni had appeared to my distorted vision to expand in proportion as the light faded, until it grew so large as to be indistinguishable from the intense gloom in which it moved. Yet the terrible eye still seemed to gleam through that sable mask long after darkness supervened. The tale that Zaroni told me before the door of the tomb, the oppressed air of the vaults, and my long fast—these surely combined to produce that faintness which conquered my proud will as the narrative ended. The trance-like unconsciousness into which I had fallen may have lasted but a few hours, or it may be that it exceeded in duration even that from which you succeeded in awaking me later. I know not.

As, on sinking into unconsciousness, the eye of Zaroni had been the last of all objects that I saw, so, on awaking, it was the *first* that met my bewildered vision.

I became aware of that terrible eye even before I had time to realise my personal condition, which had greatly changed during the interval of stupor. I was now on my feet, supported in an upright position by iron clamps, which held me by the limbs to the wall. These caused intense pain, for they were adjusted by screws, and held me so tightly that I could not move an inch. But the most terrible pain was in my head. A broad iron band encircled my brow, pressing the head against the wall. The shooting pains caused by the tightness of this band were so fearful that I felt at times that the iron must burst from the very swelling of my burning brain.

I knew now that my death torture had commenced.

"See!" said Zaroni, in a hoarse, low tone—"see, Ventronio, what is before you! You are at length in the fatal vault. At length you behold the bones of your parents. Did not I say truly, on that Carnival night, that I only could show you them! No doubt you remember that hour when, flushed with revelry and wine, your reckless mirth was suddenly checked and damped by the sombre utterances of the masked witch—of me, Zaroni; when, sobered by the weird aspect and the awful words, you fled from the companionship of your fellow-revellers, and the Carnival saw you no more!"

He loosened the screws of the band that clasped my brow, and the shooting agony in part abated. The dull mist of pain lifted from my heavy eyes, and I saw that which Zaroni had designated with his outstretched hand.

For some moments my dimmed faculties were unable to comprehend the meaning of what I saw, though I perceived the objects clearly enough. In front of me was a very large and very antique clock of carved ebony, the design of which was grotesque and horrible. Immediately before the clock was a complete skeleton, whose upraised arm grasped a small hammer, ready to descend upon a gong which stood beneath it. On either side of the clock another skeleton stood; all three seemed to look through their eyeless sockets upon my writhing and distorted face, and a hideous smile played about the skulls of each—probably an artificial smile, produced by an alteration of the facial bones, but smiles which were but too fearfully real to me whose nerves were unstrung, whose brain was on fire from bodily torture and privation. The *purpose* of these two skeletons (unless to gibe at my agonies) I could not divine.

Zaroni now began to turn the screw of the iron band, and the shooting pains recommenced.

"In the two skeleton forms you see beside the clock," said he, while thus engaged—"in those forms, Ventronio, behold all that remains of your parents!"

A shriek of horror rose to my throat, but so dry and parched was I that my voice refused to utter it. I realised now the awful purpose to which my parents' bones had been, and were being, put, but as yet I realised not all.

"He whom you see in the centre," continued the torturer, as though speaking of a living being, "was once my father. It is the three together who will co-operate to encompass your death. You can see that it wants but a few minutes of striking the hour. You must also have observed that, in proportion as the hands have sped round with the flight of time, so have the clock itself and its attendants approached to where you stand."

I had not observed the fact, but, nevertheless, it was true. The clock and the three skeletons, at first several paces away, had approached to within a few feet. What did this portend? What was to happen on the striking of the hour? A torturing curiosity began to mingle with my many agonies.

"The centre figure is Time," said Zaroni, giving the screw a final turn, "and the others—but you shall know now. Time is about to strike the hour!"

Scarcely had the words left his lips when the hammer of Time descended upon the gong. At the same instant the skeletons of my father and my mother simultaneously thrust out their arms and buried their steel-like talons in the flesh of my chest. There they remained until the hammer of Time had ceased to strike the gong. I grew sick—oh, inexpressibly sick!—on account of the horror of this sudden torture. It was so terribly unexpected, and the thought that it was by the hands of my father and mother that I suffered so horribly increased that suffering tenfold, for there now remained within me too little of that reasoning power which would at other times have rejected the hideous grotesquerie of this horror, and reduced it to what it really was—the mere ingenuity of my living torturer.

As the gong ceased to vibrate, the fangs—which were, as you know, artificial—were withdrawn from the wounds they had made, and at the same instant I felt the band round my brow slightly relax. This prevented me from sinking into unconsciousness, which would have been a relief—oh, unspeakable! But now I was condemned to linger on through the anguish of my tortures, and never know even the solace of temporary oblivion!

The anguish I suffered was surely more than mortal. With what sickness of the soul did I watch the hands move round the dial, and behold the approaching of the clock and the skeletons! How terribly nervous had I become! With what torture did the mere ticking of the great timepiece fill my throbbing brain! And those iron bands—oh, how acute was the anguish of them! What a relief would death have been—and yet I hoped for life!

The striking of the gong occurred once in each hour, and each time the steel talons were embedded in my flesh, and in the same wounds. Zaroni always entered the vault just as the clock was on the point of striking, and never failed to remind me of the fact—so hideous to my distorted reason—that it was my own parents, and not he, who inflicted on me that most appalling torture.

On the striking of the eighth hour since the commencement of the torture, despite the relaxing of all the iron clamps, I swooned from the weakness produced by the mortal anguish, not less than the intense bodily torment and the exhaustion from loss of blood and privation. But the virility of my physique withstood the effects of these agonies, and the swoon lasted but a few moments. Zaroni did not conceal his joy at my quick recovery. He spoke words from which I understood that my torture was to continue until the striking of the twelfth hour, when the awful consummation would take place. He tightened the iron bands, and my agonies recommenced—seemingly increased tenfold by the weakness which the swoon had left. But I will not distract you by recounting the details of my bitter anguish. What now disturbs me most was that my self-control was completely lost during the latter hours. I uttered things which must have made even Zaroni shudder, had they not, instead, overwhelmed him with fiendish exultation. He laughed to hear me hurling mad curses at the smiling skeletons of my father and my mother, and calling upon hell to open and engulf us all together, that the hideous torment might be, at least, varied, and that he who was causing me to suffer so horribly might so suffer himself. Then, choked with sobs, unaccompanied by tears, I begged, grovelingly, for the least respite—the slightest relaxation of the screws. And at intervals I assumed a brief stoical indifference to my torments, and maintained a dogged silence in the midst of the appalling anguish I suffered.

The ninth, tenth, and eleventh hours were past. I was now sick unto death—the sickness of the soul as well as of the body. Too weak to feel the physic anguish so acutely as heretofore, my mental torments had increased an hundredfold, and were yet increasing with every succeeding moment. A mad, an utterly reasonless terror—the complete relaxation of my shattered nerves—now preyed upon me. There were no longer but three skeletons in the vault; there were hundreds, thousands. My physical anguish distorted my power of vision; acute hunger and burning thirst formed not the least of my torments; these at times almost blinded me. The skeletons' smiles expanded into exaggerated and most horrible grins. The ticking of the clock set my teeth on edge; the hands at one moment seemed to fly, at another to stand still. The words that Zaroni uttered seemed like hideous gibes issuing from the jaws of the skeletons; he was growing more frantic than ever with satiated yet insatiable vengeance; he committed a thousand extravagances—childish acts, which were hideous for that reason; he was mad—glutted with revenge. He heaped preposterous, horrible, and most monstrous insults upon me, which I dare not repeat to you. And ever amidst his wild utterances he would pause to reiterate the words—"One hour to live, and then—the final torture!" These words he repeated so often that the fact made itself apparent even to my bewildered brain, and once, on their utterance, I involuntarily glanced at the clock. Could it be—was it possible, that his madness was making him forget? for, instead of an hour, there now remained but a fourth of that time to elapse. I was yet dimly thinking of this when once more the words, "One hour to live," struck upon my ear. Zaroni never looked at the clock.

I noted that he frequently placed himself directly in front of me, in order to fix the keen gaze of his black eye upon my dim and bloodshot one, and the better to heap upon me those hideous gibes of which I have spoken. But my great anguish would not permit of thought, though I endeavoured—oh, how painfully!—to form a train of lucid reflection. Yet a wild, intangible hope had sprung up in my heart; but of what I could not tell. What business had hope in such a place as this? Yet hope—"the hope that triumphs on the rack"—whispered to me there—to *me*, the condemned whose mind was almost destroyed with anguish more than mortal.

Another glance at the clock told me that but *one minute* remained ere the striking of the twelfth hour. Zaroni still stood before me, mocking and gibing, and repeating yet again that one hour of life was left for me ere the final torture ended my misery.

But now the power of thought had fled, though the consciousness of the mind remained. In an apathy of despair I calmly awaited the consummation of my long anguish. I had lost the will to hope, though the hope was yet there in my heart of hearts, the strength to define it had fled; thought had ceased; the beginning of that deathlike trance was upon me; this complete torpidity of the faculties of the mind, though the mind was yet capable of receiving impressions and retaining them, was the first stage of *trance*—its earliest phase.

There came to my ears a sound like the blast of the trumpet of death! It was the striking of the gong exaggerated an hundredfold to my unstrung nerves. I heard also a harsh, rending sound, and which, too, I *felt*. It was the ripping of my garment, which Zaroni had clutched with a death-grip. But the artificial grip of the skeletons, caused by some powerful hidden spring, was even stronger than his.

As the gong sounded, the hands of the skeletons had seized Zaroni in their resistless grasp, the long, sharp steel talons sinking deep into the flesh of his body. The clock retreated to its former position.

The black mask of Zaroni dropped to the floor of the vault, and *that which was beneath it*, even more horribly distorted, if possible, by pain and madness, glared at me. You who have once beheld *it*, know that the most hideous of humanity—but why dwell on so ghastly a subject? Imagine only the aspect of him who met the fearful death intended for me.

You have been astounded at the frightful rending asunder of the body—the appalling dismemberment of the corpse.

The last I remember is that, when the clock had resumed its former position, the two skeletons, with the talons of each buried deeper than ever in the quivering and shrieking form, gradually drew farther and farther apart, until the appalling mutilation was accomplished. The final stroke of the gong rang in my ears as I sank into that long and deadly trance in which you found me, and from which you have released me.

IN THE NORTH WING

My illness was of long duration; many days passed ere Nature conquered the deadly fever that burned within me, and my convalescence was inexpressibly tedious and slow.

The weary, leaden-footed hours were sometimes lightened by the presence of the dear friend who had risked his life in that act of supreme daring by which my own was saved. But his duties as host necessarily occupied the greater part of his time, for the castle was then crowded with guests.

In the North Wing, where I had been placed, so that the quietude essential to my recovery might not be disturbed by the sounds of the ceaseless gaieties, the brilliant entertainments, the wild revelries, in which Verehurst's princely munificence was displayed, and the faint echoes of which sometimes reached me in my seclusion; in the North Wing, deserted and terrible, where phantoms of past centuries were said to wander, and of which superstition whispered strange tales—ghastly tales, heavy in horror; there it was that the days and weeks of my lingering illness were passed. And there, also, occurred that awful adventure of which I have now to tell you. But you who are so well versed in the sciences of psychology and physiology must determine, from the details, whether it was the outcome of a feverish imagination, an overwrought mind, a sickness of the brain, or a real actual experience. I know only that it had all the phantasy of a potent dream-vision, and yet all the vividness of reality; and, although I cannot reconcile the idea of a dream with the memory of what I experienced in that awful hour, yet I will not for a moment pretend that the things I saw were seen with corporeal vision. Perhaps some strange trance was upon me—some state between sleeping and waking—brought about by my physical condition and the gloomy influence of the North Wing, which lent to those ghastly visions their dread reality.

As I grew stronger, both mentally and physically, the antiquity and vastness of my gloomy abode became a source of strange and powerful interest to me. This interest was increased tenfold when, one day, in turning over some old and dusty books and parchments, I found an ancient vellum-bound volume, entitled "The History of Castle Verehurst from A.D. 1354 to A.D. 1520." It was compiled by one of my friend's ancestors, Sir Hugh Verehurst. I passed many hours in perusing portions of this curious book ere I discovered that a large part was devoted exclusively to the North Wing. I glanced through these pages before reading them, and was about to return to the commencement when a heading caught my eyes:—

An Account of the Great Tragedy of the North Wing, wherein Cyril Verehurst and Alice Tremaine fell victims to the awful vengeance of Sir Phillip Margrave; A.D. 1465.

These words excited my curiosity so much that I forgot the lateness of the hour—that I should already have retired to rest, being still very weak. I began to read the pages that succeeded this singular heading, and, as I read, I felt a sense of *expectation* stealing over me—an expectation of something indefinably weird and strange and horrible, which was to come; and this sensation certainly could not have been induced by the rather ordinary and pedantic lines that introduce the narrative which I have copied below, and in which the quaint orthography is the only element omitted:—

"Cyril Verehurst, the second son of Sir John Verehurst, was a beautiful and valiant youth, albeit of a somewhat retiring disposition, and liking more the companionship of minstrels and bards than that of the gay young gallants with whom his elder brother passed the days of his life. Cyril was a scholar and a student; he had no taste for the rough pastimes that were the delight of other youths, yet he could use the crossbow well, and few dared meet him with the sword in single combat. But the life he loved was that of a student; the wassail bout never saw his face. He wandered through the woods or by the river bank; and Nature was his mistress until the lovely Alice Tremaine crossed his path like a ray of light from heaven. Then was the lonely student transformed into the gay and happy lover. His books were cast aside; his bards and minstrels were neglected; he gave himself up utterly to the abandonment of his passionate love; and all the glorious beauty which, until then, he had discerned in the stars of heaven, were now only seen in the glorious eyes of the lovely Alice. He said:—'I have never lived till now; love is life—the ideal life!' It, indeed, surpassed the life of his dreams.

"The Lady Alice Tremaine was the cousin of Cyril Verehurst, but they had never met in childhood or until now. She was noble— not alone with man's, but with God's nobility also; for her mind— of which the spiritual beauty of her face was a true index—was pure, vigorous, profound, erudite, and at all times glowing with ethereal and beautiful thoughts, born of the divine fire of heavenly genius. It was, in truth, a mind such as, perhaps, no one of those times could appreciate, or even comprehend—no one except Cyril, her cousin, whose pure thoughts answered hers—whose heart beat with hers—whose very soul held communion with her own.

"Of him who bore the name and style of Sir Phillip Margrave it now becomes necessary to speak; but the historian trembles at the very idea of attempting to delineate the strange and terrible character of this man, in that so few trustworthy facts have been handed down, the rest being, he fears, but a mass of tradition and invention—or, at the best, truth distorted. It would seem, however, that at one time he must have been a good and brave knight, full of lofty aims and noble aspirations, respected alike by men of sword and men of gown. He was something of a scholar—indeed, for those days, very learned—but his knowledge, though varied, was not profound. It appears, also, that he was great on the field of battle and in the tournament, excelling in feats of arms. But—a fact more important than all for the purposes of this narrative—he bore within him the germs of madness—of hereditary insanity, which, from his youth upward, had been slowly but surely develop- ing, until, at the period of the terrible events here to be recorded, it had, almost imperceptibly to himself, attained a dangerous and powerful sway over his reason. It is not very clearly set forth in what this madness principally consisted; there is, however, some mention of a strange and horrible passion for the mutilation of the human form, even to the extent of——"

Suddenly the taper, by the light of which I had perused thus much of the narrative, flickered in its socket, and after one last expiring flare, became extinguished. My eyes, still fixed on the pages of the history, read by that last flash a few words some lines below those at which I had broken off. These were the words I read:

"Sir Phillip, then, loved the Lady Alice——"

And as this fragment was conveyed to my understanding, it seemed to me that a current of cold and clammy air swept past me, and that it was this which in reality had caused the sudden extinction of the light. I was now in utter darkness. For some minutes there was in me a sensation of vacuity—of nonentity, as if the darkness was not merely that of absence of light, but rather the blackness of some illimitable void—of some vast abyss into which no ray had ever penetrated. I felt myself to be slowly losing consciousness under the weight of this awful sensation; yet I was dimly, vaguely aware of some subtle, indefinable change in my mental and physical conditions. It seemed to me as though some will, superior to that of man, hovered over me, to which not only mental and physical conditions. It seemed to me as though some will, superior to that of man, hovered over me, to which not only my actions, but even my thoughts were subservient. I felt no fear—I was, in fact, perfectly calm; a kind of subdued exaltation (I can find no better term) possessed me. And now, impelled by this supreme will of which I have spoken, it seemed to me that I arose and walked—though I did not appear to touch the earth in my progress, nor can I recollect opening any doors or traversing any passages or corridors. An impalpable Presence (distinct from the Will) seemed to precede me, and when, suddenly, I entered a large and lofty apartment, draped with tapestry of deep crimson, and lighted by braziers on tripods and swinging censers, which gave forth a dim, ruddy glow, and exhaled a strange, subtle fragrance—I felt, as by a sort of instinct, that here I must pause—that here all that was to happen would happen—that here, in fact, the sequel to a tale that I had somewhere read, but never finished, would be made known to me. And, as these reflections arose in my mind (doubtless planted there by that mysterious will of which I have spoken), I seated myself on one of the many luxurious cushioned seats of the vast apartment. Scarcely had I done so when I perceived, at the further end, a man reclining like myself on an eastern couch, but in a different attitude. This man I recognised as

Sir Phillip Margrave, a personage in the tale which I remembered
having half read at some period now far distant—and it actually
seemed as if I were still continuing to read this tale, or, rather, to
take it up at the part where I had left off; for the thoughts of the
man at the further end of the apartment were, by some mysterious means, made known to me, so that, even as he thought, his
reflections passed through my own mind at the same moment as
they found birth in his. A kind of double madness—partly that
which he inherited from his ancestors, and partly that which is
induced by the passion of revenge—surged within him. His teeth
were clenched; his face was white to the lips; his eyes gleamed with
a sombre brilliance—they were fixed on a small casket which lay
open beside him, and which revealed various instruments of pol-
ished steel, strangely shaped, as they flashed back the ruddy glow
of the braziers. Expectation, desire, fear, impatience, horror, were
mingled in the brain of the man, producing a chaos which threatened to plunge him into a still deeper madness—a yet greater
frenzy. Expectation of an arrival, desire for the enactment of a
hideous revenge, fear of the appalling things which were contemplated, impatience at the slow passing of time, horror of himself
and his frightful thoughts—such was the analysis of that mind into
which, by some mysterious means, I saw so clearly. Oh! it was no
dream which was upon me—of that I am sure; but I doubt if even
you, to whom years of assiduous psychical research, of profound
seeking into secret and forbidden lore, have vouchsafed such wide
and terrible knowledge—I doubt much whether even you will succeed in finding the key to this mystery.

Soft footfalls now sounded at some distance from the chamber,
but in an instant I knew that they belonged not to him whom the
maniac expected. I knew, also, though I was not conscious that the
sense of hearing was alive in me, that he muttered these words:
"Ha! it is she. Well, be it so; either of them, it matters little." And
his eyes fell once more on the mysterious casket, the use of the
contents of which even I, who read Margrave's thoughts, could
not divine. Not long, however, was I left in doubt. A young girl,
of graceful yet proud and haughty bearing, and of surpassing
loveliness, entered the apartment, and, seeing Margrave, started
with surprise, which was, however, succeeded by an air of proud

indifference. She would have passed on, but the madman seized her in his arms, and, despite her frenzied resistance and her ringing shrieks—which I could not hear, but *felt*—he took in his hand one of those strangely-shaped implements, and with it removed from the sockets both of her beautiful, brown eyes. I saw this done with feelings not of the horror and loathing which I experience in relating it to you, but of calm and attentive curiosity, which, in fact, formed not the least potent of the sensations felt by Margrave, whose hereditary madness consisted in a passion for the distortion and mutilation of the human frame, and this, his last act, differed only from his former experiments in that it satisfied both his madness and the awful revenge of which he had long dreamed.

He placed the eyes in another, and smaller casket, which he took from his pocket. Meanwhile, the Lady Alice Tremaine (which was the name of the young girl mentioned in the narrative) had swooned. It now seemed to me that many minutes of unbroken silence succeeded, during which the fires burned with a deeper, duller, redder glow, and the perfumes became so strong that my senses were affected, and I grew drowsy—so drowsy that the braziers and censers seemed to be multiplied tenfold, and yet to give no more light; and, no doubt, I would have become unconscious had not the sound of footfalls arrested my attention the same instant as Margrave raised his eyes from the casket which he still held—at the same instant, also, as the Lady Alice, recovering from her swoon, arose, and seemed to gaze at the entrance through her empty, bloody sockets, in which, it seemed to me, the reflection of the ruddy fires glowed. She stood erect and without motion, awaiting the entrance of him on whose account she had suffered so horribly. Then entered Cyril Verehurst. At the appalling sight which met his vision he staggered, dazed with a terrible fear, lost in a horror more than mortal. The Lady Alice, feeling the approach of him whom she could not see, smiled—a terrible smile of the lips alone—and pointed in the direction of Margrave. She spoke no word.

The madman started to his feet, placed the casket on the ottoman, drew his long sword, and waited. Cyril, whose aspect resembled nothing earthly—whose haggard, tragic eyes gleamed with sudden madness, uttered a cry like the roar of a lion wounded unto death. Seeing the eyes in the casket, he took them up and gazed at them with an intensity of expression for which the world has no name. Then, seizing from the trophies on the wall a Damascus sword, he flung himself upon Sir Phillip Margrave.

It was not a duel which ensued. It was a fight of madmen—a mutual butchery. There was no attempt at defence on either side. Each struck blindly at the other, and every blow, every thrust, took effect. In a few seconds both combatants, pierced in twenty places and bathed in blood, rolled on the marble floor. Sir Phillip Margrave, as he fell, breathed his last. But Cyril Verehurst lived some moments; that is to say, long enough to feel the embrace of the Lady Alice, who had seized the Damascus sword which her hand, groping about, had touched, and had plunged it into her breast. And then, falling upon the body of her lover, she mingled her last sigh with his.

A still deeper, ruddier glow diffused itself over the vast apartment—a yet more subtle and overpowering perfume emanated from the braziers and the censers, and the actors in the tragedy faded from my vision. The last I saw was the Lady Alice Tremaine, out of whose orbless sockets a crimson and fiery luminance appeared to spring, piercing a whitish mist that seemed to rise from the earth long after her form had disappeared. For the first time I shuddered with horror. Then, like the phantoms (if such they were), I seemed to sink, to vanish, to glide away into nothingness.

It appeared to me that I awoke from a long and uneasy slumber, full of ghastly and unearthly dream-visions, which, however, were so potent as to seem to be actual realities. The room in which I found myself, too, gave colour to this supposition. It was furnished in Egyptian style. All at once a light seemed to enter my mind, and memory awoke within me.

"Can this," I cried aloud—"can this be the Egyptian Chamber, of which I have heard Verehurst speak sometimes, though never without a shudder? Can this be the place in which that appalling tragedy was enacted? . . . . There are the braziers—the censers; but they are all empty and cold. Where, then, are the perfumed, glowing fires with which they were filled? There, also, is the crimson tapestry, but how faded and dust-covered! Where are its deep, living hues that glowed like the fire of the braziers? Ha! what do I see now?

Stains, dark and terrible, disfiguring the beautiful marble, and at the very spot on which the deadly conflict took place. But the bodies—the weapons—where are they? I see them not; only those sombre discolourations remain to mark the place of the tragedy. Only these? Can it be that——"

At this moment an object which seemed strangely, wildly familiar to me came within the range of my vision. It was a small ebony casket. Taking it in my trembling hands, I raised the lid.

Within, reposing on the violet lining, and rendered impervious to the ravages of centuries of time by some chemical, were two human eyes.

THE CRIME OF KARNHEIM

CHAPTER I.

THE RESCUE.

K arnheim was a Polish conspirator who entertained great ambitions. He was also an artist of singular genius and power, but lacking in application. Half of his pictures were never finished; very few were sold. They were scoffed at by the popular taste, and the critical condemned them as *outré* and grotesque. But it is with Karnheim the Conspirator, and not Karnheim the Painter, that this narrative has to do, and, although a description of some of his works would be the most graphic way of illustrating his character, I forbear to weary you. Let me, then, in future, speak of his vocation as a plotter and revolutionist, and forget, as he often did, his vocation as a painter.

Karnheim was one of the chiefs of a secret society of revengeful power, and of the most advanced views in regard to the liberty of the people of Poland. I saw him first in Paris, where, through the medium of a friend, I made his acquaintance. I was very young and romantic then, and I really believe that, but for the assiduous counselling of my friend Grahame (a Scotchman), I would have embarked my whole fortune in an enterprise which the wily Karnheim had expounded to me. The conspirator exercised all his most subtle fascinations to overcome Grahame's influence, and might, indeed, have succeeded in time, but an affair of a political nature compelled him, at this interesting juncture, to avoid all *rencontres* with the authorities, and for some years I saw him no more.

* * * * *

After travelling a great deal with my friend, who, poor fellow, died of wounds received while boar-hunting in the Ardennes, I returned to England, and lived a somewhat retired life at Grayle Abbey, my ancestral possession, which stood close to the sea. My out-door amusements consisted of riding and boating. Both gave me solitude—which at times I loved—boating the most. On a calm, sunny day I would row out of the little harbour and sail along the rock-bound coast, sometimes allowing the frail craft to drift about for hours together, while my mind lost itself in dreamy contempla-tion of the long, rolling waves that heaved so slowly beneath me, and of the grand old cliffs that frowned so dark above me. Some-times I would find myself farther away from my little harbour than was at all safe or prudent. However, the careless trust I placed in the sea, that arbiter of my destiny, was never betrayed. She was always fair and calm and smiling to me; and generous, too—for did she not confer on me the greatest of treasures?

One calm, still afternoon I had drifted several miles from shore, but had no thought of peril. Reclining on the cushioned seat, I was deep in the dreamiest of day-dreams, which lasted I know not how long. But suddenly I became conscious of something unusual in the aspect of a certain portion of the rocky shore which was well known to me, and which I called "my amphitheatre." This place was level, and encircled by tiers of great rocks, which looked like huge seats. The circle was broken, the gap facing the open sea. There was a tiny cove, where, at low tide, and in very calm weather, a small boat could approach with safety and facility and land its occupants, but great care had to be taken.

I adjusted my telescope and scanned the rocks. I saw two women thereon. The tide, I knew, was rising. I could see no boat; I concluded that it must have drifted away or been dashed to pieces among the rocks as the tide rose. The prisoners of the amphithea-tre ran distractedly to and fro. Suddenly, however, they rushed to the edge of a rock, waving their handkerchiefs frantically in the air. They had seen me.

Not even staying to answer their signal, I turned the boat shore-ward, and rowed—for there was no wind to sail by—as I never rowed before or since.

How I managed to get them off the rock I never knew. It was a miracle. All I can remember is that the ladies displayed the utmost courage, and that one of them fainted immediately the danger was past.

Her companion, while I made all haste to get out of the danger-ous vicinity, bathed her temples with the cold sea-water. I looked with much interest at the face of the lady. Its pallor was excessive. It was of the perfect smoothness and whiteness of Parian marble. The lips had paled from their original carmine to its faintest shade. It was a countenance of perfect, therefore of the purest, beauty—passionless and passive now as the marble it resembled—straight and classical in its contour as the master effort of a Greek sculptor.

While I was yet gazing, with a calm and contemplative delight, at the beautiful young face, so refreshing, so tranquillising in its pure, chaste loveliness, the other lady (a volatile Parisienne, evi-dently the maid or "companion,") talked incessantly, volunteering all information necessary for my enlightenment as to herself and the unconscious lady, and the circumstances which had led to the condition in which I had found them, interrupting herself every moment to express her intense gratitude in the wildest and most extravagant terms.

The lady, Miss Irene Grahame, was the only daughter of George Grahame, Esq., of Vingron Tower, a magnificent pile about twenty miles distant from Grayle Abbey. Miss Grahame was very fond of boating, and could row and sail with great skill. Whenever her companion could be induced to venture, they took excursions together. This time, owing to the extreme calmness and salubrity of the weather, they had ventured further than ever before, and, becoming interested in the strange appearance of the rocky amphi-theatre, had landed and explored the place. Being tired, they rested a while. When, at last, they sought their boat, they found that it was no longer there. It had slipped its fastenings. They saw, also, that the tide was rising rapidly.

The vivacious Parisienne was dilating on their extreme terror and despair at finding themselves in such dire peril, when Miss Grahame's eyes were suddenly opened. They were of the deepest, purest blue I had ever beheld. My own had been fixed on her face at the moment, and, as hers met their glance, the deadly pallor of her complexion was relieved by the faintest tinge of carmine on either cheek. Her eyes widened with wonder and mute inquiry, and presently she murmured:

"Then we are really saved? Have I been unconscious? But tell me to whom we owe our preservation?"

"My name," said I, fascinated by the sweetness of her low and full-toned voice, "is Gordon Holmes."

"Ah, the recluse—the hermit of Grayle Abbey—Oh! pardon—I am rude—I——"

Perhaps she was slightly hysterical from the effects of her recent swoon, but she spoke with a rare animation. The expressiveness of her features lent them a piquant and *riante* loveliness strangely at variance with the white, set face, so classic in its marble rigidity, which I had gazed on only a moment before, when she was unconscious. Absolute regularity of features rarely combines with piquant mobility; Irene Grahame possessed this charming combination.

"Ah, mademoiselle," said the Parisienne, whose name was Claire Dubourg, with mock solemnity, "beware how you offend him, lest he should have some secret cavern hereabouts. Who knows but that he is even now bearing us into captivity."

"Nonsense," said Miss Grahame, smiling. "But," she added, after a pause, "where *are* you taking us, Mr. Holmes? It seems to me that we are going in quite an opposite direction to that of Vingron."

I stopped in confusion. It was true. I had unconsciously commenced rowing towards Grayle Abbey. I immediately put the boat about, and took the way to Vingron Port. Miss Grahame relapsed into silence, trailing her delicate fingers dreamily in the water as we sped along. But Claire Duborg chattered incessantly. Sometimes I answered mechanically; my thoughts were centred on the lovely girl before me; my eyes caught the dreamy, far-away look of her own, and my heart seemed to go out to hers with a wistful, passionate longing; my mind lost itself in a maze of happy reverie—a reverie with "Irene" for its key-note. We arrived at length at the picturesque little port of Vingron. I drew up alongside the miniature quay, and assisted the ladies to disembark. Then I fastened the boat's painter to an iron ring. As I arose, my attention was arrested by a tall man who strolled by. This man was of magnificent build and majestic mien. He wore a broad-brimmed felt hat, rather Bohemian in style, which concealed from casual observation the upper portion of his features, while a splendid black curling beard covered the lower. But it was not his face that startled me, for I could not see it plainly from where I stood—it was the gait of the man, the carriage of his head, the swing of his arms as he walked. These I had seen before—these I remembered. But where and when? Suddenly, the man, with a peculiar gesture, threw away the cigar he had been smoking. Then I knew him; that simple act untrammelled my memory; it was Karnheim, the conspirator. Yes; it was indeed that man of endless mystery—of equivocal occupations—whom I now beheld after long years. What was it that made me tremble at that moment? What alarmed me? I know not; unless it was some mysterious foreboding of the evil—the trials—in store for me. I was aroused by the voice of Miss Grahame, who begged me to accompany her to the tower, and receive her father's thanks for the great service I had rendered them. I would fain have declined, but had not the strength of mind to part so soon from one who already exercised over me such fascination.

A few minutes' walk brought us to Vingron Tower, which stood a little apart from the hamlet of Vingron.

"There is Vingron Tower," said Miss Grahame, with some pride, as we approached. "It rivals even your Abbey, does it not? But you have surely not lived so near all your life without seeing it?"

"Oh no," I replied; "when a boy I have ridden here often merely to see it. I remember it perfectly. A splendid place—full, I believe, of historical associations."

We ascended the broad, massive steps of the beautiful terrace, and entered the tower. Miss Grahame sent a servant to apprise her father of her return and my visit. I began now to feel somewhat embarrassed at my position.

We entered a lofty and luxurious apartment—a library—which faced the ocean. A magnificent sweep of water could be seen from the battlements. As we entered this room I heard a man's voice.

"Well, ta-ta, Mr. Grahame. I shall not trouble you again for some time. I'm off to Paris."

And a tall man, with good features, but of a leering, cunning expression, passed us on the threshold, bowing elaborately to Miss Grahame, who answered with a slight and scarcely perceptible motion of her stately head.

At the same moment I heard Claire Dubourg mutter:

"Ah, it is Vernon, that detestable hound! And come for money, no doubt. How weak some men are!"

I barely caught the words, which were by no means intended for my ear. They created a wondering sensation in my mind. Little did I anticipate, however, how soon I would recall those words, and the words of the man, and the dread with which I would ponder over them in the future.

The allusion to the "weakness of some men" I appreciated the instant I glanced at the face of Mr. Grahame. Irresolution and vacillation were but too plainly written there. But these failings were more than redeemed by the impress of a kind and generous heart which was on his features, and by a noble light which was in his sad grey eyes, which told of endurance and suffering. For the rest, the face was handsome and intellectual; the hair was turning grey, and beginning to get thin.

From the fact of his former close intimacy with my father, and my friendship with his unfortunate relative, whom I have mentioned in the beginning of my narrative, I could not seem an absolute stranger to him; and, his first surprise over, he welcomed me warmly and gratefully, grasping my hand with an expression on his face of gratitude, deep and sincere, which spoke volumes for the great love which he evidently bore his daughter; and, indeed, when his glance rested upon her I fancied that his usual sadness deepened and became intensified by an expression in his eyes of pain and grief, which appeared suddenly and went away slowly.

Although his kindness and courtesy could not have been surpassed, I soon perceived that these cost him an effort to assume; that something weighed upon his mind, making this effort irksome to him. So, when Miss Grahame, doubtless familiar with her father's pre-occupation, proposed to conduct me through the Tower prior to my departure, I arose, saying that, as the day was rather advanced, I must lose no time in returning, and——

"Why," interrupted Mr. Grahame, "why not be my guest for a few days? I cannot be content with such a flying visit, especially after the great service you have rendered me in saving Irene's life. Come, stay with us a while, Mr. Holmes."

Irene supported her father's entreaty in such a charming manner that refusal was impossible. I consented at once. Mr. Grahame's eyes expressed pleasure at first, but a moment afterwards a thought seemed to strike him, and his face grew pallid and dark. This lasted only a second, and I scarcely noticed it at the time, though I remembered it afterwards.

"Thank you," said he, with his sad smile. "You may not find me pleasant company, but I am sure Irene will do her best to entertain you."

He never spoke of her as "my daughter"—it was always "Irene" or "Miss Grahame."

CHAPTER II.

A LIFE TAKEN, AND A SECRET KEPT.

I passed a happy, memorable week at the Tower. Every day Irene was my companion. Sometimes we wandered together over the vast and romantic Tower, discovering new objects of interest at every turn. Sometimes we made little voyages along the coast, and even visited the memorable amphitheatre. Claire was with us on this occasion, but she could not be persuaded to land. She remained in the boat, anxious and trembling for our safety. Sometimes we rode through the grand old wooded park—through the long, noble vistas of ancient oak that opened before us. And it was here that our troth was plighted; it was here that I drew from her the sweet confession that her gratitude had changed into love.

We were seated on one of the rustic benches that were scattered thereabouts. Suddenly we heard footsteps on the path near us. Someone was approaching. Irene quickly slipped from my embrace, and moved to a proper distance until the stranger should have passed.

A gentleman, smoking a cigar, sauntered slowly by and out of sight without having perceived us. It was again Karnheim. I trembled and turned pale, on account of an indefinable sensation that came upon me. Irene, noting my pallor, eagerly inquired the cause.

"There are times," I said, "when I almost think that this man is my evil genius. He is called Karnheim, and, when I knew him, was a Polish conspirator, revolutionist, or something of the sort. What he is doing here I cannot imagine, unless he is a political refugee. This is the second time within the last few days that I have seen him."

However, we soon dismissed the subject, being so engrossed in each other.

On the last day of my sojourn at Vingron Tower I sought an interview with Mr. Grahame, the object of which may be readily guessed. He received me in his study. When I told him of the love that existed between Irene and myself, and asked his consent to our engagement, his features underwent a curious and, to me, incomprehensible change of expression. To me, guessing at the cause, it seemed to be a great and painful internal struggle—a contest of inclination with some unknown duty. He made no objections to my proposal, and even said that I was the man of all others whom he would have selected as a husband for Irene. However, it was plain that there was an objection, and I demanded to know it.

"There is none—absolutely none," he said; "at least on *your* side."

"On whose, then," I asked, with increased surprise. "What can you mean?"

"Let us suppose," he said, after a pause, "that you married my Irene, and that after she had become your wife you discovered that *a secret* hung over her life—a secret at which your honour would inevitably recoil—a secret which would cause you to turn from your wife in horror, though you held her utterly blameless."

"Impossible!" I cried, bewildered. "Impossible, if I held her blameless. Once more, in the name of heaven, tell me *what* you mean?"

"Let us even suppose," he continued, in his low, sad tones, and still taking no note of my question—"let us even suppose your love to be stronger than your instincts of honour, and that, after your discovery of the terrible secret, your wife remained as dear to you as ever—allowing this to be possible—what would become of your peace of mind, your happiness, harassed as you would be by the knowledge that *another*, and he an unscrupulous, audacious, heartless villain, shared this secret—this frightful secret, the betrayal of which to Irene could not but be fatal to her life or her reason?"

I was silent. Crushed by the weight of this terrible blow—the more terrible on account of its mystery—I could only stare at the man who spoke these words—words that seemed to draw, drop by drop, the blood from my heart.

And when, at length, I found my voice, it was a torrent of incoherent words that I cannot now recall, which I poured forth. It was a frenzied demand to know that deadly mysterious secret—to be told all—to know the traitor who could destroy Irene's life or reason at his own wicked and treacherous will.

The old man was affrighted beyond measure by my passion, and it was some time ere he could make any reply. At length, becoming calmer, and seeming to rally his energies, he said:

"Let us end this interview, Mr. Holmes; we are both too agitated and excited to prolong it. I must think long and clearly over this. I have been weak and culpable in my conduct to you in letting you stay here; I should have foreseen what has happened. Go now; return to Grayle Abbey; I will write to you, when I have decided which must be sacrificed—love or honour."

I saw that the man, vacillating and weak as I knew him to be, was now immovable—that, wrought to a pitch of indomitable resolution by force of unusual circumstances, he possessed the strength of adamant—a peculiarity of weak natures. I departed in silence.

Irene, meeting me on the terrace, was appalled by my pallor and the wildness of my demeanour, and inquired, with loving solicitude, the cause. I felt keenly the necessity of dissembling, but had no power to do so. I told her that her father had spoken of an obstacle to our union, and that his having kept it a secret from me had aroused my anger; that anger always made me look pale and wild; that I was sure all would come right in the end. I was going to return to the Abbey, and await Mr. Grahame's letter in answer to my proposal. As I kissed her, she shuddered, saying that my lips were cold, that I trembled, and imploring me not to go until I had rested and composed myself. But I embraced her again and did not answer, for my anguish was too deep. And I rushed to the stables, had a spirited horse saddled, and was soon revelling in the deadly excitation of a mad and headlong career through the woods.

Once, like a flash, I passed a man. It was Karnheim. He could not have recognised me, so great was my speed. But I knew him at the merest glance. The sight of this man frenzied me, I know not why, and I spurred madly onward until my horse could go no farther, but stopped from sheer exhaustion.

Three or four days passed—I know not how—ere I received the promised letter:—

"I do not expect you, Mr. Holmes, to half appreciate the objection to your proposal, of which I hinted at our last meeting—the existence of a horrible, disgraceful secret hanging over the life of Irene. I know your generous nature and your great love—you would wed her in spite of all—you would make it the sole object of your life to guard Irene from all knowledge of the secret, which would, as I told you, be fatal to her life or reason. You would risk all, sacrifice all, to make her your wife. I know this; but I know also what your life would be. It would be even as my own has been, and is—full of a torture the more intolerable that it *must* be borne in silence, and without a sign—unknown to everyone, and most of all to her. A hell within sight of heaven! But apart from all this, your honour is dear to me by reason of my long friendship with your father. I could not live to see his ancient and honourable name disgraced, as this marriage would inevitably disgrace it. Let me earnestly entreat you to relinquish all thoughts of such a union, for it can never be. Something of a terrible nature has occurred since I last saw you, which has strengthened me to give your proposal my most emphatic refusal, and to forbid you to marry Irene Grahame, whatever happens. Once more I entreat you to banish all hopes of marriage with her, and to go abroad.

"GEORGE GRAHAME."

There was no occasion to read the letter twice. Every word, at the first glance, burnt itself into my memory. I have never forgotten those strange words, nor can I ever forget them.

Suddenly all the blood in my body seemed to rush into my head, and I started up.

"I will go," I muttered. "I will hear this miserable secret from his own lips. I will wrest it from him, no matter how."

I ordered a fast horse to be saddled. I walked to the spot where it waited. I placed my foot in the stirrup.

But here a deadly faintness—a horrible sense of weakness—came upon me with overwhelming suddenness, and I fell swooning into the arms of the groom.

For the last few days a fever had been in me, and the strain upon mind and body culminated in this manner.

My fever soon burnt itself out, though for hours I was delirious. My physician, an old friend of the family, who had presided at my birth, attended me. The utterances of delirium, disjointed as they were, informed him pretty well of the cause of my illness.

When I had almost recovered, Dr. Miles said to me (after explaining his knowledge of my affairs):

"When you are quite well and strong, Gordon, I have much to tell you—much that will startle and grieve you. A most melancholy and terrible event has just happened."

I was all impatient to hear the disclosure, but not strong enough yet to resist the doctor's will. Two weary days went by, and, feeling that my old strength had almost returned, I would wait no longer. With some reluctance he yielded.

He began by telling me that Mr. Grahame had been murdered. Allowing me some time to recover from the intense shock that these words created, Dr. Miles proceeded to details.

"Three days ago"—that was about a week after my interview with him—"the unfortunate man's body had been found at the foot of one of those stupendous cliffs near Vingron Tower, with a long dagger through his breast. He was discovered ere his absence from the Tower had been noticed. The corpse was recognised at once, although the features were necessarily bruised by the fall. In his pockets money and letters were found, and no articles of value had been removed from his person, for everyone who knew him in life agree that a single diamond ring and a gold watch and chain were all the jewellery he ever wore. These familiar articles were found to be undisturbed. It is clear, then, that the motive of the murder was not theft, unless the courage of the assassin failed him at the supreme moment, which has been known to happen. One of the letters found upon his body was a communication, ante-dated nearly a year, from one Saul Vernon—a most audacious missive, which informed Mr. Graham that the writer would soon be with him, and warned him to have plenty of money at hand.

It was sworn at the inquest by Miss Grahame's 'lady companion,' among others, that this man's apparent power over Mr. Grahame, and his practice of extorting large sums of money from him was no secret to the inmates of the Tower, whatever Mr. Grahame might have imagined; or, if there were an exception, it was Irene. The man—Saul Vernon—had been seen walking with Mr. Grahame in the park, not very far from the cliffs, on the very afternoon of the murder, and could not now be found. A great detective has taken up the case, and, no doubt, the murderer will soon be brought to justice."

Vernon! I remembered the name. Was it not he who held the secret? I saw it all. I pictured to myself this villain demanding exorbitant sums and uttering outrageous threats; I saw in fancy the worm turn and battle with its tyrant at last. But here—oh, mystery of the human mind!—another face, another name, came between—it was Karnheim's! Reason how I would, I could not get rid of the strange idea that Karnheim, and not Vernon, had committed the crime! It was in the last degree irrelevant and absurd, but the thought would not be driven away.

How would this terrible event affect Irene as regarded the mysterious secret? Would not Vernon in revenge, when he was captured, betray it? This thought almost maddened me.

Next day I heard the will read. It had been executed only a week or so before the death of the testator by the family solicitor, and was the only one ever made—Mr. Grahame, like many others, had always had a strange dislike and dread of the subject being broached. Irene was the sole heiress. As she was not quite eighteen, however, a guardian was appointed, but no trustees were named. The guardian would have full control over the revenue of the estate and the interest on the private fortune—in fact, he could use that splendid income as he chose during Irene's minority, although, of course, he could not touch the principal. There were a few present who were somewhat surprised by the provisions of the will. For my own part, I heard them read with a strange, illogical fear at my heart. A Mr. Henry Hargrave, brother-in-law to the testator, living in Mynton, an obscure town in some distant part of England, was named as the future master of Vingron Tower, and the guardian of Irene until she became of age. And the will contained no provision for the exigency of Irene's marriage during minority. I understood that no marriage would be legal without the guardian's consent.

"Gordon—dear Gordon," said Irene, sadly and slowly, as we stood alone in the great library of Vingron Tower, "we can meet no more; our dream is over; you must try to forget me. I thought to bring you honour as well as love, but now——"

"Honour! In heaven's name, what do you mean?"

"Hush. Do not question me, Gordon. Alas, all hope has flown away. Our union is impossible. My name is disgraced; my father—"

"What of him? Great heavens! did he tell you the secret?" I cried, in a hoarse and unnatural voice.

"*The secret!*" she uttered, catching my wrist in a steel-like grasp, while her fiercely-dilating eyes seemed to pierce my very soul. "The secret! Do you know it?"

I was too intensely agitated for a moment to reply. Her clasp on my wrist tightened as she repeated her question, and her voice rose almost to a shriek.

"No," I answered, at last; "I only know of its existence."

She shrank back.

"Its existence?" she murmured to herself—"only its existence? Its *existence!* That is strange. Could he—could he have contemplated——"

Her voice slowly died into silence.

Hearing these incoherent, and, to me, perfectly meaningless, phrases, I was for a moment almost paralysed, for a deadly fear had come over me. She knew the secret, that was clear, and the words of her father occurred to me: *"Fatal to her life or reason."* And now the deadly pallor, the wild eyes, the strange words of Irene filled me with a ghastly dread. Yet, withal, I could not think her actually mad. Her manner, at first, had been of extreme sadness and despair, but without suggestion of insanity. And, on refection, might not those singular words be relevant to the secret—might not the secret form the only clue to their meaning? But why had it been confided to her? To this there was but one answer. Grahame must have decided to, at all hazards, render our union impossible, and such a desperate course afforded the only means of effectually accomplishing that object.

Once it was on the tip of my tongue to ask Irene if she thought that Vernon would betray the secret when captured. Had I done so, some strange things would have come to light, and yet the mystery would have deepened. But Irene looked so despairing that I forbore to speak again on the subject. Her hands were clasped before her, and her eyes, staring fixedly at the wall, appeared to see far beyond it. She seemed, in her grief, to be praying for death.

I approached, and, kneeling beside the lounge on which she reclined, I took her hands in mine, murmuring words of which I have no remembrance—words that had in them the passionate eloquence of a great love—and to these she listened in silence. The trembling of her hands as they lay in mine—for she made no attempt to withdraw them—told me that her love was as strong as mine; but a slight shudder shook her as I ceased to speak.

"Oh," she murmured, "you overwhelm me. Oh, Gordon, if you only knew——"

"I do not want to know," I interrupted. "I love you for your own dear self alone."

"I love *you*, Gordon, but so well that I can never marry you. Your ultimate happiness—your honour—I think of first, and could not destroy. And, when you have ceased to love me, I know you will remember that I saved your honour—that I——"

Her wavering voice was choked in a great sob that could not be suppressed.

I urged my love upon her no longer now; my task was to console and when she at length grew calm again, I said:

"Let us, then, at least be friends, Irene, until this gloom shall have cleared away—as I am certain it will in time. Tell me about your uncle Hargrave, your guardian."

"I know nothing of him. I did not even know I had an uncle until—until some little time ago. I have never seen him."

"When will he arrive?"

"I do not know. Doubtless in a few days."

An extreme listlessness and an unconquerable apathy were upon her. Her old animation had completely vanished. Little more was said. We sat side by side, and hand in hand, for hours, buried in our own unhappy thoughts. When I rose to leave her I said—

"You will allow me to see you every day, will you not, Irene?"

A slight pressure of the hand betokened consent.

We resumed our walks and rides and sailing excursions—brother and sister in all but name. A week passed, and then the wearisome monotony was broken by the arrival of Mr. Henry Hargrave, the guardian of Irene, the sole administrator of Vingron Tower and estates. Irene and I received him much as though he were my guardian as well as hers. I had been so much her companion that to be with her at the reception of her guardian seemed quite natural, whatever Mr. Hargrave might have thought.

I was much impressed, and even startled, by the appearance of the man. He was very ugly, and to some extent deformed. His ugliness, though apparent to the most careless of observers, was not very defined. One could not tell exactly where it lay, but it was certainly there. The deformity was slight, one shoulder being a little higher or larger than the other. He was tall, rather bent and appeared to be fast approaching man's allotted years. His hair, beard, and eyebrows were iron-grey. His eyes were very dark and piercing, and seemed small, being much shaded by the heavy brows. Though bent, ugly, and deformed, the man's bearing was haughty, and at times even majestic. In his presence I could not wholly repress a slight feeling of awe, for which I despised myself. Irene was not similarly affected. Strange as it may seem, he made rather a favourable impression on her mind, and as the days passed, and they became better acquainted, a friendship grew up between them, and Irene found him kind, indulgent, and even sympathetic. Even I became to a certain extent his friend. Our tastes in literature and art were by no means dissimilar, and we often found fund for conversation in such themes, though he was somewhat chary of speech.

These were dreary days for Irene and I, but worse were yet to come.

CHAPTER III.

KARNHEIM REVEALED.

Hearing that Detective Elmsley had returned from London after a vain endeavour to track the murderer, I invited him to a lunch in the Tower. He came, looking a little crestfallen, for he bore the reputation of being one of the most acute officers in the force. I noticed, however, that he was very hopeful.

"I have been on the wrong track, Mr. Holmes, I admit," he said; "but of late I have entertained some very different ideas of this case. I have come here to get some fresh information, and I start on a new trail to-night. I was deceived at the start by the apparent simplicity of the murder. I now find that it is rather complex under the surface. I should not be greatly surprised to find that this man Vernon is, after all, *not* the murderer. I have a bold and rather startling idea, which I intend to work upon after I have gleaned more information."

Just then Henry Hargrave entered, and was introduced to the detective. The three of us talked for some time about the murder. I noticed that Elmsley scanned Mr. Hargrave very closely, and seemed much satisfied with his scrutiny. He soon after departed, to prepare, he said, for his new campaign. We both wished him success.

A week or so afterwards a most startling thing happened—*the secret* was revealed to me.

Entering Irene's boudoir one afternoon I was inexpressibly surprised and shocked to find her lying on the carpet in a dead faint. A letter was clenched in her hand.

Summoning Claire Dubourg, I aided her to restore consciousness to the unfortunate girl. At last Irene opened her eyes and looked at us. Ah, heaven! I shall never forget that glance. There was in it no light, no perception, no recognition, only the dull, stony look of despair. Irene no longer remembered her friends—no longer remembered even herself!

I had taken the letter from her. I now retired to read it, so that I might know what had caused this fearful thing. The letter was pressed as though it had been between the leaves of a large book for a great length of time. It was the fatal secret itself:

"London, 20th June, 18—

"My Dear Brother,—Yours received. You still leave me a little in doubt as to what course you are going to take; but I conclude, from the tone of your letter, that you intend to rely on my veracity, rather than risk public exposure by instituting inquiries. Such an exposure, as you seem to hint, would be indeed terrible to you and your proud and beautiful daughter. However, as I do not wish you to entertain the slightest doubt of the truth of my statements, I will undertake to prove conclusively, without the slightest risk of exposure, that your late wife was really your sister's daughter and mine, born a month after our marriage at Seawardine. Lieutenant and Mrs. Tremaine, the supposed parents of our child, were myths of your sister's imagination. All this I will undertake to prove to you beyond the shadow of a doubt. And now, my worthy brother-in-law and son-in-law (queer relationship!), I assure you that any suspicions you may have of my integrity are perfectly groundless—this I swear on my honour. It happens that I want just now much more money than you would be disposed to give me unless you were stimulated by dire necessity, such as the suppression of this interesting little secret. It was a tragic blunder to make—for you; for me it turns out rather fortunate, as I am on the brink of ruin and imprisonment. I shall wait on you on the evening of the third with the proofs, and for the present beg to subscribe myself yours *faithfully*,

"SAUL VERNON.

"George Grahame, Esq."

Now, after the years that have passed, I can read this villainous epistle calmly, and as I copy it here my hand does not tremble nor my heart beat as in those dread moments when the lines burnt themselves in upon my half distraught brain.

Well, indeed, had George Grahame said, when he told me of the possible effect upon Irene the telling of the secret would have. With her refined sensibilities and delicate nervous organisation, I cannot but marvel that the shock did not overthrow reason as well as memory. To such a mind as hers the thing was so horrible, the idea of it was so dreadful, and the lifelong shame involved was so fearful to contemplate, that it was really a mercy that the shock had resulted in a loss of memory.

*   *   *   *   *

"I will not disguise from you that it is a serious case," said Dr. Miles, who had been summoned, "but we may certainly hope for the best."

The doctor stayed some time at the Tower, in order to study the mental malady in all its phases, and to make and direct efforts for the recovery of memory.

Meanwhile I did not, of course, reveal the secret, though the doctor questioned me very closely, for he suspected that I knew something. But I loved and honoured Irene none the less on account of her unfortunate history, and jealously guarded the fatal secret.

There was no repose for me that night.

After courting slumber for many hours in vain, I arose, and strolled through the park.

It was past midnight. The moon shone clear and bright. Everything seemed still as death. I sought out the favourite rustic seat of Irene, and there reclined, awaiting the new day.

Suddenly I heard the sound of voices and footsteps. One of the voices I recognised. It was that of Karnheim. I was in deep shadow and when the two men came into view they did not see me. I remembered Karnheim's voice perfectly, though I had not heard him speak for more than three years. But when I saw the speaker, I could scarcely repress an exclamation. For he who spoke with Karnheim's voice wore the aspect of Hargrave! Or rather, it was the Pole in a sort of undress disguise. He was straight and firm as Karnheim; he was grey, and dressed as Hargrave.

I was so intensely startled that much of the conversation escaped me, and just when I began to listen, they had passed. The other man was evidently a fellow-conspirator. They spoke in French.

How Karnheim had attained such a position was a mystery to me; but, great as it was, there was one which puzzled me still more—one of which I had been thinking just before his appearance. It was this: At the time of the murder I had been led to believe that Irene had become possessed of the secret; but now it was evident that it was unknown to her until she found the letter. Could there be *two secrets*? If so, what was the other?

As to Karnheim, what ought I to do? I resolved to await the return of the detective, who would be better able to decide than I.

It was daybreak ere I arose. I strolled toward Vingron town. The early morning train had just arrived, and the few passengers were alighting. Among them I was agreeably surprised to recognise the figure of the detective, Elmsley. I greeted him heartily, and we strolled towards Vingron Tower.

"I have much to tell you," I began.

"I also,'" he said, "have a little news for you; but let me hear yours first."

"Well," I said, " this man whom we know as Mr. Hargrave, I have discovered to be——"

"Grahame," interrupted the detective, calmly. "Ah, yes. How did you discover it?"

"Grahame?" I stammered, stopping, and staring stupidly at the officer. "What do you mean?"

He, in his turn, stared rather stupidly at me.

"Have you not," he presently said, "discovered the pretended Hargrave to be Mr. Grahame in disguise?"

"No. He is in reality a Polish revolutionist named Karnheim, whom I suspect of having killed Mr. Grahame, and, by some audacious plot, put himself in the position of guardian and trustee."

"Oh—ah!" was all the officer could say.

"But why do you speak of Grahame as living?"

"Because I believed the murdered man to be not Grahame, but Vernon, the supposed murderer."

"Vernon—the murdered man!" I gasped. "Would to heaven it were so. But surely you do not forget that the body was fully identified, not alone by the dress, the jewels, and the letters in the pockets, but by the very features—incontrovertible evidence!"

"Pshaw!" said the officer. "Look you; it was the very completeness of this evidence which first led me to doubt. Tell me now, were not the colour and style of the hair, the *form* of the face, and the hue of the eyes, very much the same in both of these men? I do not speak of the *expression*, for that must have been destroyed by the death agony and the bruises of the fall."

I recollected now that what he said was true.

"Well, then," he continued, "let us suppose that we are finding the body. If we are acquainted with the usual personal appearance of Mr. Grahame, we recognise the attire immediately, and we entertain no doubt at the outset. When, however, we see grey hair and beard and eyes, the same as we were accustomed to see in the living Grahame of our acquaintance, we look for nothing more. We do not for a moment suspect that the clothes and jewels could have easily been placed on the body, and the letters in the pockets, by one who had the power, and to whose was interest it was to do so. Now, on the night of the murder, two men left Vingron. One I tracked to London, and there lost—or, rather, took no trouble to find—being convinced that he was only what he described himself to be—a book-canvasser. I returned, and making most diligent and searching enquiries, tracked the other man to Mynton, where, it seems, he stayed a few days, giving the name of Hargrave. When I learned this, I immediately returned. I found out, too, that he had never been to Mynton before. As for this Karnheim, I don't know what to make of him. Are you sure of what you say?"

"Quite sure," I answered; "but are you equally certain of the identity of the murdered man?"

"This is what I suppose:—Grahame turned on his tormentor, Vernon, and killed him. Karnheim must have witnessed the murder, and, in return for his silence, Grahame has relinquished to him his fortune or income for a specified time, while he keeps out of the way. No doubt, the man I followed to London was, after all, not a book-agent, but Mr. Grahame himself. However, we must draw all we do not know out of this Mr. Karnheim."

I agreed with him, and suggested that no time be lost.

"Well," said Elmsley, smiling, "let it be after breakfast, for I'm rather peckish."

We had arrived at the Tower by this time, and I conducted him to my quarters, where we breakfasted, or, rather, he did, for I was too anxious to eat anything.

"Oh, by the way," said the officer, suddenly, "Mr. Grahame's late wife came from this same Mynton, An old fellow there—— But what's the matter?"

I had started up, pale and trembling. "Grahame's wife!" The whole contents of the fatal letter flashed through my mind as I heard those words. Composing myself by an effort, I begged Elmsley to tell me all he knew of her. Eyeing me curiously, he complied.

"Well, this old party entertained me with the whole of Mr.

Grahame's private history. It seems that this same Vernon was the guardian or adopted father of the late Mrs. Grahame, and that Vernon's wife was an elder sister of Mr. Grahame's, who had married the worthless scamp against the wishes of her whole family. Grahame himself stuck to her pretty fairly, however, and it was through her that he became acquainted with Vernon, whom he helped with money and influence for his sister's sake. The sister had no children of her own, but she adopted, during an excursion to the seaside about a month after her marriage, the baby of the three-months' widow of a naval officer, who died penniless. The mother did not live to see her child's face, and the babe was left to the world. Mrs. Vernon, much against her estimable husband's wishes, engaged a foster-mother and adopted the child as her own, and returned from the seaside with it, rather to the surprise of her friends, who, however, were, most of them, content with the explanation that the kind, impulsive woman gave. The child grew into a beautiful woman, and was married to George Grahame."

"Are you sure," I asked, my heart beating wildly with hope and fear, "that this is the truth?"

"Well, I think it is. While I was listening to the old fellow, a decrepit serving woman of nearly eighty years entered the room, and, hearing the talk, chimed in, and querulously demanded to give her recollections of the affair. It seems that she was the foster mother engaged to nurse the infant of Lieutenant Tremaine's widow."

I grasped the detective's hand with a joy for which I can find no expression. In answer to his surprise I handed him the letter of Vernon for perusal. He read it.

"This, then," he said, "is the secret of that villain's ascendancy over, and persecution of, poor Grahame. Well, it's all over now, and——"

"Would to heaven it were," I ejaculated; and then I recounted the mischief that the letter had wrought.

"That is serious," he said; "but let us hope for the best. We will now seek an interview with Mr. Karnheim, and clean up all that is still obscure."

*   *   *   *   *

I will not pause to describe the confusion of Karnheim, and his efforts to sustain his assumed character, but proceed to briefly detail his part in the events I have tried to describe, as detailed in the statement he wrote.

Vernon had long been known to him. That person had joined his association during one of his enforced retirements to the Continent, more from the need of the lucrative employment it afforded—that of a spy—than from any sympathy with its objects. One day, however, Mr. Vernon was discovered in an attempt to betray some of its most important affairs to the authorities. He narrowly escaped with his life, and from that day it was in almost hourly peril, for the task of hunting the traitor to death had fallen to the lot of Karnheim, one of the fiercest and most vengeful of the ruthless spirits of which the association was composed.

It will be remembered that at the time I had first seen Vernon, Karnheim was in the vicinity of Vingron. This fact Vernon, almost immediately on leaving the Tower, discovered, and changed his purpose of going to Paris. He awaited Mr. Grahame in the park the next evening, and, telling him that it was his intention to leave England for America as soon as possible, and return no more, he demanded no less a sum than that of ten thousand pounds. It happened, however, that his victim could not produce so much money in as short a time as Vernon, in his impatience and craven fear, wished; and their voices rose somewhat high in dispute, arousing the attention of a man who happened to be strolling in the vicinity, and who immediately recognised one of the voices as belonging to the wretch he had sworn to slay. That man was Karnheim, who soon gathered the gist of the conversation, and instantly conceived an ardent desire to have those ten thousand pounds to devote to his beloved society. When, however, he heard the parting words of Vernon, higher and more audacious hopes sprang up in his adventurous breast. Those words were:—

"Well, then, all I can tell you is this, my dear Grahame: I will be on this spot in a week from to-day, and if you are not here with the money all the world shall know that you married your own sister's child, and that the proud and beautiful Miss Irene is—oh, well, *au revoir*. But remember what I have said."

Thus did Karnheim gain possession of the secret. A very few seconds sufficed for him to decide on the most advantageous course to pursue.

He followed Grahame, and explained everything to him—how Vernon was condemned to die, and how he had overheard all the conversation. Allowing poor Grahame time to recover from this new shock, the arch-plotter calmly unfolded his plan.

In the first place, Mr. Grahame was to make his will, so that Karnheim would have full control over the revenue of the Vingron estate. He was to meet Vernon at the time and place appointed, and lead him to think that he would receive the money that same night. Then he must retire unobserved to the Tower, and await further instructions.

All this was carried out without a hitch. Poor Grahame obeyed with the calm apathy of complete despair.

The day arrived. Vernon was obliged to be satisfied with Grahame's promise. On leaving him he was followed by Karnheim, who was agreeably surprised to find that he was going towards the cliff. It would obviate the necessity of carrying him thither.

Arrived at a convenient place, Karnheim made sure that no one else was in sight, and then confronted Vernon with his ruthless and terrible smile, which froze the traitor's blood in his veins, and calmly informed him that but a very little time was left for him in which to prepare to die. After some appropriate jests and light badinage, the Pole, who possessed twice the physical power of Vernon, forced him to the edge of the cliff, intending to cast him over. But the fear-stricken wretch struggled desperately and Karnheim's foot slipping, he was compelled to use a dagger in order to save himself from accompanying Vernon into eternity. This circumstance altered his plans a little. What might have been construed as an accident was now unmistakably a murder. But he did not hesitate in the slightest degree. Returning to the Tower (always taking the greatest care to escape observation), he airily informed Mr. Grahame that his outraged society was revenged, and directed him to prepare a suit of clothes such that he was in the habit of wearing, together with his watch, chain, and ring, and some letters and papers. This was done, and ere midnight Karnheim had sought out the corpse, changed its attire, and removed the old clothes. Returning, he instructed Grahame to play the *rôle* of a book-canvasser, for which his appearance was suited, and to travel to London, and, when there, send his address to Mr. Henry Hargrave at Vingron Tower. After a hurried, painful, and passionate parting with his daughter, on whom he enjoined silence under all circumstances, he departed without anyone recognising him, so effectually had Karnheim disguised him. Karnheim also left, but, of course, for Mynton. He now began to entertain grand schemes. What might he not do for his country with such a princely income at his command for three years? But it was not to be.

Need I say that Irene, when she heard of the murder, at once concluded that her father had killed his enemy and disguised the body, for she knew that Vernon was hated and feared, though she could not tell why. The secret that she had spoken of at our first meeting after the murder was the supposed crime of her father. She, of course, knew nothing of the other until she accidentally found the letter of Vernon.

Karnheim, on learning that the supposed secret had exploded, and that his plot had "gone up" therewith, gave me the address of Mr. Grahame, for whom I immediately telegraphed.

He arrived in due time, and all was explained to him. His joy at the discovery of Vernon's duplicity was great, but when told of the state of his beloved daughter, that joy vanished, giving place to the old despair. But Dr. Miles bade us all hope. He had a plan for her recovery which, he said, must succeed. Her memory had been lost by a great shock. It needed another—a counter-shock—to restore it. The sight of her father, he considered, would be sufficient to restore the balance of her mind, though he did not seek to conceal the fact that it was a dangerous experiment. He had tried over and over again to establish a sequence of lucid thought in the shattered mind of the poor girl—to touch some chord of memory—but all in vain. The desperate nature of the case warranted a desperate remedy. He knew (now that all was explained) that Irene, in consequence of her father's omission to explain the real cause of his departure for London, held him to be an assassin; and, therefore, even if the experiment succeeded, there might still be serious consequences attached to it.

And, indeed, the subsequent events proved this to be so.

An afternoon was selected on which Irene's mind was calmer than usual, for she was often much agitated by her earnest endeavours to remember past events.

The doctor had been conversing with her, insensibly preparing her to meet the surprise in store, and, as preconcerted, gave the signal for the anxious father to enter the room.

Mr. Grahame suddenly stood before his daughter.

She rose. At first she did not recognise him at all—he was as an entire stranger to her. But of a sudden a light seemed to break into her mind, and, with a wild and piteous look in her dilated eyes, she recoiled a few paces, and then, putting out her hand as if to ward him off, exclaimed in a hoarse unnatural utterance:

"My father? No, no! I have no father! You are not he; you—you are a *murderer*. Stand back!"

And then she sank swooning into the good old doctor's arms.

She fell into a long and dangerous fever, and was delirious for many hours, and it was for some time doubtful whether, after all, memory would altogether recover its balance in her mind.

But she rallied. My face was then the first she recognised, and the sweet, wan smile with which she greeted me I shall never forget.

A month afterwards there were two young people on their way to Italy who fully believed that they were, without a single exception, the happiest couple in the world.

Karnheim, having written a full confession, eluded the vigilance of Elmsley and lost no time in placing the British Channel between them. I should have been content to have let him escape for, after all, his crime had only rid the earth of a wretch not worthy of the air he breathed—had he not, doubtless in a moment of preoccupation, abstracted from the family jewel-case a priceless necklace of diamonds which had been wont to glitter on the fair, round throat of the yet more peerless Mistress of Vingron Tower and Grayle Abbey.

GRACE WENDELL

A TALE OF THE SEA

I had long suffered from the ills of a sedentary life and a too close application to mental pursuits. Many times I planned a lengthened relaxation, but something always intervened to cause a postponement. At last, however, shattered in health and depressed in spirits, I sought advice, and was told that a long sea voyage was the only thing which could completely restore me. I therefore took a passage in the *Aurora*, a fine, large clipper ship, bound from Sydney—where I lived—direct to England. I preferred a sailing vessel, because the voyage would be longer than in a steamer, and because those noble ships, with their great pyramidal clouds of white canvas, which I had often watched slowly sinking, sail by sail, into the horizon, appealed far more to my sense of grace and beauty than the smoking monsters that churned the waves into foam and spouted water from their sides as they rushed through the deep.

I embarked, then, in the *Aurora*. With her captain, John Hay, I had some slight acquaintance. He was a very warm-hearted, sailorly fellow, with a round and smiling face, bronzed by some four decades of exposure to all weathers—a face which, however, could become stern and determined enough when occasion required.

"You won't have many shipmates, Mr. Leigh," he said to me a day or two before the vessel sailed; "there's only one cabin passenger besides yourself, I believe, as yet, and there's not much chance of booking any more between this and Saturday."

"Don't let that trouble you on my account, captain," I said; "I shall be better satisfied with one or two than a dozen."

"You say that, sir, because you're out of health and spirits; but you've no idea of the tedium of a long voyage."

I came very near missing the ship, and I have often thought since of the vast difference another hour's delay would have made in my life.

I went to my cabin and found that my things were in order, and also that I was to have no berthmate, there being only two passengers besides myself—one, the steward said, a young lady, niece to the captain.

I stepped aft, and stood for some time leaning on the rail, watching the bustle and activity occasioned in getting the vessel under weigh, and now and then waving my handkerchief to those of my relations and friends who had come to "see me off," and who stood on the wharf staring at the ship with an expression of countenance which told of a deep-rooted conviction that she must inevitably go down ere long.

But soon the hurry and confusion of the harbour were changed for the calm beauty of the bay of Sydney; and the captain, no longer so much occupied by his duties, now that the ship was fairly under weigh, stepped up and started a conversation, in which Mr. Raynor, the other passenger, by-and-bye joined. After discussing various topics, I remarked:

"I hear, captain, that your niece is on board."

"Yes," he said, stepping aside and looking aloft, where the sails were being set, the other officers superintending the work.

"And she is the only passenger besides Mr. Raynor and myself?" I said, as he joined us again.

"Yes," he answered; "we don't get so many passengers now-a-days, sir. You see, the steamers are fitted up so grandly, and are so fast; and then 'longshore folk distrust the tightest sailers. Why it is so I don't know."

"And has your niece friends in England?" asked Mr. Raynor.

"Yes—no; that is, I daresay she will find some. She's going for—for the sake of her health, like Mr. Leigh here." He spoke with some degree of hesitation, and, thinking that for some reason he might dislike the subject, I asked no further questions. But Raynor, whose perceptions were rather dull, persisted:

"It would be a tedious voyage without a lady on board, captain. When shall we have the pleasure of seeing your niece?"

"She is not very well. I don't think she'll appear for a day or two," answered the captain, in a curt and almost brusque tone of voice.

Soon the ship, leaving the bay, began to heave with the long, rhythmical roll of the great Pacific Ocean, and for Raynor and I, who were new to the sea, the disagreeable experience of the almost inevitable nausea began. When at last we were able to appear at the dining-table Australia had long since disappeared. Raynor, who had staved off his sickness as long as he could by imbibing freely of brandy, was much later than I in recovering.

It was early in the day when I ventured on deck. The sun was shining brightly, and the scene now presented was very beautiful to me. The wind was so favourable that every sail was bent to it, and the vessel was bounding freely and gracefully through the wide stretch of waters. It was a scene such as I had often read of and as often desired to see, but the reality surpassed my warmest imaginings. For some minutes I stood as one entranced, listening to the rushing sound of the wind in the sails and watching the curling waves that glistened in the rays of the sun as they raced past the ship; and I did not perceive, so rapt was I, the form of a young girl, who was seated near the taffrail.

Just then a step and a voice aroused me from the delightful reverie into which I had fallen. The captain was beside me.

"Glad to see you're all right again, sir," he said, in his hearty tone; "a few days of this weather'll put you straight."

In turning to answer him, I saw the young girl. She was gazing dreamily across the vastness of the sea, and presented to my eyes a delicate and beautiful profile, but which plainly bore the melancholy stamp of sorrow. Her face might have been of marble, so motionless, so colourless was it. A forehead round, yet broad and low, surrounded by waving hair of glossy jet; brows dark and finely pencilled; eyes large, but a little sunken and dim, as if they had recently shed tears; nose of finely and clearly cut Grecian type; lips full, but not sensuous; the chin, though beautifully moulded, telling more of sweetness of nature than decision of character. Such may convey some faint idea of the loveliness of that pale face which I saw outlined against the dark blue of the ocean.

The captain observed my involuntary admiration of the young girl, and at once introduced me to his niece, Miss Grace Wendell. She rose, smiled faintly, and held out a little white hand. Her movements, though listless, were full of unconscious beauty.

"You have never been at sea before, Mr. Leigh?" she said presently, when, after a few remarks, the captain left us together. Her voice was full of a strange sadness, devoid of sentimentality; indeed, her whole personality bore the impress of gloom and deep melancholy.

"No," I replied, "although I have many times felt a desire to take a voyage."

"You are fond of the sea, then? I observed how ardently you gazed upon it just now," she said, softly. "For myself, I love the ocean above all things, not alone when it is smiling and glad, as you see it now, but when it is frowning and dark and angry; when its peaceful beauty is changed to warlike grandeur; I love it well in all its phases."

Her tone was that of the dreamer and the visionary, but it was indefinably sad and sweet to the ear. This love of the sea for its own sake is a passion with some deep natures, but it is, I think, very rare. He who can for hours lose himself in the calm delight of the contemplation of woodland scenery would probably grow fatigued with the monotony of the waters; yet another, whose soul would not, perchance, be wooed by the beauty to be found in the droop of leaves in verdant foliage, or the shimmer of sunlight on the bark of forest boughs, might watch the rainbow tints in sea-dust blown from the crests of curling waves with as pure and rapt a delight as that of the pastoral poet who notes the rays of dawn glimmering on autumn leaves. The love of sylvan scenery can be acquired by many, but the love of the sea in all its aspects only exists where it has been implanted by nature.

We talked but little, Grace and I. She contemplated the ocean—I looked at her; and at every glance I thought how purely beautiful she was. But this thought was always accompanied by a vague, wondering, and somewhat uneasy sensation, caused by the *strangeness* and melancholy of her expression. A conviction that she had experienced some sorrow, both poignant and recent, gradually came upon me, and this thought, accompanied by an almost unconscious feeling of sympathy, made her doubly interesting to me.

Several days of this fair weather passed. I began rapidly to recover health and strength; each day I walked with a lighter, quicker step. But not a vestige of colour appeared in the marble cheeks of Grace Wendell. Her pallor was ever extreme, and yet seemed to be perfectly consistent with health, for her lips were delicately red, and her dark eyes had become full and clear. The captain, I could see, loved her more than if she had been his own daughter, and a sadness came into his small, grey eyes and expressed itself in his weather-beaten features every time he glanced at her. And I knew, whatever her sorrow was, that he was in her confidence.

At evening, in the tropical moonlight, Grace and I often walked or sat together on deck, and though we exchanged but little speech, I began to feel, as by some instinct, that we were gradually becoming intimate with each other—so much so, indeed, that I was often on the point of entreating her to trust me with the secret of her sorrow. Our growing intimacy seemed to pass unnoticed by the captain; and Raynor, bored by the sea and the ship, was always either buried in a novel or playing euchre with any officer who might for the time be disengaged. He had given up trying to interest Miss Wendell in his commonplace conversation, and to sit or walk with her and say nothing nearly all the time was, in his opinion, the height of maudlin sentimentality.

That I would fall in love with this beautiful and interesting girl I had no thought, but it soon was so. It was not a case of love at first sight with me, for at the outset my feeling was only one of pity and sympathy. My love gradually arose out of a sense of Grace Wendell's beauty and purity of mind and soul, not less than her outward attractions.

It was not until after more than a month had passed, and we were rounding the Cape, that the conviction came upon me that I loved her. I was now in possession of better health and strength than I had ever been before, and my nerves were calm and well-balanced, my spirits high and gay.

We had encountered bad weather during the second and third weeks of our voyage, but now the sky and sea were once more serene and smiling, and, although it was by this time too cold to promenade the decks at night, we passed our days together there, and on one calm and misty afternoon, I, no longer able to keep silence, told her my heart's story.

The first flush of colour I had ever seen in her cheeks came there then, but she evinced little surprise. I might almost have thought that she had been *waiting* for my avowal. There was a tender and very sad light in her eyes, and I felt instinctively that, though she might return my affection, her secret would come between us.

"Oh, Mr. Leigh," she said, almost entreatingly, "do not think of me in that way. You fancy that you love me, but we are alone here. On shore, in cities, where there are so many people, you would soon weary of one who, they would say, spends her time in dreaming, who is useless——"

"My dear Grace—let me call you so, if only for once—you mistake me greatly if you think that I am influenced by this solitary life alone. Tell me that you love me; or, at least, tell me to hope; and then let me know and share, some day, your sorrow——"

"My sorrow?"

It had never been mentioned until now, but she surely could not have supposed that I did not know of its existence; and the accent of surprise and grief in her voice struck me forcibly.

"You have some secret sorrow?" I stammered; and the thought that I had pressed my love upon her when I knew her to be suffering, made me reproach myself bitterly.

"Ah, yes—Heaven help me!" she cried. "But forgive me, Mr. Leigh, I cannot tell you what it is—though it is my duty to do so, in order to dispel your dream."

"Dream? Is my love, then, only a dream?"

"Yes—alas!"

"You say 'alas,' Grace; and in saying so you tell me that I am not indifferent to you. Can your sorrow be such that you will allow it to destroy your life's happiness?"

"It *has* destroyed it—no happiness is possible for me. My own weakness and indecision have wrecked my life."

Her hopeless, gloomy tone conveyed to me a sense of her grief deeper than any with which her looks or demeanour had ever inspired me. At this moment it happened that a dark cloud shut out the sun, and a heavy shadow fell upon the vast expanse of ocean; and in the first shock of my despair, it seemed to me that this shadow could never be lifted, but would grow much deeper and deeper until its gloom became as the darkness of a night for which there would be no dawn.

I glanced towards Grace, and saw that her lips were quivering, and that tears stood in her eyes, which were fixed on the dark sea, and looked as if their gloom had been reflected from those sombre depths. By-and-bye the sun re-appeared, but gave forth a dim misty and cheerless light. There was very little way on the ship, and at times the sails hung heavily—it was almost a calm. And so we stood together, leaning on the taff-rail, silent and gloomily dreaming— both perhaps thinking that all light of life and of hope must have left the world forever;—such is love's egotism.

And thus some moments passed.

Suddenly there was a loud shout forward, and a noise of men rushing to and fro. Looking in the direction of the sounds, I saw with intense horror a thick volume of smoke arising from the hold. That most terrible of disasters—a fire at sea—was upon us.

How shall I describe the scene that followed? How tell of the agonising hopeless efforts that were made to cope with the dread enemy? The dense masses of water seemed but to infuriate the flames to fiercer ravages—the copious streams poured into the hold through numerous holes cut in the decks availed us nothing against the devouring element. How the fire originated I cannot tell—very likely it was spontaneous combustion of some of the closely-packed wool, which formed the ship's cargo.

The crew worked bravely, and with almost the coolness of their captain, who directed their efforts with such skill and judgment that, had success been within the bounds of possibility, it must have been achieved.

But at last even that brave man confessed that nothing more could be done to save the unfortunate ship, and that all hands must take to the boats. A few of the men had been told off to provision and equip these, under the supervision of an officer; but the fire had gained so rapidly that, although the greatest expedition had been employed, the equipment was found to be far from commensurate to the necessities that would probably arise.

But there was no time to lose now; and little order prevailed in launching the boats, which were rushed by the sailors and steerage passengers in spite of the efforts of the captain to apportion to each boat its proper number of people. However, there were enough boats to hold many more than were on board the ship, and when all had embarked in the greatest hurry and confusion in order to escape the flames, it was found that no boat was overloaded, and that each, as chance had it, contained an officer. I found myself in the long-boat, with Grace, Raynor, the second mate, and seven sailors.

The sea was calm, and the boats all withdrew to some distance, and we watched the noble ship gradually burning to the water's edge; but although she blazed fiercely, night fell ere there was any perceptible diminution in the fury of the flames, and during the time we had been watching her she had been drifting away from us.

A few strokes of the oars now and then sufficed to prevent us from following her, the captain wishing to keep in the course he had decided upon. However, she blazed so brightly that the increase of distance was not appreciable, and when at last the flames began to die out, and give place to dense columns of smoke, I was surprised to perceive that we were some miles away from her. She burnt down to the water's edge, but did not sink. Perhaps at the moment I am tracing these lines she is still drifting about, blackened and seared by the flames.

She did not sink, the officers said; but when the morning broke she was out of sight, and we were alone on the ocean. The captain had, or pretended to have, little fear, as we were in the very highway of naval traffic; and, provided that the weather kept calm, he said, scarcely a week would pass without some sail appearing; but if the wind rose, and we were blown out of the track of ships, we must rely on Providence for help.

Two days passed, and no sail appeared. The nights were calm, but very dark, and we kept together by means of lanterns affixed to the masts of the boats. On the morning of the third day a fresh breeze, with but little weight in it, arose, and sail was made on the boats, to prevent them from drifting. Towards evening the sky bore rather a heavy aspect, and the sea began to rise a little, and with good steering we hoped to get along with no mishap. But the wind increased at night, the waves were capped with foam, and the best steerers had the greatest difficulty in managing the boats so as to prevent their being swamped. The longboat's sail steadied her, but now and then she shipped a quantity of water. The mate deplored the fact of our not being in the pinnace or one of the quarter-boats, which surprised me, for I knew nothing of the qualities of light boats to run before the wind until the officer explained. "These waves would never catch a light craft like they catch this log, sir; we shall have them toppling over our stern pretty soon, I expect." We spent a night of great anxiety, no one sleeping except Grace, who appeared indifferent to the dangers which environed us.

The weather moderated in time, however, and when day dawned the sea had subsided greatly, although the wind was still fresh. But none of the other boats were in sight. They had left us behind, the mate said. He calculated that the wind had blown us at least thirty miles out of the course which had been decided on, and we found that the longboat had not been provided with the means of taking "sights." We were hundreds of miles from land, out of the track of ships, and in possession of provisions which we could easily have consumed in two days, but, by rigorous economy, could portion out to last ten. Our only hope was to sight a ship during that time.

The mate was weak, physically and morally, and by no means fitted for the position in which he found himself—a fact of which he had not the slightest suspicion. There were seven sailors in the boat; eleven occupants all told. There was plenty of room; the boat would have held forty. The men were grouped forward, while we occupied the stern-sheets, under which the provisions were, including a small cask of rum.

Two days passed, and the line of the horizon still remained unbroken. The sailors seemed contented and even hopeful.

But the third day broke, and then the fourth, and still no sail appeared. There was no wind; it was just such a calm and misty day as that on which the ship caught fire. The men began to show some signs of discouragement, especially when the mate, who was evidently the most discouraged of all, applied himself to the consumption of a flask of brandy which he had hitherto concealed in his pocket. In this action, which disgusted me, he was soon followed by Raynor, who drank as deeply, avoiding, as did the mate, the contemptuous looks of Grace and myself. This circumstance filled me with dread, which was increased when they both replenished their flasks from the rum-cask.

The crew began to murmur. The rum, they said, was common property; in fact, one intimated that, as misfortune had made us all equal, the cask should be placed amidships and used sparingly until the provisions gave out, and then the remainder of the spirit could be portioned out to each equally, to do what he liked with; this philosopher, for his part, believing that if we were to die, a state of intoxication would greatly relieve the agonies attending dissolution.

At the conclusion of this speech the mate rose, steadied himself, and prepared to reply. However, only a splutter of rage came, and wishing to display in action what he lacked in rhetoric, he put his hand in the pocket of his coat and brought out a revolver, which he pointed first at Raynor, then at the bottom of the boat, then at the clouds, and finally at the group of sailors. They rose in a body, and made as though to rush upon him, when I, suddenly forming a resolution which I had been thinking of for some time, snatched the weapon from his grasp, and pulled him back on to the seat, where, after venting divers incoherent curses, he fell asleep.

I now addressed the men, and told them that, as it was advisable to have a sober man in charge, I would in future portion out the provisions and drink, and see that all was done fairly. This was agreed to and I moved the rum, stowing it close beside me. Raynor, though nearly drunk, seemed much ashamed of his conduct, and immediately threw his flask, which still contained a portion of spirit, overboard, and then lay down. Grace approved, in a weary and listless manner, of what I had done, but seemed as indifferent as ever to the dreadful fate which threatened us.

The fifth day came, bringing no hope. The sixth, seventh, eighth, and ninth passed, and still no break in the dreary monotony of the great watery waste occurred to relieve our anguish. The mate blustered from time to time, but I was firm. On the tenth day the mournful ceremony of portioning out the last morsel of the provisions and the last drop of water was gone through. Grace gave the whole of hers away to a young sailor, who had suffered the most from the privation. She seemed now to have relinquished all hope, and to have sunk into a calm apathy of despair. My heart sank painfully as I looked at her. I could see that she almost welcomed the fate that seemed in store for us—that she gazed at the sea as if she desired it to engulf her at once, and so spare her a continuance of the sufferings she must have endured.

In the night, when the sailors appeared to be asleep, I attempted to throw the cask of rum over the side, but in this I was frustrated by the mate and Raynor. The latter, once more losing command of himself, swore that he would have drink, and defied me, in language that I will not here record. The mate was scarcely less desperate, and the two, throwing off all restraint, began to pour the fiery liquid into their throats. Their stomachs being empty, only a minimum quantity of the ardent spirit was sufficient to produce intoxication, and soon they were maddened. Their appalling screams rang through the stillness, and very quickly awoke those of the men who had fallen asleep. Only two of the sailors could refrain from following the example of the mate and Raynor, and in a short space of time there were seven raving maniacs in the boat. It was a hellish scene. The mate fancied that he saw a large ship within a few yards of the boat, and immediately sprang overboard, dragging Raynor with him. They splashed frantically for a few seconds, and then sank. Meanwhile a quarrel had sprung up among the other unfortunate wretches, through one of them maintaining that he saw a red light ahead. The others dissenting, he drew a knife, and laid about him so desperately that two of them fell dead or dying, whereupon the rest rushed upon him in a body, and quickly threw him into the sea. While this was going on I tried to seize the cask unobserved, with the intention of casting it overboard, but the two maniacs who remained perceived my action, and, with appalling cries, threw themselves upon me; I shot them both. Thus all those who had partaken of the spirit, after the last of the food and water had been consumed, fell victims to their desperate passion for the drink.

Morning broke, and, after ascertaining that there was no sail in sight, I assisted the men to heave the bodies of the unfortunate fellows who had been killed into the sea. While we were engaged in ushering in the glorious morn with this dismal task I did not fail to perceive that the two men frequently exchanged glances, and muttered one to the other. As we approached the last body, to cast it over the side, one of the sailors called my attention to the fact that life seemed yet to linger. We both paused, and our eyes met in a long and constrained gaze—and his were full of such intensity of expression, such horrible signification, that I sank down upon the seat, and a heavy sickness came upon my soul.

★   ★   ★   ★   ★

It was true that the miserable wretch who lay in the bottom of the boat still lived. But he died ere the sun went down. Although I had momentarily yielded to the desire expressed in the eyes of the men, the thought of sustaining existence by means of the dead sailor's flesh was in the last degree repugnant to my feelings, but I felt a great fear that I would in the end give way. The sight of one of the poor fellows lapping up, like a dog, the blood that had been spilt on the thwarts, horrified me, indeed, but I could not help wondering vaguely if it did relieve thirst, such as my burning throat now suffered.

The body was not touched that day nor the next, and as we were in cool latitudes the flesh did not corrupt. But on the third day since the last meal—that is to say the thirteenth since we had lost the other boats—both of the men drew their knives, and each waited for the other, gazing at the body. It was a mournful and impressive sight to see the two unfortunates reflecting upon the terrible thing that they were about to do, and having no power to withhold themselves from it. I also *waited*; almost mad with extreme privation. I felt that the moment one of them tasted of the human flesh I should be obliged to follow his example, when I suddenly turned towards Grace. Her pale face was haggard and worn, her eyes were sunken, her lips were white. She gazed at the men, I thought, with the profound pity of one who sees suffering, but does not so suffer; yet there was in her looks an expression of immeasurable disgust, contempt, repugnance. She seemed to be a mere spectator of this hideous drama, mentally not *personally* interested in its details. The horrible thought that she might be mad now struck me; but at the same time the expression of her eyes influenced me to a greater degree, and seeing with what loathing she regarded the imminent cannibalism, I resolved that I would endure the most intolerable anguish rather than merit her contempt. With this intention I turned completely round, and she turned also. She held out an emaciated hand. I took it in mine and bathed it in a flood of tears that sprang from my eyes. There was a movement in the forward part of the boat, but we would not look round, knowing but too well what it meant.

★   ★   ★   ★   ★

We sat hand in hand for hours, but neither could utter a word, less on account of our parched throats than the fulness of our hearts. I knew that I was loved; she knew that she loved me; perhaps she thought that it would be no sin to *die* loving me. . . . Awaking from a long and painful slumber, I found that day was once more breaking. All the others slept, and the men were breathing heavily, and apparently with difficulty. I endeavoured not to look at the carcase in the bottom of the boat, but could not withhold my gaze. The head and extremities had been separated from the trunk, and, I supposed, cast overboard, for on looking more closely I saw that flesh had been taken from the side of the corpse. It had evidently been consumed immediately, for, although the means of kindling fire were in the boat, there was nothing to justify a supposition that they had been used.

The men awoke. It was a heartrending sight to watch them gradually regaining a consciousness of their fearful position. They uttered deep groans, and turned with loathing from the corpse. Thirst appeared to be now their chief torment. They remembered the rum, which was still in the stern-sheets. They advanced, and I did not oppose them. They took the remainder of the spirit forward in silence, and quickly consumed it. While I watched them, Grace had awakened from her sleep, if such it can be called. I did not know that she was awake until I heard her give utterance to a stifled shriek. I was about to look round, when the strange conduct of the two men attracted my attention. They stood up, tottering, on the thwarts, waving their arms and laughing inanely and wildly; one of them seized an oar, but let it fall through sheer weakness; then, as if actuated by one impulse, they jumped, or rather fell, over the side of the boat, and commenced to swim feebly away. But they had not proceeded more than half-a-dozen yards ere their strength failed, and they were drowned before my eyes—a horrible spectacle for me, for I was far too weak to propel the boat to the place where they were struggling. While watching their throes and seeming to actually feel in my own soul the bitter anguish that must have dwelt in theirs, I could not help vaguely pondering upon the cause of their actions. When at last the inscrutable waters closed over them I turned to Grace, and beheld her on her knees, with her hands clasped as if in prayer, and her eyes fixed and distended, and staring in one direction the while—the same direction, I remarked, as that in which the unfortunate sailors had tried to swim.

I followed with my own eyes her enraptured gaze, and there, looming large and shadowy through the mists of the morning, was a ship and she was stationary upon the deep, as though waiting for us. With a bursting heart, I sought to take Grace's hand, but immediately I touched her she fainted.

I laid her gently on the sail of the boat, and then began to watch the ship. I noticed now that there seemed something strange and unusual about her, which the pitiable weakness of my faculties would not allow me to determine; and I also failed not to remark the extreme silence in which she was wrapped. A rather strong breeze sprang up while I watched the ship, and the boat was wafted along towards her. Soon the intervening distance was very considerably lessened, and all at once the secret of that strangeness which I had vaguely remarked in the vessel's appearance broke in upon my reason. She carried not an inch of canvas. But that was not all. *Her masts* were gone! Her bulwarks were torn and broken in numerous places, and she was very low in the water. It was a wreck—too probably an abandoned wreck—to which we looked for succour in the extremity of our suffering and despair.

Prostrated by this terrible blow to my hopes, I sank into a state of insensibility. I awoke with a vague feeling that a sweet but haggard face was bending over me, and that I was being brought back to life by the coolness of waterdrops sprinkled over my face from white and emaciated hands. On one side of me was the sea, calm and waveless; on the other a great black shadow. It was night. From time to time I felt slight shocks and heard low sounds, but could not determine in my mind the signification of these, although I felt that if I could only employ my ordinary powers of thought I would not long remain in ignorance. And in a few moments I knew all. I sat up on the seat and looked intently at the black shadow.

"It is a ship," murmured Grace. "We have drifted against it; but there is no one on board, and I think it is only a deserted wreck."

Then I remembered all, and felt sick at heart to think that we were to reap but this negative deliverance as the harvest of our hopes. However, there might be food on board, and that we needed so much—suffered so much from want of it—that either of us would have died willingly to procure the smallest morsel for the other.

We decided that I should first endeavour to get aboard and search for something eatable; if I found anything, I could bring it to Grace, and when our strength was sufficiently recuperated, I would assist her to the deck of the vessel. To give me the temporary strength necessary for the effort I was about to make, I drained the rum-cask into a tin cup, and, having succeeded in getting nearly a quarter of a gill, I swallowed it. The effect was marvellous for a time, and, grasping a rope that hung over the side of the ship, I managed to swing myself through a gap in the bulwarks. Fastening the boat's painter, which Grace cast to me, I started on my search. I thought if I could find the pantry I would have the best chance of obtaining what I required, but by this time the rum had taken effect on my brain, and I became greatly confused. Staggering hither and thither, not knowing where to go, I stumbled against a fixed cask, with a square hole cut in the uppermost side. I put my hand in this aperture, and drew it out wet—here was water at all events. I drank some from the hollow of my hand, and felt greatly refreshed. After this, fortune favoured me. Turning by accident into one of the deck cabins aft, and groping about in the darkness, I found some large biscuits, and a few bottles that seemed to contain wine to judge from their shape. Two were full, the rest uncorked and empty. I gathered together all the biscuits I could find, and took two of the bottles, one full and the other empty; then I felt my way to the water-bulk and filled the empty bottle, after which I went to the place where I had fastened the boat. I lowered the bottles into the boat very carefully by means of a piece of halyard line which I found, and then descended myself, with the biscuits in my pockets.

I now remembered a fact which I had unfortunately forgotten before—namely, that there was a lantern in the boat, with which I could easily have searched the wreck, and doubtless, with more success. I found and lit it now, however, and by its light we broke our long and painful fast. The bottle contained port, which we poured into tin cups and diluted with water; then we soaked the biscuits in the wine, and began to eat—very sparingly at first, though we could with difficulty restrain our appetite. In this way, we were soon sufficiently strong and invigorated to leave the boat and establish ourselves on the gloomy and shattered wreck.

I led Grace to one of the deck cabins, which had not been much damaged by the storm that had wrecked the ship, and left her there to sleep, while I sought shelter in another.

I did not sleep, but lay in the berth thinking dreamily of the strangeness of my destiny, and the mercy of Providence in saving me when so many had perished, and also of the patient, unmurmuring endurance of poor Grace, who loved me at last and whom I now loved more than ever. And I lost myself in a maze of vague conjecture as to the nature of that secret which stood between us. The sliding-door of the cabin was not quite closed, and admitted a view of the stars; by-and-bye, after some hours had passed, the moon rose slowly from the deep, and her pale light shone through the aperture. Although I was so weak, sleep would not come, but at length a sort of semi-consciousness, caused perhaps by the stillness and silence, broken only by the melancholy sough of the sea against the vessel came over me. At the time of falling into this half sleep, a somewhat vivid impression of the door, the moonlight, and such portion of the broken bulwark as could be seen had been stamped on my mind. Something aroused me—I knew not what it was, but supposed it to be a heavier wash of the waves against the ship—and I raised my eyelids and gazed dreamily through the slightly-opened door. Some change, some alteration which I could not locate or define, for many minutes held my attention. The impression which my mind had received of all the objects within range of my vision was sufficiently vivid to enable me to perceive that some alteration had taken place; but what could it be? For many moments I taxed my faculties in vain endeavour to comprehend the nature of this mysterious change.

At length, wearied by the efforts I had made, I closed my eyes; but a strange and uneasy feeling came upon me, and caused me to open them once more. I looked again, and this time the mystery was revealed. At a few inches from the top of the door, and grasping its edge, was a long and emaciated hand. The moonlight shone on the brown knuckles, and it was the faint glimmer that had so vaguely arrested my attention.

I was intensely startled by this strange circumstance, and could do nothing but stare at the hand for a few moments. Reflection, however, soon came to my aid; this hand must be that of Grace, who, unable to sleep, like myself, had arisen and wandered over the wreck. Knowing her love of the sea by moonlight, I could easily suppose that she would walk about in the silent solitude rather than lie awake in the dark cabin; and, pausing here by accident, her hand had closed on the door, perhaps involuntarily, or as a support in her weakness. I was about to speak, when it suddenly occurred to me that the hand I saw was both too large and too brown to be that of Grace. This fact occasioned me great uneasiness. I tried to persuade myself that the hand really had no existence, save in my unstrung brain, or that it might be a piece of moulding which the phantasy of night and my own imagining had so transformed that it appeared to be the hand of a man. But I looked at it intently, and I was convinced that it was really a hand.

And now a great hope arose within my heart. Perhaps a ship was near and had sent a boat, and this hand was that of a man about to enter the cabin, and—but why had I heard no voices and why did the stranger pause so long? Nevertheless, I started up as quickly as my weakness would permit, and, perhaps because of the noise I made, the door quickly slid back, and a wild face looked in, but recoiled on seeing me. I stepped from the cabin to the moonlit deck, and confronted a man. He was tall, well built, handsome, and bore the appearance of wildness peculiar to people who have dwelt in solitude. His hair and beard were long and uncared for, and his head looked like one of those drawn by Titian—savage and grand. My own looks could not have been less strange, though I did not consider that then.

For some moments we stood in silent wonder, utterly unable to speak. At last, the stranger said, in a quick and strange tone:—

"How did you get here? Where did you come from?"

Still unable to utter a word, I pointed to the sea. A ghastly, mirthless smile writhed his lips.

"How?" he said.

I leaned over the bulwarks and indicated the boat.

"You came in that boat?"

"Yes," I said, huskily, finding my speech at last; "and you?—how did you come here?"

"In somewhat the same manner as yourself," he replied. "I was on my way to England, and one night, when the sea was rather high, I fell overboard. A lifebelt was thrown to me, and by chance I caught it, and slipped it on. The steamer stopped as soon as she could, but I don't think a boat was lowered; probably the sea was too rough. I was washed to and fro until morning. The steamer was out of sight, but in its stead I saw this old wreck. The sea was calm now, and I had little difficulty in swimming to her. It was not so easy to get on board, but I managed it at last. I have been here ever since—some weeks, I think, and during that time but two or three sail have come within the range of my telescope. I kindled a fire, and made as much smoke as I could each time, hoping to attract attention; but in vain. That is my story, sir; and now I hope you will return the compliment by telling me yours."

"With pleasure," I said. "In the first place, however, I must tell you that there is a young lady on board. We were both passengers, and our ship was burned. All hands took to the boats, and on the second day ours, the long-boat, was left alone. We two alone survived of the boat's occupants—the rest dying in the most horrible manner. We were four days without food or drink, and this night we broke our fast."

"Strange that you should come aboard and I not know it."

"It was; and I never thought but that the wreck was entirely deserted."

"Ay, it looks so. But tell me the name of your ship that was burnt."

"The *Aurora*."

He fell back a step, and his hands trembled.

"The *Aurora*!" he cried, hoarsely. "And her master—quick, her master's name?"

"John Hay," I answered, in bewilderment at his strange manner.

"Great heaven! The very ship that I was in pursuit of—that I intended to wait for on my arrival. And burned at sea! My God! But you say that all hands took to the boats. None perished in the flames?"

"None," I said. "Had you relatives on board?"

Instead of answering he started violently, and gave utterance to a sharp and sudden cry; then he caught my arm in a painful grasp.

"This girl—this young lady who is on board—tell me her name quick!"

"Grace Wendell," I replied, and even as I spoke a dreadful, though undefined, fear sprang up in my heart. "What—what is she to you?" I asked, faintly.

"To me? What is she to me?" he said, trembling violently with agitation. "She is my wife!"

"No, no; it cannot be," I stammered; "we love each other . . . it cannot be true. You are mad."

"Mad!" he repeated, in a strange, hoarse tone; "well, I may be mad; I ought to be. But stand aside, if you please. I wish to see my wife. Or, rather, do you show me where she is."

And he advanced a step.

"No, no," I cried, wildly; "not now, I implore you. Think of her frightful sufferings. It would kill her to see you—if—if you are——"

"Her husband? Your doubts shall soon be set at rest. As for the shock of killing her—why, they say that 'joy never kills.'"

The bitterly sardonic tone in which he spoke these words caused me to shudder. He once more attempted to advance, but despair and horror made me mad; I drew the mate's revolver, in which some shots still remained, and pointed it at the man's head. He fell back, clenched his brown hands, and seemed for a moment as if about to spring upon me. But suddenly he broke into a hoarse laugh, and assumed an indifferent attitude, saying—

"Well, well! we will wait until daybreak."

I have marvelled since—I marvel now—that I did not shoot him where he stood. I know not what stayed my hand. I felt no compunction when speculating upon his death. I only knew that he purposed to rob me of her I loved so much—to take her from me by virtue of earthly right. And yet, was his story true? Was she really his wife? Could it be a fabrication? I tried earnestly, but in vain, to think that it might be so. I called to mind his surprise when he heard the name of our ship, and my heart sank as I remembered how unaffected was that surprise. And here I recalled the secret of Grace—her gloomy sorrow, her sad words that "no happiness was possible for her; her own weakness and indecision had wrecked her life." These words must refer to an assent to a marriage at which her soul revolted—an assent drawn from her, forced from her, by others. The marriage must have taken place; she must then have been horrified at the consequence of her weakness and indecision. Instead of becoming reconciled to the hated match, she recoiled with loathing from the unholy embrace of one she could not love; and then she had flown for help to the only true friend she had, Captain Hay, her uncle. That good-hearted sailor had consented to take her away to England, thinking little of any possible consequences. I felt certain, knowing Grace's character so well, that my conjectures were very near the truth.

While we waited for the dawn, Grace still sleeping, those were the thoughts that vexed my mind. What passed in *his* I know not. He stood, like myself, silent and gloomy, leaning on the shattered bulwark, and contemplating the slowly heaving sea, wherein was reflected the pale cold light of the moon.

As I gazed upon him I felt a hideous hatred rising in my heart against him—a hatred at which I shuddered, for even then an undefinable fear of what was to happen seemed to shake my soul. And this growing hatred and loathing I could not resist.

Of all the millions in the world, what accursed fate had thrown *this* man here? I groaned at the thought.

And now a plan—a plot—began to form itself in my mind. Grace might not wake for hours; there would be plenty of time to kill this man—to drag him, weak as I was, to some remote part of the wreck. I would wait some days, and then propose to Grace a journey all over the vessel, in which we would stumble upon the body. She would recognise it as that of her husband. She would perhaps faint, and on recovering, she would explain why she had fainted, and tell me who the man was. I would then remind her that she was free, and that I loved her. . . . But how to accomplish the act?—a shot might wake her; and how else could I, so weak, compass the death of this man, who had gained his health and strength while on the wreck? I was almost glad to find such good reasons for not attempting the man's life, for strong as was my desire for his death, I shuddered at the thought of destroying him.

As I was yet revolving these hideous thoughts in my over-wrought mind, streaks of dawn appeared in the east, and the moon waned.

The man still leaned upon the bulwark, but now and then he moved, and cast a sinister and sidelong glance upon me.

My faculties became confused now that day was so near, and I tried in vain to conjecture what was to happen on the appearance of Grace. Would the shock of seeing him, in her weak condition, prostrate her? Would she submit to fate and to *him*, or would she fly from his touch and throw herself upon my protection? The latter I devoutly hoped, and in that case I resolved to shoot him like a dog should he attempt to approach her. I looked upon him as a savage enemy—as an evil genius in our path.

The glory of an ocean sunrise burst upon us. But what was this miracle of beauty to hearts wasted by passion—to souls laden with grief and sinking under the weight of fatality?

The man turned and confronted me.

"Now," he said, in a tone that made me tremble.

But I still stood in his way.

"Wait," I said, "until I prepare her."

He made a gesture of dissent and impatience.

"Then, at least," I said, "let her awake and come herself."

In reply, he pushed me with his hand and tried to pass. Mad with rage, I drew the pistol and fired. The ball passed through his hand as he attempted to ward off the weapon. I was about to fire again when he started back, gazing fixedly in the direction of the aft part of the wreck.

I followed his gaze, and saw—Grace.

The noise of the shot had awakened her, and she had arisen and come from the cabin.

The man stood still as before, the blood dropping from his wounded hand to the deck. It is certain that Grace did not recognise him from where she was, and a great hope sprang up in my breast. But in a moment I was undeceived.

She advanced to within a few paces, stopped, and for an instant seemed about to speak. But suddenly she reeled, caught at the air, and then sank into my arms. I had sprang to her assistance, but the man, her husband, had not moved.

She did not lose consciousness—perhaps from having been unable at once to realise this terrible thing that Fate had prepared for her awakening.

She gazed fixedly at the man, with starting eyes, as a child would gaze at the serpent which fascinates it.

I could not speak—my brain whirled.

The man advanced, and she clung convulsively to me.

"Grace," said he, "leave that man, and come to me—to your husband." But she clung the closer.

"Is this thing true?" I murmured in her ear.

"Alas, yes," she replied, and how strange seemed her voice! "He is my—husband—on earth, as you are mine by our marriage made in heaven; you will not let him take me? You will—"

A deep groan interrupted her, and I saw the man leaning against the bulwark, with both hands pressed over his eyes and brow, and the red drops falling from his wound seemed like tears of blood.

Suddenly the man turned towards us. A wild and terrible light shone in his black eyes. His brow was smeared with blood. He faced us uttering disconnected and meaningless words—addressing them apparently to Grace, who, naturally fearless, and thinking perhaps that he was losing his reason, relinquished her convulsive grasp upon my arm.

But suddenly, and before I could even suspect his purpose, he sprang to his feet, and seized the light form of Grace in his arms.

"You are mine!" he cried, in ringing tones, "mine in death!" And, springing swiftly to the gap in the bulwarks, he prepared to leap with her into the sea. At that moment I aimed at him and fired. The bullet struck him between the shoulders. He threw up his arms with a wild cry of pain, and fell backwards, while Grace tottered a moment, lost her balance, uttered a stifled shriek, and in a moment the waters closed over her.

Throwing down the pistol, I leaped into the sea, where she had disappeared, hoping to save her. And I was not disappointed. Soon we were both in the boat which still lay alongside; but, so violent had been the exertions which I, in my weak condition, had undergone, it was many minutes ere I could take any steps towards the recovery of Grace, who lay like one dead. But at last, I took the half empty wine bottle that was in the boat, and succeeded in pouring some between her pale lips. The dark red fluid flowed over her chin and neck, and gave her an appearance so ghastly that I dropped the bottle in nervous terror. But her vitality was great—she recovered soon, and looked wonderingly at me as I chafed her cold and emaciated hands.

"You are saved, dear Grace, once more, thank God!" I murmured. She replied not, nor seemed at first to understand, but suddenly, and with a start, she glanced above, towards the deck of the ship, and then, with a wild, piteous, fearful expression in her dim and sunken eyes, she shivered violently.

I started up. There was no time to be lost; she must have succour—warmth, and dry clothing. I collected my strength, draining to the lees the wine bottle, and taking the—alas!—too light form of Grace in my arms, succeeded in gaining the deck. Then, passing the body of her husband as I went, I placed her in her cabin, and searched the others. In one, fortunately, I found a woman's wardrobe, which I at once took to her, beseeching her to change her clothes ere the cold and wet could have ill effects. Then I left her, to change my own clothes and procure some nourishment. There was, I found on inspection, abundance of provisions on board, and when Grace, attired in dry clothing, and with her glossy, sable locks hanging damp and heavy over her shoulders, came forth from the cabin with trembling steps, we partook of some refreshment.

Soon we were both greatly recuperated. I proposed to Grace that she should try and sleep, or at least lie down and rest; but she shook her head, and pointed to the side of the vessel, and scarcely more than whispered:

"Is he alive?"

These words caused my heart to sink, for I had forgotten in my joy that the man still lay on the deck where he had fallen, dead or dying.

Grace rose, led the way, and I followed her at some little distance. She knelt beside her prostrate husband. I saw him move slightly. She raised his head, and some words were spoken by both, words which I could not hear, nor shall ever know. Then she beckoned me to approach. I did so. The man, dying fast, raised his dim eyes to mine, and said in a faint and altogether indescribable voice:

"I—forgive—you."

I fell on my knees beside him, and took his hand in mine, but even as I touched him his spirit fled.

★　★　★　★　★

"You know my secret now, Philip," said Grace, sadly, next day, when, her tumultuous emotions having settled into a gloomy calm, she sat with me at evening on the deck of the deserted wreck.

"Ah, yes; but not your story—not your past life, dear Grace," I answered.

"But you can surely guess what that has been—it is so simple! merely the story of a fatal mistake, made in a moment of indecision, and, perhaps, of terror. But I will tell you. He—his name was George Herapath. I never saw him until six months before my marriage. I lived in Sydney with my aunt and uncle (not uncle Hay). They were poor, mercenary, and grasping; Herapath was very rich. A very little while after our acquaintance began, he told me that he loved me passionately—that life without me would be madness; in short, that if I did not consent to be his wife he would destroy himself; and, oh, I can never forget the wildness of his passion as he pleaded for my consent! I was affrighted by his manner, and trembled to think of the consequences of a refusal—trembled also to think of marriage with one whom I feared, and at times almost hated. My guardians were never tired of expatiating on the advantages of a union with such a 'rich, handsome, amiable, and accomplished gentleman,' as they called him, and tormented me night and day with their persuasions and 'advice'; and at last, in a moment of madness or weakness, I gave my consent. Herapath was wild with delight, and my guardians sought not to conceal their base satisfaction. We were wedded, and then I realised what I had done, and what my true feelings were toward the man—fear, aversion, bordering on actual hatred. But in a little while I learned something more—something that struck me with renewed terror; my husband was almost a maniac. I inadvertently overheard a conversation between two gentlemen who knew him well, and from the words spoken I gathered that the man I had married bore the taint of an hereditary insanity—that it had always been assiduously concealed when possible, but that there had been occasions when it had escaped control, and showed itself in acts and words that left no doubt of its existence. I was horrified at learning this, and when I had endured outrages at his hands, such as I dare not speak of—dare not think upon, I made up my mind to fly from him. Captain Hay, my uncle, visited me at this time, and to him I confided everything, and gained his complete sympathy. I entreated him to take me away in his ship, and he consented at once, his affection for me annulling all other considerations. You know the rest. Ha!" she cried suddenly, clutching my arm, "look—look!"

It was a ship—a noble square-rigged vessel in full sail, bearing down upon us.

In a little more than a month we were once more in Sydney, where we were welcomed back by no other than Captain Hay. All the boats except ours had fallen in with an Australian bound steamer; he had given us up for lost.

My story is not yet ended—I mean, as most stories end. Grace is not yet my wife, but her every action promises me the realisation of my dearest hopes, and at a day now not very far distant.

THE RED CHAMBER

For some years prior to the disappearance of my father he bore the reputation of being a miser, and I cannot but admit that the epithet was in some sense deserved. From being thought a miser, he gradually came to be credited with the possession of immense wealth. But misers, I believe, are always supposed to be rolling in gold; and so, when my father suddenly disappeared, it was fully expected that a fabulous sum would be found secreted somewhere about the house, or that he had acquired large properties and lands at home and abroad. However, on the discovery that all the money in the place amounted to a few odd pounds, and that he had possessed no other property than the old house and some small farms, people did not know what to wonder at most—this fact, or that of the old man's disappearance.

I knew very little of my father. There was not much sympathy or love between us. Indeed, in my boyhood I scarcely ever saw him, and as soon as I was my own master, I hastened to gratify a long-felt desire to travel. He placed sufficient funds at my disposal, telling me that if ever I overdrew so much as a shilling I would escape mention in his will. He made no will, by the way.

My mother had died when I was very young—soon after the birth of my sister Vera, who, unlike myself, became much attached to our father. During my absence abroad, they lived together in the old, rambling house. Vera must have been very lonesome, as our father was not a good host, and seldom entertained anyone; but she had one friend, a young lady of a wealthy family, whom she visited every week, riding on her pony to the grand mansion, where she was always welcome. Her visits were often returned by her friend, whose name was Miss Myrtle Rivers. The two residences were some miles apart, and on the day before my father's disappearance, Vera had paid a visit to her friend, and had been prevented from returning home by a heavy storm. When she did return, she found the three old people, who were the only servants of the house, in a state of the greatest consternation, consequent upon their discovery of the unlooked-for absence of their master, who had left without their knowledge—left, too, without making the slightest preparation or taking anything with him, not even a valise. Inquiry at the nearest railway station failed to elicit anything. The old gentleman had disappeared without leaving the slightest clue as to his destination or purpose in going away so suddenly.

This happened, strangely enough, but a day or two prior to my return home. I found Vera in great grief and trouble, though she rejoiced much at seeing me, and at having someone to care for her in her loneliness. I employed skilled search for the old gentleman; the house itself was scrutinised, the cellars and disused rooms were looked into, but all in vain. And now we discovered that not only had he made no will, but that, unless he had taken his money with him or hidden it somewhere, he had been comparatively poor. There was nothing left for us but the old house and a few farm rents; even some rather valuable family jewels had gone. But Vera still had a small annuity inherited from her mother; so we decided to still live together in the home of our childhood, and make the best of circumstances.

I was naturally much surprised to find that we were now comparatively poor—nearly as much surprised, indeed, as those kind people who made it their business to interest themselves in our affairs. The prevailing opinion was that my father had, for some reason best known to himself, deemed it advisable to remove with his money to some country where no one was likely to find him. Of course, neither Vera nor I listened to such ungenerous imputations; but, unless he had somehow met with foul play, what else could we think? We spent many hours, Vera and I, in talking and puzzling over the mystery. My sister was not nearly so much surprised as I at our poverty, for the old gentleman had never allowed her to understand that he possessed any considerable fortune or property.

We now lived together in calm contentment. We possessed more than sufficient for our own simple wants. Our natures were sympathetic, and we never wearied of each other's society. Vera had a talent for music and painting, and I dabbled in literature. Each took great pride and interest in the other's work. I regarded Vera as

an artist and musician destined to achieve renown, and she looked
upon me as a poet and author, who would yet do great things. Each
of us knew that the other was mistaken, but had no suspicion that
we both were. In fact, we dwelt in a state of happy mediocrity, from
which each intended one day to emerge and surprise the world—in
the meantime falling into a state of indolence most fatal to any
flickerings of genius that might have once existed; but such sparks
need to be fanned by the soaring wings of ambition or the cold
breath of want, ere they mature into the divine flame, whereas we
merely enjoyed ourselves, which was very pleasant, if inglorious.
One amusement we took much delight in (especially in winter),
this was the study, construction, and solution of cyphers and cryp-
tographs. Vera showed herself possessed of much analytical ability,
both in inventing and solving these enigmas, and shared a great
writer's opinion, that human ingenuity could not construct a cryptogram which human ingenuity may not, by proper application,
resolve.

I had had some slight acquaintance with Myrtle Rivers before
going abroad, but had certainly never expected to find the tall, hoydenish girl transformed into such a lovely, graceful, and dignified
young lady as she now was. Neither had I expected ever to regard
her otherwise than as a friend. Judge, then, of my surprise when I
woke one morning, and found myself—not famous, but—in love!
I was fortunate—in the sense that it is happiness to love; but I was
unfortunate in that the fair object of my devotion was not intended
for so poor a suitor by her fond parents. Vera suggested this to me;
I had not thought of it. We spent many happy moments together,
thanks to my sister's contrivance, at parties on the river-bank, and
in the extensive gardens belonging to Myrtle's father; on such
occasions we generally found ourselves apart from the rest, and it
was not long before I was made happy in the consciousness that I
not only loved, but was loved in return. But the task of presenting
myself, in all my poverty, before old Rivers, to ask for the hand of
the richest heiress in the country, at first shook my nerves considerably. Still, the forlornest hope has no terrors for the true lover, and
I set about storming the position; as I expected, I was repulsed with
loss. Mr. Rivers was naturally astounded at my presumption, and I
was then the most hopeless of lovers.

"But why despair, Arthur?" said Myrtle; "in a year I shall be of age, and may do as I please; surely you can wait a year."

"Ah, my dear Myrtle, I should be unworthy of you if I accepted such a sacrifice; how could I ask you, who have been reared in such a profusion of wealth and splendour, to share a life of comparative poverty?"

"Nay, I know you are proud, Arthur; but we would be just as happy in what you call poverty as in this oppressive superfluity of riches. Do not despair; let us wait and hope—we are young."

Vera, too, would not let me despair, and many were the hours that we spent conferring together and making divers plans to resuscitate our fallen fortunes. These conversations always ended in our wondering what had become of our poor father, and what he had done with all his wealth—whether he had lost it in some gigantic speculation, or had taken it with him to a distant land, or had been murdered and robbed. This latter conjecture seemed to me to rest upon very slight grounds, and I was surprised to find that Vera entertained it persistently, especially as she would give no reason for so doing, beyond the rather weak one that she "did not know what else could have caused him to disappear so mysteriously."

One night we had sat up rather late talking on this subject, and Vera was still airing her theory of murder and robbery. There was an old disused well near the house, and she began to entertain an idea that the old gentleman had been killed and thrown into this pit, which was very deep.

"Some night," said she, in a tone of awe, and with a shudder, "we may see his pale shadow emerge from the well to warn us of—oh, heaven! what is that?"

"What do you mean?" I cried, startled by her wild looks; "do you hear anything?"

"Hark!" she cried.

I listened intently, and presently a faint and peculiar sound came to my ears. At first I imagined it to be a hoarse human voice, and for a moment gave way to a feeling of superstitious terror. But I heard it again, and this time I thought it was caused by the opening of rusty-hinged doors.

"What can it be?" I said.

"Burglars, perhaps," said Vera. The idea of burglars selecting

Stanton House for the exercise of their talents made me smile; but the next moment the sound was repeated. I started up, and, arming myself with a stout stick, I went cautiously in the direction of the noise, followed, at a few paces, by Vera, who would not remain alone.

The old house was large, and the eastern half of it was, and had been for years, almost entirely disused. I traversed several apartments of this portion before hearing anything more. I then paused and listened.

After a brief interval (which seemed an age) I fancied I heard a soft footfall in the next room. I immediately opened the door leading to it.

As I did so, the tall figure of a man turned round, and, letting fall a dark lantern, sprang for the door.

I struck at him with my stick, but missed. As he passed, however, I managed to clutch his coat; to my surprise, he slipped out of it with the agility of an eel, and disappeared, leaving the garment in my hands.

I pursued him by the sound of his footsteps, for, it being dark, I soon lost sight of him; but the burglar, if such he was, knew the house well, for he was out of it before I could ascertain which way he went. An open window subsequently showed his means of entrance and exit.

Vera and I returned to the room from which we had been startled. I still had the coat, and when the excitement had in some measure cooled down, we examined it. It was a well-made and somewhat costly garment, with rather more inner pockets than usual. I turned out the pockets, and we examined the contents. These were mostly papers, but there was also a pocket-book, with some notes and gold in it. The papers were all roughly-written letters, without envelopes, so that it appeared to have been an object with the late possessor to carry nothing about him which might lead to a discovery of his identity; no names were mentioned in the letters, but persons were referred to by initials. The phraseology of the epistles was to us almost as an unknown language, so much interspersed was it with slang.

Suddenly Vera uttered an exclamation—she had found a half-sheet of note-paper, with a plan drawn on it, a plan of the eastern portion of Stanton House. It was very nearly exact, too; and what surprised us most was that three of the rooms were designated by their names. They belonged to a suite of apartments, and were known by the colour of their hangings and tapestries as the green chamber, the red chamber, and the blue chamber. On the plan the space allotted for the red chamber was marked with a cross.

While we were lost in wonder at this discovery, I was mechanically turning out the contents of the pocket-book, fingering the crisp notes it contained. Presently my fingers touched something much smoother than the paper money. I looked at it—it was a piece of writing-paper similar to that on which the plan was drawn. In fact, so much did it resemble it that I placed them together, and found that it was the other half of the sheet.

But for this fact we might possibly have thrown it aside. Now, however, we examined it, and found it to contain nothing but some figures, all jumbled together, with the letters "Cr. A.K." above them. The figures ran thus:—

522141436221125231133353225243
411321425452212111535421524263
113434314252211413241141122152

"What is it?" asked Vera.

"I don't know, unless, perhaps, it is a memorandum of the number of the bank-notes."

"Let us ascertain."

But a glance showed us that I was mistaken in my conjecture.

Vera took up the paper, looked at it a moment, and then said—

"What can this 'Cr. A.K.' mean? It must signify something, and—why—Arthur!"

"Well."

"This is a cryptogram."

"Nonsense."

"I am certain it is. This 'Cr.' is evidently a contraction of the word 'cryptogram,' and 'A.K.' must refer to the key, or, at least, to some particular order of cypher it belongs to."

I readily fell in with Vera's opinion, and now we were in our element. The fact that the cryptogram had been written on the same paper as the plan of our house, and then torn off, evidently to take care of it, increased our interest tenfold.

"We most solve it," I said; "but you, Vera, being the ablest, must conduct the solution. I will make suggestions."

She thereupon took the paper, studied it a while, and began—

"Well, then, we have here an assemblage of figures which we think may contain a meaning. Until we prove the contrary, let us assume that each of these figures signifies a letter of the alphabet."

"If such is the case," I remarked, "there must be very few letters used, for the highest figure here quoted is 6."

"True; and as six letters would not suffice to construct a sentence of sufficient length to give it coherence, we may consider our assumption disproved; unless, indeed, only six letters *have* been used, and the rest are to be supplied to complete whatever words may require them. However, that is a theory which we will look at afterwards, if at all necessary. We will now proceed with the supposition that each letter necessary to the sentence has been expressed by a combination of figures, and, as the hidden sentence would otherwise be too short compared with the importance which we are to suppose the owner or constructor attached to it, we cannot think that more than two figures have been used for one letter. Let us count the figures."

"There are ninety."

"Then the number is even, and my theory is not yet refuted. Ninety figures will, then, give forty-five letters."

"But I am afraid, Vera, the shortness of the sentence will increase the difficulty of solution."

"How so?"

"Well—that is, if we proceed, as we have done on previous occasions, by ascertaining what character occurs oftenest, and assuming it to be the letter *e*, the next *a*, the next *o*, and so on; for it must be apparent that such a rule will hold only in the solution of a cypher of much greater length than this."

"True; but we may search for repetitions of the same combinations of figures, in order to obtain the word *the*, thus gaining three letters. Unless, indeed, the articles have been omitted."

"They are almost certain to have been in so short a sentence, especially since brevity appears to have been an object with the writer."

"Well, then, what are we to do?" said Vera, rather petulantly.

For some minutes we were both silent. At last Vera's face lighted up, evidently with a new idea.

"I think I have it," she said. "How many letters are there in the alphabet?"

"Twenty-six."

"And the highest figure in the cryptogram?"

"The figure 6."

"Yes. Well, divide the alphabet into six parts, leaving *y* and *z* out, and we have four letters for each portion."

"Well, but——"

"Do you not perceive? Let us call the first part No. 1, the second No. 2, and so on, as thus"—and she wrote the following:—

1	2	3	4	5	6
abcd	*efgh*	*ijkl*	*mnop*	*qrst*	*uvwx*

"You see," she continued, "that each division has its number. Well, if we give each *letter* its number also, from 1 to 4, the letter *a* will be the first letter of the first division; place the figures representing each together, and we get 1—1; and for *b* 1—2, assuming, of course, that the number of the division is placed first, and followed by the number of the letter in that division. Let us now look at the cypher. The first two figures are 5 and 2—the second letter of the fifth division—viz., *r*; the next combination is 2—1, or *e*; the next 4—1, or *m*; the next 4—3, or *o*; the next 6—2, or *v*; and the next 2—1, or *e*. Thus we have the word *remove*; and there is now nothing to do but to translate the rest."

This was done, and the result was the following sentence:—

"Remove bricks from centre eastern wall in Red Chamber."

"The Red Chamber!" I exclaimed.

"The Red Chamber!" cried Vera.

Then we were both silent, not knowing what to say or to think.

"What can it mean?" I said, at length.

"Let me see the plan," said Vera. She looked at it, and then said—

"It is marked here, Arthur—the Red Chamber is marked with a cross."

We had remarked this fact before, but now it assumed much more importance.

"I am certain," said Vera, excitedly, "that poor papa was murdered, and that his wealth, or a great portion of it, has been concealed in the Red Chamber!"

"But how singular," I said, "for the murderer to have hidden it there, instead of taking it away."

"I have a theory to explain that. Papa had become, as you know, childishly averse to letting any of his money leave his hands—of trusting it to the care of others—and he never of late years had any banking account. He may have had a hiding-place in the Red Chamber, and perhaps a thief—who knows?—surprised him in the act of concealing it. *The well* is near the Red Chamber. If a thief murdered our father, how easy——"

"Say no more!" I cried. "This very night we will search the Red Chamber, and to-morrow the well."

"Oh, Arthur, let us go at once."

The night was now far advanced, but our excitement was so great that, had the phantoms of all the previous dwellers of Stanton House marshalled themselves to stay our progress, we would scarce have flinched.

Providing ourselves, then, with candles and matches and a crowbar and pick, we passed through the long corridor that led to the eastern wing, and went from thence to the Red Chamber.

But we now remembered that we had never known of the existence of any bricks in any part of the chamber. Yet the cryptogram said "Remove *bricks* from centre eastern wall." We now looked all along this wall, and could see nothing but the massive oak wainscot. However, on striking the centre of the wall with the crowbar, a duller and heavier sound was produced than at any other portion. We scrutinised this part very closely, and at length discovered, near the floor, a small knob, which at first sight resembled merely a knot in the wood. This I pressed, and a panel of oak slid to the right, disclosing a wall of bricks. They were not ordinary bricks, however, nor were they cemented together. They were glazed and very finely made, and fitted into the space allotted for them with the greatest nicety. Indeed, at first sight, this wall appeared to be one solid stone, so well set were the bricks.

While Vera held the light, I, much excited, endeavoured to insert the blade of my pocket-knife into one of the fine crevices. For some time, so nicely did the bricks fit, my efforts were fruitless. But at length, by dint of much labour, I succeeded in forcing one of the bricks a little out of position, and the pickaxe did the rest. I piled the bricks on the floor as I dislodged them, one by one. When they were all out, a small iron door was revealed. It had no handle, but there was a keyhole, and on trying the door we found that it was locked. It was strong, but not sufficiently so to resist the leverage of a crowbar in the hands of a moderately powerful man, and in a few seconds it gave way, opening outwards, and revealed a space about four feet wide by two deep.

Vera advanced, and the taper's light feebly illuminated the recess.

I dropped the crowbar in horror, while Vera uttered a shriek, and let fall the light, which was extinguished, leaving us in total darkness. We were about to fly from the chamber, but mastered the terror that had seized us, and relighted the candle.

We had seen in the recess a human skeleton!

And now, subduing my fear—or, rather, nervousness—I took the light, and peered into the mysterious tomb.

The bones, around which clung some remnants of male attire, had been thrown upon a large iron-bound chest. The skull was broken.

Plucking up courage while Vera, deeply agitated, sank into a couch near at hand, I removed the bones, and drew forth the chest, which was extremely weighty. It was massive and old, with a wonderful lock, which extended all over the inner side of the lid, and which required a dozen or more keys to fasten it. These were all in their places; the chest, moreover, was not locked.

Closing the iron door of the recess upon the gruesome spectacle within, we now examined the interior of the chest. It was divided into numerous compartments, but the contents were not so various. They were of but four kinds—gold, jewels, silver, and paper.

The gold, which formed the greater part of the box's contents, was all in coinage, excepting that which composed the setting of the jewels. The silver consisted entirely of rare and ancient money, worth more than its weight in gold; and the paper was all bank notes of recent date, ranging in value from five to one hundred pounds each. These were soon counted; they amounted to £56,580. The jewels we recognised as, for the most part, old family heirlooms. We did not count the gold, but subsequently ascertained it to amount to something over £50,000. In fact, independent of the magnificent family jewels, and of the almost unique collection of curious coins, we, lately so poor, found ourselves in possession of over £100,000.

But this sudden acquisition of wealth could not drive from our minds the horror we felt at finding our poor father's bones in such a place, and it was some time ere we quite recovered from the shock; Vera, especially, being much affected.

The remains of the unfortunate master of Stanton House were laid with all due ceremony in the family vaults. His skull, as I have said, was broken—evidently by a blow from some heavy weapon.

The letters found in the pockets of the coat afforded the police a clue to the burglar, and led to his arrest. He, however, was able to prove that he had obtained the cryptogram and plan from a friend, whose name he would not divulge. This friend was the real murderer, and was, he said, dead. He had tracked the old gentleman to the Red Chamber, watched him secrete some money in the chest, and had then been discovered by and forced to kill him. He hid the corpse in the recess, and, only taking a handful of gold and notes from the chest, he fled, intending some time to return and steal the rest, but death overtaking him, he gave the plan and the cryptographic memorandum to his friend.

The ancient glories of our house were now revived, and at no lengthy period from our discovery of the chest, the stern parent of sweet Myrtle Rivers was prevailed upon to reconsider a certain decision—with the result that a wedding took place, in which ceremony, as will be guessed, I was a chief performer.

A TALE OF THE SEA

The collision was terrific. The gigantic bows of the stranger towered above us for one fearful second, and then bore us down with a hideous crash into the black profundity of the ocean, whose waves we could not see—for it was a night of unusual gloom, and the dim lights of the lanterns failed to pierce the thick darkness that reigned over all. There were shrieks, and groans and curses, quickly stifled by the waves, as the shattered vessel sank. All was soon over. A few minutes after the collision silence fell upon the ocean—or that quiet which we call silence; for there was still a vague sound—it was that of the winds, which seemed to be moaning a funeral chant for the unfortunates, over whom the black waves had closed so placidly.

Although the night was starless and very dark, the sea was calm; long rhythmical billows rolled, foamless and smooth and black, along the deep. The lights of the strange ship could not be seen; whether she had sunk or had been swallowed up by the intense darkness of the night, I could not determine, and have never known. When we were struck I had had time to snatch up a life belt, and now, a few moments after, I found myself floating among those great foamless rollers, apparently alone. I shouted; the wind sighed, but no other answer came to my hail.

All through the long night I was lifted from billow to billow with a slow and regular motion, so gentle and rhythmical that it almost induced slumber. The deep gloom continued, and my condition was unutterably dreary and lonely. But all my life I have been a dreamer, and my soul has drunk in the shadows of ancient cities and immemorial ruins ever since the deaths of those dearest to me made me a wanderer among men, so that now the darkness of the heavens and of the silent, ghostly billows lulled rather than depressed my heart. Nevertheless, it was with anxiety that I watched the skies for some indications of the breaking of the heavy clouds. But no star appeared, nor any light, until the dawn of the new day grappled with the gloom and slowly forced it back, replacing it with a soft gray radiance; the clouds in the east now began to break and draw apart from each other; soon some gleams of sunlight shot up into the heavens, and then others sped across the immensity of the ocean, tipping the erstwhile pitchy billows with golden light.

But, grand as this beauty was, I noted it little; not because I had seen it so many times before, but because another object now rivetted my attention. As I was lifted to the summit of an unusually high wave I saw, within a mile of where I then was, the tempestshattered hulk of a ship, apparently deserted. She seemed to me to have the build of a schooner, but, as both masts were gone by the board and the hull was rather low in the water, I could not be sure. Not that it was of the slightest moment, but in the midst of stirring and terrible events I had often found myself taking an unaccountable interest in trifles, and now, for many minutes, I busied myself in bootless endeavours to determine from the shape of the hull whether it was that of a brig or of a schooner, and wondering if I should ever know the truth.

A deserted wreck is a dreary and sorrowful spectacle, and the sight of the hull gave me but little hope. But it would, at least, afford me a prolongation of life, though to what extent I could not, of course, divine. Therefore, cramped and weak and chilled as I was from long immersion in the water, I exerted myself to reach the vessel, which, as I have said, was distant from me about a mile. The struggles I made to swim gradually loosened my stiffened muscles, and soon I found little difficulty in propelling myself towards the hulk. From time to time, as I found myself raised upon a billow, I endeavoured earnestly to ascertain whether the wreck was entirely deserted, or whether some unfortunates yet remained on board; but I saw no sign of life. True, I thought, they might be below, but surely a watch would be kept for some passing ship. A sinister gloom seemed to pervade the shattered hulk. It brought to my mind an old house, said to be haunted, that had been the terror of my lonely boyhood.

When, at length, I had arrived quite near, I looked about the sides for some assistance in clambering aboard. I did not hail the wreck; why, I know not. Perhaps its antiquated build, which I now perceived for the first time, lent an additional air of mystery and gloom to its dreary appearance, and compelled my silence. At length, after swimming round the hull, I perceived a piece of rope hanging over the port bulwark, which was very much damaged. I grasped it and prepared to climb on board.

I had scarcely raised myself out of the water when a succession of loud and horrible screams, coming apparently from three or four different throats, caused me to relinquish my hold upon the rope and fall back into the sea. The cries appalled me—for they were unearthly, inhuman; yet I felt that they were uttered by human voices. They lasted but a few seconds, then all was still; nor, though I listened intently, could I distinguish the slightest sound beyond that made by the sea against the side of the vessel.

I have said that I was appalled; I was, but not so much as to induce me to abandon my attempt to board the ship—for the instinct of self-preservation was stronger even than the feeling of horror that came upon me; besides, terrified as I was, curiosity formed no slight portion of my sensations. I therefore grasped the rope once more, and this time reached the deck without the former ghastly interruption.

The cries had come from aft, and thither, my mind full of strange conjectures, I proceeded, slowly and cautiously. There was a broken skylight near the wheel. Creeping towards it, I peered down into a dark cabin. At first I perceived only some vague forms, but, as my sight became accustomed to the obscurity, I distinguished five men in the cabin. I drew back with intense surprise, and looked again to be sure my vision had not deceived me.

The five men I saw were each of a nationality different to the others. One was a wrinkled and meagre Chinese; another was a savage-looking Malay; the third was a spare Hindoo of miserable aspect; the fourth a European. The fifth man, who was most remarkable of all these singular beings, was, to all appearances, a full-blooded negro, whose build and stature brought before my mind the Farnese Hercules. He was naked to the waist, and his chest and shoulders and arms seemed to be sculptured, in heroic size, from ebony. This man must have been more than six feet in height, and was magnificently proportioned. At the moment I saw him he was standing over his fellow-occupants of the cabin in the grand attitude of a victorious gladiator, while they, prostrate on the deck, grovelled at his feet. The visage of this living statue—such, for an instant, he seemed—wore an expression at once demoniacal and triumphant. While yet I gazed, fascinated, on this strange scene, he relaxed his attitude, and, spurning with his foot the man nearest to him, walked to a chest and sat down; the others then gathered themselves up, and limped or crawled to the opposite end of the cabin, casting looks of hate and fear at the terrible negro on the chest, whose face, having now regained its composure, appeared to me to be more regular in feature, higher in expression, but also fiercer, than that of any negro I had ever seen.

I knew not what to do. The scene I had witnessed was far from inspiring me with confidence. But I was famished, for I had been in the water many hours; I saw the impossibility of concealing myself for any length of time on the hulk. I determined, therefore, to make myself known at once. I sought the door of the cabin, and, opening it, boldly entered.

As I had expected, the negro immediately sprang to his feet. The European also arose, but sat down immediately, in obedience to an imperious sign from the negro; the others, who seemed to be hurt, looked up eagerly from where they lay.

The negro confronted me.

"What are you? Where do you come from?" he asked, in excellent English, and with a deep and resonant voice.

"My ship was run down in a collision," I said, "and I have been floating about all night. When day broke I saw this vessel, and came on board."

"How long have you been on board?"

"A few minutes."

"You are cold and wet. You want food."

"Yes," I answered.

He spoke some peremptory words in a language unknown to me, and the Malay arose feebly to his feet, and staggered from the cabin.

"What was the name of your ship?" asked the negro.

"The *Hermione*," I replied. "She was bound from England to Batavia. And, now, will you tell me how—how you came to be floating about in this old hulk, and why you do not keep a look out for some ship to take you off?"

The negro made no reply. He smiled, but having smiled he frowned in a terrible manner. At this moment the Malay came in with some coarse food, which he set before me. I satisfied my hunger, and then, not wishing to appear to be daunted or awed by the giant negro, terrible though he was, I again questioned him about the hulk, which I now observed, by the fittings of the cabin, to be of even more ancient date than I had at first imagined. At my questions I thought the European looked at the negro with intense eagerness, but the latter, rising and drawing his massive and towering form to its full height, spoke, in a low and even tone, as follows:—

"While you are here, sir, beware how you cross me. If I do not choose to reply to any questions you may put to me, think well before you dare to repeat them. Your life is to me as a single straw floating on the great sea yonder. Guard, then, your words and your actions."

This speech was given with the unconscious dignity of an all-powerful monarch whose voice had never been opposed, and, strange to say, I was awed into silence. I strove to frame a haughty reply, but the words refused to come. The negro seemed to expect no answer. He left the cabin, saying two or three words to the miserable beings on the floor as he went out. They immediately arose, and opening the chest on which he had been sitting took out therefrom some pieces of a brownish substance, which I recognised as pure opium. The Malay and the Chinese immediately swallowed sufficient to kill twenty men unaccustomed to the drug, while the Hindoo filled a pipe and smoked. The European, who looked like a Spaniard, mixed together equal parts of opium and tobacco, and likewise smoked. The Malay and the Chinese soon relapsed into unconsciousness, and in a few minutes after the Hindoo also succumbed to the narcotic influence of the drug. The European, seeing their condition, laid down his pipe and looked at me intently. I addressed him in Spanish.

"Can you explain to me," I asked him, "the mystery of this vessel—who or what this negro is?"

"I am almost as much in the dark as yourself, señor," he replied, in the same tongue; "I have not been long on board. The negro himself rescued me from a piece of wreckage on which I was floating. My ship foundered in a storm. These men could, doubtless, explain much of what seems so mysterious; but they speak no language save their own—and, indeed, they appear too much awed by the negro to tell anything."

"However," I said, "you can at least explain the meaning of those fearful screams that I heard just before I came on board?"

"I can, indeed, explain their cause," said the Spaniard. "Ever since I have been on this vessel the negro has, while allowing these men to indulge in opium as much as they list, treated them otherwise with the greatest cruelty. To me he had seemed indifferent, merely cautioning me not to baulk him in any way; but very often I have, when witnessing his inhuman atrocities on the others, felt terrible fears for my own safety. Last night he himself indulged in opium—a most unusual practice with him—and these men, it would seem, plotted to kill him while he slept, and made signs to me to join them in their design. Although I had not forgotten that the negro had saved my life, I had good reason for wishing him rendered incapable of harm, and so I made them understand that we should bind him with ropes and keep him so until a ship hove in sight. This was agreed to, but it was daybreak ere the cowards could pluck up courage for the assault. Then, however, we sprang upon him in a body. He immediately awoke, and, throwing us off as if we had been children, he became frightful in his rage, and, seizing us all in turn, twisted and wrung our limbs until the bones and muscles seemed to crack and snap; and this it was that drew from us those awful shrieks that you heard."

"Good Heavens! But have you no theory to explain this systematic cruelty that you spoke of?"

"Ah, señor, I have been trying to unravel the mystery ever since I saw its existence. Perhaps we shall never know this fiend's motive, or his previous history. I have thought that it must be some terrible vengeance he is perpetrating on these men, and, again, that it is madness; but, if so, that madness is consistent and full of method. I know not what to think."

"You have, then, no idea how *they* came to be on this ship—or *what* the ship is; for you cannot have failed to observe her great age."

"These things, too, have caused me a world of vain conjecture. Horrible fancies have occurred to me at times. For some days I was haunted by the thought that these men are but the remnant of what was once the vessel's crew—that the others have all been put to death by this wretch at different periods. But I am far from penetrating the mystery; and I have even a presentiment that I shall not live to know what all these things mean. It is, indeed, singular that the vessel should be so old—and wonderful that it should be tenanted by such strange beings."

"One of them is a Hindoo, I think?"

"Yes."

"I will speak with him," I said; "I have some slight knowledge of Hindustani."

"Be very careful, I pray you."

"Yes. But now, as my clothes are wet, I will go on deck and dry them."

"Wait. There is another mystery. You must not appear above the bulwarks unless the horizon is clear. I myself seldom go on deck, not wishing to offend the negro; and *now* it would be doubly dangerous to cross him. So be careful."

"Listen to me. This state of things must not continue. We must circumvent this savage—we two—if he has not heard our conversation; do you think he has?"

"No; I do not think so."

"Why?"

"Because—another mystery—there is a small cabin amidships, which he keeps locked, and into which he often retires for hours together."

"And you think he is there now?"

"He is always there when he allows the opium to be used."

"Do you think *they* know the secret of the closed cabin?"

"I believe they do."

"Then—we may yet unravel the mystery. But to return to what I was about to say. Does the negro know your language?"

"He does; he addresses each, I think, in his own tongue. He speaks Spanish well."

"And English too. But you understand English, do you not?"

"Yes."

"Then we can pretend to be ignorant of each other's language, and seek the first opportunity of convincing him of the fact. The others converse among themselves, do they not?"

"They have, I think, a sort of *patois* which they use; but they seldom talk."

After a few more minutes' conversation with the Spaniard I went on deck. I determined to submit to no one on the ship—not even the negro. When, therefore, I reached the deck I looked around for something that might serve me for a weapon in case of emergency —a bar of iron, or a piece of heavy wood that I could fashion into a club. But there was nothing of the kind to be seen upon the deck. It appeared as if the sea had swept away all things moveable. But now I remembered that I had a large pocket-knife, with a blade nearly three inches long. I determined, on occasion, to use it without scruple in defending my life.

The wreck was, indeed, *very* old; and the great fractures in the bulwarks seemed almost as ancient. The deck had the appearance of having been washed by the waves of a century of years. The ropes were black and rotten with age.

The sun shone warmly. My clothes soon dried. I laid myself down on the deck to rest; and, thinking over my strange position, I fell asleep. When I awoke the sun was low. I had slept long, and was much refreshed.

As I arose, I saw that the negro was approaching me. Suddenly he stopped, sprang upon a bulwark, looked intently towards the horizon, and then cried—

"*Una vela—una vela! Llégate acá, señor! Una vela!*"

"*Dónde?*" I exclaimed, unwittingly replying in Spanish; and spring up—"*dónde es ya?*"

"So," he said in English, while a cunning smile writhed his lips— "you understand Spanish, and speak it."

"Why not?" I replied, endeavouring to conceal my vexation at having been entrapped.

"'Tis no matter," he said; "but remember what I told you—as you value your life."

"I shall soon cease to value it," I answered, with all the haughtiness I could assume, "if I am to be treated as you treat those men; and when I no longer care for life, look to your own. I am an Englishman, and if you know the English as well as you know their language, you must be aware they are not easily subdued."

"This is of very little moment to me," he said, with a disdainful smile; "I shall easily subdue you, whatever you may think to the contrary. Even Englishmen must bow their proud heads to death. Plot as you may, you cannot harm me—all your efforts will but recoil upon yourself. Therefore, unless you are weary of life, relinquish all such thoughts."

"But tell me," I exclaimed, curiosity overcoming my fear and anger, "what is your intentions in regard to—to the Spaniard and myself?"

"The Spaniard, in all probability, you shall never see again. For yourself, if you prove obstinate, and endeavour to circumvent me, you shall die, as I have said; but it shall be no ordinary death."

I did not reply—for at the last words he spoke, he fixed his eyes upon mine, and how can I describe the consternation I felt on perceiving that they were of a *light blue!* As he turned away I noted also his stately walk, so unlike the peculiar gait of the negroes. I glanced instinctively at his head to see if he had the *wool* of an African black; but neither hair nor wool was to be seen, for the head was covered by a skull-cap of red velvet. In deep agitation I watched his majestic form until it disappeared beneath the deck.

Long, long, I pondered, over the mystery that enshrouded the ship and its strange people. But this negro (if such indeed he was) engrossed my thought the most. Moreover, his last words to me raised an undefinable horror in my heart. I felt that, if I ever aroused his real enmity—if I ever provoked him to actual vengeance—I should indeed, as he said, die no ordinary death. With a man of such extraordinary physical powers it was useless to cope without weapons—and what weapons had I? Here, I instinctively felt for my knife, but it was gone! Could I, indeed, cope with him in *cunning?* It seemed almost hopeless. Yet, I thought he *must* be suppressed. I *must* find means to divest him of his power, and that soon. The Spaniard, he said, I should never see again; I must, then, mature my plans alone. Even now a thought arose in my brain; if I could only secure him in that "secret cabin " until a ship appeared! But his ferocity, and, above all, his terrific strength, behoved me to be exceedingly cautious.

★ ★ ★ ★ ★

A week passed away. During this time I had frequent opportunities of observing the Asiatics, who seldom left the cabin. Their whole existence seemed to be given up to the vice of opium-eating. Never had I seen or heard of such quantities of the drug being consumed as these wretches contrived to swallow. They rarely touched ordinary food. I observed, also, that they bore traces of an extreme old age, but whether these were the effects of their opium orgies or of actual longevity I could not determine. The Chinese, especially, seemed prematurely old. I have reason to believe that he was almost blind; and the others had all the appearance of aged and decrepit men.

But the strange being whom I must call the negro—*he* seemed young, almost youthful. I saw but little of him during this week. Once I made bold to follow him to his secret cabin amidships, and fancied myself unseen, but as he entered he turned and looked at me with his mirthless and demoniac smile, and then closed the door behind him. I could never think of him *then* but as a maniac, though I am at this day by no means certain that he was wholly such. Despite of the extreme ferocity of his features, there was in them at times much of bitterness, of deep sorrow. But the "heart of his mystery" shall, perhaps, never be plucked out. I relate these things as I witnessed them, and will advance no theories to explain whatever of them may seem to need elucidation.

One day a sail appearing on the horizon the negro scanned it through a powerful glass, and reflected for many minutes, and then compelled me to go below.

Once I addressed some words in Hindustani to the Indian, but he replied only by a meaningless stare. The Spaniard I never saw again in life. During the whole week I had busied myself in endeavouring to mature some plan by which to render the negro powerless; but there seemed no chance. Once I thought of making an attempt to throw a rope round his neck, half-strangle him, and then bind him fast; but as I glanced at his muscular throat I saw the folly of such a proceeding. Then I thought that if I could gain access to his cabin while he was absent I should, I felt certain, find some weapon there.

At the end of the week an opportunity was afforded me. The

negro, after maltreating the Asiatic in a fearful manner, gave himself up to indulgence in opium. Seeing this I at once lay down, and pretended to sleep. Soon he seemed to be overcome by the drug. I then crept out and went to the secret cabin. To my surprise the door was unlocked. I entered. It was night, but an oil lamp, suspended from the deck overhead, burned dimly. The cabin was small; there was a table and a chest—the chest was locked. In the corner was a shelf, by the side of which hung a large pistol, loaded. I immediately possessed myself of it. On the shelf were several papers which looked like legal documents, and also some newspapers about a year old. These latter were very dirty, but the documents looked new and clean, and were fixed to the shelf by large clasps. I was about to examine them, when I heard a step without.

I crouched in a corner behind a large cloak that hung there. As I did so the negro entered. He did not appear to suspect or think of anyone being in the room, but sat down on the chest, and stirred not for many minutes. At length he arose wearily, and throwing off his velvet skull-cap disclosed to my astonished view hair of a rich chestnut.

Uttering a low groan, he sank back again upon the chest. Once more rising he took up a small mirror from the table, and stood gazing at the reflection of his face for many moments.

"Black, black!" he muttered; "black for ever. Oh, accursed, ever accursed wretches! Vengeance! vengeance! And yet—what—*what* torture could suffice to punish them? Oh——"

He shuddered, let fall the mirror, and smote his brow with his clenched hand in a paroxysm of mental agony.

At length, becoming calmer, and reflecting, he took the legal documents—or what I considered to be such—and burnt them to the last scrap. Then he unlocked the chest and took out therefrom a suit of wearing apparel, such as is worn by the English gentleman, and dressed himself. This done, he searched in bottom of the chest and found a belt of chamois leather and a small wooden casket. From the latter he drew a little bag, which he emptied on the table, and I saw that it had been filled with a number of remarkably large, unset diamonds. These he began slowly to put into the belt, muttering the while, but so very low that I caught only a word here and there—

"'Tis time—next ship that appears—end all—for this—must die—the Spaniard—kill, kill the cursed——"

Here he paused, and drew from the casket what seemed to me to be a miniature portrait, gazed at it awhile in silence, and then, with a deep, shuddering sigh, he looked from it to the mirror, which he took up, and moaned these words, that seemed to well up from the bottom of his heart—

"Oh, Heavens! what a fate, what a doom! Oh! hellish villains, who did this thing!"

Then, to my inconceivable horror, he approached and took down the cloak that concealed me.

On seeing that I had been watching him he uttered a roar of terrible fury, and sprang upon me. I fired. The ball tore through his cheek. Snatching the weapon from my hand, he struck me a terrific blow on the head with its butt, and I instantly became unconscious.

I found myself, on my return to life from that deadly swoon, in the hold of the vessel, bound fast to a bulkhead with ropes. Light fell dimly from the open hatch far above me.

"Now," said a voice near me—a voice low, but acrid with hate and bitterness—"now shall you know what it is to die. You rejected my warnings; you persisted in your struggles against my will; and so you perish."

"But," I said, "why do you persecute me? Think! I have never harmed you."

"Have you not angered me? Have you not discovered my secret and my shame? Have you not completed my disfigurement? One of these things were enough. And yet, what is *your* life? I would kill—destroy the world—ay, the universe! I——"

He stopped, apparently overcome by the pain of his wound, for articulation seemed to cause him intense anguish. Stooping, he withdrew several round pegs from the bottom of the ship, and as many streams of water immediately leaped up through the holes.

He gagged me with a handkerchief, and then ascended to the deck without once looking back; and from that time forth I never again beheld this mysterious and sinister unfortunate.

I now heard the sound of voices and the splash of oars; I saw shadows fall across the hatchway far above me; then all was still. I bit the gag, and strove to cry out, but was unable to utter any sound above a low moan.

Clearly I perceived the fate devised for me by an ingenuity practised in torture. I was tightly bound—so tightly that I could not move. The water spouted its jets higher than my head. Yet it was long before there was sufficient to cover my feet. Many, many hours elapsed ere my ancles were submerged. But steadily, surely, inexorably it crept up, and its deadly chill penetrated to my very bones. Yet higher—still higher—it rose.

And now, to my intense horror, I beheld, as the water rose, dark forms floating here and there. And as they by chance emerged from the shadows of the hold into the dim light, I recognised the corpses as those of the Spaniard, the Chinese, the Hindoo, and the Malay.

The day closed, and I was alone with the darkness, the rising water, and the corpses. But the night, although its every minute seemed to me an hour, waned at last, and the morning broke, and the rays of the sun streamed down dimly into the black hold and on the black water, which continually crept upwards.

But why dilate on the horror of that time? Why tell of the more than earthly anguish of those leaden hours? Why attempt to express the loathing inspired by the hideous visages of the floating corpses? Why recount the burning thoughts—the struggles of the body to be free—the struggles of the mind to devise a means of freedom? For the memory of the reality of these things mocks all attempts at their portrayal.

Stealthily, slowly, unremittingly the water rose. At length, after, perhaps, many days, I felt it on my neck, its ripples washing against my chin. And even yet it rose; for *why* should it not? *What*, indeed, should stop it here? Oh, God! what chance, what accident could now prevent it from overwhelming me?

But in very truth it seemed to stop there; or was it that the hour which marked its advance from my neck to my lips was expanded, by my agony, into weeks, months, years of weary waiting and dread suspense? I cannot tell how long it was; but the thoughts or fancies that crowded into or rushed through my mind during that time were of a magnitude that even now, as I write, appal me.

But when the saltwater entered my parched and burning throat (for I had bitten and chewed the gag away) I felt that I was really doomed. Again the brine washed my lips—again and yet again. I stretched my head forth to escape the black waters, but they followed it, and rose continually. And now the corpse of the aged Chinese floated with its face against my own; its chilly lips touched mine—its sunken and glassy eyes looked into my own with a hideous meaning. And still the water rose—I gasped!—I choked!

There was a sound above as of the tramp of many feet; there came to my ears the vague echoes of human voices. And as the ripples rolled around my mouth, I uttered a last despairing shriek, half-stifled by the water and the lips of the corpse. Then I heard a loud shout—the water rose above my nostrils—and a blindness came before my eyes and there was a ringing in my ears—and I knew no more until, on recovering, I found myself in the well-furnished captain's cabin of a large English clipper.

IRENE

At no period of my life have any of the ordinary or esoteric doctrines of the supernatural obtained a positive hold upon my belief. That I have always been a dreamer by day as well as by night may appear, at a casual glance, irreconcilable with the fact that in my heart there has never dwelt the slightest faith in preter-nature; but although in earlier years my fancy was not uninfluenced by whatever might present features of the strange or mystical, it was rather an indulgence in an idle pleasure—a sort of mental luxury which led my imagination to lose itself in the pursuit of the *ignes fatui* of mysticism and superstition—than anything even approaching to serious belief. Thus my mind presented the curious anomaly of the antithesis of a habit of rigid thought and a Pyrrhonian of opinion regarding all speculative matters, and an insatiate love of revelling in the interminable mazes of fantasy and reverie.

Even now, although the long and earnest endeavours which I have made to explain the seeming incomprehensibility of the event I have here to record by reference to merely natural causes and effects have been attended in every case with unequivocal failure, still I cannot fully persuade myself that some mind better versed in the multiform phases of psychological science than is my own may not yet "play the Œdipus to the riddle."

Having failed, however, to entirely reconcile the apparently supernatural character of what I shall relate with my own long and settled disbelief in the existence of "night side" to nature, it would be supererogatory to obtrude any suggestions bearing on the subject during the course of narration, and I shall, therefore, content myself with simply presenting the facts themselves.

Irene and I were intimate and devoted friends long before we first became aware of the impalpable presence of the god Eros. We had, indeed, been happy enough in the days of our friendship; a similarity of predilections and of tastes in the realms of intellectual life had imparted to our intercourse a fascination which, although sub-dued and comparatively colourless, was none the less all-sufficing for mental enjoyment. But not long did we dwell in ignorance of the "myrtle and the vine," for love at length entered our hearts.

We wedded, and our happiness was, perhaps, as nearly complete as that of mortality can be. My own joy was heightened, even while I was a little puzzled, by the intensity of Irene's love and devotion. No ordinary passion was that which reigned in her heart; I am bound to say that it far transcended my own in the utter abandon-ment of its adoration.

The only shadow that rested upon our happiness was one that arose from causes quite beyond our control. We had all that Mrs. Browning defined as the desiderata of earthly bliss—"love, life, and Italy." More than these, we had fortune, friends, and that equable temperament which is a bar to discontent. It was Shelley, I think, who wrote of—

> Sweet basil and mignonette,
> Embleming love and health, which never yet
> In the same wreath might be.

And such was the shadow on our lives—we had not health. Yet this circumstance, if possible, endeared us to each other but the more. We sought in our love, in our constant companionship, the mitiga-tion of our physical pains.

In Irene a very distressing tendency to epilepsy began to mani-fest itself during the first months of our marriage, and was a source of nervous apprehension to her, chiefly, I believe, on account of that intensity of affection for me of which I have made mention. She feared always that my anxiety concerning her might serve to aggravate my own malady.

This latter I will not pause to describe, beyond saying that from my earliest years I had been afflicted with a certain spasmodic dis-ease, the pangs of which I was wont to assuage by means of copi-ous doses of laudanum whenever they came upon me.

This practice did much towards making my general health uncertain, besides keeping my nervous system in a highly wrought condition and exciting my imagination to a degree little short of frenzy. It must not be supposed, however, that the attacks of my malady were of frequent occurrence. I often passed whole months in complete immunity from pain.

In the beginning of the second year of our wedded life Irene rapidly grew worse. Her original ailment had not increased, but it seemed to have induced others, and she became very feeble. The skill of her physicians was completely baffled by the abstruse and complicated nature of her malady; and at length they did not disguise from me that they despaired of ever effecting a cure. Yet in the appearance of Irene there did not seem to be much to warrant any fears for her life. True, she was very slender, even emaciated, but her eyes, albeit that their size and length and heaviness of lash gave them an air of drowsy voluptuousness and languor, were still full of energy; and although her cheeks, her brow, even her lips, were fearfully pallid, it was with the clear whiteness of Parian marble rather than the waxen hue of the dying. Her voice was indeed low, but then it was clear, calm, and not in any degree tremulous or distraught.

She had no thought that the hand of death was upon her—nor had I. And yet, one sultry midnight, not long after I had left her composed, as I thought, for sleep, one of her physicians sought me, and told me that all was over—that Irene had succumbed to the complication of disorders by which she had been prostrated.

Of my thoughts I cannot speak; the suddenness of the blow seemed to deprive me of all powers of reflection. Even to the physicians the event, though not by any means unexpected, had come sooner than they had imagined it would.

I looked upon her as she lay, still, and white, and cold. Her beauty had always been great, but now there seemed in it a very pronounced, though indefinable, weirdness that rendered it almost superhuman to my eyes, and I shuddered as I thought how soon would this matchless handicraft of nature be the food of the worm. For many minutes I stood gazing at the motionless face, the closed lids, the heavy raven hair, the slender but exquisitely moulded arms, the delicately perfect outlines of the bosom. I had been suffering acutely, and my nerves were highly strung by excessive draughts of laudanum. It may be that I uttered some wild words, for I have an indistinct remembrance of an agitation of some sort within the room; however, I was led away, and found myself next morning in my own chamber.

In the afternoon Irene was interred.

At night I sat alone in a little remote room in the old *casa*, watching, with an intensity of painful abstraction, the dim shadows that danced incessantly to the flickering of the firelight. The curtains of the single casement were drawn, and a broad white moon could be seen as it "tottered up its pathway to heaven." A solemn silence reigned over all.

The pains of my disease had increased since the interment of Irene, and a large phial of the ruby-coloured fluid which I used to mitigate them stood near me on the table. Every few minutes I drank from it. I had become so habituated to the use of the drug that there was no need for any admeasurement. On this occasion, however, I must have swallowed a most unusual quantity, for, although my pains had subsided and almost disappeared, my brain seemed to reel as with a species of frenzy. All objects on which I gazed assumed to my sight a refracted and unreal importance. The moon appeared much larger and nearer than usual; the sound of an ember falling from the fire vibrated in my ears with a sonorous magnificence. I lost all sense of physical being, and all memory of past events—even of that recent one which had so terribly bereaved me.

Whether this condition was but the natural result of inordinate indulgence in the opium I know not. It may have been, but then I had at previous periods swallowed more without experiencing the same weird effects—at least, not to such a degree.

Of my thoughts during this condition it would be the utmost folly to attempt a description. Indeed, I could scarcely be said to think at all, any more than one can be said to think in a dream. But it is very certain that I did not dream, for never were my impressions of outward things so vivid, so accentuated.

As I sat thus, gazing now on the white, filmy face of the moon, it seemed that a thin, ethereal, almost imperceptible shadow passed between me and the casement. It was like a white silken gossamer veil hung for a second before the light and then withdrawn—if, indeed, this is not much too gross a simile for that shade which, but for the powerful effect of the opium, my eyes might have been too dull to see at all. I felt my heart thrill, yet it was with a feeling rather of expectation and joy than of astonishment or fear. I looked intently, but it came not again.

Scarcely a minute elapsed, however, when I distinctly heard the soft sound of a *footfall* near me. I have said that the slightest sound vibrated in my ears with a strange loudness; this of the footfall, however, was inconceivably soft and faint. My heart beat violently, but still with a vague expectation, and not in any degree with fear. I felt that some indefinable influence was gradually stealing over me, but what it was I neither knew nor felt any desire to know. Although all my senses were exaggerated to a high degree of acuteness, my powers of thought were almost dormant. Yet my brain was transcendently calm—all traces of dizziness and frenzy had disappeared.

As I had seen the shade but once, so the sound of the footstep fell but once upon my ear.

While I listened eagerly for a repetition of it, I became aware of a still more startling circumstance than either the footfall or the shadow. I now felt the soft *pressure of a hand* upon my shoulder!

Then a light seemed to break in upon my mind—and then I *knew*. The shade and the footfall I had failed to recognise—but the touch of the hand! How could I mistake *that!* The lucid light of an all-sufficing intelligence filled my brain; and, as I became conscious that the impalpable hand no longer rested on my shoulder, I arose, took up a long and heavy cloak, and moved slowly from the room—preceded, it seemed to me, by the unseen presence of what *might be* a spirit, which was to lead where it would, for the accomplishment of some mysterious purpose.

We, then—the Presence and I—went out into the weird Italian night. As we passed the north wall of the *casa* I possessed myself of some object, the nature of which did not, strangely enough, present itself to my apprehension; nor did I feel the slightest desire to know anything regarding it; my will seemed in complete abeyance, and subject solely to that of the impalpable Presence which preceded me.

Our way led through an avenue of cedars, where the light of the moon could be seen only in indeterminate glimpses. The shadows were deep and ghostly and fantastic. The ground was uneven, but I

strode onward as if it had been broad daylight. And the consciousness that some Presence led me never once left my mind, but gradually became more and more accentuated until the end of the vista
was reached.

I stepped from the thick shadow of the cedar trees into the
bright moonlight, and then, for the first time, a vague feeling of
wonderment came upon me. This feeling continued to intensify
and to gain definitiveness as I proceeded, and at last, as I saw before
me the white stones and monumental sculptures of a *cemetery*
gleaming in the still moonlight, I stopped involuntarily, and a kind
of shiver passed over me. Then the strange influence that was upon
me resumed its power, and I entered the gates of the silent field of
death.

I threaded my way through a labyrinth of graves, and at length
paused before one that bore no stone, but which seemed strangely
familiar to me. My feeling of wonderment was now mingled with
a desire to know why I was acting thus—why I was *here!* The thing I
carried on my shoulder now seemed to become heavier, and I grew
sensible of its weight, and then curious to know what it was.

I lowered it to the ground, and regarded it for some minutes
with a feeling of the most profound astonishment, strangely mingled with a sensation of acute anxiety. It was a gardener's spade.

However, I proceeded without hesitation to thrust it into the
newly made grave which was before me, and to throw out the
earth which filled it. I soon found myself toiling with the most anxious haste and precipitation, as if I feared interference or preven-
tion. Indeed, I was beginning to feel that the mysterious Presence
which had attended me hitherto was now leaving me—that I was
becoming more and more my natural self—and I wished, with a
sense almost of agony, to complete whatever it was that I had been
intended to perform—as when we dream and know or feel ourselves to be near the awakening we vaguely, yet fervently, desire to
finish the dream ere sleep entirely departs.

The minutes flew by, and still I toiled strenuously at the grave.
At length the spade struck upon the wood of the coffin with a dull
and ghastly thud. Soon it was wholly uncovered. The grave had not
been made very deep, and by a powerful effort I raised the coffin,
with its burthen, to the surface.

The moon was high in the heavens and shone down full upon the coffin and upon a silver plate in the centre of the lid, whereon some words were graven.

I looked at them, and a cry of horror escaped me. The influence which had led me hither and impelled me to violate this grave had now entirely disappeared, and left me a victim to a species of intolerable and uncontrollable terror. For some moments I failed to comprehend the meaning of the words engraven on the plate— their very obviousness may have confused me—but in an instant I understood perfectly. The coffin was that of my wife, Irene.

"I have been mad," I muttered; "I have been distraught with grief or frenzied with the drug; and this horrible deed is the result. Let me repair it, however, and then none may ever know of my madness."

And then I prepared to re-deposit the coffin in the grave, and fill in the earth again. But just as I was about to try and lower the coffin as gently as I could I was intensely startled to hear, close to me, a sound resembling a low, muffled sob.

I arose, trembling, but could see no one. Again I seized the coffin—and again there came to my ears that low, half-stifled sob. Unable to move, I listened intently. I thought my mind must be wandering again—that this sound existed only in my imagination, as, doubtless, had the footfall I now remembered having heard in the room of the *casa*. Still I listened, in extremity of agony and agitation.

It came again, and louder, much louder, and then I could doubt no more; *then* I knew whence it had proceeded.

In a moment I had seized the spade, and with its edge wrenched off the lid of the coffin, revealing the enshrouded but still palpitating, still breathing form of Irene.

Her eyes were open, clear and full of life; there was colour in her cheeks, and she smiled faintly as she murmured my name, and in a low voice—

"You have come!"

In the next instant, however, she relapsed into unconsciousness.

I wrapped her in my cloak, and bore her home with all speed.

In a few days she no longer needed the attendance of her physicians. That epileptic trance seemed to have been the turning point of her illness. She rapidly grew well, and has since had no relapse. As to the part I played in her rescue from the most hideous of deaths, I have, as I said in the beginning, no explanation to offer. To me and to Irene it is a mystery, and such, I fear, it will remain.

THE CURSE OF THE EMERALD

A TALE OF THE SEA

"Yes," said the passenger, thoughtfully, "it is as you say, a remarkable stone, and most remarkable is its history, if I may credit what I have been told."

"It has a history, then?" said Fenwick.

"A strange one; but, although I think it may be partly believed, yet I cannot accept *all* I have heard as truth. That would require more credence in the supernatural than I have at any time been disposed to entertain."

"There are certain properties, or virtues, ascribed to the stone, are there not?" asked Williams.

"Yes," replied the passenger, smiling, but growing involuntarily more serious in his manner; "I have heard it said that—that—but, really, it is too absurd."

He stopped abruptly; and Fenwick, who had narrowly observed him, noticed that he had become unaccountably pale.

"Still," said the skipper, "there can be no harm in telling us what tradition is associated with the gem; my curiosity is piqued, I confess."

"Well," said the passenger, who had regained his colour, and seemed half-ashamed of having displayed anything like emotion, however momentary, "if it be of interest, I will tell you. The emerald was found—or, let me say, stolen—from an Aztec temple in America. It passed through many hands there, and, by what must have been a series of extraordinary coincidences, each successive possessor met with a violent death. These coincidences—for, of course they can be nothing more—were too strange, or *seemed* too strange, to be received as such by those acquainted with the emerald's history, and soon a belief arose that the stone was accursed— that no one could possess it long and live."

160

"Very strange," said the second mate.

"Yes; but not so much so when the lawless state of that part of America, the value of the gem, and the cupidity of the adventurers there are considered. Indeed, it would have been strange had no blood been shed over such a stone, and stranger still had no superstitions been the consequence."

"How long have you had it?" asked Fenwick.

"Only a few weeks; but I am not to be intimidated by the ignorant tales I have heard. From Manilla I go to Amsterdam, where I can dispose of it to the best advantage. Till then it shall remain in my possession, come what may!"

"And its former owner—I mean the person from whom you—"

"Oh, my brother? Well, I must confess that I profited by his absurd belief in the extravagant stories told of the gem. I bought it of him for about a tenth of its value. He was very glad to get rid of it."

"And from whom did *he* obtain it?" asked Fenwick, who was much interested.

"Well, to tell the truth, from a man of notorious and rather shady repute, well known in Singapore and other places. My brother knew that this man was said to be connected with certain pirates in the China Sea, and would not have purchased the stone of him had he been aware of the tradition associated with it. The emerald, however, was soon recognised by some connoisseurs who had seen or heard of it."

"So then he hastened to sell it to you, his brother?" said the skipper.

"Oh, not exactly. I believe he would have destroyed it rather than have sold it to *me*, but I easily obtained it through an agent. He does not know I have it, and be sure I shall rally him smartly over the transaction when I have realised the profits. Ha! ha! ha!"

"At all events," said Fenwick, thoughtfully "the stone's deadly charm, if it ever existed, may be fairly said to be broken, since to your own knowledge two men have successively possessed it and are still alive."

"That is true," said the skipper; "but you must not forget that these two men hastened to rid themselves of it; neither intended to keep it longer than he could help."

"Well," said the passenger, "nothing but an offer of its full value shall ever induce me to part with it till I reach Amsterdam."

"You are quite right," said Fenwick, who then went forward to attend to some ship's duties.

"It would perhaps be well," said Captain Gould, "to keep your possession of the stone a secret, Mr. Westbrook. We have a mixed crew, and there are more than one who would not scruple to uphold the tradition of the gem in a very practical manner." So saying, the skipper went below.

The passenger, leaning against the taffrail, became lost in thought as he watched the fleecy fragments of cloud passing swiftly before the moon. The memory of a savage face, with a pair of gleaming eyes, which had passed swiftly by while he was showing the emerald to the captain and the two mates, somewhat disturbed him after hearing the words of the skipper. He was by no means sure that those eyes had not caught sight of the gem. He blamed himself for disclosing it at all, even to the captain. Though, as we have seen, he was perhaps a little proud of his freedom from all superstition, yet, as he gazed upon the beautiful gem as it flashed in the fluctuating light of the moon, he thought he saw sinister gleams dart from its many facets. He pondered long and deeply over this fancy, holding the emerald between his fingers the while.

Suddenly there was a soft step behind him; a hand deftly snatched the stone from his fingers, and, ere he could utter a cry, a powerful pair of arms lifted him boldly in the air, and in the next instant the black waters had closed quietly over their victim.

The murderer glanced around. All was still; the man at the wheel had not heard the sullen plunge; in his ears it would be but a louder sough of the billows against the ship.

The assassin looked down into the dark sea. Probably the passenger sank immediately, or was drawn under the vessel, else he would surely have cried for aid.

The murderer placed the gem in a small tobacco-box, and then walked composedly forward.

The *Albatross* was a fast and well-built schooner, of three hundred tons burthen. She was bound from Singapore to Manilla, with a various, but valuable, cargo. Captain Gould and his mates, Fenwick and Williams, were Englishmen. As to the crew, the skipper, in calling it mixed, did it no injustice. There were ten men—two Lascars, a Spaniard, a Frenchman, three Swedes, and two brothers, who were, in some sense, cosmopolitans; they had lost, it seemed, whatever distinctive traits of nationality they originally possessed. Speaking all languages indifferently, they were taken for Frenchman by the Spaniard, Maltese by the Frenchman, French-Canadians by the Swedes, and English or American by the skipper; they had shipped under the name of Lambert. The tenth man was a young Englishman, of education, and even refinement, who was a sailor partly from choice and partly from necessity; able in the rough profession he had adopted, but sadly out of place among such a nondescript crew as that of the *Albatross*.

This crew was not easily managed; but Skipper Gould was a man of strong individuality, possessing that decision which is the chief essential of ship government, and combining with it an admirable tact and a sound judgment. He was experienced in these "hard" crews, and he ruled each according to its peculiar characteristics. He might often have been observed to chuckle or wink to himself after some little piece of seeming indulgence or concession which only made his authority firmer. His mates were capable men—subordinates whom he could handle with precision. Thus everything hitherto had gone well with *Albatross*, despite the threatening clouds, with vague flashes of the lightning in them, which occasionally hovered over its internal government.

On the morning following the conversation, a portion of which opens this narrative, the captain was somewhat surprised at the non-appearance of the passenger at breakfast. Westbrook was an old sea traveller, and the slight roughness of the weather could not be held accountable for his absence. On a small ship the slightest divergence from a routine or a custom is an event, and a matter for conversation; but in the captain's thoughts there was something more than mere interest, though it could scarcely be said what. Williams, the second mate, had not seen the passenger; Fenwick was attending to his duties above.

However, occupied by the difficulties of navigation in those waters and the gradually freshening breeze, the skipper forgot all about Westbrook until dinner. Again the passenger was absent.

The captain's vague thoughts now began to assume some definitiveness; he asked himself some serious questions. The steward,
sent to inquire if Mr. Westbrook were coming to dinner, returned,
saying that the passenger was not in his cabin, nor near it.

"Perhaps he is forward; he often takes a stroll over the ship,"
said Gould, quietly. But he was not forward, and a rigid search was
made with no success. The skipper had now to face the fact that his
passenger was no longer in the vessel. A rigorous inquiry failed to
account for his disappearance; indeed, it seemed that the captain
himself was the last man who had seen him alive. He had, however,
some reason for doubting this and for drawing certain conclusions,
to which he gave no utterance as yet.

"If," thought he, "Westbrook has been murdered for that emerald, it must have been by Williams or by Fenwick; but it won't do
to accuse either outright. One thing is certain, though—we three
alone knew of the emerald."

The captain was not more superstitious than the generality of
those who spend their lives face to face with the incomprehensible
wonders of the ocean, but he could not repress a shudder as he
called to mind what had been said of the emerald—of its apparent
sinister influence upon the fate of its possessor.

"Now what," reflected he, "could have induced the man to reveal
his ownership of a gem with such a reputation, and to strangers?
Pride of possession, scorn of concealment, arrogant defiance of
superstition, or fatality?"

Fatality! Despite of himself, the skipper's thoughts inclined the
most to this apparently least plausible explanation. But one thing
seemed certain: if the passenger had not fallen overboard, which
was extremely unlikely; if he had not committed suicide, an idea
altogether untenable—then he must have been murdered. Indeed,
the skipper had not the slightest doubt that he had. The real question was, was he murdered for the emerald? He could imagine no
other motive. If so, the assassin was one of two men, and the jewel
was still on board the vessel.

He knew not how to proceed. It would be unwise to let the
existence of such a gem be known among his lawless crew; equally
unwise would it be to charge either of his mates with the crime, for
they might easily turn the crew against him; indeed, if one of his

subordinates were innocent, that one must think him (the captain) guilty, unless he took some decisive action to elucidate the truth. But what could he do? He waited and watched.

On the night of the day after the search the skipper, watching narrowly the actions of his two lieutenants, observed Fenwick standing alone very near to the place where he had last seen the passenger. He approached as near as possible, screened by the shadow of a deck-cabin, and looked attentively at Fenwick. The mate was leaning against the taffrail, smoking. He held his tobacco-box in his hand; he was gazing into it steadily, it seemed reflectingly. Just then a man came from forward to "take his trick at the wheel." The tobacco-box closed with a snap and disappeared at the sound of footsteps, and the mate turned round hastily. None of these actions was unmarked by the skipper, who now stepped forward.

"Ah, Fenwick," he said, in his usual manner, "all going well? She creaks a bit, eh? Still rather new."

"Yes," rejoined the mate; "that's her only defect—a small one."

"Breeze still fresh," went on the skipper, taking out his pipe; "going down a bit, though." Here he commenced an elaborate search in his pockets. "We've had better weather than I—confound it! I've left my 'bacca below; let's have a pipe."

Fenwick handed him a well-filled pouch.

"A pouch, eh?" said the skipper, easily; "thought you always used a box."

"I did," said Fenwick, clearing his throat, "but I've lost or mislaid it. After all, a pouch is the best for Cavendish; I don't smoke ship's now."

There was a pause, during which the skipper manœuvred so as to get Fenwick in such a position that the moonlight shone full upon his features.

"But what," said Gould, quietly, as he puffed away at his pipe, taking care to keep his eyes fixed upon Fenwick's face—"what do you use that little box for that you were looking at just now?"

"Box?" stammered the mate, turning livid in the moonlight. "Oh, yes, this box! A few papers, a little gold chain of my mother's, and my certificate; the box is watertight, and—and—handy."

"Ah, yes."

There was another pause. The captain continued—

"I'm greatly disturbed about the affair of Westbrook. What do you think ought to be done?"

"It's hard to say," replied the mate. "Do you think it possible he could have made away with himself?"

"Decidedly not," said the skipper; "a man of his temperament rarely ends in that style."

"An accident, perhaps?"

"It must have been a very strange one, then. The man was as much a sailor as a landsman well can be. No, Fenwick, murder has been done, and we must find out who did it."

"That is the best course. But what motive?"

"The emerald."

"Ah, that emerald of his—yes," said Fenwick, calmly, "certainly that may have been the motive."

"But you and I and Williams alone knew of its existence."

"That is likely, but not certain; Westbrook was very much taken up with the stone. Why may we not fancy him standing here, or anywhere, fancying himself alone, and making it flash in the moonlight?"

"And the villain slowly creeping upon him, knife in hand——"

"There would be traces of blood."

"Or a rope deftly slung round his throat, like the thugs."

"Perhaps; but it's a mystery."

"Not for long, I hope. So you would advise an investigation among the crew—a search for the emerald?"

"Yes; but would not answer for the result. We have a crew of thieves and rascals, and it would be like letting off rockets in a powder-magazine to accuse them."

"After all, it might be better to wait until we reach port, and let the authorities deal with the affair."

"That's much the safest plan."

They smoked awhile, exchanged a few commonplaces, and then the skipper left Fenwick alone and went below.

Captain Gould was a man of decision; but his judgment had never been so sorely taxed. He was morally almost sure that Fenwick had the emerald in his possession; yet there was no absolute certainty. True, he could have the mate searched, and, indeed, this was no time for delicacy; and finally he resolved to submit everyone in the ship to a rigorous investigation. He would call the crew together, tell them the facts, representing the emerald of small value, and state clearly the necessity of a thorough search. Satisfied at having at length come to a decision, he retired to his berth, intending to carry out his plan upon the morrow.

But when the morning came the steward (one of the Lascars), on entering the captain's cabin, was horrified to perceive him lying motionless in his berth, his right hand clenched tightly round the haft of a large clasp-knife, which was buried in his breast.

At the steward's cries the second mate, Williams, and Fenwick appeared. Williams examined the body; it was almost cold. The knife was one belonging to the dead man; it had been plunged into his chest to the haft, but the hand that still grasped it had evidently attempted its withdrawal, without success.

"Good God, Fenwick!" cried Williams, with starting eyes, "what are we to make of this?"

"Evidently a case of suicide," said the other, who was pale, but calm; "you know how cut up he was about the passenger."

"Cut up, eh? I suppose he was; but I—oh, yes, of course, he must have been."

"And, perhaps——" began Fenwick, in a significant tone.

"Perhaps what?" said the other.

"Oh, nothing. I don't like to say it of a dead man, but——"

"Ah, I understand you. He was the last who saw the passenger alive; he——"

"Yes; but I may be wrong."

"If he killed the passenger, it was for that emerald, surely?"

"It must have been. We had better search for the stone, and take charge of it."

They searched, but the jewel could not be found.

The first mate announced the mysterious death of the skipper to the crew, and formally took command of the *Albatross*.

Of course, these two strange and sudden deaths created much commotion among the crew. Whether any of them knew of the emerald is not certain; at all events, nothing was said of it, even by the two mates. But a feeling of ominous gloom spread through the schooner. Few words were spoken; each distrusted the others, without knowing why. The germ of anarchy was in every breast.

Captain Gould had been at once trusted, feared and respected. He was the true compass of the ship, and he was dead.

Williams was a man who knew his duty, and could do it well under supervision. Directed by a man to whom he felt his inferiority, he was thoroughly reliable. But Fenwick could not inspire him with the confidence necessary to his proper management. Knowing himself to be "as good a man" as Fenwick, he was not likely to feel easy under the first mate's command. Possessing that fearlessness which is the result of robust health, a hardy frame, and a coarse nerve-fibre, Williams, as a soldier, would have been intrepid to ferocity—a trusty weapon in the hand of a chief—admirable food for powder; but his was the courage which, in ordinary life, approximates closely to the spurious bravery of the bully. The crew disliked him, respecting only his somewhat unusual physical powers.

Williams, at the outset, had no definite intention of in any way resisting the authority of the chief mate, but, ere many days had passed, a misunderstanding occurred which engendered a coldness between them. The second mate felt a sort of impatient contempt for Fenwick, who, being of an exacting temper, gave his inferior officer many opportunities for an explosion. Williams, however, was too honest a seaman not to have some regard for the safety of the ship, and bore up as well as he could under what he thought, perhaps justly, an attempt at malicious and petty tyranny.

But Williams had a hasty and even ferocious temper; and one day, receiving an order which seemed to him obviously unnecessary, he broke into a tirade of contemptuous and angry words, and refused to execute "this piece of foolery." Then Fenwick (very unwisely) threatened to have him placed in irons, at which Williams' passion got the better of his judgment, and he instantly stretched Fenwick at his feet with a heavy blow.

Fenwick, no match in physical strength for his opponent, seized an axe from the stand near, and raised it to strike. The other dashed in, received the blow on his arm, wrested the weapon from his adversary, and, enraged beyond description, buried it in Fenwick's brain.

The struggle was so hideously brief that it had attracted none of the men, who were nearly all below. But a sailor (one of the brothers Lambert) came upon the scene just as the blow was struck.

"You've killed him, sir," said Lambert, keeping a wary eye on Williams, who still held the blood-imbued weapon in his hand; but the mate threw it down, fell on his knees at the side of the man he had murdered, placed his hand on the breast and held it there for some moments, as if in hope that all life was not yet fled. But there was no pulsation.

As Williams withdrew his hand he felt something hard in the inside breast-pocket of the mate's coat. Mechanically he took out an iron tobacco-box; at a touch the lid flew open, revealing a large and beautifully-cut emerald.

"Ha!" cried Lambert, "is that what you killed him for?"

"No, no, no!" cried the mate, shuddering; "we—we quarrelled."

"Oh," said Lambert, in a very significant tone. "Look here," he continued, glancing cautiously around—"look here, Mr. Williams, you must be sharp if you don't want the men to know. I'll help you; but we must go halves in that stone. Eh?"

"Yes, yes! Anything!"

"Come, then; there goes the axe"—throwing it overboard—"now let's get the mate into his cabin till night. I'll swab up the blood for you."

They carried the body unobserved into the cabin, and locked it in. Then Lambert washed the deck.

Williams had involuntarily put the box in his pocket. He fell into a gloomy reverie, from which he was aroused by Lambert, who said, in a low voice—

"It is understood, then, about the stone?"

"Yes."

"Let's have another look at it. A pure emerald—eh? I saw it that night when the passenger disappeared—I mean when he showed it to you."

"Ah!"

"Yes. Fenwick must have killed him for it."

"Fenwick? The captain——"

"Well, no. The skipper wouldn't have done it, sir. Fenwick killed the passenger, and the skipper must have found out——"

"I see, and then Fenwick murdered Gould, too? Well, he deserved death—the first mate, I mean."

"That he did. But what will you do? There'll be an inquiry made into all this, and it'll be found out that the emerald was on board, and——"

"Yes, yes, all will be discovered," said Williams, in a tone of despair.

"It needn't be. Listen, that stone's a fortune; there are very few emeralds so large and fine. It'll set us up for life. But these three men killed—how can you account for them? Nohow. You must lose the ship and get away."

"Lose the ship?"

"Yes; run her on some rock, or start a hole in her. But we'll talk of that another time. I must go back to the wheel; it's lucky for you I was there."

"Be silent about this."

"Have no fear. I'll help you dispose of the body to-night. I must go back now; she's beginning to go off her course."

The mate remained buried in dark thoughts, which half attracted, half repelled him. He understood Lambert's suggestion. Lose the ship! That meant the deliberate sacrifice of nine men, to say nothing of the schooner and her rich cargo. The alternative—ignominy and death for himself. Was there no middle course?

Lambert's brother presently came aft to take his turn at the helm—their "tricks" were consecutive. He who had witnessed the crime of Williams was the elder. As his brother took the wheel, he said, in a low tone—

"Williams has it."

"What? The em——"

"Hush! yes. He's just done for Fenwick. Not a word till to-night."

He went forward.

When darkness came the disposal of the body was successfully accomplished; and now that the ghastly object was lost in the sea—that great receptacle for hideous secrets—the mate became more composed. He excused himself in great measure—his passion had seduced him to the deed; and if Fenwick had not attempted to strike him with the axe the thing would not have happened; and the man, himself a murderer, was justly killed. But no such sophistry can satisfy the conscience; and, when all was said, the fact remained that Williams was an assassin—he could not explain away his crime. Yet the past disturbed him less than the future. To escape, he must plunge still deeper into infamy. He had taken one life; to avoid the forfeit, he must take nine more. Nine? Why not ten? How could he rely on this man who knew his secret? And what was one life more or less among so many?

To lose the schooner and ten lives, then; but how? And was there no alternative? To be sure, he might steer the ship close to some island, and go ashore in a boat secretly. But then the fear of pursuit, discovery, retribution—it was hideous to think of. After all, a dozen rascals——

That night the brothers Lambert, who were united by one of those half-savage, half-chivalric attachments often found among adventurers who have planned, plotted, swindled, perhaps even murdered together—that night the Lamberts consulted. It were doubtless supererogatory to explain how they came to know of the emerald, or even to say that their present consultation, held on the lee side of the forecastle, was to find a means of obtaining the stone for themselves, and of leaving the schooner. The reputation of these two men was extremely shady, and they knew that if, on the inquiry which would be made on arriving at Manilla, the emerald were found in their possession, it would go hard with them. They decided to kill Williams, secure the emerald, lower the skiff that hung over the stern, and leave the *Albatross*. Strange to say, they did not count upon the elements; they believed, as most scoundrels do, "in luck." They knew the China Sea well and, with a compass, had no fear of not being able to make some island, whence, representing themselves as shipwrecked men, they could take passage for America or Europe.

As they concluded their plan and were about to go below, a tall, lithe figure, which had crept near and listened for the last few minutes, drew away, and seemed to fade into the gloom like a ghost. Neither of the Lamberts had seen this spectral form. Yet it was not a shade, but a tangible body. It had a man's voice, too, and might have been heard to mutter some fragmentary phrases, interspersed with low chuckles—

"*Voila une fière affaire! . . . C'est une contremine vraiment gaillarde! . . . Rien de plus facile—un coup de main! Ho, ho! Admirable!*"

On his side the second mate had come to a decision somewhat similar to that of the brothers Lambert. The *Albatross* had now more than half completed her voyage. She was about a hundred and fifty miles to the north-west of the coast of North Borneo. Williams had the course a little changed; he intended to steer close to a cluster of small islands to the south-west of Palawan. Once on one of these isles he could easily reach Palawan, or even Borneo, and trust to chance for the rest. It was a desperate and difficult plan, but preferable to the fearful crime involved in wrecking or sinking the ship, as Lambert had suggested.

It soon became known that Fenwick had disappeared. The crew were now in a state of nervous agitation beyond description; they felt, and with reason, that these horrors might go on indefinitely. "First the officers, then the crew," thought they. The poor, inoffensive Lascars were looked upon with no favourable eyes; the superstitious Swedes told terrible tales of malignant spirits, who were said to have a preference for the Asiatic form as a disguise; while the French sailor related horrible cases of homicidal monomania which had been known among the Malays and other islanders; he expressed himself to be in constant terror for his life. Nor were the Lamberts slow in taking up the theme, as may be supposed.

The night of the second day after Fenwick's disappearance was calm, but very dark. As has been mentioned, the Lamberts' turns at the wheel were successive. This was favourable to their plan. The wind was steady and very light.

While the elder Lambert steered, his brother crept stealthily towards Williams' cabin. It was intended, as soon as the deed was done, to lash the wheel and leave the vessel to its fate; there was, however, little danger of an accident happening before the next man came to take his place at the helm.

The elder Lambert waited, at first composedly enough; but presently he began to grow a little impatient. "He's a long time about it," thought he. Half-an-hour more passed, and he became anxious. Soon the clouds began to clear away and the stars to peer forth. He could wait no longer; lashing the wheel, he made his way towards the cabin of the second mate. All was dark and silent there; the door was ajar. He listened for some minutes; no sound—not even of breathing. Then he entered; still nothing. "Perhaps the fool's courage failed him," thought he, "or the mate is not here." He struck a match, but no sooner had the dim light diffused itself over the cabin than he dropped it in horror.

He struck another. A ghastly scene was before him. The mate lay stretched upon the deck, with his throat cut from ear to ear. Beside him, horribly contorted by a death spasm, lay the body of the younger Lambert; the haft of a dagger protruded from between his shoulders. The mate seemed to be floating in blood; a razor lay beside him.

The match burnt down to the gazer's fingers; he lit another. He searched for the emerald; it was gone. Then, overwhelmed by rage and grief, he aroused the crew, retaining sufficient presence of mind, however, to send one to the wheel.

The men were wild with terror; the French sailor advised that the Lascars should be "slung up to the maintruck" forthwith. They fell on their knees, protesting their innocence and ignorance of all participation in the atrocity. Lambert himself interceded for them, but he swore a terrible oath to be revenged for his brother's death.

The wind fell towards dawn, and when the sun arose the schooner was becalmed. There was not a breath of wind; a feather, dropped from aloft, fell straight down like a plummet. Though the mate, had he been alive, could have told them that the schooner was within sight of the island of Palawan, no land was visible, on account of a peculiar haze or mist, which seemed to veil the horizon, and through which the sun gleamed redly. A silence like that of the tomb encompassed all things. At mid-day the bodies were committed to the deep, and the men saw with astonishment that they sank nearly twenty fathoms before they were out of sight. The day, which was insufferably hot, closed at length, and the deep darkness came. The stars shone with unusual brilliancy.

Lambert had assumed, by a sort of tacit consent, the direction of affairs. He had the sails furled, the topmasts sent down, and all safely stowed.

These preparations were not made in vain. Towards morning a dark cloud spread with a rapidity quasi-miraculous over the heavens, and seemed descending like a pall upon the stagnant and ebony sea.

Suddenly a terrific wave arose and hurled itself upon the devoted vessel; it was accompanied by a blast of tremendous power. Then were the furies of the tempest loosed. Thunder pealed, lightning flashed with a weird, unearthly glare, and the sea was lashed into a rage that seemed almost sentient. For some minutes the *Albatross* was completely buried in foam; the three Swedes, the Spaniard, and one of the Lascars were swept away like straws, and never seen again. The mainmast snapped off short like a twig.

At length the schooner arose, staggering, from the gulf of waters. The mainmast was not yet clear; it hung over the side, held by the straining ropes. The young Englishman (whose name was Walters), the Frenchman, and the Lascar seized axes, and, with great difficulty, freed the vessel from its incumbrance, while Lambert endeavoured to get her before the wind.

Again and again the gallant schooner was submerged by the tumultuous waves; presently the foremast went by the board, carrying away the remaining Lascar. The loss of the mast relieved the schooner somewhat, but each gigantic wave threatened to destroy the little vessel.

For nearly three days the storm continued, during which time the *Albatross* drove swiftly before the tremendous blast. Then the weather moderated, and finally grew calm, but on sounding the well it was discovered that the ship was sinking; several planks had started during the fury of the tempest, and the water was flowing in with horrible rapidity. The three men who remained could not hope to save the schooner, and so, provisioning the only boat that remained from the ravage of the storm, they abandoned the *Albatross*, which sank a quarter of an hour afterwards.

Their whereabouts they had no means of knowing. It was possible that they were somewhere between the Philippines and Formosa. They hoped that some ship bound for Hong Kong, Manilla, or other ports, would sight them before many days had passed. They bent a sail on the boat and steered northward.

But weeks passed, and no sail appeared; and, as the provisions grew scanty, they lost hope. Few words were exchanged.

Walters, buried in his own thoughts, did not at first notice a very singular circumstance. The French sailor never sought sleep until he was sure Lambert was not awake; and they watched each other furtively. Walters at length perceived their strange behaviour, but, though he was puzzled, he felt no alarm.

At length the last meal was shared and eaten, and the boat's occupants resigned themselves to despair.

On a calm and misty day, the third of their fast, Walters fell asleep. He was suddenly awakened by a violent rocking of the boat, and, on opening his eyes, he saw his two companions locked in a terrible struggle. While he was considering how to act Lambert overpowered his adversary, and wrested from him what appeared to be an old tobacco-box, which he put in his own pocket. Then, by a great effort, and before Walters could interfere to prevent him, he hurled the Frenchman over the gunwale into the sea.

Throwing a threatening look at Walters, he seized the oars and began to row. The Frenchman rose to the surface quickly, and swam lustily in the wake of the boat.

"Swim, swim!" half shrieked the rower—"swim for it, you murderous villain! Ha! ha! ha! So it was you, was it, who stabbed my brother, and cut the mate's throat, too, for all I know? Swim, swim! Don't give in! Keep it up, you lubber! Hand over hand, come on! We will see who shall tire first, you or I!"

Walters sat still, paralysed with astonishment and horror. Lambert, keeping up his taunts and demoniac laughter, rowed on, sometimes pausing until the gasping swimmer almost grasped the stern of the boat, and then urging it on again by a vigorous stroke.

"*Grâce! Grâce!*" spluttered the drowning man. "Mercy!"

"You don't swim fast enough, you dog!" cried the exulting rower.

"*Mon Dieu! Avoir un peu de pitié!*" gasped the swimmer.

"Pity!" howled Lambert. "How much did you show to *him*? Come; if you can catch the boat, I'll see."

There was a piece of rope in the bottom of the boat. Walters seized it and threw one end to the Frenchman, who, eagerly clutching it, began to draw himself towards the boat. But Lambert, with a savage oath, raised an oar and struck the young man senseless on the sternsheets. The swimmer continued drawing the rope towards him, while Lambert urged the boat forward. The rope soon payed out, until it was all in the water.

Lambert laughed long and loud; he stopped rowing several times to jeer at the now rapidly failing efforts of the desperate swimmer, whose face became hideous in its agony of despair and rage. He turned on his back and rested. The sea was very calm, and a strong and skilful swimmer might sustain himself above water for hours. The French sailor had evidently decided to combat the inevitable; it is probable that he did not even consider the utter impossibility of entering the boat, even if he could reach it, without the consent of his terrible enemy.

As soon as he regained some strength the appalling race recommenced. It were equally vain to attempt to describe either the fiendish exultation of Lambert or the half-pathetic, half-horrible struggles of the swimmer. From time to time the miserable wretch uttered curses and supplications at random; but Lambert replied only by bursts of insensate laughter, mingled with jeers and gibes and imprecations. At length the Frenchman, after mustering up his remaining strength for one last effort, suddenly cried, in a loud and piercing voice—"A sail! A sail!"

And while Lambert stood up in the boat and glanced wildly in all directions over the great waste of waters, the French sailor, in three rapid strokes, came up with the boat; his hand was on the gunwale, but at the very moment when he was about to draw himself into the boat his enemy turned and saw him. With a savage oath, he hurled the exhausted swimmer back into the sea. This time the unfortunate man sank for ever.

When Walters recovered his senses Lambert was in the bow of the boat, gazing fixedly upon some glittering thing which he held in his palm. The young man glanced round, surprised to see no one else in the boat; then he remembered all, and shuddered.

Several more days passed; the two men were so weak and exhausted that they could scarcely move. Yet hope did not even then entirely desert them.

The crime-stained Lambert hoped, and the innocent Walters hoped; but of the two Lambert was the least resigned to the fate that seemed imminent. The guilty fear death more than the innocent.

No doubt the little water that remained served to prolong their lives to some extent, but it was soon gone.

There was no wind. All the sea, sky, and air seemed to be awaiting, in motionless suspense, the end of these two unfortunates. To Walters, who was somewhat of a thinker and much more of a dreamer, the silence seemed full of mysterious voices—the voices that call to us sometimes in the realms of sleep—and vague, shadowy doubts and fears overwhelmed and oppressed his mind. He listened to these imaginary sounds with an intensity of reasonless interest. The commingled gloom and grandeur of the watery desolation bore like a weight upon his heart; the immensity overpowered and appalled him. To be alone in the presence of the Infinite is oppressive to the mind; and, knowing that he had but a few hours more to live, he felt the vague anguish, the strange tremulousness of the soul pausing upon the threshold of the unknown.

Sometimes he gazed into the lucent depths of ocean, which seemed to him the very home of Oblivion, and he longed for the dreamless sleep of death; but then there would throng through his brain wild tales of unearthly things—the weird superstitions of the seas, and his fading mind pictured terrible places within those mysterious depths, the secrets of which no human eye has seen, and where the kraken slumbers in the serenity of absolute and eternal silence.

Lambert's thoughts were condensed into the one (to him) appalling reflection "I must die!" He repeated these words so often that, by constant iterance, they at length failed to convey any meaning to his mind; but the terrifying thought was never absent. This man had scoffed at religion, but now he shuddered at the memory of his long life of crime. Yet he gazed continually at the emerald—that stone which, though it had destroyed the *Albatross* and her crew, could not prolong his life one second there.

Walters, rising languidly from an uneasy sleep, found his companion motionless in the bottom of the boat. The sea was still calm. The sun was low in the sky. Lambert did not stir. Walters stretched out a long and emaciated hand, and touched the shoulder of his fellow-castaway. The man was dead. The iron tobacco-box was still in his hand.

This box had excited Walters' curiosity when he first saw it; he felt little interest in it now. Yet he took it from the dead man's hand and opened it. Within lay the emerald—that sinister stone, that Avatar of blood. He gazed upon it for some minutes; then, with a shudder, he cast it into the sea and watched it sink down, down into the clear azure depths, until it disappeared—he hoped for ever.

Even this exertion completely overpowered him. He knew he

could not live many hours more. Yet hope—hope that triumphs over the tortures of the rack, that gives the lie to the inevitable, that smiles back defiance on despair itself—hope was with him even then, and, raising his eyes full of the shadow of death to the gleaming dome above, he murmured, "Mercy!" But there was no change in the pitiless serenity of the sky, and the deaf and imperturbable sea still smiled on.

Then he sank back and moved no more. This time he felt that the icy hand of Death had indeed clutched him; he yielded; the will succumbed; and soon the last faint gleam of light went out from his eyes.

At that moment the sun sank beneath the blue line of the horizon; his golden light was replaced by a soft grey radiance that filled the sky, from the hyaline depths of which the evening star arose. Gradually the gloom deepened, other stars appeared, and slowly over the great sepulchre of the sea the brilliantly jewelled pall of the night extended.

THE HOUSE IN THE SUBURB

Were it not for the simplicity of the few facts hereinafter to be set down, the horror of what I have to tell might indeed baffle belief. But here, in this gloomy prison, with the shadow of an ignominious death hanging over me, it can scarcely be supposed that I will in any way distort or exaggerate, for whatever purpose, the details of my crime. I have been convicted, and will now confess; and it will be seen that a narration of the truth and such relief as a full confession may afford me are my sole objects.

The house in the suburbs belonged, as is known, to my brother. It is very old, and for some years has been only occasionally tenanted. Its architecture is extremely irregular and faulty; it might be thought to have been constructed by some maniac who had once been a builder. Its utterly incongruous, unnecessary, and annoying windings and turnings were the chief reason of its remaining without an occupant—though I believe its gloomy appearance had given rise to certain hideous superstitions; certainly it was said to be haunted by the more ignorant of those who dwelt in the vicinity.

My brother and I had long desired the old man's death. To set forth the full reason of this would entail the recital of our life-history. Suffice it here to say that a long, bitter, and implacable hatred, the suppression of certain family secrets which Halston had for years held over our heads, like the Sicilian's hair-suspended sword, and several advantages which would result from his death, had created in our hearts a passionate desire for his demise, and at length my brother hinted that we might ourselves compass our wish. I cannot say that I was at all reluctant in my acquiescence; and so we decided on the murder. The causes of our enmity were unknown to any but ourselves. We agreed to quietly kill Halston in the old house, and conceal the body in a deep hole prepared under the brick floor of one of the cellars. One of us was sufficient to do the deed, and the lot fell to me. My brother, however, was to

179

help me in the disposal of the body and the careful re-setting of the bricks.

The chief difficulty was to contrive that the old man should consent to pass a night in the house; but we must also be sure that his visit was unknown to anyone without—that he could not be traced. It were tedious to relate here how many abortive attempts we made to attain the consummation desired. At length we succeeded; nothing, we thought, but a highly-fortuitous conjunction of circumstances could direct suspicion towards us, or lead to an investigation of the house; but at the worst we relied on the scrupulous care with which we intended to conceal the corpse.

We contrived, then, to persuade our enemy to stay in the old tenement until morning. We entertained him with the most flattering and assiduous hospitality. It was late ere he retired. The rich wines we had set before him had the effect of making him extremely loquacious. He professed eternal friendship in the future, and tearful regret for the past. Yet at intervals he would remind us, with a self-satisfied chuckle, of the power he possessed, and the effect it would have if he chose to wield it maliciously, so that his professions of friendship were extremely distasteful to us, qualified, as they were, by half-veiled threats. I, especially, who had drunk deeply of the generous wine, felt rage, disgust, and contempt rising within me as I listened to his maudlin speeches and saw the drunken tears streaming down his cheeks.

At length he retired to the room prepared for him, assisted by my brother, whilst I, to gain more nerve, drank still deeper of the red and fiery wine. My brother returned.

"He will soon sleep," he said, calmly.

We sat drinking for some time. My brother was very cool. He seemed to consider the deed in which he was a participant as an ordinary affair—or, at most, as a troublesome and dangerous but necessary task. I, on the contrary, was much excited, and profoundly surprised to hear my brother discussing "the affair" in such an easy tone; still more so when he spoke of going to bed to "get some sleep," and told me to be sure and awaken him before the dawn, so that he could assist in the disposal of the body. These things, I say, surprised me, but I thought little of them; moreover, they accorded well with my brother's character. I am assured that he would have been almost as little excited had the task fallen to him; would to heaven it had!

When he had gone I prepared to accomplish my ghastly work. But for many minutes, despite the copious draughts of wine I had imbibed, I could not gather sufficient nerve. There was a stand of liqueurs in the room; I drank several glasses of pure hollands in quick succession, and then, feeling the ardent spirits working like fire within me, I seized the long dagger which I intended to use, and, staggering, half-blinded by the drink I had so lavishly taken, I ascended the tottering staircase of the old tenement. I reached the top.

I was not familiar with my brother's house, the irregular construction of which I have already mentioned. And now, in my bewildered and wildly-intoxicated condition, I forgot the position of the old man's chamber, and scarcely knew which way to turn. I rushed forward at random, endeavouring to recall the corridors and passages to mind. At length I seemed to recognise the way; the old man's room was, I knew, at the end of a short passage—such as the one I was in.

I reached the door at the end and listened. To be sure, thought I, this is it, for I heard a heavy breathing within, and through the door, which was not quite closed, there came a very faint ray of light.

I listened for some moments. Assured at length that the occupant really slumbered, I gently pushed open the door and crept into the room. There was a lamp on the table, burning very low, and giving only the faintest light; it was, however, sufficient for my purpose. I moved stealthily towards the bed. The victim lay on his right side, with his face turned from me. I was glad of this, for I feared to look on the old man's features at such a time, lest I should be unnerved.

He breathed stertorously; a faint odour of wine was in the air. The bedclothes had been thrown partially off, so that he was uncovered to the waist.

Leaning over him, I carefully selected a spot upon his left side as near the heart as I could guess, and then placing the keen point of the dagger thereon, I ran it swiftly through the sleeper's body. A low, gurgling groan, and a long and violent tremor followed; then all was still—then I knew that he breathed no more.

And the deed was done. I crept slowly away; the horror of the crime I had just committed now rushed upon my heart, and in some measure neutralised my intoxication. But, above all, I felt intolerably weary and depressed; the excitement was gone. I felt that I must have repose—I must regain my strength. The night previous my brother and I had worked hard at the grave in the cellar; it must be that, I thought, which, coupled with the wine and spirits I had drunk, had so exhausted me. A distant clock sounded the hour—three a.m.; it was early yet. I sought my own chamber—finding it more by instinct than by memory—for I was still bewildered and distraught.

I had scarcely thrown myself, dressed, upon the bed when I fell asleep.

Never before had I ever *suffered* from any dream. My slumber has always been full of strange visions, but never had I derived until then anything but a sort of shadowy or negative pleasure from them. This I ascribe not to the dreams themselves (for they have often been horrible enough), but to their effect upon my apprehension *during sleep*. Though in these shadowy dramas I have always been the central personage, yet never have I *seemed* other than a mere spectator. I have seldom felt, while dreaming, the slightest emotion beyond that which I might feel when sitting at a play.

But in *that* sleep I had a dream—or, let me rather say, a succession of dreams—which caused me the most vivid and exquisite agony. As might be supposed, the deed I had done formed the chief part of my visions; yet with it were interwoven many long-forgotten and irrelevant memories and reminiscences of the distant past. But let me here speak only of the *last* of these terrible feignings of the slumbering mind. The anguish of this dream arose from the Tantalus-like impossibility to make use of easily available means of hiding the evidences of my crime—of disposing of the body.

The most trivial things interposed between my wish and its effect. Assisted by my brother I bore the corpse of the old man to the cellar, where the hole was prepared to receive it. But we found that this hole was much too small. We tried to enlarge it, but the implements we used bent and twisted like wire on the bricks. At last we forced the body into its grave, but were disturbed by a violent knocking at the street door. A more vivid sound than this knocking

I never heard before in a dream. We left the cellar and ushered in a visitor, who kept us talking of trivial things for many minutes. When at length we returned to the cellar we hastened to replace the bricks over the body; but they would not fit in. Our hands trembled, and the face of the corpse seemed to smile with ghastly disdain at our frenzied efforts. The bricks crumbled away in our fingers, and the fragments fell upon the body. My brother procured others, but they were different, and we dreaded to place them in. Meanwhile the smile on the dead man's face became more accentuated; the white lips writhed about the clenched teeth, and the eyelids began to rise. They opened, and the eyes fixed themselves upon my own so that I could not move or speak, but remained motionless with horror. Then the body began to stir; with a slow, stealthy, gliding movement it rose to a sitting posture in the grave. I trembled in every limb; and glancing around I perceived with terror that my brother had left me.

When I looked again at the corpse I saw that it had risen from the shallow grave, and now stood looking at me with a questioning expression as it slowly drew the long, keen dagger from its side and thrust it into my hand, muttering some strange words, which were all the more frightful to me because they were utterly meaningless. Overcome with terror, I awoke. It was day, broad and garish.

Then rushed upon me the memory of my crime. But so vivid had been the dream that I yet seemed to hear beside me the low tones of a man's voice. Could I be mistaken? Was it all a dream? No! Almighty God, no! There—there beside my bed he stood—*he*, the murdered man—he who was dead—whom I had killed!—*he*——

Was it possible? Yes; the old man stood and gazed, in astonishment, at my wildly-staring eyes and pallid lips. He spoke some words; but I—not for worlds could I recall them. As soon as the fulness of the hideous truth had forced its way in upon my shuddering brain, I uttered a wild shriek and swooned.

* * * * *

The old man had arisen and gone to my brother's room (which was near his), and had found him dead, with a dagger buried in his body. He then sought me—with what result I have told. Afterwards he communicated with the police. The rest there is no need to tell. My crime has destroyed us both—my brother and myself. I neither expect nor desire mercy on earth, and can hope for none beyond the grave.

A TALE OF TOKIO

It was during my residence in Japan that the somewhat peculiar and decidedly unpleasant adventure which I am going to relate happened to me. In those days Tokio (or Yeddo, as it was formerly called) was not what it is now. Yet the changes which have taken place are not so much, I think, referable to outward or physical developments as to that rapid moral and social evolution which has of late years excited so much interest and comment. To the superficial observer the general aspect of the Tokio of to-day is, perhaps, not radically different from that of the old town I knew so many years ago. Still, I doubt very much if the locality in which stood the quaint old house of my ancient *bête noir*, Yohla Kusima, is not metamorphosed from a sort of mysterious and sombre faubourg into a busy and populous thoroughfare.

How I first excited the enmity of this man I scarcely know. The Japanese are not a specially vicious or vindictive race; but Kusima was one of those abnormal characters which are to be found under all skies. His fierce malignancy and utter fiendishness were of such a nature as to suggest some taint of madness in his blood. Shelley, or rather his Beatrice, says, in "The Cenci"—

> Horrible things have been in this wild world,
> Prodigious mixtures, and confusions strange
> Of good and ill; and worse have been conceived
> Than ever there was found a heart to do.

Kusima, however, could both conceive and execute anything in the way of vengeance. How the man lived, if not by robbery, I cannot say. He had been a wrestler, and it was in this *rôle* that he first crossed our path. But as a wrestler he was, as Artemus Ward would say, "not a success." Indeed, it may have been our hearty and uncontrollable mirth at his futile and ridiculous efforts to vanquish his opponents that implanted the germ of his deadly animosity towards us. My friend Elliston, I remember, called my attention at the time to the tigerlike glare in Kusima's eyes as he swaggered past. But to me the man appeared a mere harmless impostor—a braggart—knave and fool in one. We were soon tired of the wrestling, which is a national sport in Japan, or was in my time, and in a few days forgot all about our "Mongolian tiger," as Elliston called him.

We were in the habit of strolling through the city at night—a proceeding safe enough in Tokio. But one evening, while passing through a rather gloomy street, we were suddenly set upon by five men, led by our *ci-devant* athlete, Yohla Kusima. We carried no weapons, so there was nothing for it but to stand shoulder to shoulder and use our fists. We were neither of us strangers to that class of exercise, and two of the fellows were on their backs in a second. Then, as luck would have it, I found myself confronted by Kusima himself. I caught the glitter of a blade of some sort in his hand, and knew he would not scruple to use it. I therefore stepped forward at once, made a feint, and then delivered a blow with all the strength and address of which I was master. My right fist struck him fairly between the eyes, and he dropped like an ox.

Elliston, in the interim, had put the others to flight. We could thus return home, and laugh over our adventure. When the excitement had subsided, I became conscious of a sharp pain in my hand. I found that a large diamond ring I wore had been broken by the blow I had dealt to Kusima; the stone bed been forced out of its claw and lost. I had some difficulty in removing the ring itself, and I reflected that the forehead of my antagonist must have suffered rather severely from the effects of the blow. I felt half sorry for the fellow, but one cannot be expected, in an impromptu fight, to think of removing a ring. The loss of the stone concerned me more than Kusima's hurts. One or two of our Japanese friends advised us to try and obtain redress, but, considering Yohla punished enough, we allowed the matter to drop.

However, the redoubtable Kusima was by no means satisfied.

Some weeks later, when we had ceased to think about the affair just described, Elliston and I resumed our nocturnal perambulations. It was, in fact, a habit to which we were both very much addicted—to stroll wherever chance or fancy might direct us, while we discussed some subject of interest. One night we were walking along as usual, engrossed in discussion on a favourite topic, when suddenly Elliston uttered a faint cry, and fell backwards. Before I could even turn round, something in the nature of a sack of thick cloth or canvas was cast over my head and shoulders. I was thrown down, and ropes were passed round me, one of which encircled my throat so as almost to cause suffocation. I then felt myself carried quickly and silently away—how far I could not tell, for the pain of the tightly-bound cords, the compression of the rope about my neck, and the almost total deprivation of air caused me to sink into unconsciousness.

On recovering, I found myself in darkness; the dense gloom around me seemed to have enveloped my mind, for I lay still for many minutes, trying vainly to recall my memories of the late event. I endeavoured to move my arms, but they were still tightly bound. I found I could not even turn my head. Gradually a clear comprehension of all that had occurred came to me, and I shuddered to think what might yet be in store.

Suddenly a feeling came over me that I was not alone. It was too dark to see—besides, I could not turn my head. I strove to speak, and then discovered that one of a number of broad bands which encircled me in all directions was drawn tightly over my lips, and that some adhesive substance in which it was soaked—pitch, I believe—prevented me from opening my mouth. I could only await, in an agony of apprehension, the event of "the unborn hour."

Soon a soft light began to diffuse itself over my surroundings. It seemed as if the day was beginning to break. I could see dark beams and rafters above me, and presently some faint pencils of light shot through certain interstices in the roof. As well as I could judge, I was in a sort of loft or attic. The rafters and beams, however, looked far more cumbrous and substantial than any I had yet seen in Japan. From my position I could observe but little. As far as I could see, the den was entirely without furniture. As the light increased, however, I saw, on a kind of stand near, what seemed to be the model of a piece of machinery, though it represented nothing with which I was acquainted. I thought I could perceive a spring in the centre, and there were numerous wheels and cogs. It looked like a piece of grotesque clockwork. A sort of arm projected from one side, to the end of which were fastened two small discs of thick glass, each about two inches in diameter, such as might have been taken from a telescope or a pair of field-glasses.

Nothing happened for several hours, during which it was natural I should regard the strange machine, since it was the only object in sight, the purpose of which I could not divine. But apart from this, it had a peculiar fascination for my eyes which I could not resist; and at times it inspired in me a vague terror. I gave myself up to a sort of conjectural reverie, in which I fancied all kinds of improbable things in connection with the mysterious object. But at certain moments I was surprised and even terrified to find myself—at least so I thought—on the very point of divining the use or purpose of the machine. I longed yet feared to know the why and wherefore of its construction—above all, the purport of its presence. All this time I still remained conscious of the proximity of some person. A man, I knew, was near—just out of range of my eyes. Meanwhile my body, cramped, immovable, was racked by increasing pains.

At last, he who was behind me stepped within my sphere of vision. It was Yohla Kusima. Strange to say, I had not associated him with the outrage. Why I did not I cannot imagine, for on seeing him I was in nowise surprised.

He gave me one glance—and there was in his gleaming eyes a depth of baleful malignity indescribable, utterly irreconcilable with the idea of sanity. I tried to, but could not, sustain that burning gaze. Kusima did not speak, but stood upon a box and unfastened a sort of trap-door in the roof, letting in a flood of sunlight which came within a foot or so of where I lay. Kusima glanced towards me, made a gesture of anger or impatience, and closed the door again, thereafter resuming his station behind me.

Not many minutes elapsed ere he again opened the door. This time the sunlight came a little nearer. Kusima was about to close the trap, when a thought seemed to strike him, and he began to move the ponderous wooden frame to which I was bound. He shifted and adjusted it until part of the sunlight fell upon my face. Then, while I watched his every movement with a nervous intensity of interest, he busied himself with the mysterious machine of which I have made mention. My heart beat violently, though I could not conceive the purpose of his sinister preparations. He fixed the machine so that the arm to which the glass discs were fastened could be swung over my face. He then set in motion a pendulum which had hitherto been hidden from my sight by a portion of the framework on which the machine was mounted. A sound somewhat resembling the ticking of a clock ensued, and I could see that the machinery was in motion. Kusima then began carefully adjusting the glasses, and I waited in an agony of fearful expectation. Even yet I could not divine the purport of his actions. But I was not long left in doubt.

Suddenly a terrible pain shot through my head. It was intense, intolerable, overwhelming—so fearful that for a moment all power of thought, all mental volition, was suspended within me, so that I failed utterly to realise its nature or its cause; nor could I even tell on what portion of my head or face it was centred. Thought at length returned, and then the hideous truth flashed over me like an inspiration. The sun rays passing through the glasses were concentrated into two points of intense fire, and these, about three inches apart, fell upon my forehead just at the roots of the hair.

Anyone who has used a burning glass may, perhaps, form some faint conception of the terrible agony I suffered. The points of heat seemed not merely to burn, but to drill and bore through my skull into my very brain. I could move neither hand nor limb; the relief of cries or shrieks was denied me, for my mouth was effectually closed. The intensity of the silence, broken only by the soft noise of the machine, added to my anguish, if that were possible. Kusima never spoke, but stood before me contemplating, with an appearance of calm interest, the ceaseless contortions of my face. His hellish eyes alone spoke of the infernal exaltation in his heart.

At certain moments, the unnatural intensity of my suffering made it seem impossible. I felt that such agony could not be real—could not belong to mortality. But a new thought—a new terror—distracted me. I saw that the machine, in working, moved the arm to which the glasses were fixed, so that the concentrated heat-points travelled slowly downwards, yet it was some minutes before I fully comprehended what this meant. I feared, in fact, to look forward—to contemplate what might lie in the immediate future. But soon, as the piercing points of fire still moved steadily downwards on my forehead, I could not but realise in full the fearful fate that awaited me. I knew, in a word, that the fires must ultimately reach my eyes!

As this terrible conviction forced itself upon me my heart almost stopped in its beating, and for a second of time I forgot even the hideous anguish that never passed. My tormentor evidently read in my face the horror which consumed me, for he allowed a sombre and demoniacal smile to writhe his lips.

I glanced wildly round. I struggled with my bonds. My most furious efforts caused not even a vibration of the heavy structure to which I was bound. My head was firmly fixed in some contrivance of iron. I could only wrinkle up my brow, but this rather increased than mitigated my agony. And still the points of fire crept inexorably with the ticking of the devilish machine.

Horrible thoughts, fearful ideas, found birth in my tortured brain. Had I been able to speak I shudder to think what hideous curses I would have launched at heaven and its God. In my complete helplessness I thought with agony unutterable that it needed but the shadow of a cloud to stop the fearful doom that awaited me, and of the cruelty of the Creator who could gaze down upon my unnatural torment and offer not even that intervention. But far more blasphemous thoughts dominated my mind—thoughts too terrible even for memory. And the fire-points still crept down— steadily, stealthily, relentlessly downwards to the eyes that seemed destined to be burned and withered in their sockets, while the fiend Kusima looked calmly on.

In a brief moment of lucidity a thought occurred to me. I remembered having read, in a romance called "Michael Strogoff," how the hero of the tale is sentenced to be blinded; how a white-hot sword is passed slowly before his eyes; and how his sight is preserved by the tears that have gathered under the lids from the of his mother's fate. If I could weep—if I could fill my eyes with tears—might not the fiery point—but no! *they would stop at my eyes*, and no tears could save me. As well think of so quenching the sun itself. The hope vanished; all the horror of the impending event returned, accentuated by its increased imminency, for the points were now upon my brows; I could even smell the burning hair. In a few minutes more I should be blind—perhaps dead.

In moments of intense pain we frequently fancy a heavy, throbbing sound within the ears. Such a noise I now heard, but gave it no attention in the stress of my agony. It ceased. The fiery points had now almost reached my eyelids. I felt sick unto death. The torture was reaching that point at which the last reserve of human vigour is exhausted, and I knew that my strength would succumb under the last and greatest torture—that a merciful insensibility would save me from an anguish beyond mortal endurance.

As this thought—grateful as that of death to the dying—crossed my mind, I heard again the strange sound of which I have spoken. But it was louder, more definite—and I could no longer fancy it within my ears. It was a low, ominous rumbling—a sinister murmur, which seemed to arise from the very bowels of the earth. At the same moment I felt a peculiar, tremulous motion. The cause of these things I could not divine. I glanced at my torturer; I saw on his face a look of amazement, in his eyes a glance of fear. And then the sound came again, still more accentuated; again the singular tremor was felt, this time much more pronounced.

Kasima cast one wild glance around, and then rushed away. At that supreme moment a merciful cloud swept before the sun; and as, conquered by pain, I sank into unconsciousness, I felt the earth convulsed beneath me, I heard sounds as of deepest thunder, in which were mingled distant cries, the crash of falling timbers, and the rush of a terrified populace.

My next memories are of a comfortable room, a soft bed, the kindly face of my friend Elliston bending over me with deep commiseration, and the murmur of hushed and sympathetic voices. I had been rescued from the ruins of Kusima's house. An earthquake had intervened in my behalf. The body of my fiendish tormentor was found among the ruins of the den. He had been crushed to death by a falling beam.

VANSTEIN

"And horror, the soul of the plot!"

—Poe.

The sensation created by the tragic death of Edgar Vanstein, not merely in his own little world of intense friendships, but among the populace also, had reached its culminating point and subsided gradually into a settled wonderment before I had become aware even of its existence or conscious of the interest centred in myself. And it is not singular, perhaps, that this should be so, borne down as I was by the almost intolerable burden of sorrow and despair which the event itself occasioned. I now feel, however, how great must have been the amazement of all.

It is not, nevertheless, to satisfy the mere popular curiosity that I pen these remembrances of the noble but peculiarly unfortunate being whom it was at once my happiness and my despair to love with an intensity of passion and devotion for which I can find no adequate expression—it is not, I say, for the satisfaction of these people that I am about to disclose the few simple facts connected with the history of Edgar Vanstein. These pages are intended for the perusal of his friends alone, and the general public will, perhaps, remain for ever in ignorance of the terrible circumstance which was the chief, though not the immediate, cause of his melancholy death.

I feel—I know—that my own end rapidly approaches; therefore, it behoves me, perhaps, to break the silence I would willingly have preserved. It is necessary, my friends tell me, to vindicate the character of Vanstein if I can, and, above all, to refute the widely entertained supposition that remorse for some fearful crime committed during his absence in the East was the real cause of his mysterious suicide.

It has not been fear of misconstruction or censure, nor dread of notoriety, which has hitherto prevented me from confiding my secret to the dearest of my friends, or even from making it public, for, in the desolation of my heart, all such considerations have been lost sight of, and are matters of indifference to me. The real reason of my silence lies in the very depth of my grief and despair, which has precluded all thought of seeking the sympathy of my fellow-creatures, for such would not only be distasteful to me, and a bitter mockery, but—if possible—would increase the intensity of my pain. I know that relief is nearly always sought and gained by confiding our heart-wounds and their causes to a dear and tender friend; but there are some sorrows that cannot be thus told—that cannot be assuaged in any degree by the sincerest of human sympathy—and mine is of that order. But, now, because I know the shadow of death is upon me, I raise the veil of mystery which has for so many months enshrouded the real Vanstein—the noble, self-sacrificing, but, ah! how unutterably ill-fated being, whose spirit, in taking flight, bore with it my last hopes of happiness on earth.

We were children together, but my memory of our earliest years is merged in the grey shadow of dim, feeble, vague, indistinct rec-ollections, above which ever rises the figure of the boy Vanstein, always noble, always admirable to my childish apprehension.

The estates of our families being contiguous, and our parents living on terms of the closest intimacy, we were thrown very much into each other's companionship, and a certain easy familiarity, of brother and sister, was naturally engendered by our childish inter-course. The only unhappiness I can now recall as pertaining to my early girlhood was that brought about by the inevitable preference of Vanstein for companions of his own sex. I remember more than once weeping bitterly in secret because the young Edgar repeatedly discarded my society for that of my brother.

Edgar was an only child; I am the youngest of three. My brother and sister, being several years older than I, had, of course, different and more advanced tastes and predilections. My temperament, too, had very little in common with theirs, or, indeed, with any-one's save that of Edgar Vanstein. In my studies—in the develop-ment of my faculties—I was strangely slow and backward, and an unconquerable love of reverie and solitude shut me out from all companionship except that of my boyish friend, who, at certain times, was similarly addicted.

It was rather, I think, an invincible distaste for study—and, indeed, for anything in the form of a task—than actual incapacity to learn which retarded my educational progress; but it is not the less a fact that the two first lustra of my life had passed before I could even read. Then, however, I astonished my preceptors by the speed with which I mastered the various branches of elementary knowledge. Still, the quaint simplicity of my mind—of my habit of thought—and of expression, did not leave me; and at the age of fifteen I was regarded with the same feelings of unsympathetic wonderment which I had inspired from my earliest days; I was yet spoken, and doubtless thought of, as "that strange child, Lucille."

At this age, however, I began to emerge a little from the visionary and fantastic world with which I had, with a peculiar perverseness, surrounded myself. External things now began to assume, in my eyes, a different and more natural aspect; I contemplated those around me more as real beings of the earth, earthy, than as the abstractions of such beings; for I had hitherto been wont to regard all people, myself especially, as possessing attributes of an unreal—of a weird and fantastic character. It is not my present purpose, however, to attempt any analysis of such an abnormal, though not altogether unparalleled, condition of mind; I have mentioned it at all merely because it has ever been an inseparable memory of my solitary girlhood—a strange, haunting reminiscence of an epoch of my life which I cannot now regard, unhappy as I am, without feelings of the most intense interest and wonder.

It was at this period, however—that is to say, when in my sixteenth year—that I experienced the first great joy, and the first great sorrow, of my life.

Edgar Vanstein was then about twenty. Our companionship had been broken only by the necessities of education; and he had now become, I thought, more fond of my society than in our early childhood. For my own part, I never even sought to hide my admiration of him, nor the happiness I experienced in being near him and in listening to his conversation. Scarcely a day passed at this period without our seeing each other. Sometimes we rode, and drove, and boated; but more usually we wandered, like children, through the woods and by the streams of the two estates, discussing and dilating upon the subjects dearest to us—poetry, romance, art, music, nature.

It was with an indefinable feeling of uneasiness that I listened to Edgar's enthusiastic expressions of an ardent desire to see the world—to travel in the far-off lands of which we had so often read together. For hours he would dilate upon this theme, while I listened in silent abstraction, not altogether free from pain. I felt that I would perhaps lose the only companion whose sympathies were identical with my own; but it was not this in itself which created in my heart the vague anguish, the sense of impending sorrow, that dwelt there. Could I have looked into my soul at that time, I would have perhaps seen that my friendship for Vanstein was already merging into love—but of this I thought not then.

Suddenly Edgar's only living parent, his father, became ill, and we were, for a little time, almost entirely separated. The patient rapidly grew worse, and at length died. Edgar was now left alone in the world, for he had no other near relatives. Between the father and son there had been but little in common, and the grief of the latter was not enduring. Still, the sense of his loneliness weighed on his mind, and one day, as we stood gazing dreamily upon a stream that skirted his domain, he told me he had decided to carry into effect the project he had so long contemplated, and that I should in all probability not see him again for some years.

I said nothing; a deep shadow seemed to have fallen on all things even as he spoke—and a sense of depression heavier than I had felt at any time before came upon my heart; but I made no reply, for the nature of the feelings within me was still vague and indefinite, and altogether beyond the power of lucid expression.

He noticed what seemed my abstraction, and said—

"Are you listening, Lucille?"

"Yes," I replied; "You—you are going away. When?"

"In a week from to-day I shall leave for the East. Of course, we shall correspond?"

"Yes."

Silence fell between us; this was by no means unusual, for we had often wandered slowly on for hours without speaking a word; but now the silence was painful and awkward—on my side at least. I felt that I ought to say something—to express regret at his approaching departure, or interest regarding the particular direction of his travels. But no word passed my lips for some minutes.

"I shall be sorry to leave the dear, old place—and—and you, Lucille," he said; and then he added, with slight sigh, "Ah, if we could only go together!"

I glanced up quickly, though I knew not why I did so; but he was not looking at me. He seemed to be contemplating, in anticipation, the scenes of his future wanderings.

"But, of course," he resumed, with a short, quick laugh, "that's out of the question."

There was an irrepressible yearning in my heart which seemed to cry No! But, then, as before, I did not, and could not speak.

We met twice ere he departed. On both occasions his mind seemed divided between exulting expectation as he thought of his travels, and the natural regret at leaving his home and friends.

He departed; and it was not until I felt that he was really gone that I saw, as it were, my heart unveiled before me. I knew then that I loved him—loved him with all the wild passion of my nature, all the *abandon* which the solitary and unique existence I had lived had engendered within me. That in his own heart dwelt only friendship—sincere, devoted, ardent, but still friendship only—I knew too well, but it caused no alteration in my own sentiments. I loved the more, the more hopeless seemed my passion. But on this I cannot bear to dilate. Let me say only that during the two years which intervened between his departure and his return, my soul was for ever absorbed by this one sad theme—everything reminded me of him—every tree, every meadow, every little path, every clear, silent stream, and, above all, every line in the books we had read together.

It happened at this time that reverses befell my father, so that we became comparatively poor, and though we still dwelt in the old ancestral mansion, we lived alone, receiving few visits and making none. Thus I resumed my solitary life, and remained buried in dreams—dreams that were as fanciful as those of my childhood, but never in any degree pleasurable. My mother had died in my infancy; my sister loved society and pined in her enforced seclusion, until, by her marriage, she gained access to the life she loved;

my brother degenerated into a mere country squire, and I seldom spoke to or even saw him, though he had always been kinder and more considerate towards me than the others. As for my father, he remained brooding over his fallen fortunes and his wine until death came to end his disappointments. I cannot tell why, but his demise gave me relief rather than otherwise. Not that I had never loved him, or had really any reason to be glad that he was dead, but, with a strange spirit of perverseness, I tortured my heart into a belief that I could not possibly feel any sorrow for the event that left me almost alone in the world.

During the first of these two years I had received, at irregular intervals, letters from Edgar Vanstein recording some of his experiences and thoughts during his travels. I could never divest my mind of the idea that these missives were written in a tone of sadness altogether at variance with the nature of the occurrences they described, or even of the reflections they embodied. Yet it may have been simply that my own melancholy tinged them with a gloomy hue. My answers were, however I might try to avoid it, peculiarly cold and constrained; and so painfully was I sensible of this that I often re-wrote them in the vain hope of imparting to their contents a more genial, familiar, or "natural" air.

The last epistle I received from Vanstein was dated at the Indian city of Benares, upon the holy river. It detailed, with all the youthful enthusiasm of the writer's nature, an exciting event in which he had played a prominent part. A house in one of the suburbs of the city had caught fire, and he, at the imminent peril of his life, had succeeded in rescuing several of the inmates. This letter, as I have said, was the last I received from Edgar during his absence, although it was written nearly eighteen months prior to his return. I answered it, but received no reply, and a sense of pride and mortification prevented me from writing any more.

Some six months after the death of my father I saw once again the man whose image had never faded from my heart, though his absence seemed to have extended over ages of time.

We met in a large, gloomy room of the old house wherein I was born.

Could I live to extremest age I should never forget that meeting. Yet there were no strongly-coloured circumstances—at least in the ordinary sense—connected with it which might be calculated to leave a definite impression upon the memory. I know that, in the midst of my joy in seeing him once more, I shuddered and turned pale as I looked into his eyes. But not for worlds could I tell what that was which created in my heart so terrible a sensation of vague and ambiguous horror. What—ah! what *could* it be? A certain bias of mind had always imparted to his countenance an appearance of indefinable but by no means unpleasing melancholy. But now there was something more—much more—than this; but what—what was it?

We stood in silence. An immense antique clock stood in a corner of the room, and its measured tick seemed, like my own excited soul, to ask continually—*"What was it?"*

Unable to utter a syllable because of the strange awe that oppressed me, I involuntarily riveted my eyes upon his face, as if to seek there that inexplicable something which had so vaguely appalled me. I scanned the large, hazel-grey eyes. I regarded the broad, placid brow, the solidly-cut nose, the fine mouth that slightly smiled, and the nobly-rounded chin; and in all these I seemed to find the strange expression of which I have spoken. And in the tones of his voice, far more even than in his eyes, I was made aware of its existence.

"I have come home, you see," he said. "Do you find me changed?"

"Yes," I replied, almost in a whisper.

"Ah, I am . . . and so are you. You are quite a stately lady now, Lucille—more beautiful than even I ever thought you would become."

"But you—you, Edgar! What—what——"

I could say no more. How, indeed, could I attempt to express the inexpressible, or give words to that which could not even be distinctly thought? But, as he saw my looks, he started violently and averted his eyes. I felt the necessity for saying something to relieve our mutual embarrassment, and asked, falteringly—

"Are you going to stay at home?"

"No, no!" he said, while a still stranger expression diffused itself over his features. "I—I shall stay but a little while here, and then—then leave England for ever."

"For ever?"

"Yes—for ever. I shall die in the East."

It were vain to attempt to embody in words any idea of the peculiar infection of mingled gloom and resignation which accompanied his utterance of that sentence—"I shall die in the East;" and equally vain would it be to tell of the vague and irrelevant fancies which rushed tumultuously through my agitated brain as I listened.

"What—what do you mean?" I faltered.

"I mean—of course I mean that I shall make the East my home for the rest of my life, Lucille. But let us talk of other things."

We did so; but ere long the conversation flagged and became painful and constrained, and soon Vanstein took his leave. As we parted I thought he looked into my eyes with an uneasy, inquiring expression, as though he sought the confirmation of some idea, or the removal of some doubt.

I did not see him again for some days. On the occasion of our next meeting he assumed a kind of nervous gaiety which rather accentuated than concealed the gloom beneath. He avoided, for some time, all allusion to his approaching return to the scenes of his travels. But at length I spoke of it, impelled by the pain at my heart, not less than by an insatiable desire to penetrate the vague mystery which seemed to surround him.

"Yes, I am certainly going," he said; "I have returned only to look for the last time upon my old home, and to relinquish all my landed property to relatives; I shall retain, in fact, simply a small annuity—sufficient for a life of indolence somewhere in the East."

"But why—why——"

"You are my dearest friend, Lucille," he said, sadly, "and I shall confide to you as much as I dare. The whole truth—the real reason for my retirement from the world—is a secret I must bear to the tomb. My life, as far as regards the hopes, the enjoyment, the ambitions of men, is over, for these can never be mine. At one blow the common aspirations of humanity have been struck down before me. Henceforth the occupation of my existence must be to dwell alone, and, far from populous cities, to dream away the hours, the days, the years, until death shall transport me to a land of real dreams, where even I may be at rest."

I knew not what to reply to these strange words; but he seemed to expect no answer, for he turned away as if oppressed by his own thoughts or emotions. The tone in which he had spoken was one of unutterable melancholy and despair, and I felt moved to tears by it more than by the words themselves. I now remembered his last letter, so full of life and enthusiasm, and then recalled the fact that he had not written since. A feeling of something akin to horror prevented me from making any mention of this circumstance to Vanstein. I turned aside, trying to restrain the tears that fell from my eyes, and half wondering why I wept. When I looked up I found that he was gazing attentively at me with a puzzled expression in his eyes—an expression, I thought, not altogether free from a nameless dread of something ill.

"Edgar," I said, at length, "whatever has happened to change you thus, you are wrong in refusing to confide all, if not to me, at least to someone on whose advice you could rely. My brother——"

"'Twould be useless," he interrupted. "If any good could come of it, I should not, perhaps, hesitate, but—I have decided on my course of action, Lucille."

"It cannot be that you—that is—that——"

"You would ask me if my misery springs from remorse—if I have committed some crime?"

"Yes—forgive me; I know it cannot be that."

"You are right, Lucille; it is not."

"And you will confide in no one?—not even in me?" I murmured, with an intensity of yearning in my heart.

"No—no!" he said, with a shudder. "You would pity me, perhaps, but it would be a pity far more intolerable to me than your hatred or your scorn."

"Oh, Edgar, you know me better—you *must* know me better than that!" I cried, wildly; and then all the long pent-up emotions of my heart burst forth in a flood of tears, which I sought not to restrain nor even to conceal.

He neither moved nor spoke, but when I had recovered I looked up and was startled to perceive that he was deadly pale, and that his eyes were dilated with horror. He seemed to have just conceived some thought—some idea which filled him with a ghastly dread.

"Tell me," he exclaimed, in an intensely agitated voice—"tell me, Lucille, is it that—oh, God!—*is* it that you love me?"

"Yes—yes!" I cried, impulsively; "but why—oh! *why* should I not?"

He was silent. The shadow of a mirthless smile flitted over his pale lips, but he was silent.

"You have never loved me, I know," I continued, in a calmer voice; "and perhaps it is another's love or another's perfidy which has caused——"

"You are wrong," he murmured, in a voice so faint that I could scarcely hear it. "It were best, perhaps, that you should believe so, but you are wrong, Lucille. When I told you that the object of my return was only to see my home I lied. It was—it was to see *you*—to look once more on your sweet face—to hear your voice again. Yes, I love you—I have always loved you—God help me!"

"You love me—you love me," I faltered, for his tones were so unspeakably hopeless that my joy at finding my affection returned was all changed to a hideous fear—a ghastly terror. "You love me," I said. "Why, then, did you go away? Why did you ever leave me?"

"Ah, why—why?" he murmured, dreamily. "Listen, Lucille," he resumed, after a pause. "It was only after I had left England that the full consciousness that I loved you came upon me. The passion had been awakened within my heart so gradually, so insensibly, and I have never been given to analysing my sensations. I could not tell—and then—you were so cold at parting."

"Cold—cold!" I cried, in agony. "No! my heart was breaking. It was—oh, Edgar, forgive me!—it was my pride. I thought you cared so little for me——"

"Lucille," he said, "I would die a thousand deaths rather than you should suffer! Ah, what fiend directed my steps to that accursed city? And why—*why* did I ever think of returning here? Oh! it is horrible to reflect that——"

I approached him.

"You will not," I said—"you will not refuse *now* to tell me all; you will not shut me out from your heart *now!* whatever your sorrow, I will share it—it is my right; I *demand* to know the cause of your unhappiness!"

"You demand to know," he repeated, wearily. "Well, perhaps it were best. It may help you to forget me—to cease to love me."

"Never, oh, never!"

"When you know all, your love will be merged into pity, per-haps—that is the most I can hope for. But I cannot—it is impossible that I can tell you with my own lips. I will write, on the eve of my departure, I will write, Lucille."

"No, no! Tell me now—it cannot possibly be worse than your words have led me to anticipate; its horror *must* fall short of that which fills my heart; it *cannot* be so horrible as the vague terror which consumes me!"

"Nevertheless, I must write it, Lucille. We had better part now—and for ever. Your love is the sweetest, but yet the most painful memory I shall bear to the grave. We must part now; lingering can only increase our anguish."

I bowed my head as beneath a blow. But just then a little ray of light entered my darkened brain; "All is not lost," I reflected, "we may be happy yet."

"Good-bye, Lucille," he said. I wished to throw myself into his embrace, but he held me aloof, while a strong shudder convulsed his frame.

But I cannot bear to dilate on the agonies of our parting. I heard him murmur the word "Farewell;" I sank down in a half swoon; when I raised my eyes again he was gone.

That night I did not close my eyes. A dreamy stupor, wherein the senses were partially awake while the power of thought remained supine, oppressed me until the succeeding day was far advanced.

At the closing in of night a messenger from Edgar Vanstein brought me the following missive:—

"Dearest Lucille,—I now redeem my promise. You will perhaps remember the last letter I wrote you, in which I described a fire in the outskirts of the City of Benares. That letter was written while I was still in ignorance of the fearful misfortune which had already befallen me. The burning house from which I rescued four or five miserable wretches was a leper hospital. The unfortunates I dragged from the gloomy rooms were all leper patients in an advanced stage of that hideous disease. I was warned of my peril, but in the mad fervour, the delirious excitement of the moment, I disregarded all advice, and, indeed, thought of it but little, even after the excitation of the event had completely subsided. Scarcely a month had elapsed, however, when a French physician, with whom

I had become intimately acquainted, discovered the terrible truth—that I was infected with the awful disease—that I was, in dreadful fact, a leper! He did not conceal from me that there was not the slightest hope of a cure; the only consolation he could afford was that for some years the disease would be scarcely manifest, even to myself—that, by aid of strict hygienic rules, and the use of certain palliatives known only to himself and a few others who had made leprosy the study of their lives, I might, for a great length of time, if so I wished, conceal my true state from all, and move among uninfected people with little or no danger to them, the disease being, his experience had told him, contagious only in its more advanced stages. I resolved, however, when the first agony of my despair had worn off, to isolate myself—to live in utter seclusion for the rest of my existence. In pursuance of this design I purchased a house at some distance from the city—a house near the magnificent Ganges, and surrounded with beautiful gardens. I filled it with everything that could in any way interest me or distract my thoughts; and the many friends I had made in the city insisted on visiting me from time to time in order to cheer me and relieve my weariness. The French doctor took a special interest in me, and scarcely a day passed without my seeing him, and we revolved many plans for the improvement of the condition of those afflicted with the disease. But an irresistible desire to see my old home again—above all, a desperate yearning to look upon and speak with *you* once more—at length decided me, with the concurrence of the doctor, who knew all, to visit England for a brief time, returning as soon as possible to my new home upon the holy river.

"So, my dear Lucille, you know my secret. The most I can hope is that you will not loathe me—that you will, perhaps, pity me, for the terrible days which, in the future, will inevitably be mine. Think sometimes, if you can, with kindness of one whose happiness and whose despair is to love you as man has seldom loved. Farewell—forever.

"Edgar."

As I made an end of the perusal of the letter, it fluttered to the floor. But of my thoughts or sensations it would be the uttermost of folly to attempt a description. My action only let me record.

The night had fallen. I heard the bell of the clock strike the hour of eight. The sound seemed to come from the remotest ends of the earth.

I hurried to the stables; a groom, by my order, saddled a favourite pony. I mounted and urged him onward, at a delirious, breakneck pace towards the house of Vanstein.

I found myself within the gloomy hall. He stood before me.

With an hysterical, yet intensely passionate cry, I threw myself into his arms. Then all was blank—I had swooned.

When I recovered we were in a small apartment of the northern wing. I lay on an ottoman; Edgar Vanstein was seated near.

I arose. I was calm; it seemed to me that there could not be the slightest fever, or even agitation, within my brain. Yet my voice sounded strange.

"I have come," I said. "We will go together; we will dwell with each other in our Indian home, we will forget all—and be happy—"

"Lucille!" he cried, in a tremulous tone. "Lucille! This is madness."

"Yes! Well, let us be mad, if so we may be happy. Tell me, Edgar—when do we go?"

"My poor girl," he murmured, "you are delirious—the horror of this thing has unhinged your mind. You must——"

"Edgar," I said, in as calm and natural a tone as I could assume. "Edgar, you *know* that it is not so. But let me speak plainly and clearly, so as to convince you that I am not distraught. I ask you—I implore you—I *demand* of you by all you hold sacred—by *our love*—to take me with you! If you refuse, I shall go mad indeed."

As I spoke, a light like a ray from the highest heavens dispersed the clouds that had darkened his face—a light of love and gratitude ineffable.

"Ah!" I cried, in rapture; I knew you would not—I knew you *could* not deny me what I ask. When shall we go—to-morrow?"

"Yes," he murmured, with a strange smile—"we will go to-morrow. But you must return home now, my darling Lucille; we shall meet again."

"No—let me stay! We must not part at all."

"But this is folly, dearest. Besides, you—you must have preparations to make. To-morrow, then——"

"Yes, yes! But tell me, Edgar—did you really believe I could desert you, just—just because of *that*?"

"Forgive me, my darling. You can never know how happy you have made me. But I might have known. However, you must go at once—it is late; I will ride with you—come."

We rode to my home. At the threshold we exchanged a last lingering embrace, and then we parted—for ever on earth.

In the morning I arose, feverish and weak, yet with a strange exaltation of mind and heart.

I hastened to my lover's house. All seemed buried in silence and gloom, and a deadly chill ran through my frame, though I was burning with fever. I rushed to his favourite chamber—a study. He was there.

He lay stretched on an ottoman, asleep. Asleep?—There was a strange, subtle odour in the air—an odour that seemed familiar to my perceptions; but for some moments a dreamy abstraction—a kind of *interregnum* in thought—prevented my reason from at once arriving at the truth. Soon, however, the truth wrested its way into my mind, and then I knew—then I could doubt no longer—that the odour came from an open phial beside the ottoman—a phial still containing a few drops of *laudanum*.

For a moment I staggered, lost in horror. Then I threw myself hurriedly down beside the yet breathing form of my beloved. His eyes, bright with the prophecy of death, turned for an instant towards mine; his lips parted in a slight smile; and his last breath whispered the syllables of my name.

Then my heart stood still and my brain reeled; there came upon me a sensation (if such it can be called) as of a wild rushing descent into the depths of chaos; then darkness and nothingness reigned over all.

My swoon had been so sudden that I had not perceived a note that lay in Vanstein's hand. And not for many days did I know even of its existence. It is almost unnecessary to give the contents of that paper here, since it has been published in all accounts of the judicial proceedings that followed. Nevertheless, it will serve to complete my narrative:—

"Dearest Lucille,—Throughout the long and weary night I have reflected—I have endeavoured to stifle in my mind the voice of duty—to persuade myself that we might really be happy, as you think; but in vain. To accept such devotion as yours would be but to make myself an object for the contempt and loathing of all men—of myself more than any. Forgive me—oh, forgive me, Lucille! I die blessing and loving you.

"EDGAR VANSTEIN."

★   ★   ★   ★   ★

These pages will be given over to my friends when I am dead—And by the mist that floats ever before my eyes; by the veins on my forehead that throb tumultuously with the gentlest emotion; by the semi-transparency of these emaciated hands; by a strange languor of both mind and body, I know that even now the cold finger of death is resting on my bosom—that the faint vital spark that holds eternity aloof is flickering low and fading fast away, soon to be swallowed up forever in the thick darkness of oblivion.—Be it so.

MERVALE ABBEY

S aving the cold realities of misery, there is, perhaps, nothing more pathetic to contemplate than the inscriptions on the wall of an ancient prison cell. The unhappy wretch, pining away in the obscurity, with no companion but Despair, is aghast at the thought of quitting the world utterly forgotten and unknown. He feels that he *must* leave some record of his identity, some hint of his sad story—the thought of sinking into the great black gulf of oblivion without creating even a ripple on its stagnant surge is intolerable. Hence the writings on the wall.

Something of this thought is upon me now. My soul, imprisoned "in a body like a grave," pining in its solitude, yearns like the captive in his cell to give some expression to its sorrow.

It may, then, be indeed something akin to the pathetic egotism of the solitary which impels me, at this late day, to reveal the simple story of my life. I have survived all who ever had any knowledge of the circumstances I am about to relate; and now, feeling that my end is, perhaps, very near, it seems meet that the truth be told.

The estate of Verehurst, my father's property, was contiguous to that of Mervale Abbey. Little trace of it now remains. It has long since been parcelled out into a number of petty villas, "country seats" of successful tradesmen, and cottages. From my earliest years, under the cloud of misfortune that hung over our house, I lived a life of isolation and gloom; my mother continually, as it seemed, hovering on the confines of the grave—my father's exist-ence embittered by the criminal extravagance and profligacy of his only son, which had so involved the estate as to leave no hope of its ever stemming the tide of adversity. No smile, no kindly word, no sympathy for the child who grew up almost unnoticed in the care of her nurse. But it would be cruel to blame them; the one, intense and unremitted physical suffering confined almost continu-ally to a sick-room; the other, loss of fortune, loss of hope wherein hope had been most passionately centred, rendered a misanthrope, morose, silent, and forbidding.

I remained at home. Neither parent gave a thought to my education, and friends we had none. My nurse was not ignorant, and between her and the musty volumes of the old library I acquired a strangely ill-assorted gathering of scraps of knowledge. From an old German lady who lived in the village I learned the rudiments of music, and, as I soon developed an unusual talent for the art, the hours spent at the piano greatly outweighed those occupied by other learning. I could analyse the most intricate harmonies long before I had mastered the "rule of three," or knew how to conjugate a verb. A discord in music I could easily detect; not so the simplest blunder in a sentence. Lindley Murray was neglected for Bach.

But for music, my girlhood had been as dreary as the grave. How many were the hours I spent—far away from my mother's sick-room and my father's study—dreaming over the subtle beauties of Mozart, awed by the solemn grandeur of Handel, thrilled with the tempestuous energy of Beethoven! What names more revered than these? True that I found delight in the poets, but the inarticulate poetry of music was to me infinitely more divine than the articulate music of poetry.

But the time came when music and dreams ceased wholly to suffice. I longed for something more—though I knew not what. However, these undefined longings vanished with the attainment of their unknown object. I had pined—as any young girl in my position must have done—for human sympathy, for someone to love. Due allowance being made for poetical exaltation, I might compare myself to Shelley's

> Highborn maiden
> In a palace tower,
> Soothing her love-laden
> Soul in secret hour
> With music sweet as love which overflows her bower.

My days were not all spent at the piano; many times I wandered among the old woods around Verehurst, or read by a small, silent stream which divided our land from that of Mervale Abbey. It was on one of these occasions that my first meeting with Gerald Hawthorne occurred. I had seen him once before, under very different conditions. *Then* he was dashing along, at a reckless, neck-or-nothing pace, on a splendid hunter, following the hounds. Now he held a fishing rod in one hand and a book of poems in the other. The two things he most dearly loved, as I afterwards found, were extreme excitation and extreme quietude. He was a dreamer, capable of infinite energy and passion.

I forget what trivial incident led to our friendship, it is so long ago. The meeting itself is involved in the grey shadow of distant remembrance. But we met, and our friendship grew apace. Our meetings were perforce unknown to our respective parents, who had long been at war with each other. My father had, in his moroseness, put insults upon the father of Gerald which could never be forgotten.

Time passed on, and what was boy-and-girl friendship ripened into love. We met more frequently, and Gerald began to speak to me of marriage. The feud between our parents, not less than the impoverishment of Verehurst, seemed an inseparable bar. On the one hand, to give his daughter's hand to a Hawthorne were more than my poor father's pride could bear; on the other, the master of Mervale Abbey had set his heart on Gerald's alliance with an heiress—and in any case would never consent to his so marrying the portionless daughter of a ruined enemy. Gerald often urged on me an elopement, or a secret marriage; but to this I would not listen, seeing clearly enough the misery, perhaps disaster, that might ensue.

Then came the first of a series of dire misfortunes that came upon us both, almost without intermission. This was my mother's long-expected death. My grief was greater than it might otherwise have been, for she had latterly much altered in her attitude towards me—as though a sense of her approaching demise impelled her to seek her long-neglected daughter's sympathy and love. Just as I was beginning, then, to feel that I really had a mother, she died. I cannot say whether my father was much affected; I know only that I saw less of him than ever now, and that the few servants who remained to us spoke of him as "fast breaking up."

My mother's death was followed by an event altogether unlooked for. Mr. Hawthorne contracted a serious illness—the result, it was said, of an accident while hunting. In a few short weeks he died, and Gerald became the master of Mervale Abbey.

Following close upon the death of Mr. Hawthorne came the climax of my father's misfortunes—the foreclosure, long threatened, of the mortgages on the Verehurst estate. My father was now utterly ruined. His son was far away, on the plains of the new world, a penniless adventurer. The only person who would have helped us keep Verehurst together—Gerald Hawthorne—was the last of whom my poor father's pride could accept a farthing.

Alas! what misfortunes were crowded into those two fleeting months!

> When sorrows come, they come not single spies,
> But in battalions.

The dismemberment of Verehurst was too much for its last owner to contemplate. He died by his own hand.

By courtesy of the creditors, a small portion of the estate, with a cottage, was to be set apart for the suicide's much-pitied daughter. But something of my father's obstinate pride forbade the acceptance of this magnanimous gift.

In the respite allowed me—a respite which I was anxious to make as short as possible—I waited impatiently for a word from Gerald. It never occurred to me to doubt his love. His sudden inheritance of Mervale Abbey would, I well knew, bring no change in his plans for our future happiness. The worst I feared was his mother's probable aversion to our marriage. But from what little I knew of her, I expected that Gerald could easily win her over to his views. After all I had suffered, the thought of our happy union came over my soul like balm. The slightest suspicion of his fickleness would have been intolerable. Fortunately, my trust in him was so deep that, as I have said, nothing of the kind suggested itself. Yet I could not help growing anxious as the days passed, and he did not come. However, when my faithful old nurse told me that she had heard of some imperative business connected with the management of his estate having called him away, my fears vanished, and I again became patient—only wishing he had sent some lines to reassure me. The only letter I had ever received from him had reached me soon after my father's death, sympathising with me, and assuring me of his unaltered affection. It said nothing of our next meeting; perhaps he had thought it better to wait until I had recovered from the first bitter shock of my misfortunes.

At last a letter was brought to me. I received it with a tremulous joy; but my heart sank again as I saw that the superscription was in a strange hand—a lady's. I opened it in trembling. My many griefs had made me fearful. And this was indeed the climax of my sorrows. I must let the missive explain itself:—

"Mervale Abbey,
Friday, 16th June.

"My Dear Child,—From what I have learned of the relations that existed between you and my son, I am afraid that this letter will prove a great shock to you; unless, indeed, the sad news has already reached your ears. My poor Gerald died on Tuesday morning, after lingering in great agony through the previous night. You must forgive me for hurrying over the details. He was shooting with some gamekeepers—or inspecting the preserves, I know not which—but there was a desperate affray with poachers, in which Gerald received a dangerous wound. This might not have proved fatal, but just as he was going to fire the gun burst in his face. The injuries resulting from this terrible accident, together with the wound, left no hope of his recovery, and he succumbed as I have stated. He never regained consciousness until a few minutes before his death, when his thoughts were all of you. Your name and mine were the last he spoke. The shock of this terrible misfortune so prostrated me that some days elapsed before I could arouse myself sufficiently to communicate with you.

"And now, my dear Muriel—my almost daughter—you must come to me, as to a mother. I have heard of the wreck of your home—that Vere-hurst can no longer shelter you. But what your pride forbids you to take from strangers, you will accept from me, the desolate mother of him who would soon have been your husband. Come, then, I beg; if there be consolation left on earth for us, we shall find it in each other.

"MARGARET HAWTHORNE."

Of the effect of this blow I cannot speak. There are griefs which have no tongue—and mine was of them. Compared with this, all my other misfortunes faded into trivialities. This sorrow was the climax. It so filled my mind as well as my heart that I had no thought of anything beside. Were it otherwise I might have occupied myself with such details as the burial—the absence of any news of the catastrophe until the letter came, three days after, and other matters. The only being left me to love was dead, and despair filled his place in my heart.

The letter remained unanswered—the offer it contained forgotten. I was plunged, for I know not how long, in a sort of stupor, seeing no one save the faithful old nurse, and never more than half conscious even of her presence. At length I was partially aroused by the noise of a carriage. A moment later a pale, sad, sweet-faced lady appeared before me. She was Gerald's mother.

"I have come for you, my child," she said, in gentle tones. Then I vaguely remembered the letter, and murmured an apology for not having replied.

"You must return with me, Muriel," she said. "Share with me the home which should have been yours. Henceforth you are my daughter."

I suffered the nurse to dress me for the journey. Grateful as I felt, I could not express my gratitude then. She seemed to understand, however; and when I was ready we entered the carriage. In an hour we were within the walls of Mervale Abbey. We had spoken little on the way. Our grief was still too poignant for words.

Mrs. Hawthorne herself showed me the rooms which had been set apart for my use. They were bowers of luxury and taste—far different, indeed, from the dusty, decayed old rooms of Verehurst. Adjoining them was a little music-room which she had prepared.

"He told me how fond you were of music," she said, with her sad smile.

This was the first time Gerald had been directly mentioned. She now told me all he had said in those few moments of consciousness which, as she had written, preceded his death. It was not much, but very dear to me. He had spoken of our love, commended me to his mother's care, and had even told her, as she said, of my passion for music.

But many, many weeks elapsed ere I made any use of the beautiful little music-room. It was only very gradually that I began to recover something of my former calm, and to take any note of things around me. Mrs. Hawthorne seemed to be suffering much, not alone from grief, but from bodily ailment also. Old Dr. Grahame was in almost continual attendance upon her. At length, however, his visits became less frequent, though they never ceased altogether. He was a very kindly old gentleman, who regarded me with great interest and sympathy on the few occasions that brought us together. By his advice I took long, solitary walks in the park—always returning by a particular route which he showed me, thus avoiding the curious eyes of the servants.

Mrs. Hawthorne and I now began to spend our afternoons in the music-room. I found that she was scarcely less fond of music than myself, and that our tastes were congenial. It may well be supposed that the saddest and most solemn compositions were those which gave us the most pleasure—if that peculiar emotion may be called pleasure which springs from a contemplation of that which suggests sorrowful reflections.

The music was interspersed with conversation, of which the subject was ever the same. At first every mention of Gerald's name was the key of tears; but in time the sharpness of our grief was replaced by the tranquillity of a sad remembrance.

I was never tired of playing, nor my companion of listening. The music selected was of that kind which is seldom played in public, being neither complex nor artificial, neither "effective" nor very difficult. But people do not go to concerts to dream. The beautiful sonatas of Mozart, certain of the more solemnly-melodious adagios and andantes of Beethoven, a few of the richest of the mysteriously-suggestive compositions of Chopin—ballades, nocturnes, and polonaises—these were among the selections which beguiled many an hour which otherwise had been filled with weariness. We loved those harmonies that were vague, ideal, dream-like; that rebus-music which pretends to elaborate extraneous ideas, to present definite images to the intellect, thus usurping the domain of poetry and painting, was never played. I thought then, as I think now, that no tangible idea which can be expressed in music is ever worthy to be so expressed—for the conveyed will always be found inferior to the vehicle; and it is a canon of art that the jewel should be of more importance than its setting.

But now a strange thing began to create uneasiness in my heart. Often while playing I felt a sensation scarcely describable. In the midst of some soft phrase a feeling would come over me that I was not alone—that, besides my companion, there was another person in the room. It was always merely momentary, and at first I thought little of it, attributing it to nervousness, or to that kind of hallucination with which every dreamer is familiar.

Once the feeling came upon me so strongly that I stopped abruptly and turned round.

"What is the matter?" asked Mrs. Hawthorne.

"I—I thought you had gone," I stammered, ashamed to confess the real cause of my uneasiness. I had been playing the beautiful first movement of that strange sonata of Beethoven's which has somehow acquired the name of "Moonlight," and now, without finishing it, I plunged at once into the tempestuous agitation of the concluding part. It seemed that thus only could I shake off the ghostly sensation which had so disturbed me.

"You must spend more of your time in the open air, Muriel," said Mrs. Hawthorne, "and retire earlier. You are growing nervous."

It happened that I had not taken much exercise of late, and had had wakeful nights; so I set down my strange agitation to the cause suggested. I endeavoured thereafter, by rigidly observing the rules of physical health, to regain something of a mental "tone."

The calm peace of my present life, the kindness of my adoptive mother, and the immunity from all petty care combined to soften the great grief which otherwise might have been too much for me. The memory of Gerald was, indeed, ever present, and at certain hours the thought of "what might have been" overwhelmed me with heavy sorrow; but I succeeded in vanquishing the demon of despair—or, at least, in holding it aloof.

But this mysterious thing I had attributed to nervousness—that would not be shaken off. It haunted me as a ghost, and though I betrayed no more uneasiness in Mrs. Hawthorne's presence, I felt it just the same. The strangest thing was that, when alone in my chamber, through the long intervals of insomnia which occasionally divided my rest, or while wandering in the vast park, the feeling never came upon me. It was only while playing some simple, dreamy melody in the little music-room, where our afternoons were almost invariably spent. Was the room haunted? Mervale Abbey was very old—quite ancient enough to have its ghost. Could it be that the spirit of some former occupant of the room still visited it unseen? This thought so fastened itself on my imagination that I felt certain that if I entered the music-room at night I should see some dim, ethereal phantom floating among the tapestries or gliding over the carpet.

The time came, however, when this strange feeling no longer caused me any uneasiness. It still seemed as weird as ever, but it had lost its fear. I even found a peculiar pleasure in it—I wondered and dreamed over it. Some author says—"It is a happiness to wonder; it is a happiness to dream." At such times as I felt that mysterious presence, it seemed that I played with more subtle delicacy—that the music carried with it a diviner tone—than might be possible under ordinary conditions.

Thus several months passed away.

Mrs. Hawthorne again became ill; or, rather, the visits of Dr. Grahame again became frequent. You will say it is the same thing. I could not, however, help wondering how it was that little or no trace of her supposed malady was ever apparent. Certainly, I could detect none. I saw clearly enough that great grief, mingled with care and anxiety, was stamped upon her face. But what could be her disease? Some insidious one, no doubt, which was eating out her vitality, and leaving as yet no trace of its ravages.

I saw her now but seldom. Once or twice, at her desire, I played some of her favorite pieces. On the last occasion, during a *pianissimo* passage, it seemed to me that I heard a sound strongly resembling a stifled sob, coming, as it were, from without, but still very near. It startled me so much that I turned abruptly towards Mrs. Hawthorne, just in time to catch a strange expression of fear in her eyes. Before I could question her she had left the room, while I remained to wonder. I resumed my playing, listening intently the while, strange fancies thronging my brain; but no repetition of the sound occurred, though the sensation that I was not alone was now even more pronounced than ever.

Becoming tired of playing, listening and wondering, I took up a book, and lay down on a couch to read. The day was very calm and drowsy. I had not read many lines when I felt a strong desire to sleep.

I made a half struggle to rouse myself, and then yielded. I remember the book slipping from my hand. My dreams were fantastic and confused. The "ghost" of my imagination flitted through all. Sometimes it took the shape of a child clad in filmy white, then it was a stately something which I could not determine. At last, however, it assumed the form of my lost love, Gerald Hawthorne, as I had last seen him. But now it was no ghost, but himself. We stood by a dim, silent stream, which he was about to cross, while I was compelled to remain till he came back for me. The moment of parting arrived. He kissed me on the brow and vanished. I heard the echo of his departing step and felt the impress of his lips as I awoke.

This dream was so intensely vivid that for some moments I could scarcely realise that it was indeed but a vision. Above all, I seemed to feel the kiss. I hurriedly left the room, fearing I knew not what.

I passed the next day alone, marvelling over the strangeness of the things I have related. I did not go near the music-room; something akin to awe prevented me. The sob I had heard or fancied, the strange look I had seen in the eyes of Mrs. Hawthorne, my vivid dream—all these weighed upon my mind, and formed material for a world of solemn and mysterious meditation. A presentiment, vague and terrible, hung over me. I seemed to be in momentary expectation of some strange event. But I had not the remotest suspicion of the dreadful surprise that Fate was preparing for me.

The night had nearly fallen, and I was still buried in reverie. Suddenly I heard a step. Mrs. Hawthorne stood beside me.

"Come," she said, solemnly.

I arose. She led me into the music-room. There she paused, and once more spoke.

"You must be brave, my dear child; a great shock awaits you. Call up all your courage."

She moved towards the wall near which the piano stood, and it appeared as though the wall opened before her. In reality she had touched a spring, and a panel had moved aside.

In another moment we stood in a small, irregular chamber, luxuriously furnished. In a bed at one end someone was lying motionless, with a sort of white mask over the face. Dr. Grahame stood near. On my entrance the occupant of the bed moved slightly. A corner of the white mask fell, revealing one of the eyes and part of the forehead. It was enough. I rushed forward with a frantic, breathless cry.

"Gerald!"

"Muriel!" he murmured.

I threw my arms about him, and snatched at the white cloth. It was securely fastened; I could only kiss his brow. Suddenly it seemed to me that his eye was becoming glazed. I shrieked; I felt an arm drawing me away—I knew no more.

In the affray with the poachers Gerald had not been killed, but his wound was mortal. It was but a question of weeks or months how far his life could be prolonged. The bursting of the gun had not caused any dangerous injury; but it had transformed his noble face into something too hideous to contemplate. The day after the accident he had decided on his course. A poacher had been killed in the affray—some wretch unknown and friendless. He was buried in place of Gerald. The latter, with his mother's solicitude and Dr. Grahame's skill, to a certain extent recovered. The wound would never close, and must soon prove fatal; in the meantime he suffered but little pain, and could end his life in peace.

As soon as this was definitely decided by the doctor, who was an eminent surgeon, Gerald told his mother of our love, and induced her to act as she had done. In the morning the unfortunate heir of Mervale Abbey looked down from his window, and saw his affianced depart on her way to the woods; he counted all the weary minutes of her absence, and again thrilled with joy to see her return. In the afternoon he listened in rapture to the beautiful music he had always loved—music which seemed far diviner now, because it was played by her whom he idolised, and to whom he was dead. For it had been Gerald's intention that I should never know the truth. He did not wish to re-open the wound in my heart; but when death was so near the desire to hear me speak to him once more could not be resisted. The doctor's visits, which had so puzzled me, were, of course, to Gerald. The strange sensation I had so continually felt was, no doubt, caused by his close proximity. And my dream was really not all a dream. Guessing that I was asleep, he had glided through the panel and kissed me while I slumbered. It was, in fact, the effort of doing this which hastened his death.

There is but little to add. An ancient vault in the old abbey received the body of Gerald. The burial was, of course, kept secret; besides ourselves, only an old servant who assisted us knew anything about it.

The poor mother survived her noble son but a few years. She died beloved by all—and by none more than me. A youth at Eton is the heir of Mervale Abbey. I am its nominal mistress. In the hearts of the people in and around the abbey my name has, I am proud to say, succeeded the beloved one of Mrs. Hawthorne. As for myself, I am content to await the time, which I feel is not now distant, when it shall please God to remove the frail barriers that separate me from my beloved.

MARGRAVE'S MASTERPIECE

The pleasant little suburb of Ravenscroft is, in regard to its inhabitants, very fashionable and exclusive; its social structure most intricate, the upper and innermost circles being exceedingly small and select, the others gradually widening in their descent to a less rarefied atmosphere.

Among the least pretentions of those dwellings, which bear about them such a solemn air of aristocratic seclusion, is a residence which, though surrounded by trees and shrubs, arranged with an eye to picturesque effect, is yet not so far back from the sidewalk but that the curious passer might discern, near the street-door, a small brass plate—or even read the legend it still bears—"Edward Margrave, Artist."

The house, and land attached, belongs to this Mr. Margrave, who holds a fairly good position in Ravenscroft society, in virtue of his possessions, and the fact of his brother being a baronet. At the time when occurred the events of which this narrative purposes to treat, Edward Margrave was a somewhat different man from what he is to-day, though but a very few years have passed. He was then gloomy and discontented. His "establishment" consisted of a gardener, a housekeeper, a "man," and a trap.

Whenever he drove up to his own gates in the last, and it happened that the legend on the door caught his eye, his lip would curl with a curious expression of contempt or impatience, and some such remark as this would escape him—"Artist! Edward Margrave, *artist!* Pshaw!"—not always *sotto voce* either. Now, had he not been Edward Margrave himself the apostrophe might very well have been interpreted as a sort of challenge of the artist's right to his title—an imputation, suggested rather than expressed, that he was *no* artist, only a *painter*, as Zanoni says of Nicot. In point of fact, this is precisely what the young man, though he apostrophised himself, really did mean.

And he was not far from being right. A man in whom vanity is abnormally developed may persuade himself that he is a genius, but one who is sincere and candid will always at least approximate the truth. Genius, too, can gauge itself better than is generally supposed. Byron, loaded with adulation, was surely not one to underrate himself, yet his words—"If people only understood Shelley, where should *I* be?"—show that he could form a pretty accurate idea of the limit of his powers.

It had more than once occurred to Margrave to erase the "artist" from his plate and put "portrait-painter" there instead—he could fairly call himself that—but it seemed to him too much like an abdication. He was not *sure* that he had no artistic genius. Had the success which always attended his efforts at portrait-painting ever crowned but *one* of his many attempts at original conception, his doubts might well have been set at rest; but *they* seemed inspired by the very genius of the commonplace.

"It is not her portrait; it is herself!" said Mrs. Eversleigh, on receiving the finished picture of her eighteen-year-old daughter.

"Surely I *am* an artist!" the painter had thought, as he put the last touches to the portrait.

And, indeed, it was, as far as a portrait can be, a work of genius. The old lady's remark did something less than justice to it; there was more than fidelity to nature in the work—a certain vague, abstract, all-pervading expression, not to be explained—even by the artist himself—which threw over it a charm that was lost on none who ever beheld it. As for the *likeness*, that was beyond all praise. What, perhaps, struck the ordinary observer most was that the work did not appear to be a portrait at all, and no one unaware of the young lady's existence could have supposed it to be other than a purely ideal conception. Everyone is familiar with that indefinable something by which we recognise a portrait—the stiff, strained, unnatural attitude that ninety-nine out of every hundred sitters think proper to assume. Here, however, the "subject" might have been totally unconscious that her portrait was being painted, so entirely natural—above all, so characteristic, were her pose and expression.

The painter's success in this regard was, undoubtedly, due in some measure to the spirit of genial *camaraderie* which existed between him and Margaret Eversleigh, and which made anything like constraint on either side impossible. For many years they had known each other—nearly all their lives, in fact. He had given her lessons, though she had no more aptitude for painting then he for music, in which art she was remarkably proficient. She was all life, light, and motion; she could never have sat, or, rather, *stood*, for her portrait, which was a "full-length" one. He painted her while she flitted about his studio, laughing and chattering as she turned over numberless sketches of projected masterpieces. With such form as hers every attitude was inevitably full of a lithe, subtle, unconscious grace. Now and then she would be still for a second or two, as a little interval of reverie divided her laughter and merriment, softening and subduing the light that seemed to cling around her like an irradiation. He liked her best thus, and let none of these moments escape his eye, and it was in such a pose that he painted her.

Margaret had much more of this facile grace than of beauty. She was—at least, while a girl—by no means so stately as her name. The artist called her "Airy, fairy Lillian." Her face, without possessing one feature above criticism, except, perhaps, the eyes, yet gave the effect of beauty. It was not really beautiful, but it seemed to disdain classical perfection—to be in no need of regularity.

Whatever its faults, it was a face admirably adapted for breaking young men's hearts, and Philip Waltran, whom many mammas with grown-up daughters "on their hands" did especially favour, on account of his wealth, family, and distinguished appearance, was in a state of much uneasiness. In early youth he had nearly been decoyed into a marriage with a most notorious adventuress, and had since cicatrised his heart wounds by a pronounced cynicism on all matters pertaining to Hymen. He now felt himself succumbing to the power unconsciously wielded by this simple girl of eighteen; but it was not the smiles with which he knew the announcement of his marriage would be received among his acquaintance that caused the uneasiness he felt, for he possessed that rare gift, a mind ridicule proof. His first love affair having ended disastrously, he had decided that in some object of unceasing pursuit alone could he find his happiness. He distrusted love. The painful truth of Shelley had assumed an undue importance in his mind—

When hearts have once mingled,
  Love first leaves the well-built nest;
The weak one is singled
  To endure what it once possessed.

His own heart might not, perhaps, prove the "weak one," but there would be suffering in any case. Besides, he had found, he thought, the object in the pursuit of which his real happiness was to be attained.

Philip Waltran was a being of no common order. At the age of thirty travel and intercourse with the world had enlarged his naturally high intellect. An inveterate habit of self-anatomy enabled him to analyse the minds of others even better than his own. He had a very extensive acquaintance, but his friends were few. Those who failed to comprehend him he understood but too well. As time passed he withdrew more and more into himself, and his "eccentricity" became proverbial. It was said that he lost himself in the study of certain abstruse sciences—one especially, in which, as it was rumoured, he had, in conjunction with some mysterious associate, opened up vistas of surprising interest.

However, the time came when Waltran saw plainly that his intellect, character, and philosophy were no safeguards against the common fate of man. He loved Margaret Eversleigh.

Added to his natural aversion to marriage was the fact, patent to his discerning eyes, that the young lady by no means reciprocated his affection. Thus it was that he hesitated longer than might have been expected in a man of his decision. But, at length, he resolved to lay siege to the young lady's heart without delay. They were on easy terms; Mrs. Eversleigh had done all in her power to encourage their friendship, in the hope of its ripening into love.

Edward Margrave was not unknown to Waltran, who took some degree of interest in the discontented portrait-painter, mainly on account of the latter's candour and sincerity with respect to his art. Waltran had easily come to a conclusion on the subject which caused Margrave so much dissatisfaction and bitterness. He knew that the young portrait-painter really possessed a certain order of genius—an intense aptitude for *imitation*. In his own domain, reproduction of what he saw, he need fear no rivalry; but out of this field he would do well not to venture. Unfortunately, it was in creation—original conception—and in that only, that the young painter desired to excel.

When Waltran saw the portrait of Margaret he was not a little surprised—more astonished, perhaps, than pleased. He knew well enough the spirit of goodfellowship that subsisted between Margaret and the painter, and he knew, or divined, how imperceptible the transition might be from one kind of intimacy to another. The picture was so far in advance of Margrave's previous achievements that it suggested to Waltran the probability of the artist being indebted for his success to some such inspirational excitement as love might induce.

"And Margrave," he said to her, as he stood contemplating the picture; "is he still the same?—still dissatisfied as ever with his prospects of future greatness?"

"Indeed, yes," she answered, lightly, yet with a shade of sadness. "I can't make him out at all; but I suppose it's the nature of men of genius to be discontented, is it not? Always aspiring to something beyond their reach."

"Yes, it certainly seems so," he answered, somewhat reassured; "but Margrave's would appear to be an extreme case. His morbid desire to attain greatness is rapidly growing into a sort of monomania, it seems to me."

"Indeed, I think you may be right," she said, in a much more serious tone. "I used to consider him foolish, and had no patience with him; but now, would it not be delightful," she said, suddenly, "if one could only bring this greatness within his reach? Oh, I would give—— But that's nonsense!" And she laughed in a somewhat constrained manner.

He, ever observant, lost not a single inflection of her tone or phase of her expression. But for once his divination was at fault. It is one thing to read men's minds, and another to unlock the secrets of a woman's heart. Waltran was of a noble nature, possessed of a kind of haughty, disdainful unselfishness. He would have scorned to press his love on one whose heart was already given. But here there was nothing like certainty.

Margaret, on her side, noted his inquiring glance, veiled as it was, and felt instinctively that he was probing her soul. Something more than maiden shame armed her against succeeding attacks, and she gave Waltran no more indications of her hidden love. For she loved Margrave—loved him without hope of return; and the pride of unrequited affection made her resolve to guard her secret closely. Had her love been reciprocated, all the world might have known; but, as it was, no corner of her heart was too deep a hiding-place for the unvalued treasure.

A conversation with Margrave soon convinced Waltran of one thing—the artist had at present no thought of aspiring to the hand of Miss Eversleigh. He was buried in his other aspirations, of which he had never made any secret to Waltran, although the latter was the only friend, with the exception of Margaret, in whom he had ever fully confided.

Waltran did his best to convince Margrave that the success he had attained in his last portrait was sufficient to bring him fame and fortune, and that he would be foolish to trouble himself longer about the unattainable.

"You are right, I know," said Margrave; "but I can't settle down to portrait-painting all my life. If I merely wished to make money I might rest satisfied as I am. That Eversleigh portrait has brought me in more commissions than I know how to execute."

"Well, work away at them, and forget your profitless ambition."

"Yes; but you must recollect that all my sitters are not airy, fairy Lillians—I mean Margaret Eversleighs. I *must* paint people as they are, and that doesn't always please them, though it rarely fails to delight their friends. Look here." He showed Waltran a portrait, nearly finished, of an eccentric old maid, well known in Ravenscroft. Waltran agreed, with a smile, that it was probably far too characteristic to please the lady.

"However," he said, "she will not be able to find any fault; there is nothing tangible for the most prejudiced critic to grasp at. How *did* you manage to get that look into the eyes?"

"It's in her own. That's just what I'm afraid of. *She* won't recognise it as one of her idiosyncrasies of expression, and her friends—especially her relatives—will be polite enough to say *they* don't."

"Yet you are too much of an artist to alter it."

"I *can't* alter it—that is, I can't bring myself to do so. Of course, it's of little consequence to me; but I hate a thankless task."

Waltran soon after took his leave of Margrave, wondering if that young man would ever attain the acme of his ambition; but thinking still more of his own love affair, which he resolved to push forward without delay. He sought every opportunity of seeing Margaret, whom he found quiet, dignified, and self possessed—much more serious now than he had ever known her. He was aware that she still saw Margrave often, for the artist loved above all things to pour out his whole heart to her sympathetic ears, and to listen to her warm wishes and hopes—warmer now than ever—for the ultimate realisation of his dream. She often recounted her conversations with the artist to Waltran, always showing how intense was her desire for Margrave's success, but never giving her interlocutor any decided glimpse of the secret that preyed continually upon her heart.

"His desire to produce something great," she said one afternoon, "is becoming more and more intense. It haunts him continually, and fills his sleep with the wildest visions. The most remarkable of these dreams is one he had quite lately. He dreamed that he had bartered away his soul to Satan in return for undying fame. And how do you suppose the fiend was to perform his share of the bargain?"

"By allowing our artist to set up an easel in the nether regions, perhaps."

"No; simply by sitting for his portrait. Mr. Margrave awoke just as he was preparing to take the first rough sketch of the Satanic countenance."

"And, on awaking, I presume he seized his pencil and tried to recall the features of his distinguished sitter—as Tartini tells us he took up his violin to reproduce the demoniac strains he had heard."

"I've never believed Tartini's tale till now. But Ed—Mr. Margrave could recall nothing of what he had seen, nor could he remember having seen anything at all definite."

"Well, if the demon *should* ever desire to have his portrait painted he could not patronise a better man than Margrave. What does he say—Margrave, I mean? Does he regret not being able to——"

"Oh, yes! Anything, you know, that should be a great, original picture would satisfy him."

"Ah! of course; and an authentic likeness of such a celebrated personage would certainly confer immortality upon the artist who painted it."

Margaret seemed slightly piqued at the tone of levity in which Waltran spoke, and did not reply. Both fell into a reverie, from which Waltran was the first to awake. For a moment his face wore something of the look of one inspired.

"If," he said, "it were in your power to give this artist what he desires would you do it?"

"Oh! can you ask? I would make any sacrifice! He is so old and dear a friend," she added, meeting his eyes bravely. "But why do you put such an inconsequential question to me?"

"It may be by no means inconsequential," he said.

She waited, with feelings of wonder, to hear more; but he merely said, after a pause—"Will you sit down at the piano for a few minutes, Miss Eversleigh?"

She immediately obeyed, for there was a mysterious inflexion in his tone which seemed to compel her acquiescence. "What shall I play?" she asked, in a voice that seemed a little strange to her; she felt, too, a curious sensation stealing through her limbs, but so vague that she scarcely realised it. There was no alarm—only a feeling of undefined wonder and expectation—in her mind. Waltran took up a position whence he could command a view of her face. At length he said—

"Have you ever tried to improvise?"

"No," she said, dreamily; "I am like Edward—I have no gift for creation."

"Well, then," he answered, fixing his eyes upon hers, "do so now!"

The next instant a wild minor chord was struck, and then, for two or three minutes, the room rang with the most weird and unearthly music—the wildest and strangest combinations of sounds that the player had ever heard or dreamed of. When she stopped, her hands fell listlessly to her lap. Then she started to her feet, pale and trembling.

"What—what is this?" she cried.

"Calm yourself," said Waltran, gravely; "and, pray, forgive me for subjecting you to this experiment. Recall what we were speaking of."

"You—you hinted that it might be possible to——"

"To give Margrave his desire. Now, supposing you were ambitious, and wished to astonish the artistic world with a great and original musical conception, do you not think, with my assistance, you might compass your desire?"

"I cannot doubt it. But what—what is this power?"

"It is a phase of what is now known as hypnotism," said Waltran, with something of a sneer. "Were I ambitious I could—but no matter. The science is very abstruse and little known, even among its so-called professors, who usually dally upon the outskirts. To none, perhaps, save myself and one other, is it given to unveil—but I cannot tell you now; some day, if——"

He broke off, looking at her with a strange expression. She was very much surprised, but not in the least disturbed. Waltran's whole person breathed a kind of solemn candour. He no longer exercised his strange power over her, and ere he spoke again she divined what he was about to say. In a few impassioned sentences he besought her to be his, offering his whole life's devotion, just as any ordinary man might have done.

It was a strange position for Margaret. A less noble nature than her own might, in view of the power the hypnotist had shown himself possessed of, have been affrighted. But no protestations on his part were needed to assure her of his scrupulous honour. He, well knowing that he could compel her assent, yet scorned to accept any other than her own heart might give him.

Reflections passed rapidly through her mind. This man was of a higher nature even than he whom she loved. The latter, save in friendship, cared nothing for her. Her mother and her friends ardently desired her to accept Waltran. It was clear that Margrave did not love her; and where else could be found one so good, so noble as Waltran? These arguments would not of themselves have impelled her to accept him, but if, by so doing, she could secure the happiness of him she loved——

"If I consent to become your wife," she murmured, "can you—will you—place within the artist's reach the greatness he covets?"

"I can, and will," he said. Her condition, though not unexpected, pained him a little. It raised once more the doubt—was her interest in Margrave born of love or friendship?

"Why," she said, "have you not already so befriended him?"

"My dear Miss Eversleigh, you do not know—I cannot explain. Let it suffice that I am bound not to trifle with the powers which I owe partly to another. And then, fame does not always mean happiness. However, I am ready now to give Margrave his desire; but in the plan I mean to pursue with him hypnotism will play a minor part. Above all, he must have no suspicion that the work he shall produce does not emanate solely from his own genius—in fact, I intend that it shall, as far as possible, be really *his own* work."

"In justice to himself?"

"Of course. Now, tell me—will you give me your hand—plight me your troth on the day that Margrave completes an indubitable masterpiece?"

"Oh!" she replied, "you must not suppose, Mr. Waltran, that if I accept you it is merely out of gratitude for any service you may do my friend. If I thought I liked you well enough to marry you, you should have my answer now. But—you understand?—I require time."

"Exactly. My proposal has been rather abrupt, I know. At all events, you will give me an answer at the time I mentioned?"

"Yes, certainly."

"Then," said Waltran, with a smile, "I shall commence operations without delay."

He would not tell her how he intended to proceed. When he left her she sank down into a seat, and pondered long and sadly over the strange conversation she had had with a still stranger being. To be the wife of such a man—what a glorious privilege, if she could but love him! Ah! if her heart were only free! Now that she had, if not promised to be Waltran's wife, at least led him to hope, she realised more than ever her love for Margrave. To her self-sacrificing nature it would be a great pleasure to see the artist happy; but she could not help feeling hopeless and miserable. Her mother, entering the room unobserved, found her weeping.

Mrs. Eversleigh desired nothing but her child's happiness. She divined in part what Margaret's emotion arose from; but she knew not that her tears were of despair. She thought, and her daughter encouraged her to think, that they were merely a result of the emotion natural to a young girl who has received an offer of marriage.

Margaret said nothing, of course, about the strange compact, if such it may be called, which she had entered into with Waltran.

The artist's dream had kindled his imagination to a considerable degree. Waltran found him buried in Milton, and with Goethe's masterpiece at his elbow. Margrave at once spoke of his dream. He was, he said, making a study of the two most celebrated pictures of the Fiend in literature—Milton's "Satan" and Goethe's "Mephistopheles." He had already projected a painting which, if successful, should realise a subtle mixture of the godlike grandeur of the one and the sardonic laughter of the other.

"But will that be an original conception?" said Waltran.

"As original as I can ever hope for," replied the painter.

"Well, I wish you success; only beware of overstepping the limits of the sublime. It would be unfortunate if——"

"Yes, yes—that's just what I'm afraid of. I may succeed only in painting a common devil, such as one sees occasionally in the pantomime."

"Better give up the whole idea. Turn your thoughts to something else. You were not meant for a misanthrope. Have you ever contemplated marriage?"

Margrave smiled at this abrupt question.

"Would *you* recommend such a panacea for disappointed ambition?" he said, with significant emphasis.

"In your case I might," replied the other, coolly. "This Margaret Eversleigh, now—a girl to whom, I fancy, you are by no means indifferent."

"Marry Margaret!" exclaimed the painter. "Why, she's—no, she's not a child now, certainly. But I am not to be distracted from my idea by any girl. Besides, I'm like you, not a marrying man."

"But suppose you heard of her engagement to someone else? How would that strike you?"

Margrave made no reply. It was evident that he did not relish the thought.

"You see," he said, at last, "we've always been such friends—comrades, as it were; there's a sort of Platonic love between us. Now you speak of it, I am surprised I've never thought of falling in love with her. But enough of Margaret. Let us return to my *chef d'œuvre*."

"Well, are you going to paint the single figure—Satan alone?"

"Yes. I won't trust myself with anything in the way of a scene. I shall throw my whole soul into a delineation of the Fiend's countenance."

"You are right. Paint him just emerging from the Cimmerian gloom, with nothing really distinct save the face. Make the form perceptible, but indefinite, and don't commit yourself to anything tangible in the way of costume that the critics can grasp at."

"Thank you; I will follow your advice."

As Waltran rose to leave he turned his eyes full on those of the painter, saying—

"Set to work at once, Margrave, and paint as man never painted before!"

Margrave could not have answered him for worlds. Something in the tone, but much more in the glance which accompanied Waltran's speech, thrilled him with a sensation entirely novel. For some moments he stared at the door by which Waltran had taken his departure; then he arose, and, with that air of unconscious deliberation which characterises the actions of the sleepwalker, he began to prepare his materials.

Meanwhile, Waltran was buried in thought. His doubts in regard to Margaret Eversleigh were gradually melting away before a conviction that her heart was really given to the dreamer who valued an empty ambition—for so Waltran deemed it—before the priceless gift of woman's love.

When he next saw Miss Eversleigh the expression of her face served materially to strengthen his conviction; her eyes told that she had wept bitterly, and he divined too well the origin of her tears. Bravely as she had guarded her secret, it was no longer inviolable. He knew now that she was lost to him, for, as has been said, he was too haughtily honourable and unselfish to accept the hand while he knew the heart was another's.

"It is all over," he reflected, with a painful sigh—"all over, as far as I am concerned."

"Well," she said, with an assumed lightness, which of itself was sufficient to apprise him of the truth, "and what of our friend the artist? Has he begun?"

"Yes," he answered.

"Really!" she cried. "Is he—I don't quite know how to express it—is he working under your spell? Have you inspired him?"

"No, not yet," said Waltran. "You know what we said about doing him justice. Well, the fact is, he has been seized with a strong inspiration of his own, and that is the spell I found and left him under. I should like to see what comes of it before endeavouring to help him."

"Yes, yes—you are right. Oh! I hope he *will* do something—something *entirely* his own, you know. Of course, what you proposed would be interesting in itself; but I can't bear to deceive a friend, even for his own benefit."

"Nor I, Miss Eversleigh. So noble a young fellow as Margrave were scarcely a fit subject for idle experiments."

A faint blush deepened the delicate colour of her cheeks at this praise of the man she loved. He saw it, and went on expressing his admiration of the young artist until tears of commingled pleasure and grief stood in her eyes, and warned him to desist.

"Nothing remains now," he thought, as he took his way homewards, "but to bring them together—to persuade this young fool that he loves her—and, in the conventional phrase, to tear her image from my heart." He laughed bitterly as he thought how much easier the one would be to him than the other. Marvellous as his powers were, they could not accomplish both.

Next morning, early, he called on Margrave. In the hall he met the artist's servant, whose face wore a very troubled look. Late on the previous night his master, usually very regular in his habits, had positively refused to retire, and his voice, countenance, and actions all tended to convince the man that "something was wrong."

"He's there still, sir—painting away as if his life depended on it; but what the deuce he's painting is more than I can tell, for he wouldn't let me get a glimpse of it. He's popping on plenty of black stuff, though."

Waltran easily succeeded in laughing the good fellow's fears away, and passed into the studio.

The artist was not painting when Waltran entered, but had thrown himself back into an arm-chair, in an attitude of extreme exhaustion. The room was still lighted, though the sunbeams were filtering in through the window curtains. For some moments Margrave did not perceive his visitor, who, nevertheless, was looking full at him. The painter's face expressed a passionate delight, subdued by extreme awe. His eyes were fixed upon the canvas before him, to which Waltran presently turned his glance.

He had counted on seeing something novel, perhaps even wonderful. But he was by no means prepared for the terrible sight that met his startled eyes. He involuntarily closed them, as if he distrusted his senses. The picture was not nearly completed, but so much was done that the rest might have been painted by a tyro. As he gazed upon it Waltran experienced something of the terror that might strike one who should lift the veil from some mystery too fearful to be revealed, and find himself unable to cover it up again. Not that the dreadful countenance that looked out upon him from the Rembrandtesque gloom was merely horrible. It was majestic in its hideousness—grand in its tremendous terror. Its effect was somewhat similar in kind, though infinitely superior in degree, to that of the Medusa of Da Vinci; in it horror was carried to a point at which it became beauty, and it was *that*, more than anything else, which "turned the gazer's spirit into stone."

As soon as Waltran could collect his bewildered faculties he took the hand of the artist in his; it was icy cold. Margrave started violently.

"You have succeeded," said Waltran, in a low voice; "I congratulate you."

"Then it is real—it is no dream?" said Margrave, faintly.

"No; it is a splendid—a triumphant—reality," said Waltran, in a louder and heartier tone. "You have your desire at last. This effort far eclipses all the pictured incarnations of the Fiend in existence—including those of Retzch, of which I have heard you speak so enthusiastically. I must confess I expected nothing like it of you."

"It is very strange," said the artist, speaking more to himself than to his friend; "I was certainly quite calm and collected all the time—I remember everything—yet it seemed as if some power other than my own will impelled me to——"

"Inspiration, my dear friend—inspiration so intense that it must have seemed strange to you."

"I suppose you are right," said the artist, who was willing enough to believe so. "And what do you suppose its effect will be on——"

"On your friends? Oh, there can be no doubt of its effect. I can judge by my own sensations. Miss Eversleigh will be delighted with your success."

"I hope so," he answered, a little doubtfully, "It's hardly a picture to please a girl."

"She's no ordinary girl, Margrave. Do you know, there is but one thing which, as your friend, would delight me even more than your success."

"What is that?"

"To hear of your marriage with Margaret Eversleigh."

"Nonsense! Can I think of love while——"

"Oh, all in good time, of course. Had you not been so blinded by your artistic ambition, you would, perhaps, have seen——"

"What?"

"Why, that the young lady's heart is lost to you already."

"You are joking!"

"How could I jest on such a subject? But you had better rest yourself now. I'll inform Miss Eversleigh of your success, and you will, no doubt, see her soon. In the meantime," he added, lightly, "as you value your future happiness, fall in love with Margaret."

"Nonsense! As if one could command one's affections!"

As Waltran, with a last glance at the painting, left the studio, the artist threw himself upon a couch and fell asleep. His dreams, strange to say, were not of future fame, but of Margaret Eversleigh.

Waltran's self-control was perfect when, after telling Miss Eversleigh of the artist's great achievement, and again hinting that it was entirely the product of his genius, he announced that he was compelled to go away on business, and would probably be absent for some months. "So that," he said, as he pressed her hand tenderly, "you will have plenty of time to give me my answer." He allowed his eyes to linger on her face for some moments and then left her. She has never seen him since—knows nothing of him save that she has heard he is immersed, with his mysterious friend, in his favourite study—in what part of the world no one seems quite able to say.

*   *   *   *   *

No single picture ever rendered its painter so famous as Margrave's "Satan" made him. In view of the fact that he never, in any other instance, succeeded in painting a great original picture, his friends are wont to make merry over the circumstance, pretending to think he must have invoked the aid of the arch-fiend himself; that the picture is in reality a portrait, to be ranked properly with his other wonderful successes in that department of the painter's art.

Margaret Eversleigh, now Mrs. Margrave, is, in the midst of her happiness, strangely puzzled at times. She cannot help suspecting that both Margrave and she owe more to Waltran than to chance or good fortune. Her knowledge of his strange powers is the only secret she has from her husband. He must never doubt the genuineness of that "inspiration" which resulted so splendidly; nor, above all, must he ever suspect what, happily, it would be difficult to make him believe, that the love which sprung up so suddenly, yet so unmistakably, in his heart might never have had an existence but for his friend Waltran.

SEAGRAVE'S MANUSCRIPT

It was in an opium den in the purlieus of the city that I found Seagrave. He was a fearful wreck, and it was some time before I recognised him as an old schoolfellow. He himself could not remember me, but took my word as to our former friendship—which, he being within a few weeks of his demise, interested him sufficiently to induce him to confide his manuscript to my keeping. He had written it, he said, in the intervals of his opium torpor; and he assured me that, however incredible I might consider some of its contents, it was all perfectly true. He then sank back upon his padded bench, took up the tube of his pipe, and speedily relapsed into the opium smoker's oblivion. A young girl lying near him raised her heavy eyelids and said to me—

"He is nearly gone. Do not disturb him again, please. Let him rest. It was no common trouble that sent *him* here, that's certain. So, please, don't plague him anymore."

"How long has he been in this place?" I asked.

She shook her head slowly, much as Seagrave himself had done, in response to the same question.

"Was he here before you?"

"No," she replied, drowsily; "but he used laudanum, I think, and so—well, well, I don't know—don't trouble me, that's a good fellow. I can't answer questions after three whiffs." She thereupon replaced the mouthpiece of her pipe, and closed her eyes once more.

The manuscript is short, and bears neither title nor signature. I append it without further comment:—

"There are many who smile or sneer, and there may be some few who weep, over lives wasted in dreams—lost in the clouds of reverie. Mine, then, may afford amusement, or excite tears; I care not which. I doubt, indeed, whether I shall find strength to shake from

my mind the accumulated mists of vision sufficiently to enable
me to make clear what I have to tell; but that, in common with
everything else, matters little to me now.

In all my life I had no such friend as Basil Winter. Our love was
as that of David and Jonathan. Winter was unlike me in many
respects. In character he was far stronger. *He* could think and act—*I*
could only dream. Yet misfortune weighed with equal heaviness
upon us both. But, then, his sorrows came from without, and
might be combated to some extent; whilst my misery germinated
within, like *fungi* in a stagnant tarn. His poverty, for example, was
crushing to him on account of his aspirations and hope; but I never
noticed mine.

It is to energetic natures that despair is most terrible. When the
realities of life are keenly felt, passion is great and grief intense.
With me, and such as I, every feeling of the heart becomes merged
at last into reverie—that quicksand of the intellect—and there presently becomes illegible.

Winter was of those whose sensations are always clear and
defined, and thus he suffered greatly when sorrow came. His
grief, though not by any means unparalleled, was yet of the most
heart-rending kind. It was his fate to see, day after day, the being he
loved approach nearer and nearer towards the grave—to note how,
as time fled, the eyes grew larger and more unearthly bright, the
cheeks more pallid, the form more fragile; and to hear the voice
he worshipped grow more melodious and strange, as if it were
going through some mysterious evolution which was to fit it for
the songs that are sung in heaven. Her loveliness was painful to
behold, but its luminous spirituality was intensely fascinating. Her
step was that of a ghost; her every motion was endued with grace
and majesty not of earth. She was my sister Marion. Many times
have I beheld her since, in my dreams, with her large, limpid eyes,
her pure brow of the whiteness of a vestal taper, her lips with their
sweet yet poignant smile. It is thus that she now haunts my nightly
dreams—why, I may not know.

Alas! it was another dream which destroyed me—a dream more
hideous than this is beautiful. When did I dream it first? Was it
before she died? I cannot tell; but it matters not. Yet I think that
it was after Marion's death that the terrible dream first filled my

sleep with horror, my waking hours with fear. I dreamed of being a murderer—of slaying with my own hand my dearest friend. Night after night this vision was repeated, in all its ghastly, vivid details, making my sleep a torture. It is in dreams that my sensations are the most acute and definite.

The most dreadful feature of my dream had little or no connection with the visionary *events*; it was a sense of charnel horror, of unutterable *loathsomeness*, clinging round them from first to last like the black filmy robes of a ghoul, which so tortured and appalled me.

My sister died, and Winter was lost in despair. No comfort or consolation was possible—certainly I had none to give. He went about his affairs as usual, but his high hopes were in the dust. Condolement had been a mockery to one so bereaved. My own grief was soon swallowed up in the new and secret misery which now dominated my whole being.

And this dream—what was it? Whence came the terrible curse? How long was it to continue? Sometimes the horror of the thing would awaken me; then what unspeakable relief it was to listen to the quiet breathing of my poor friend—to know that it was, after all, but a dream. I would fall asleep once more, and then yet again would I enact the drama of my visionary crime. In the morning, shuddering and bathed in sweat, I would awake, and again praise Heaven that I had but dreamed.

This horrible persecution so absorbed my thoughts that I had little time or inclination to think of other matters; yet Winter's condition was such as forced itself upon my consciousness. No reference to Marion's death, it is true, ever passed his lips or mine, but I knew that his whole despairing heart was filled with her alone, and that it was doubtful whether he would ever succeed in conquering his grief. Once, in my hideous dream, just as the blow was given—just as the knife entered his heart—he shrieked, "Marion!" This was the first and only variation in my nightly vision. I awoke with the sound of his voice still ringing in my ears; he had called upon her name in sleep.

On the morning that followed this incident I resolved to make an effort to cast off the tyranny of the dream, lest insanity should overtake me. For several days I took long walks, visited public pleasure grounds, thoroughfares, and theatres—I forced myself to take interest in the affairs of the day, and projected certain studies. I would even have left Winter if I could have done so, but it was impossible without telling him the reason, and of *that* I never even thought.

My efforts were all in vain. Every night the dream returned with its inexorable persistency, filling my sleep with its accustomed horror. Its *accustomed* horror? Alas! it was only on awaking that I ever knew the dream to be the nightly haunter of my sleep. During its progress there was never the slightest shadow of memory mingled with the enactment of the horrible tragedy; the dream was always *new*. When I awoke, this circumstance would cause me the most intense wonder and bitterness of grief; it always seemed to me that, if I could recognise and remember it in sleep as I did on awaking, the dream's terror might be gradually attenuated. I should, in time, grow used to it.

All my efforts to conquer the tyrant having failed, I resigned myself thenceforward to despair. Once the idea of suicide presented itself to me as a means of relief, and I might have closed with the offer death made, but that a singular fear withheld me—a fear at once fantastic and terrible. It was this. I imagined death as one long, unbroken sleep, and my dream, expanded in length and horror so as to be commensurate to the eternity of my slumber, torturing me for ever and ever without a hope of respite. Sometimes I forced myself to remain sleepless for several consecutive nights, but my terrible and impalpable enemy, as if eager for revenge, swooped down upon me the moment my eyelids closed, and was more hideously potent—above all, more loathsome—than ever.

One night I entered, unobserved by Winter. At first I did not see him, but when I turned my eyes in his direction I was intensely startled. He held a long and glittering dagger; yet it was not the sight of this weapon in itself that so disturbed me; it was the awful and unaccountable fact of its precise and absolute identity with the dagger of my dream—the same blade, bright as a surgeon's lancet, and fluted near the curiously wrought, silver hilt. Hearing my step, Winter turned towards me, but made no attempt to conceal the weapon.

"Will you take charge of this?" he said in his quiet, melancholy voice. "I am growing afraid of it; it is too tempting. Suicide is the coward's resource. Besides, *she* would not approve it."

I took the dagger mechanically and in silence. Even as I touched the haft, warm from the pressure of Winter's feverish hand, a dreadful thought shot through my brain—so swiftly that at first I failed to grasp its full significance, though it filled my soul with horror unutterable. And yet it seemed that there was in it something that resembled hope. It was as though some demon had whispered in my ear the words—"Why not deliver yourself from the hideous thraldom of your nightly tyrant? Do that in reality which you do in your dream, and you are free!"

This reasoning of a distempered brain seemed endued with unanswerable logic. It was the sophistry of madness, which counsels men to horrid deeds—deeds that become the wonder and the detestation of all who have never suffered from a mind diseased, an imagination warped and perverted by its own horrible creations. But the heart of him who does so suffer is a gulf of dim, intangible mysteries, hideous and strange. Various causes, it is well known, produce the same result. I know little of the *rationale* of nervous derangement or cerebral affections; I know only that in my own case a predisposition to inordinate reverie, that most invidious and pernicious form of sloth, is the fatality that has destroyed me.

I was now the victim of a double tyranny—the dream by night, the temptation by day; and the thought of its continuance was intolerable. Again and again did I hear the hideous voice counselling me to crime. And the dream—it seemed even more fearful and loathsome now that I had, as I never doubted, the means of deliverance at hand. And then the identity of the dagger of reality with that of the vision—what could that mean? I locked the thing up in a bureau without daring to think of the future.

For three nights I abstained from sleep, but on the fourth I felt that I must succumb. And the temptation of the voice grew even more potent as I yielded to the desire to sleep; it was in my heart, it was in my very soul, and close—how terribly close—beside my ear. And the voice said:—"Be free!—brave not again the unutterable horror—tempt madness and hell no more. Be free—be free!" And the words rang in my ears and reverberated to the very depths of my soul as sleep rushed upon me.

And now once again the tyrant of the night asserted his dominion—again the hideous dream clutched my helpless imagination, and held me in its dreadful thrall. But this time the torment was too intense for slumber to contain. As the blow was sped, I awoke, bathed in icy sweat. The light was burning dimly. Winter was asleep. There was a vague sound somewhere as of mocking laughter. It may have been within my ears, but I fancied it came from beneath me.

I arose. I unlocked the bureau slowly and softly, and took out the bright, keen weapon. I gazed upon it for many moments, in a kind of gloomy trance. Then something aroused me. I saw the lips of the sleeper move.

I bent over him and listened, but his utterance was broken and inarticulate. Presently, however, I distinguished a few German words—a line from some song; they were half said, half hummed— *"Wie weit noch bis zur Bahre!"*

Suddenly I felt my muscles grow rigid, and, almost without thought or volition, I plunged the dagger through his heart. A kind of galvanic shock seemed to seize him; his right hand mechanically closed upon the haft, almost touching my own as I withdrew it. I was vaguely conscious of an indeterminate humming in my ears, which insensibly resolved itself into a portion of the melody of the *lied* that had apparently been in the sleeper's dreams during his final moments. But I gave no thought to this, or anything. I threw myself again upon my bed, which was still warm, and fell asleep almost as soon as my head touched the pillow.

The dream did not return! In its stead there came a vision of an angel face, which I recognised as Marion's; its expression was one of radiant and spiritual joy—of an ecstasy not the less intense because it was so calm. Apart from its divine expression, my sister's face was just as I had last seen it in life; it recalled, suggested nothing—I saw and recognised it, and that was all.

In the morning, delirious with joy, neither looking at nor thinking of the body of my friend, I sallied out into the bright sunshine. It was the season of spring, and everything appeared to be steeped in the deep calm of perfect happiness; but not to anything could I compare the terrible rapture that surged and throbbed in every vein. I walked on and on, not caring where I went, possessed by the one glorious thought that I was *free*—that the tyrant was over-thrown—that henceforward I could sleep in peace. Day followed day, and still this satanic joy reigned in my soul. Events passed before me like shadows. The inquest, the suspicions that had at first attached to me, the searching investigation, the ultimate verdict of suicide—these things left no more impression upon me than the minor incidents of the drama leave upon the playgoer. I still had but the one thought—the reign of the tyrant was past; the dream would never come again.

One morning, however, I awoke, and looked towards the place where Winter used to sleep. It was vacant; the bed had been removed. Then, for the first time, the consciousness of the deed I had committed burst upon my soul in the fulness of its horror, and from that moment to this it has never left me. The tyranny of the night is indeed cast down, but another is arisen—a tyranny of the day, the despotism of conscience. Yet it would be rash for me to say that the latter, which has driven me to opium, is half so ter-rible as the former was. And then my sleep is invariably filled with that most peaceful and beautiful of visions. Sleep is as welcome as death will be. One day, not now far distant, the magic drug will open for me the portals of the infinite; but what prison awaits me there, I who have eluded human justice—in whose custody I shall find myself when the grave is passed—belongs to the mystery of the Unknown.

THE LADY WITH THE VEIL

I blame nature for it all—nature and heredity. It seems to me that I have been but the sport of these; and I cannot feel, as so many do when ruin overwhelms them, that different circumstances would have altered my case. Generations ago my fate was sealed.

Early in youth I developed a strange nervous affection that sapped my otherwise strong physique like a poisonous parasite. It revealed itself chiefly in an inordinate abhorrence of the various perfumes commonly used by women, more particularly the one called patchouli. Therefore, although the attraction of the graces and refinements of the opposite sex was for me at least as powerful as for the average youth, I shunned all women, for no effort of will could overcome my antipathy to the sickening scents they indulged in. My disorder survived adolescence; in manhood it possessed me like a demon of the age of miracles. I have said that I shunned women, yet it was through a woman that I was to fall.

They say my wealth attracted her; it may be so. But however that may be, she plucked out the heart of my mystery, purified herself of all perfumes, save that of her own glorious youth, and took entire possession of my soul. She was one of those women whose love is fatal, whose passion is a devastation. Years have not dimmed the vision of her beauty: there is no single detail that cannot be at will recalled. But details would convey no adequate picture of such a creature. Pieces of lead will not reconstruct an idol cast in fine gold.

Mine, not hers, was the surrender. Her physical charm—I know now that she had no other—conquered me absolutely. And I, blind fool that I was, thought I had conquered her! There was a rival, too, to spur me on—a dreamer, who made miserable attempts to transfer her beauty to his second-rate canvases. I think she loved this artist, who was cold to all outside his art. She loved him, but she loved love more. The wild passion in her blood claimed a fiery response, which he could dream of, perhaps, but could not act. My heart, preserved in its freshness by my malady, was noble prey to her. Yes, my wealth was a secondary consideration; it was the love of a youth, reserved, unworldly, mystic, that she desired.

Let it be said, then, that she married me for love. But it was the love of a vampire; and, like a vampire, she fastened upon my heart, and drained it to the last drop. And then there came that financial crisis that swallowed up the moiety of my worldly wealth, together with a portion of her own. Of this epoch of my gloomy life my memory is confused; I am unable to piece facts and conjectures sufficiently to form a coherent, consecutive record. Whether she merely wished to drive me away, now that she was bankrupt both in property and passion, or whether she was actuated by a darker purpose, I cannot tell. Whatever her object, she approached it with the ruthless cynicism of her kind.

Jealousy, betrayal—such vulgar methods she despised. Her knowledge of my secret infirmity gave her readier—and, she thought, safer—means. A slight, very slight, odour of vervain in her room was the first intimation I had of her treacherous return to the perfumes, the use of which she had relinquished for my sake. I had then, as always, the uncontrollable temper of a nervous man; yet for a time the love she still inspired lent me strength to endure the strange martyrdom she made me suffer. But the end came soon. Recriminations were followed by haughty contempt on her part and a more flaunting indulgence of those vicious distillations. In patchouli she reached the climax. That penultimate scene of our connection is burnt in upon my memory, like colour in glass: but I cannot dwell upon it. . . . In her insolent defiance of my anger, she sprinkled the horrible perfume over me, laughing cruelly the while. I knew this was the end. Rage and despair, not less than the maddening fumes, overleapt the last barriers of self-control. I dashed the bottle from her hand, and then, seizing the largest of the jagged fragments into which it broke, I hacked at her face until that fatal beauty was destroyed for ever. And as I fed from my dreadful work the smell of blood and patchouli filled my distracted brain.

* * * * *

Was it the persistence of the vitality within me which, in the midst of my passionate longing for the end of all things, withheld me from self-destruction or surrender to the law? I know not. . . . The woman did not die, however; nor, for reasons best known to herself, did she denounce me as her assailant. Ignorant of her fate or intention, I remained hid in the covert of the crowded city for many weeks. But my sufferings during that period must remain untold. They would have sated even the vengeance of that wretched creature, my wife, could she have known them. How could I describe the torment arising from the vastly-increased acuteness of my malady which the crime brought about? Remorse was, I verily believe, the least of my agonies; nor was it so much that all odours were now a horror and an abomination, but that in every one of them I could smell nothing but that indescribably loathsome mixture of patchouli and blood which had flooded my brain as I rushed away from the horrid deed.

But enough of this. Let me get as quickly as may be to the end.

Gradually—with what agony of effort the pen refuses to tell—I roused myself from the thraldom of my disorder, and projected a plan which seemed to promise a measure of peace and rest. With the remnant of my fortune I had a house built far in the depths of a wooded district in the north, where I hoped to live a recluse, with books and nature for company. And in this I was not wholly disappointed. For more than a year I dwelt alone—laboured in the field, studied from my books, fought down my sufferings—till at last the gum leaves began to lose their odour of patchouli, and to give forth a wholesome smell once more.

Then the bush fires came. The country was devastated. I joined the fire-fighters leagues away, working like a demon for the sake of the excitement, and the oblivion it gave me—helping poorer (but not more unhappy) people to save their homes.

Returning at the close of one awful day, I rode over blazing logs and past falling trees, and revelled in the dangers of the burning forest. The road was strewn with fire. A light waggon dashed past me, the horse urged onward by a frantic driver. Out of the back there fell a child—a little girl of three years—and lay insensible on the hot earth.

I reined in my frightened horse, dismounted, and gathered up this little waif. I brought her to my home, and had her tended. Love sprang up again within my heart—the pure love of a father for his child. Oh, God! if anything could make one believe in the angels, surely it were the divine grace of early childhood! A deep thankfulness possessed me at having secured this lovely little thing; it was the beginning of a new life.

A year passed, and I was almost happy—almost, for sometimes in my dreams I felt the fumes of warm blood mingled with patchouli, and saw the woman's lacerated face, always with fierce eyes that lusted for revenge.

But little Mamie, my good angel, stood between me and my terrible memories, and evil thoughts. . . . Shall I find her where I am going, and will she save me then?

It was in the midst of this peaceful life that the blow fell.

One afternoon, as I was leisurely polishing a Burmese dagger that I possessed, Mamie began telling me of some strangers—ladies and gentlemen—whom she had met whilst out on her pony.

"One of the ladies had a dark veil on, and I couldn't see her face; but she had a lovely voice. She talked to me a long while, and asked me about you, papa. She said they might come here today. Won't that be lovely!"

I paid slight heed to her prattle; but suddenly strange voices sounded without, and Mamie ran off, crying, "There they are!" I felt annoyed at the intrusion, and went on polishing the Burmese blade. I was still at this task when she returned, breathless, with something in her hand.

"Oh, papa!" she cried, "see what the lady has given me—the lady with the veil! Let me put some on your handkerchief!"

And before I could realise what was happening, she snatched the handkerchief from my pocket and sprinkled it heavily with—patchouli!

Instantly the hideous fumes rushed to my brain, red fires flamed before my eyes, and in another moment the murderous dagger struck out the innocent young life in which I had so vainly hoped to find happiness and peace. . . . And she—"the lady with the veil"—she was with those who rushed in and saved me for the scaffold or the mad-house—it matters not which—and her distorted smile of triumph danced before me as I swooned away, overcome by that thrice-accursed odour!

THE PURPLE DEATH

I first met Dr. Wainwright in a Melbourne club room. His appearance, which was what is called "distinguished," caught my eye, and I carelessly asked young Holgate, with whom I was talking at the moment, who he was, little dreaming how closely—I may say tragically—I was to be associated with the man.

"Oh, he's an old member," said my friend; "hasn't been here, though, for a long while. Been under a cloud, I think. His name? Dr. Wainwright. Some say he's a distant relation of the famous criminal; but I reckon that's a libel."

"Does he practise in the city?"

"No; not that I know of. Don't think he has any regular practice at all. Private means, I understand. Have an idea he's been going the pace in some form or other—absinthe, chloral, morphine—something of that sort. He fell foul of the police a few years ago—vivisection, I think. Fad for experimenting. Have a cigar?"

"Thanks. An experimenter, eh? Scientific enthusiast, I suppose."

"Yes, in a way; but only to satisfy a sort of morbid curiosity, I believe. There's a horrid tale of his playing electric light on a boy's eyes till the poor little wretch went mad; but I hope it isn't true. I don't like the man myself. Somebody does, though, it appears."

"Indeed?"

"Ay—my cousin, too—Marie Seymour."

"Good heavens! You don't mean to tell me that a mere girl like Marie——"

"Would marry a world-worn medico of close on forty? Why not? Seriously, though, I'm much concerned, though, as yet, nothing is said of an engagement. But you'll admit that the fellow has a certain debonnair grace; and Marie's an impressionable girl, rather more romantic than the average."

"You know, Holgate, I'm a good deal interested in Miss Seymour myself——"

"Good on you, Coverdale, old chap. You can count on me to shove you along in any way I can. Something tells me Wainwright is a rotter, and if you can cut him out in Marie's good graces, you'll deserve well of all of us."

I laughed confidently, as a young fellow will; but somehow I felt a vague, uneasy sensation at my heart. I am not wont to look on the dark side of things, yet this Dr. Wainwright exercised somehow a sinister effect upon me, like a sudden darkening of the landscape to a wayfarer far from home. However, I shook off the feeling, and thought little more of Wainwright for the next few days.

A week after the conversation with young Holgate, I dined at the Seymours', and was more annoyed than surprised to find Dr. Wainwright among the few friends who had been invited. Mrs. Seymour introduced him with what seemed to me a somewhat ostentatious display, as of one exhibiting a social lion. And as such I soon found Wainwright was regarded. He had recently published a remarkable book on obscure lesions of the brain, or something of that sort—I never read the thing—and certain daringly original hypotheses therein had won for him a passing fame, as such things will: and this, in association with his vivid and striking personality, made him an object of more than ordinary interest in fashionable circles. Like all such ephemeræ, he soon faded out of notice; but he was in the enjoyment of his brief renown when fate threw him across my path.

He was tall and slight, with strong, saturnine features, black hair, and piercing grey eyes, in which a look of resolution and power warred strangely with a dreamy, far-away expression. Without showing the traces of dissipation too markedly, it was evident that he had warmed both hands at the fire of life; or it may have been that scientific research, too intensely persisted in, had begun to impair his physical energies. Though his equal in stature, I could not help feeling, for the moment, commonplace and ordinary beside him. He had certainly the advantage of me in looks, and what is somewhat vaguely called "presence."

In conversation he also outclassed me. He was witty, brilliant, keen, quick. My own little social gift of easy insouciance and quiet humour (called "smug self-sufficiency" by my more critical friends) seemed a poor thing beside the lightning flashes of his raillery and wit. I tried hard to persuade myself that the doctor's influence was due to the meretricious glitter of a charlatan; and I exceedingly rejoiced to find that the one whom I would have wished above all others to see this man through my own spectacles did, to some extent, detect a want of solid human qualities in the brilliant doctor. Marie had, it is true, succumbed in a measure to the spell of his personality, and still enjoyed listening to him; but her native discernment and intrinsic purity of mind and heart made her at least suspect that the man was little better than a living mask. And I make no doubt that Wainwright, who seemed to read us all like open books, saw that his star was declining. We who were most intimately concerned in these events know now that he had staked a great deal upon winning the richly-dowered young lady, for of his private fortune but a remnant was left, risky speculations, ruinous living, and costly experiments having made serious inroads upon his patrimony.

It would be tedious to narrate in detail (even if I could trust my memory to recall them correctly) the incidents that marked the course of our love, and Wainwright's disappointment and jealousy. I really believe he loved Marie in his own way. He had a passion for her, just as he had for his experiments, of which strange tales were whispered. And the loss of the lovely young girl and her fortune kindled within him the fires of hatred and revenge, which found in his strenuous, unbridled nature the kind of furnace wherein they could rage freely. So I am forced to think, in the light of after events; otherwise I should have considered the man too much of a stoic philosopher to give way to the common emotions of ordinary mortals.

A stoic he was, to be sure, in his power of outward self-control, for I am certain no one suspected his true feelings. His frank, open manner deceived me completely; and, whilst I never quite lost that sense of something false or disingenuous in his character, I no longer thought of him as an enemy, and scarcely even as a rival. His attitude towards me seemed like that of a beaten man who resigns himself to the inevitable. This was flattering to my self-love, and no doubt helped considerably to dissipate any lingering suspicions.

Friends, in the true and sacred sense, we could never have become; but it is certain that my liking for him as a brilliant talker, and an interesting guide in many subjects of inquiry, made me feel rather sorry when he spoke of leaving the Commonwealth. He had in view, he said, certain experiments which could be conducted successfully only in the interior of Borneo or Java. Sir Miles Grangerford, a wealthy friend, had placed at his service a steam yacht, and he invited me, with "other choice spirits," to what he called a farewell symposium at his rather ostentatious flat in Collins-street.

I could not complain of the company, unless it were for their intellectual superiority. I felt myself to be distinctly the least brilliant person present. Wine flowed freely, and witty dialogue more freely still; and I had certainly never enjoyed a similar gathering so much. I was both grateful and indignant with Wainwright for the pains he took to give me all possible opportunities to "come out" and display my poor little knack of quiet humour, which he was indulgent enough to pretend he valued higher than the most brilliant of repartee or wit.

No doubt, like the others, I took too much wine; but I am now satisfied that what I did take was skilfully "treated" by the adroit hands of Wainwright himself. The closing scene of that wild night I cannot recall. There is a vague memory of being hustled or carried into a vehicle; but that is all. When next I woke it was with a feeling of rather comfortable weakness or exhaustion. I call it "comfortable," because I can find no other word that quite expresses the strange state of quietude and of mental and bodily satisfaction in which I found myself. At first I supposed that I was in my own house and that it was the morrow of Wainwright's farewell gathering.

The discovery that I was mistaken in this supposition came upon me gradually, and without shock or apprehension. A sort of lazy wonder or curiosity was my dominant feeling. It was novel and interesting to know that I was in a strange place, and I felt in no hurry to solve a mystery which in itself constituted a mild form of pleasure. So I lay perfectly still, steeped in the drowsy luxury of dreamy wonder. How long I lay thus I cannot tell, nor what fancies floated through my mind. I think the deep silence, which at first had lulled me, at length caused a feeling of vague oppression, merging into anxiety. It was the silence of a tomb. Not unlike what one might conceive some splendid tomb to be, also, was the apartment in which I lay, in its absence of windows and pictures, and the strange configuration of its walls and vaulted roof. Light entered through many narrow strips of stained glass, forming part of a wild, arabesque design, that twined and twirled and capered all over the ceiling. Decidedly I was not in the house of any of my friends.

For a bedchamber, the room was of rather more than ordinary size, and the paucity of furniture made its dimensions appear still greater. Besides the bed on which I lay, and which I afterwards found to be of richly-carved wood, but small, there were an octagonal table, two curiously designed chairs, a small, carved bookcase, and a piano, shaped to the fancy of some eccentric dilettante in art furniture. The walls were not papered, but were panelled in a unique style, and decorated in varying shades of purple, though the range of colour was not extensive, nor the different shades very distinct.

Endeavouring idly to trace the design in its endless involutions, it became apparent to me that the whole scheme of the apartment had been carried out in this one tint—purple. Strange it was that this fact should be so late in definitely impressing itself upon my mind. Even the stained glass which admitted the light was of purple. I fancied for a moment that this coloured light was the origin of the purple tinge I saw all around me; but it was not. The entire room, and what it contained of furniture, were of the prevailing hue. The whole effect was strange, but not bizarre. Whilst its novelty added to its attractiveness, it was soft and pleasing, yet, somehow, it only served to deepen that sense of vague anxiety which had for some time been growing upon me. Into whose house had I fallen? Evidently the owner was an artist of a kind, rich enough to indulge his fads and materialise his theories. I knew of none such among my acquaintances. Even Dr. Wainwright, who, I supposed, was by this time upon the high seas, had never, so far as I knew, interested himself in art furnishing or decoration. His town flat was richly, even splendidly appointed; but it differed in no important point from a hundred others. He had simply given *carte blanche* to the furnishers and upholsterers.

Yes, in its way, this room was a masterpiece of decorative art; but I soon found myself thinking that if one had to live in it always it

would become a purple monotony. Why were there no windows?
A view of the street, or the garden, or whatever might be outside,
would make all the difference. But evidently the designer had been
so much in love with his purple symphony that he was jealous of
any note of distraction.

I was fast becoming weary of that soft purple light, when
the door opened, and a man appeared. At first I thought it was a
woman, for he wore a long robe, and his face was beardless and
smooth. He bore a large tray, on which was a chocolate service,
with some food. Drawing a tiny table to my bedside, he set the tray
upon it. Then, pointing to the wall opposite to that through which
he had entered, he said, in a very low tone—

"That door opens into your dressing-room. You will find a bath
there, and everything necessary."

He was turning to go, when I said—"Where am I? Who are
you?"

"I am a servant of the master of the house."

"And who is he?"

"You will see him when you have breakfasted and dressed."

I was opening my lips to ask another question, when I stopped
in amazement, not unmixed with horror. Not only the man's robe,
but his face and hands also, were of a soft purple tint. Before I could
speak again he had disappeared.

My eyes fell upon my own hands; they were of purple. I looked
about me for a mirror; there was none. Then I tore open the garment I wore, and saw my breast was of the same prevailing tint.
All the bedclothes were dyed purple. I leapt out of bed on to the
rich purple carpet, and opened the door indicated by the attendant.
I found myself in a plainly furnished dressing-room, with a bath
at one end. Everything was of purple, and the mirror reflected no
other colour. There were hot and cold water taps. I turned them,
and clear, but purple-tinted water flowed forth. And the silence was
that of death.

I am not of a nervous or highly-strung temperament; and,
though I had drunk so deeply at Wainwright's party, I was by no
means "shaky" or unsettled. My courage seemed to surge up within
me, and for the moment all sinister fancies were driven away.

"This is a trick," I said—"an elaborate practical joke, and I shall know all about it presently. In the meantime the chocolate is cooling."

With something of a lightened heart, therefore, I returned to my breakfast, and found it much to my taste. Then, ignoring the colour of the water, I had a purple bath, using plenty of the purple soap provided, which, however, had no effect upon my stained skin.

There were no outer garments save a rich purple dressing-gown, somewhat similar to the robe worn by the attendant. There was a second door to the dressing-room, but it was locked. It began to dawn upon me that I was a prisoner; and, returning to the bedroom, I beguiled myself with wondering who were the authors of this fantastic jest, and how long they intended to keep it up. Apart from the mystery, which was disquieting enough, I had business interests and engagements, and therefore, in a mere worldly sense, was bound to suffer from what I now began to look upon as something verging upon an outrage.

Whilst I was busied in these reflections, the door again opened, and the attendant entered, followed by a man similarly attired, but taller. The servant quietly took up the tray and disappeared.

"Good-morning, Mr. Geoffrey Coverdale."

It was Dr. Wainwright. His clean-shaven, handsome face was stained purple, as were also his hands.

I arose and looked at him steadily. "So you, Dr. Wainwright," I said, "are the perpetrator of this stupid practical joke. I hope you have enjoyed it sufficiently. But I must ask you to return my clothes, to give me something to remove this idiotic stain, and let me go. I have important business matters to attend to." I spoke as sternly as I could, but near the end of my speech I was conscious of a queer faltering in my voice.

Wainwright's thin lips relaxed into an inscrutable smile.

"Why, how long do you suppose you have been here?" he asked.

"Since last night, of course—the night of your symposium."

"My dear fellow, that was months ago. You are now in Andiang, a town in the interior of Java, which my friend Grangerford and I have fixed upon as the scene of our experiments."

"Impossible! Why, it was only last night——"

"Gently, gently, my dear fellow. Cerebral affections like yours leave one very weak as to notions of time and place. You are progressing famously, however. In a few more months I hope to restore you to your friends; but you must be calm and patient."

My heart beat wildly. Could there be any truth in all this? I in Java! "But," I stammered, "why bring me here?"

"Certainly, it was not absolutely essential," he said, softly. "But as the peculiar lesion of the brain from which you were found to be suffering made it desirable that you should be placed in my hands, and as I did not wish to delay my departure, it was arranged that you should accompany us."

A lesion of the brain. And ill—mad, doubtless, for months!

"Softly, softly, Coverdale!" purred the specialist; "excitement of any sort may undo all that has been so laboriously accomplished. Be patient; you are doing splendidly."

"But why—why this purple?"

"It is part of the treatment. The effect of colour on the mind has long been known; but never before (here he smiled strangely)—never before has it been tried as I am trying it."

I calmed myself by a strong effort. It was evident that, whether Wainwright spoke truly or not, nothing could be gained by argument or opposition. I inquired after my friends in Melbourne. He smiled again.

"Miss Seymour is well," he said, suavely—"well, but anxious, of course."

I pressed him for particulars of my misfortune, but he had little to tell me. He said that I was found wandering about the streets at dawn after the symposium, and somebody took me back to his rooms. A consultation with two well-known physicians was held, my friends were apprised of my calamity, and the result was that I became Dr. Wainwright's patient and Sir Miles Grangerford's guest. Such was his story.

"I really feel, Wainwright," I said, rather plaintively, "that sunlight and fresh air——"

"Not on any account, Coverdale," he said, smilingly; "it would be disastrous."

"But—this seclusion—this solitude—it will become so depressing——"

"Ah, yes, depressing; quite so. That is the effect desired. During the state from which you have so happily emerged, Coverdale, the least thing excited you—even a gleam of sunlight would send you frantic. I have been trying colour effects for the last month. Green was very helpful—calmed your maniacal outbursts wonderfully. But the influence of green is only transient—it ends by irritating. Purple is slower, but much more efficacious."

I knew not what to make of all this, but there was no use doubting or contradicting. Whether I believed him or not, Wainwright would certainly tell me only what he chose.

"I suppose," I said, "that as I progress towards recovery some at least of this purple will be dispensed with. I can't see why——"

"Patience, patience," said the specialist, in whose soft voice I fancied at times there lurked a mocking undertone. "In a little while you will get quite used to the purple. You may even come to like it. You may grow a little melancholy, but that means mental rest, which you need greatly. The main thing is to accept everything as you find it, and don't worry."

I felt a chill at the heart upon hearing these words. Knowing this man to have been my rival, whom I had dispossessed of both love and lucre, I could not feel at my ease in his hands.

"I suppose I shall see your friend, Sir Miles Grangerford?" I said.

"He is away at present hunting after rare moths and things," said Wainwright. "He's quite an enthusiastic entomologist, you know. But doubtless, when he returns, he will be curious to see his queer guest." And Wainwright smiled—a very sinister smile, or his purple lips made it seem so. He then left me, saying he would look in again, perhaps, next day.

Alone once more, I reflected deeply, staring at the purple carpet. Surely such an adventure had never happened to mortal man before. But the more I pondered over Wainwright's words the more firmly was I convinced that his every statement was false. Yes; the man was lying. He had compassed my disappearance from the world, and his motive was not hard to guess. He had set his heart on winning Marie Seymour and her money.

I knew that his voyage with Sir Miles Grangerford had been arranged. But had they sailed and taken me with them? That part of the story might be true. In the wilds of Java he could do with his supposed patient what he pleased. But why such an elaborate scheme I could not imagine, unless he had found it necessary to dupe Sir Miles, whose reputation was undoubted.

While I was reflecting upon these things, a deep melancholy seemed to settle upon me. I knew that it was not natural, for the usual effect of untoward circumstances upon my mind had been to stimulate it into action. But now I felt like De Quincey's dreamer, who, "through languishing prostration in hope and the energies of hope," lies down before the lion. I had a vague dread that, however great the need, however pressing the emergency, I should fail. I, too, should "lie down before the lion." There is a kind of luxury of defeat into which the human mind is prone to sink. The failures, the "deadbeats," of life enjoy that sad luxury. Despair has its voluptuousness. But I am by nature energetic and sanguine, therefore it could only be by some artificial depressant that my mental powers could be so relaxed. No doubt Wainwright had it in his power to produce this effect with drugs; but I now believe that he relied solely upon the exclusion of all colours but purple from my range of vision.

When the attendant (who was evidently of British nationality) brought my lunch, I scarcely observed him. Appetite had left me; but for want of occupation I ate and drank. The food (which, as before, was tinted purple) seemed designed to avoid any stimulating effect. It consisted of some fine form of wheaten meal, deliciously cooked, and served with milk. There were some purple grapes by way of dessert, and, instead of wine, cocoa. When the servant came to take away the dishes, he found me gazing intently at the pale green of a grape from which I had removed the purple skin. He snatched it from me. I made no resistance, but looking up at him, saw that his face wore a terrified expression.

In the midst of a deadly silence, weighed down by an overpowering melancholy, I languished for several hours. Then I made some sort of effort to analyse my mental condition. I felt a dull fear at the view I found myself taking of my worldly affairs—the singular falling away of all care, all anxiety. Vaguely I realised that I was lapsing into a state of indifference, of pure contemplation, with little thought of myself as a concrete being. I had still a feeling of revolt against the indulgence of this mental sloth, which, I dimly reflected, might prove hurtful to the interests of others as well as myself. And I seemed to know, in a shadowy sort of way, that many days of this purple horror and deathlike silence would plunge me into a state of melancholia, from which I would never emerge by any effort of my own will. With an effort I arose, and walked up and down the room for a while, forcing myself to think clearly and coherently.

The action had some effect. I reflected for several minutes. It became evident to me that Wainwright was indulging a strange revenge, and at the same time, perhaps, testing a theory. I could have no doubt but that he intended to allow my purple surroundings to exercise their full effect upon my brain, even to the destruction of my reason. I also felt sure that my friends were unaware that I was in his hands. Holgate alone would never have consented, for he regarded Wainwright as little better than a charlatan. Marie, too—her instinct would warn her against the man.

But what could I do? Even if I found means to combat the effect of the purple, Wainwright, having me in his power, could easily and quickly resort to other ways of getting rid of me. The only plan I could think of was a resort to brute force. A sudden attack upon him and his servant, and their disablement, might procure me the means of escape. But, first of all, it was imperative that I should find some relief from the purple colour, which now began to fill me with horror unspeakable—not that it was at all painful in itself; it was insidiously soft and soothing—but the anticipation of its ultimate effect upon my reason filled me with a nameless dread.

I tried the books, tearing some to pieces in the hope of discovering even the smallest portion of white paper; in vain. I turned up the carpet; the floor beneath was stained purple. I wrecked the little table, splintering the woodwork; but it was stained right through. So was the leathery composition used for the decorated walls. It seemed that all my efforts to find some non-purple substance had been foreseen and provided against.

I felt an almost unconquerable desire to surrender myself to what seemed the inevitable. I sank down upon the bed and closed my eyes, but I could not shut out that all-pervading purple. I tried to rouse myself, but my lethargy was too great. I forgot my fears, and relapsed into a profound and melancholy contemplation, through which ran funereal melodies, such as Schubert's "Raven,"

Chopin's "Marche Funebre," Beethoven's mournful andantes—music which, I must confess, has but little attraction for me when in my right mind. These strains seemed to come from without, yet I knew that they did not; and they were more than sad—they were lugubrious, dirge-like. I did not seem to suffer from this mental state; on the contrary, there was in it a kind of negative enjoyment, such as we often experience in dreams.

So the afternoon wore on, and the attendant came again. I dimly remembered my plan of escape, and looked at the man. He was not tall, and I felt that I was more than his equal in strength. He glanced at the broken table, and smiled. I roused myself.

"Look here, my man," I said: "I must get out of this. I'll give you my note for a cool thousand——"

"No good, sir," he replied. "Not if it was millions. Money's no use to me, sir."

"But you must be aware that you are aiding and abetting——"

"Yes, yes, I know, sir. Leastways, you can say what you like. But don't break any more things, sir. It ain't no use."

When he was gone I made another effort to think, and for a few moments collected my faculties sufficiently to come to a sort of decision. I knew that if I let another day go by I should be beyond all self-help. The insidious purple would triumph over the remnant of my shattered will, and I should be a hopeless prey to melancholia. I must act speedily. When Wainwright came next day I would overpower him, and deal with the attendant later. The master must be settled first.

Darkness fell, and, as before, they gave me no lamp. I slept—if it could be called sleep, which was filled with dreams that were not dreams, but only dim and varying phases of a shadowy world filled with purple—purple solitudes, mountains, skies, forests, cities, palaces, theatres, crowds of people—surging seas of purple, billowing waves of human faces, all stained with that treacherous, soul-destroying hue.

The mental condition in which I found myself next morning I know not how to describe. Everything that had happened to me seemed to have receded to an incalculable distance in past time. It was almost as though those events belonged to a former state of being. All the people to whom my fate most bound me—Marie,

Wainwright, Holgate, and the rest—were to me but phantoms of the past; the first sadly remembered and regretted, the second no longer feared or hated, the third a mere shadow. I felt as though I were in some borderland between this world and another. Memory, however, was not lost. I recalled that I had resolved, by fair means or foul, to overpower my enemy and force him to release me; but now this resolve seemed the uttermost of folly. My former life was done with; it was too remote, too alien; it belonged to the eternity of the past.

When Wainwright came I did not move. I looked at him with the indifference of an opium-eater. He was no longer an enemy. The word had no meaning for me now.

"Well, Coverdale," I remember him saying, "the experiment is succeeding beautifully. In a few days your cure"—I observed his sinister smile—"will be complete; you will no longer need the purple."

"I shall not be taken away," I murmured, for in the notion of any change or disturbance there was a peculiar irritation.

"Not until the last," he said, still smiling. "When the purple has quite killed Geoffrey Coverdale, and left a mere case of melancholia, and my pompous medical confreres can be trusted to recommend you to Yarra Bend or Kew, or some other such comfortable place of residence, then I shall be done with you. This little episode will be over, you know. But we may come and see you sometimes—Marie and I."

For a moment I felt something almost like an emotion, but it died out instantly. His brutally frank statement that I would soon be a maniac was singularly unmeaning in my ears. If I could be said to think, my thoughts inclined vaguely to a sort of conception that Wainwright himself was mad. I had, if I remember correctly, a dim feeling that all who busied themselves with worldly plans or affairs were using up their energies in an insanely foolish way. This led me into one of my interminable reveries, and when, I know not how long afterwards, I looked up, he was gone.

After this I lost all count of time, and my memory grew weaker and weaker. Stagnation fell upon my mental being, and my bodily energies succumbed to an overpowering lethargy. I ceased to distinguish between my nights and days—if, indeed, many passed—

for dreams and realities seemed to have merged into one mass of vague, indeterminate sensation. The quicksand of melancholia had all but engulfed me.

It was night when the fire broke out. I awoke, half-suffocated. Flames and smoke were breaking through one of the walls. I heard the crash of falling woodwork, the shouts of men; and through the burning wall a stream of water came, falling upon me, and drenching me to the skin. But I made no attempt to move. I lay still, fascinated by the noise, but still more by the varied colours of the fire, smoke, steam, and water. Then I lost consciousness.

I was rescued by the firemen, and, after considerable delay, my identity was established, and my friends took charge of me.

The shock resulted in brain fever, from which I only recovered as by a miracle. In my convalescence I had my dear Marie, now my wife, for a constant companion and nurse.

I had never been to Java. The house in which Wainwright had immured me was in one of the outer suburbs of Melbourne. He himself perished in the fire, which was supposed to have occurred through the explosion of some chemicals with which he was experimenting. His attendant disappeared.

I have since been told that the doctor's choice of purple with which to destroy my reason was a merciful one; that blue, for instance, or yellow, would have produced mania of the most violent kind, preceded by fearful experiences. Whether he chose purple to spare me that suffering, or as being likely to give himself the minimum of trouble and risk, I leave those who knew the man to decide.

THE STRANGE CASE OF ALAN HERIOT

[The remarkable lapse of memory which afflicted my friend, Alan Heriot, on his return from a long absence in Japan and other Eastern countries, and which culminated in a very dangerous attack of brain fever, presented some features so extraordinary that I induced him, after much persuasion, to relate the story of this part of his life. It will be seen that the phrase "loss of memory" is far from correct, if what he has set down be true; but whether his narrative is to be taken as a record of actual facts, or as the weird adventures of a sick brain in the shadowland of dreams, the reader must judge for himself. I append Mr. Heriot's MS. without further comment.]

It was in a Japanese coastal village that the long-sought "Word of Power" was revealed to me. The old bonze, Atzu Sumangala, whom I had journeyed so far to see, would, however, tell me nothing, except that I was not deceived in my conviction regarding the potency of certain of the ancient mantras or spells. He refused to teach me the least of them, and I wanted the greatest.

For many years psychic research and other occult studies had been my ruling passion. Latterly, it is true, the beautiful Miss Alison Grant had drawn a good deal of my attention away from scientific and pseudo-scientific pursuits, for which she had but scant sympathy. The rupture between us, however, was not caused by my studies; it was the work of a very cunning and unscrupulous enemy —a rival in fame and love—Gregory Hawke, the well-known Orientalist. This man, who, I must admit, loved the lady with all the strength of his nature, had, by a most adroit presentment of half-truths, against which it was impossible to fight, succeeded in poisoning her mind to my injury—an injury so serious that it seemed irreparable along ordinary lines. It would he painful to both of us for me to go into details on this matter; so I must leave the bald statement as it stands.

Now, this Gregory Hawke was an old colleague of mine. We were engaged in the same great search. It was the quest for a certain formula of words, or rather sounds, of a class known in the East as "mantras"—sentences so constructed that they possess peculiar powers. At first we had both laughed at the claims made for such things, treating them as mere superstition. Determined investigation, extending over many years, had, however, made one fact very clear to us—viz., that all so-called superstitions, or nearly all, are the fragmentary or corrupted traditions of what in far-distant ages were great truths. A study of ethnology reveals the fact that all races have their infancy, their maturity, and their decay. When a nation declines it loses the mental power of its prime.

In the East this rise and fall is explained by the theory of reincarnation. The decline of a race means that the more advanced egos, or souls seeking re-birth, no longer find in that race the necessary environment for their further evolution, and so it becomes the training school for lower and lower grades of egos, until, reaching its nadir, it is either absorbed by conquering nations, or dies out. However this may be, the fact remains that decaying races no longer preserve their ideals, nor cherish their best traditions; yet these ideals and traditions are never wholly lost. Here and there a great soul is compelled by its "karma" to reincarnate in the dying race; and the sacred truths, debased by the multitude, are preserved by the few who can see their inner meaning. Much, of course, is lost; yet not a little survives. A conviction of this fact led Hawke and myself to form a theory that behind many of the seemingly absurd superstitions of the East there may lurk not only much valuable knowledge, but even some great and portentous secrets of nature—the discoveries of long-forgotten sages, not yet recovered by orthodox science. Further research tended to the conviction that amongst the more erudite and exclusive of the Brahmins and Buddhists there yet lingered men of extraordinary wisdom and profound knowledge—men who, knowing well the folly of casting their pearls before swine, or throwing that which is holy to the dogs, preserved an unbroken silence to the outside word.

Urged by such conclusions as these, and passionately desiring knowledge not yet vouchsafed to our own race, we embarked upon an enterprise not less difficult than extraordinary. It was our purpose to wrest from those who guarded it a "Word of Power"—which had the virtue, when chanted in a certain prescribed way, of enabling him who used it to pass out of bodily consciousness and to function mentally in that mysterious division of the great realm of nature which lies next above the physical. The vista which this possibility opened before us was alluring beyond expression, yet the love of a woman came between us, and our search for forbidden knowledge was interrupted by mutual jealousy, and ended finally in death and disaster. But this is anticipating.

After my quarrel with Gregory Hawke over his treacherous conduct, I pursued the search on my own account. I threw myself into it with all the more determination, now that my hopes of winning Alison were wrecked. I did not follow Hawke's movements; my jealous fancy pictured him relinquishing the great search in order to win a dearer prize; though something seemed to tell me that Alison would never surrender her life to his keeping.

So I wandered over the East in search of the "Word of Power." The quest of the Holy Grail was, apparently, not more hopeless, but this was not less fascinating. From a Hindu kajayogi I at last learned that a certain Buddhist bonze, Atzu Sumangala, of the Tendai sect, in Japan, might by a bare possibility give me a hint. This yogi saw, or pretended to see, that my "karma" was bound up with that of Atzu, who, he said, owed me a debt contracted in some bygone life.

But Atzu smiled pityingly when I spoke of this.

"If the yogi has attained samadhi, he might know this thing," he said; "and the mere fact that you are here shows that your karma is mixed with mine. But what of that? Our Dharma says we should do no ill, and surely it is ill done to reveal the secrets of the wise to the vain and foolish."

I thanked him rather ironically, though I could not help liking and respecting the old fellow—he was so obviously a man of high development, intellectual and spiritual. I urged that I was perhaps not foolish above other men, that I did not want the mantra for any selfish purpose—but here I stopped, for his eyes seemed to be looking straight through me.

"Not till one has conquered Trishna," he said, solemnly, "can wisdom be imparted; and you have scarcely attained Vivella; in your inmost heart Vairagya is only a name"—meaning that I could not yet discriminate between reality and illusion sufficiently to have a clear grasp of the former. Though a Buddhist, Atzu used Sanskrit terminology in preference to the Pali but this, I believe, was because he had studied the former in his old age, and liked to display his knowledge, many Buddhist priests being ignorant of both tongues.

Returning to my quaint little lodging, who should I meet but Gregory Hawke! Well for him that I was unarmed. The great Orientalist, however, greeted me as coolly as if we had never parted in anger.

"No hard words, Heriot," he said. "Let this be a business interview. I've got what you are looking for!"

"You—you've——"

"Found the mantra—yes. Got it from a hoary old Chikku of the Malwatta Vihare at Kandy!"

Though I feared he was lying, my heart beat wildly.

"And—and what is it?"

He laughed.

"What should you say, Heriot, if I told you that it was simply the well-known so-called Thibetan prayer—'Aum! Mani Padme Hum!'"

I made a despairing gesture.

"You've come all this way to laugh at me!"

"Not likely. I'm not that kind of humorist. It's as I say. As with all extant mantras, everything depends on the correct intonation and the rate of repetition. Once you produce the requisite soundwaves the effect follows."

"I know—I know. Vibration is the whole secret. And—you've seen it tried?"

"Without doubt. The old rascal of a Chikku chanted it seven times, and then—the separation was effected, palpably. Not content with that, I tried it myself. I very nearly followed the Chikku—only just stopped in time."

"Why did you stop?"

"Caution, Heriot—or fear. It's a deuce of a thing to tamper with. One mightn't get back, you know. Besides I've other plans now."

"And you are willing to teach it me? On certain conditions, I suppose?"

"One only, which I see you guess—that you give me a free hand with respect to a lady I need not name."

I repressed my anger, and reflected. I had lost all hope of winning sweet Alison Grant by any effort exerted on the physical plane. On the other hand, I had little fear that Hawke would gain the prize. I knew the proud girl too well; she was the wrong sort to encourage with the suit of a slanderer.

"I will not interfere with you down here," I said, emphasizing the last two words significantly. "You have my word."

"That's enough for me," he replied. "And for any other sort of interference you may attempt, I care not; she is no sensitive."

"Very well; that's settled. Now for the mantra."

Gregory Hawke had not deceived me. The long-sought mantra was mine at last! To the commonality of the East, "Aum! (or Om!) Mani Padme Hum!" ("Oh, the pearl on the lotus!") is a prayer to Buddha—the pearl representing the illustrious teacher, and the lotus his heavenly abode. But to the more enlightened it becomes an invocation to the inmost spirit—"O Thou! the God within me!"—and is used by the religious devotee in his effort to raise his worshipping soul to as great a height of spiritual exaltation as it may be capable of attaining. Chanted in a peculiar way, known to very few, it has the extraordinary—it will be said the incredible—power of so affecting the purely mental part of the human constitution as to cause a separation, similar to that which takes place at death, except that the body, instead of disintegrating, remains in a kind of trance. My friends, who look upon me as having suffered a "loss of memory," will smile sceptically, I fear, at these statements, and the still more remarkable ones to come; but the thing is as much a scientific fact, and as susceptible of scientific analysis, as is "wireless telegraphy," the germ theory of disease, or any other now accepted hypothesis. This, at all events, I know—that as the Word from the darkness spoke the universe into being, so is it possible, given the secret formula, to command the spirit, the real man, to leave his tenement of flesh and range at will over the phenomenal world.

Before I left, something prompted me to go and inform the old bonze of my success. He was deeply perturbed. Raising his withered arms, he uttered a solemn warning against the use of the mantra. It was a sacrilege for which I would surely suffer. Nameless perils would beset me. I was not fitted—not sufficiently advanced upon the "Way"—to use such awful powers with impunity. He quoted a Buddhist adage, the equivalent of our own proverb—"fools rush in," &c. He spoke of the "Gunas," the three qualities. I was not beyond the second, "Rajas"—the quality of activity, passion, desire; whilst the human love of life—physical sensation—"Trishna," would drag me down and destroy me. But I heeded not his jeremiad, though I was struck with the gentle old ascetic's evident anxiety, and I had an uneasy feeling that much of what he said was true.

In a month I was back in Melbourne. Anticipating experiences unheard-of among my countrymen, I made elaborate preparations for my physical safety. I need not describe these, since they proved futile. During this time I had more than once, by cautious experiments carried to a certain point, proved the mantra's power; and now I was ready for the full trial.

When the time came my heart almost failed me. The old bonze's solemn warning, added to my own theoretical knowledge of that condition of existence bordering on the physical—known in India as "Pretaloka," or "Ghostland"—was not encouraging. But, relying upon my trained mental forces—above all, upon a will power developed along unusual lines—I determined not to recede from my momentous enterprise.

It was necessary that I should chant the mantra in that "bitter hour before the dawn," when physical vitality is at its lowest ebb, and the principles of man's being are most readily separable. At length I conquered the shuddering body, the quivering nerves; and, having attained to a state of complete mental and physical tranquillity, I began that weird chant. Seven times I repeated the fatal syllables, and then—the awful separation of soul and body was consummated!

There was no loss of consciousness, though my form sank down upon the couch prepared for it. I was still in the room, but all was changed. I saw with rising apprehension that, without having moved more than a few feet, I was in a strange world, to the conditions of which I should have to grow accustomed, much as a new-born child has to accustom its senses to their proper use. What bewildered me most was that all objects seemed to be pulsing with life, and to have lost their appearance of solidity. Moreover, I could see all their sides at once, as if they were spread out flat before me, while yet retaining their natural shapes. It was some time before I realized that this was merely the result of the enlarged perception belonging to my new condition; I was in a realm of more dimensions than the familiar three known to physical eyes. The vibration of everything, too, meant that my new sight was more than microscopic, so that I could see plainly the atomic life with which even the densest or heaviest matter is permeated.

As I was trying to accustom myself to these strange conditions, I suddenly became aware that I was held in the room by some force which I could not overcome. This seemed the more remarkable because my prevailing sensation was that of lightness. I felt that I could will myself anywhere with the speed of thought—that I *was* thought, in a vehicle of desire—if only I could tear myself away from the spot. Then I knew that my body was the point of attraction, and with that thought came an almost unconquerable impulse to return to the fleshly tabernacle. Would that I had obeyed it! But my will prevailed. After an indescribable struggle, which lasted I know not how long, I found myself free, and gliding, much as I had often done in dreams, over the surface of the sleeping earth.

A description of the sights and scenery of Pretaloka—could it be rendered intelligible to the physical intellect—would make a bulky treatise. Some day I may attempt the task, but here I must confine myself to my personal history. My chief motive in thus daring to tamper with the mysteries of life and death had been the quest of knowledge. Of this I had assured my friend the bonze—to say nothing of the yogis, swamis, bhikkus, shamans, &c., whom I had vainly besought to help me. Evading the toll usually paid, I had slipped through the gates of death; I had pushed into the beyond—an alien adventurer without a passport. A spiritual law-breaker—such I was; and a bitter penalty I paid. But I had reasoned that my purposes were not entirely selfish, even though the desire for knowledge was now mingled with another motive less pure. That motive concerned my love for Alison Grant, who had, as I have said, been turned against me by the half-truths of a cunning slanderer. Although the passion for knowledge would alone have impelled me to dare the perils of the unknown world, a novel and entrancing motive was added in the singular chance offered me to regain Alison's esteem, if not her affection. Denied physical access to her, I would seek her presence on another plane, and endeavour to influence her mind—to undo the evil work of my enemy. This, surely, was but just to herself, for I felt—nay I knew—that she loved me.

It would be interesting, but apart from my main purpose, to detail the experiences I went through in my efforts to accustom myself to this new state of existence, and to the very bewildering and sometimes terrifying sights of Pretaloka. The millions of shadowy beings like myself, and others of a higher and a lower order; the vast expanses of what I must call scenery for want of a fitting term, but which far transcended the scenery of earth in glory, and in many other qualities which are quite incommunicable in words; the light that was not light; the sounds that were not sounds—how can they be described? Only by constructing a system of metaphors and symbols could even an approach be made to anything like an intelligible account of the wonders of Pretaloka. And yet this realm is coextensive with the world we live in, and is separated from us merely by the limitations of our consciousness.

As soon, then, as I had accustomed myself, in a degree, to my new condition, I "thought" or "willed" myself into the presence of Alison Grant. It was morning. She was in a garden, gathering flowers. I saw her in the luminous cloud that surrounded her—the many-coloured envelope of etheric mist which psychics call the "aura." It was an object far more beautiful even than her bodily self—as well it might be, for it was her "robe of glory," the true vehicle of her spirit. It projected from her figure several feet; its size and purity of opalescent colour were eloquent of her lofty development of heart and mind. My own smaller and comparatively turbid vehicle rebounded as I sought to mingle it with hers. Yet I succeeded in impressing her, for I saw her start, grow pale, and fall into deep thought. Then she turned, and plucked a scarlet carnation—my favourite flower—and gazed upon it intently. I saw that I was remembered, but that was all—unless a sudden flush of rose-pink in her "aura" might indicate that love mingled with her memories. A passion of desire surged through me as I beheld it, and I hurled myself against that protecting wall of luminous ether, invisible to mortal eyes, but impervious as granite to the intrusion of unwelcome or alien influences.

Then a strange and solemn thing happened. She drew herself up to her full height, dropping the flower; her eyes hardened and flashed; her hands were clenched; and faded from my sight! Thus it seemed; but it was I who departed. She had willed me away!

It was clear, then, that such high-souled purity was proof against the influence of a desire-nature so ill-controlled as mine. With the expanded intuition of my present state I grasped the position instantly. To regain her confidence, to teach her the mantra, to have her for companion and helper in my occult investigations—above all, to show her, more plainly than by any physical means, the essential honour that underlay all the natural dross of my being, and the manly as well as the manlike quality of my love for her—such was the framework of the fabric I had raised, and it had fallen like a house of cards.

I was aimlessly drifting about in the etheric currents, wrapped in gloomy thoughts, when suddenly I felt that my physical form was in danger. I flew to it with the speed of thought. Too late! My body—mine no longer—was seated on the floor of the room, with a large scientific work on its lap, the pages of which it was turning with quick, jerky motions, now and then tearing out a coloured plate. I felt the vibrations of babbling laughter, of baby glee; and despair seized me as I saw that some ego waiting for reincarnation had drifted into my soul-deserted body. I tried frantically to drive out the intruder, but in the newly-incarnated "Trishna" is strong and I only succeeded in frightening the child-soul, which thereupon used its physical vehicle to set up a prolonged and lugubrious howl.

I fled in horror. I knew that only by the aid of beings usually called "supernatural" could I regain my physical tenement; and who was there to help me? I was doomed. It was exactly as if I had "died." I should have to wander in Pretaloka for centuries, perhaps—until my "vehicle of desire" aged and fell away, leaving me another of still finer texture, which would respond to the rarer vibrations of a higher state of existence. The only gleam of hope left to me was that, in course of time, Alison must also "die," and that she would voluntarily descend from her own loftier sphere to cheer my purgatory. But the immediate prospect was too appalling to admit of any comfort in such attenuated hopes.

Losing the mental balance so essential to the dweller in that realm of spectres, I abandoned myself to the agonies of despair. This left me a helpless prey to all the horrors of Pretaloka. I was instantly surrounded by a host of grinning demons—foul and loathsome shapes, such as not even the diseased imagination of a mediaeval hermit could have conjured up. In my normal state I could easily have willed away such base creatures, who are the mere refuse or scum of the lower levels—souls of debased savages and of criminals, degenerates, &c.; but now, given over to terror, I fled—a disembodied Tam o' Shanter—before the horde of my goblin persecutors. Through sulphurous clouds, down flaming cataracts, into more than volcanic gulfs of living fire, I was harried—fearful hells, the illusive but all too realistic thought-forms created by my own senseless terror and their hateful exultation—hells such as Dante saw in his immortal vision, and such as only he could have described. I fled in vain. Horrible eyes glared into mine; great mouths, with red vampire lips, hovered hungrily about me; I shrank from beastlike fangs and talons, from hands armed with gigantic weapons. Forgetting that no injury could be inflicted upon me save that of terror, I became a fitting object for the mocking sport of these degraded beings.

How long this persecution lasted I cannot tell. But suddenly the fiendish myriads left me, and with them the scene so easily shaped from the plastic matter of Pretaloka by artist-egos, whose ruling passion dies not with the bodily form; and my old friend, the Japanese bonze, was beside me, soothing my still agitated being. He it was who had rescued me from my hellish tormentors before I had, as I might have done, sunk to their level through a kind of dreadful perverted sympathy, the effect of my terror. I thus owed him more than life itself.

As is customary in Pretaloka with those who have not long quitted earth, we "thought" ourselves into the semblance of our bodily forms, and, stretching ourselves upon the grass of that lovely, though illusive place, we conversed in the telepathic language of the plane, which I translate.

"You are here?" I said.

"Yes. My body fell away at last . . . My poor friend, you heeded not my warning, and now—what suffering!"

"Yes, you were right, Atzu. But what you have saved me from is not all. I cannot return—my fleshly vehicle——"

"I know. But do not despair . . . The ways of Karma are strange. I am here to help you. I must dwell in this dense and gloomy medium till you are free."

"What do you mean? This is not, then, your place?"

The old man smiled sadly, yet with a certain gentle pride.

"My place is in Devachan (heaven)," he said. "There might you also dwell but for Trishna. Ah, how strong is Trishna! This terrible craze for physical life—how enduring it is! I have seen the Blessed Ones, the Devas (angels)—and they, even they who possess all knowledge, gaze with awe and wonder at the myriads of souls madly pressing downwards into incarnation, content with misery, pain, sin, and all forms of earthly suffering, so that it be but physical life! Oh, mystery of mysteries!"

"Old man," I cried, passionately, "for a year—ay, for one day—of earth-life with my beloved I would accept annihilation, could such be!"

"I know," he said, sadly. "Many, many lives must you endure before you will even begin to tear Trishna from your heart. Karma is just—she gives unto each his desire; but the nature of the desire may be moulded by the reason; and thus, in some degree, man is the master of his fate, and every man must and will work out his own emancipation. Thus have we heard," he added, with true Buddhist humility.

"But, Atzu," I said, for I was in no mood for philosophy, "what will happen to my unhappy vehicle?"

"I know not yet. A soul has been permitted to enter it. That soul remembers not its former life on earth; thus it is an infant on the physical plane, and must acquire knowledge like any other. But this kind of incarnation is quite abnormal—though not unique—and there are ways . . . Well, my poor friend, we can only watch and wait. In the meantime, if you choose, I will be your instructor in the lore of the superphysical planes."

I had to submit. Intensely interesting was his instruction— strange beyond credence were the secrets he revealed; but Trishna held me constantly in her thrall, and the passionate longing to re-enter physical life never left me. Here there was a vast freedom of motion and of intellection; the ills that flesh is heir to, and the clogs that thought, working through a physical brain, must contend with, did not exist; knowledge, within limits, came by intuition. But the feeling that I was shut out from all that I had been accustomed to regard as solid realities made me desire to get back at any cost—even if it were in the form of a cripple, a dwarf, a savage—so wildly did I desire to quit this world of shadows. The bonze told me that this feeling would wear off in time, and that if I brought it under control I should get rid of it in the course of two or three centuries—a cheering prospect.

"Give yourself up to knowledge, my son," he urged. "Knowledge will conduct you to Devachan, where there is bliss; and in the ages to come, when you have conquered Trishna, knowledge will bring you even unto Nirvana, where there is supreme peace."

Of course it was chiefly my love for Alison Grant that drew my thoughts constantly back to earth. Lacking this powerful magnet, it is possible that in time my Buddhist friend and helper would have won me over to his benevolent plans; and that, under his direction, I should have taken the first steps upon that long and difficult path which leads the neophyte to higher and higher states of consciousness. But this is "taking the kingdom of heaven by storm," and I shrank appalled at the magnitude of the task, preferring, like the majority of men, to progress towards perfection in the normal way.

Be sure that I lost nothing of what took place in respect to my fleshly form, so strangely lost. The baby soul that inhabited it soon played such havoc that he had to be restrained; and I had the mortification of witnessing the wonder and grief of my friends, not to speak of the somewhat contemptuous pity of certain acquaintances who "had always doubted Heriot's sanity," and who were "not at all surprised!" Alan Heriot's "strange loss of memory" made quite a sensation in scientific circles; and the papers "wrote it up" rather more fully than the real Alan Heriot, whose memory was only too distinct, relished. It was thought that the "famous scientist," as they were good enough to style me, had dropped back into infancy, as far as the mind was concerned; and many noted brain specialists were much interested. I succeeded in impressing the mind of one of these men with a vague idea of the true facts; but the only result was that he became alarmed, and fancied himself suffering from brain-fag, the result of overwork, and he gave himself a long holiday.

My mortification was strangely added to by the self-sacrifice of Alison Grant. As soon as she heard of my supposed condition, she undertook the task of nursing me, and lavished a world of womanly care and tenderness upon a perfect stranger—a baby-ego who came from heaven alone knows where. It was a peculiar situation—a painful one for her, poor girl. She naturally thought my psychic studies had cost me my reason. This was bad enough for her but the fact that she could never arouse the slightest gleam of recognition or memory in her helpless charge, try how she would, was a terrible affliction.

How I strove to gain access to her mind; how at times I almost succeeded; how she once or twice trembled on the very verge of comprehension; my despairing struggles to lead her on to the right train of thought—these things must remain untold. And there was no respite for my sufferings, for sleep comes not in Pretaloka. The bonze would not help me in these attempts, but besought me to desist from them, pointing out that the mental strain that Alison was enduring was sufficiently great without making further demands upon her. But for the soothing and strengthening influence of this truly great and highly-evolved being, I must surely have sunk into a condition which would have left me a prey once more to the rabble souls—if souls they can be called—of Pretaloka, to whom the sport of harrying and torturing some weak-willed or affrighted spirit of a better class than themselves is a kind of frantic happiness—not without its counterpart on earth, by the way.

The bonze could not always be with me. His life was as full of work as it had been when he was in the body; in fact, he was far more constantly occupied, as there is no sense of fatigue in Pretaloka, and thus no need for rest or recuperation. Probably the help and sympathy he so ungrudgingly gave to me formed the lowest or basest kind of all his occupations. I gathered, also, that he was receiving spiritual instruction from certain very exalted beings who were helping him upward, even as he, in his degree, was helping others. I found that the higher the stage of spiritual evolution attained, the greater is the responsibility of assisting those on the lower rungs of the great ladder; that sacrifice becomes more and more the life principle of these lofty spirits, and that the greatest of them exist for nothing else.

How well I remember my last interview with Atzu Sumangala! We stood in the midst of a sylvan scene surpassingly beautiful; it was wrought by the thought-power of one of the masters of landscape painting, who, since his "death," used the plastic matter of the spirit-world instead of earth's dull pigments, and realised his grandest art dreams unhampered by the difficulties and obstacles inseparable from physical resources. Pretaloka is indeed a "land where our dreams come true," but, alas! our dreams are what we make them, and many that I saw were far different from this. I saw the dreams of the vain and foolish, the narrow and the bigoted, as well as those of the earnest and sincere, the kindly and the single-hearted.

We stood and gazed, he with the calm, sad eye that recognises illusion but does not despise it; I with that yearning joy which seizes one in presence of supernal beauty. But my thoughts could not long stray from my personal concerns.

"Atzu," I said, wearily, "is there no way? With your great powers, surely you could drive away that baby-soul that is keeping me out of my body."

"That could easily be done," he said, calmly.

I felt my being vibrate wildly.

"Then why, if you desire to help me——"

"My poor friend, a great danger menaces you. You have an enemy on the physical plane—one Gregory Hawke."

"It is true. He it was who discovered that accursed mantra, and taught it me."

"I know. And he uses it, too. He, like you, is waiting, waiting for that infant soul to be driven out. And his will is stronger than your own. He has trained it more assiduously, and on a better plan. His object is to abandon his own body and to steal yours. Thus he will win the lady that loves you, for she will imagine that it is you, and that your memory has been restored ... Gently, friend Alan, gently; you attract the pretas, the Shûtas, and all evil beings by these swirling passions. Alas, poor friend! why hunger so for the things of earth? Let them go; give yourself to me—to wisdom—and I will teach you how to will your desires away, how to kill this Trishna that drags you down. And I shall take you with me to the higher realms, and you shall be initiated into the knowledge of the Buddhi—the Pure Reason—knowledge too glorious, too divine, even to be approached in the language of the physical intellect, which you must use on earth. And this knowledge, this divine wisdom, will make you a guide and helper of the humanity that you already love, when, in the course of time, you return to earth in a new incarnation."

But I could not listen to his gentle entreaties ... So Hawke had outwitted me after all. I had thought he lacked the daring to cast off his physical form and enter Pretaloka. Yet he had done so, and even designed this double robbery, impelled by his passion.

I calmed myself.

"How will he proceed?" I asked.

"He will find a way to cause your body to fall into a sickness—brain fever. Then, awaiting his opportunity, he will take possession."

"I will fight him for it," I cried passionately.

"He is the stronger," said Atzu, "but the more evil, and therein lies your advantage in the fight. Yes; you must battle with him for the physical existence that you value so much ... And now, friend Alan, we must part. It is not my karma—alas!—to help you further. Not until you have trampled Trishna under foot may we meet again. Peace be with you. Farewell!"

Overcome with sorrow at the parting, I found no words in which to reply. He faded from my sight, withdrawing himself into some higher state of consciousness whither I was powerless to follow him. I saw him no more.

Soon after this, as Atzu had predicted, my body fell sick. I expected to see the etheric vehicle of Gregory Hawke in its vicinity, but he did not appear. The idea struck me to will myself to him, and see how he was occupied. I found myself in a secluded house in the great city of San Francisco. Very soon I discovered that Hawke had prepared a safe place for his body, even as I had done. At this moment he was alone, idling away the time with some magazines. I did not stay long. There was something abnormal in the etheric currents of this place which I could not understand, though I had a vague feeling that it boded ill. I returned and watched unceasingly beside my unhappy body.

The fever advanced rapidly. In my savage resentment against my unknown supplanter I at first rejoiced to see him suffer; but very soon that feeling gave way to pity. I felt that neither of the two beings I most revered—Alison and the bonze—would admire me for such a hateful sentiment. Besides, the poor creature's agonies would have disarmed an anger even greater than my own. Alison's hospital training made her an invaluable nurse; but she needed all her fortitude, and more than once the strain was almost too much for her. Indeed, my desire was that she should break down and be taken away, for I dreaded the effect that her sufferings would have upon me. In Pretaloka the joys and sorrows, the pleasure and pain of those we love on earth have a powerful effect upon the fine and sensitive matter of the mind's vehicle; and I would need all my thought-power in the conflict with my desperate and determined enemy. I drew some solace from the reflection that he also, in his reckless passion for her, would suffer with her even as I; yet I knew him to be made of sterner stuff than I could boast. He showed his wisdom, too, in keeping away. For many days I saw nothing of him, and even began to hope that, after all, he had not the hardihood for such an unheard-of adventure.

But at last, I saw a spirit-vehicle hovering near—larger than my own, and of a portentous and sinister luminosity. It was the ethereal counterpart of Gregory Hawke. I felt that his will was indeed more powerful than mine, but, happily for me, also more evil. He passed continually through and through my prostrate body, except when Alison bent over it; but the infant soul held strongly to its new-found home, and would not be ejected. Sometimes, in the delirium of the fever, it left the body and hovered near—a pallid, almost shapeless cloud—but at the approach of either of us it regained its position. I saw, however, that, as the fever advanced, its hold would be weaker, and that a strong-willed spirit might easily drive it out. Then would come our strange contest. Hawke would have the advantage, being the stronger; but then, after all, the body was mine, and perhaps would more readily accept my return. This thought was suggested by despair rather than knowledge, and it gave me but little comfort.

I learned then, as I had learned in my flight from the "bhûtas," as Atzu called them, that suffering does not belong to flesh alone—the vibrations of the spirit-vehicle, set up by mental perturbation, may cause the most terrific torture; but what I endured cannot be told. In these moments I often thought of my friend the bonze, and almost wished I had yielded to his entreaties and joined him in the calm pursuit of wisdom and knowledge, leaving to unevolved humanity its unquiet passions and distracting desires.

The fever raged more and more fiercely, and I saw that the time was near when the baby-soul, too weak for a man's agonies, could no longer cling to a body that caused it such excessive torture. In what I may truly call an agony of spirit I waited for the crisis, watching the delicate vehicle of the child-spirit, and the passionate crimson and black cloud that embodied the soul of my enemy.

Suddenly the vehicle of Hawke vanished! A few seconds later the agonised baby-soul fled, and I leapt into my fever-racked body, glad of the pain, glad beyond expression of the weakness, the parched throat, the burning heat that possessed my limbs; glad to suffer any tortures, only to know that I was once more a denizen of earth, our mother—so cruel, yet so well beloved!

"The delirium has ceased," I heard a gentle voice say. "There is a change!"

"Thank heaven for that," was spoken in still sweeter tones—those of Alison Grant. "And look! his eyes—he knows me! Oh, God! he knows me at last!"

I was too weak to utter a word—too weak to return the pressure of her hand, or her fervent kiss. They led her away, weeping hysterically, and I was left in a half delirium of joy as well as of fever.

How was it that Gregory Hawke had fled just at the moment when he must have been anticipating a speedy victory? For many days, during my convalescence, I pondered over this question. But when I was strong enough, Alison told me of the death of my younger brother, whom I had not seen for many years; he had been killed in the San Francisco earthquake. I was grieved; but almost instantly my thoughts flew to that secluded house in the doomed city where had last seen Gregory Hawke. I knew then that disaster had overtaken his physical form, and that the sudden danger had drawn him irresistibly to it; the "Trishna" instinct had betrayed him and saved me. Subsequently, the fact that Hawke really perished in the calamity, together with a careful comparison of dates and times, confirmed this theory. Further, Hawke had willed his whole fortune to his "friend and colleague, Alan Heriot," expecting, of course, to enjoy it himself when he should have exchanged his physical vehicle for my own. I relinquished the money to his next of kin.

Wonderful indeed was my enforced sojourn in the strange realm of the Pretas; vast is the knowledge, too, that may be gathered there. But I have done with mantras, and not for all the wisdom of the ages would I chant that spell again.

THE POWER OF THE SEVEN

The story of my connection with the mysterious Seven dates properly from the threatened bankruptcy of Mr. Richard Westlake, who had inherited from his father a flourishing mercantile business, founded in 1848, and extremely successful during the years following the discovery of gold in Victoria, when large fortunes were easily made in trading. This estimable gentleman's one great weakness was a love of pre-eminence in philanthropic effort, which constantly tended to overbalance his prudence. A long course of ill-considered munificence, combined with a very reprehensible neglect of his personal affairs, culminated at last in a state of things which left him face to face with impending ruin. To him the cruellest part of it all was the inevitable cessation of his charitable gifts—a sad blow to a vanity that had long fed on the applause of the press and the gratitude of beneficiaries; but to his only daughter, Joan, the threatened calamity meant something far different.

Miss Westlake, a beautiful and amiable girl, had many admirers, and, at least, two very ardent suitors—Percy Hastings and myself. Now, the position was a simple one. Joan had chosen me; but Hastings, a very wealthy man, found most favour in the father's eyes. Not only were they men interested in the same objects and aims, and, therefore, in sympathy with each other, but Hastings' wealth could avert the coming bankruptcy, and save the old man's name and pride. Joan loved her father, and was blind to his faults; and she hesitated to consign him to ruin when a single word from her would restore his happiness and honour.

Naturally, I was angry with the poor girl that she should hesitate; and I was mean enough to doubt that sweet whispered confession which should have been sacred to me for all time. I failed to fully realise the extreme difficulty, nay, the cruelty, of her position. To a man the world may seem well lost for love; to an affectionate daughter the deliberate desertion of a loved and honoured parent may appear almost a crime. We were both proud, and that icy barrier of pride rising between us threatened to divide us for ever.

It was my friend, Gavrowski, the Russian violinist, who convinced me that I was unjust. Moreover, he promised to help me.

"I don't see how you can do that, Leo," I remarked gloomily.

"Leave it to me, my friend," he replied. "It will be some poor return for what you did in my behalf. But, first, my dear boy, you must—how would you call it?—abase yourself before Miss Joan, and convince her of your regret, your contrition."

He nodded in his friendly way, and smiled, as he always did when he achieved a sentence or two in his careful English.

He would say no more; but some days later I was very much surprised to read in the morning paper that Mr. Westlake had received a large gift of money from an unknown donor, in appreciation of his well-known philanthropic services. My first idea was that the gift came from Hastings; but reflection convinced me that he was not the sort of man to adopt that method of transferring his money to Westlake's coffers.

The same day I called on Joan. She received me calmly, but there was a subtle, underlying encouragement in her manner, and I soon made my peace with her.

"I knew you would see more clearly how I am situated, Gilbert," she said, in the low, thrilling tones habitual with her. "But now, it seems, the peril is averted, for the present at all events. My father has decided to accept this money as a sort of trust. It will tide him over his difficulties, and, when his affairs are in order again, he will disburse the amount of the gift, with interest, to the charities. That is his plan."

"Well, it's not for me to find fault with it, my dear Joan," I said; "but what a pity to have to live in a world where money has such power! And I suppose we are not the only two people whom someone else's financial troubles have affected."

"Truly, it seems to be the root of all evil. And those who care least for it are not exempt from the sufferings it brings."

"Unless they can will themselves to be free," I ventured; but she only smiled sadly. Joan was not assailable by argument. The appeal must come from another quarter. I was resolved on one thing, however—that I would never let that icy wall of pride arise between us again, no matter what it cost me. Such love as hers was too priceless a possession to be trifled away.

I was by no means satisfied that Mr. Westlake's windfall would do more than put off the evil day. I knew the man too well. I felt that, sooner or later, he would again be in a position in which Hastings' money would jingle sweetly in his ears. My own means being so modest, and my financial genius so undeveloped, I was helpless in that respect. As a music teacher of some ability, I earned enough for a comfortable, quiet life; but, as for assisting ruined philanthropists, except with good advice, it was wholly out of my power.

I was reflecting upon these things one morning, and wondering how it was that men of no education or ability, except a certain kind of shrewdness, can grow rich, when my friend Gavrowski called upon me. I had been acquainted with him for some years, and had saved his life in a boating accident; but I really knew very little about him. He occasionally brought his violin of an evening, and played strange Russian and Magyar melodies, with a power and spirit which drew forth my delight and admiration; but, as I never heard of his performing for money, or teaching, I concluded he had other means, and that music was a hobby and not a profession with him.

"Well, Forde," he said, "and how is the grand affair proceeding?"

"Excellently—at present," I replied. "Of course, you've heard of that famous gift to old Westlake?"

"It was mentioned in the papers," he said calmly.

"Coming as it did so soon after your promise to help me," I remarked, "it seemed to me that you must be able to work miracles."

"Miracles! There are no such things," he said, in a serious tone.

"I have certainly little faith in modern miracles," I replied smiling. "Of course, it was a coincidence."

"Then you are not inclined to give me credit for a part in the matter?" he said, with a laugh. "Such is your gratitude."

"I should be only too glad to believe myself indebted to you, old man," I said. "But, unless you gave the money yourself——"

"I have barely enough for my own necessities," he remarked. "But what if I could persuade some rich man to do so? Would that be a miracle?"

"Depends on the man. Or if you played him into a hypnotic trance with that magic violin of yours——"

"No, no. I know of only two people who love music more than money, and those two are with us now. But things can be done, even nowadays, when the world is doing its best to forget everything really worth knowing, and toiling so hard after such barren learning. Yes, there are some things——"

He broke off abruptly, and fell into a sort of reverie.

"Have you, then, some treasures of knowledge in your keeping, Leo?" I asked lightly.

He raised his eyes, and subjected me for a moment to rather a close scrutiny.

"You are not one of these—what is your name for them? Babblers. Yes. You are not a babbler. You have larger interests, and you have not the time, nor the inclination, to be a babbler."

"Accept my thanks. I humbly believe that your estimate of my character is within the bounds of truth."

"I am not joking. If you will submit yourself to a little experiment, I will convince you, perhaps, that there is yet something to be known not dreamed of in your philosophy."

"I shall be delighted," I said: "and I promise not to go round the town babbling about it."

"You will not have the desire to do that," he said, with some significance in his tone. "But let us proceed. I see you still play chess."

He waved his hand towards a chess table at which I had been playing the evening before with my old housekeeper. We had left the game unfinished, and the chessmen were still upon the board.

"This will do as well as anything else for my little experiment, which, I am sure, will amuse you," said Gavrowski. He carefully moved the chess table to within a few feet of my chair.

"Now," he said, in a low and rather strange voice, "I want you to consider that these kings and queens and knights and bishops standing so still upon the board, might be made to move, as it were, of their own volition."

"Without the aid of spirits," I suggested; but somehow the intended levity of my tone miscarried, and I felt myself becoming unaccountably serious.

"Without any such aid," he said, deliberately, and his voice seemed to come from a distance. "Now, please fix your eyes upon the board, and concentrate your attention upon these little figures."

Wondering, and somewhat ill at ease, I did as he directed. For some moments nothing happened, but presently the chessmen began to move about, seemingly endued with life. At first the movements were slow and deliberate, as though invisible hands were playing a game; but gradually they increased in speed, until my eyes could scarcely follow them.

For a few seconds I was almost stupefied with surprise, not unmingled with a kind of vague terror. But soon a feeling of revolt arose within me; I felt that I was being made the victim of some illusion—that I was being practised upon; and, with a sudden effort, I set my will strongly against the fancied movements of the chessmen. For a time they still continued to oscillate upon the board, but, as I struggled yet more against the illusion, the motions gradually ceased, until the pieces finally resumed their former positions, and were still; and then I knew they had not moved at all. But my effort had almost exhausted me, and I sank back in the chair with a queer feeling of languor.

I became conscious that Gavrowski was gazing at me with an enigmatical expression, in which I seemed to perceive a mingling of approval and admiration.

"You will do!" he said, emphatically; "you have the will-power—in posse, at any rate."

"You will oblige me by explaining," I said, in no very cordial tone.

"First, I must apologise for the liberty I took in thus experimenting upon you. It is a phase of hypnotism; and I think not many could have resisted and conquered the illusion as you did. This is the way those Indian fakirs perform most of their marvellous tricks. Some of my friends and I have a—a club, which we call the Brotherhood of the Seven. We have this secret, and others of more utility and importance. Recently a member has been removed from us by death, and I believe that, without great difficulty, I could procure your admission to fill the vacancy."

"Do you refer to the late Mr. Trent? I know he was a friend of yours."

"Yes. Trent is dead, as you know. He was a powerful member, and, without him, we are weakened—what you call handicapped—in our work."

"Your work? I do not understand."

"True. I must explain. Well, to speak in general terms, our Brotherhood has for its chief objects the protection of the weak against the strong, the adjustment of social injustices, and the advancement of the good and the true. We work on very unusual —I should say unique—lines, and the results we obtain will be incredible until you actually see them."

"If I may hazard a guess, you seek to hypnotise people into doing, not what they desire or intend, but what you think they ought to do."

"Speaking roughly, you are right, though, when you know our methods, you will be able to put it with more accuracy. Hypnotic suggestion, as commonly understood, is not a part of our work. We have got beyond that a little. In the experiment in which you have just participated the result was obtained, not by hypnotism, for your ordinary consciousness was not disturbed: no, it was sheer will-power on my part, and you met and finally defeated my efforts by an exertion of your own will. That does not mean that your will is the stronger; a struggle of this kind between two persons is always unequal. I mean that the defence in such contests has a decided advantage over the attack. It is for this reason that we cannot work efficiently with fewer than seven members, all of exceptional will-power, with knowledge and training added. It is, briefly, by bringing our sevenfold will to bear on a given point that we are able to achieve some very remarkable results."

It is needless to say that I had become intensely interested. Yet I could not restrain a very uncanny feeling as I looked at Gavrowski. It seemed as if I met the man for the first time. The Gavrowski I thought I knew was a different person altogether. This man assumed a formidable aspect, as a wielder of powers which I had until then little dreamed of.

"You spoke," I said, with some hesitation, "of a vacancy in your brotherhood?"

"I did; and I believe your proper place is with us. I think you have the necessary power, combined with the equally necessary ethical sense. On that point, however, we are not too quixotic. But, if you join the Brotherhood of the Seven, it will be for some weeks, perhaps months, as a novice. It will take time to learn even the rudiments of our great science. But in a little while you will see a glorious vista opening before you of usefulness to the world, of untold interest to yourself, and of knowledge undreamed of by ordinary science."

His eyes glowed with enthusiasm, and I felt an answering thrill of anticipation; but my native caution made me hesitate.

"As a small example of what even the six of us can do," he resumed, "witness that little gift to Mr. Westlake. It came from old Trevor, the reputed millionaire, as miserly a wretch as you would meet in a day's march. He shall disgorge a few more thousands before we have done with him, too."

"Do you really mean to say that you forced Trevor by sheer will-power to give that money to Westlake?"

"Briefly, we willed him to do it—how, you shall know later."

"But isn't that a sort of robbery?"

"Not at all. No man can honestly earn half as much as Trevor has acquired, nor should any man be allowed to retain such huge sums. Besides, by willing these men into a benevolent frame of mind we do them the best service possible—that is indisputable. There was old Bannister; you will remember what a sensation he caused by suddenly growing liberal, and not only giving, but helping personally in charitable work. He was one of our successes. We made Bannister a better man—and a richer, in the truest sense."

"And is this—this bleeding of the rich for the benefit of the poor—your chief work?"

"By no means. It might almost be termed our recreation. Our real work lies in more important fields. But, even in such a case as what you would call the bleeding of Bannister, the money aspect was not the most essential part of the design. Our success really consisted in the entire transformation of the man's character—a permanent change, for he died with the most fervent expressions of gratitude that it had pleased Providence to let him make some amends for his past life. We have even reformed criminals—though that, too, is not part of our regular work."

"What, then, is your real work?"

"I cannot yet give you more than a few hints. Consider, for instance, that the human mind, even in its highest development, is still most imperfect—that the greatest men have their foibles, their weaknesses, which prevent them very often from realising their most cherished ambitions. In many cases we have succeeded in directing the earnest attention of such men to their weak points, have helped them to strengthen their characters wherever they were vulnerable, and have even tided them over crises that threatened to wreck their lives. Consider, further, how many obstacles the great reformer has to fight against. He is commonly opposed by men of ability and wealth whose interests lie in another direction. Suppose we are able, once in a while, to bring those opponents round to the great reformer's way of thinking, making them his friends and co-workers instead of his enemies, what is the result? Reforms are realised in a year for which mankind, otherwise, would have to wait for a generation."

"If your work is of this nature, Gavrowski, and you wish me to join you, I should be a fool not to accept. But I trust you have not painted your picture in colours too glowing?"

"Rest assured I have not. Neither the colours nor the words exist that could adequately portray the splendour of our work and our life. You will not, however, have an easy time. The work is the hardest, the most exhausting, you can imagine. It is work that requires a man to be at the top of his condition; and you must be prepared for a life of self-sacrifice, of obscurity, and even of contempt, for the world looks upon us, as I fear you have been accustomed to look upon me, as idlers and wasters. What say you?"

"It must be a grand privilege to take part in such work. I may not, after all, be equal to it. But I am strongly inclined to try."

"There is a sort of novitiate, lasting a month, or perhaps two or three. After that, if you become a full member, there is no turning back, no escape, except by death, for the secrets imparted are such as can be held only by the Brotherhood. But we need not speak of that now. We may count upon you, then, as a novice?"

I bowed assent, and we clasped hands in silence.

"One moment," I said, as he was about to leave; "I have omitted to thank you for the great service you did me in that matter of Mr. Westlake."

His brow clouded a little.

"We had not thought of you as a member then," he said gravely; "and I may tell you at once that we do not work for ourselves either individually or collectively. There are certain occult laws which forbid that. We can, and do sometimes, strengthen each other for our work; but, as to advancing the personal interest or desire of any member, you must put all such thoughts out of your mind at once. Our Brotherhood would soon go to pieces if the slightest element of selfishness entered into its counsels."

This chilled me a little, but it was not in my nature to look back once I had set my course, and, having made up my mind to see this strange adventure through, I was determined to go on.

The Brotherhood of the Seven met in a room of moderate size, very plainly furnished, in the house of the president, a man with whom I was already slightly acquainted. I need not name him, nor any of the rest. They were all men of singularly striking appearance, evidently persons of high mental development, and I did not fail to notice that they were all of unusually robust physique. At the same time, to a casual observer, they would have seemed to bear the traces of a rather dissipated life. On closer inspection, however, this idea would have given place to a clearer conception of the men's character and pursuits. If they appeared slightly worn, and even haggard at times, it was the effect, perhaps, of thought and study, but certainly not of dissipation.

The president welcomed me in a cold and formal manner, well calculated to make me feel my position as a mere novice. I was informed that my novitiate would be spent entirely in the development of the power of concentration—the fixing of the mind on a single point; and it was left to Gavrowski to explain to me the best methods and exercises for the attainment of the necessary standard of power. I was then, with very little ceremony, dismissed, leaving the six to proceed with their own business.

Gavrowski called early next morning, and gave me my first lessons. The work of concentration was excessively laborious and exhausting, but the scientific methods known to my instructor made it much less so than it would otherwise have been. After a week of this, he professed himself surprised and delighted at my progress, and told me that I should in time more than supply the loss of power the Seven had suffered by the death of Mr. Trent.

During my probation I saw Joan but seldom. Had I been less absorbed in my new work I should not only have seen her oftener, but would certainly have noticed a subtle change in her manner towards me. As it was, I observed nothing, and, as time went on, and I had to cope with tasks of increasing difficulty, I could give but little thought to her at all. Once, when I chanced to remember her, I caught myself wondering whether, after all, there might not be something in life more glorious even than the winning of a woman's love—and that woman Joan Westlake. At that moment the six were assembled at their work—a circumstance I recalled in after days with curious feelings. But my time was too precious just then for indulgence in reverie.

A month passed, and Gavrowski at length pronounced me sufficiently advanced for the first initiation as a member. There was but little ceremony, for initiation meant scarcely more than the disclosure of a portion of the Brotherhood's secret methods. I was simply asked, and promised, never to divulge those secrets. I took no oath, but I was told plainly that the Brotherhood had but one punishment for treachery, and that was death.

The actual work of the Brotherhood was not conducted in the meeting room, except on special occasions. But it was necessary that all the members should work at the same time, wherever they might be, and the meetings were held to discuss and arrange for the Brotherhood's activities. For some time, of course, I was hardly of any value in the work, but in a few months I progressed so far that the second of the three initiations was spoken of as near. This meant that some even more important secrets would be imparted to me. I have reason to believe that the dual initiation involved some very startling knowledge in regard to thought transference and kindred mysteries. This knowledge, however, I was fated never to acquire.

I was surprised at the lofty and ambitious nature of the enterprises undertaken; but at times I seemed to see a darker side to the work of the Seven. Whether my ethical sense was finer than theirs I cannot say; but certainly I felt at times that I was assisting in enterprises the possible results of which I could not contemplate without more or less serious misgivings. I solaced myself with the thought that at least our motives were above reproach; and the feeling that it was given to us to play the part of Providence in matters great and small was so tremendous, so fascinating, that I believe I could have consented to far more than I ever did rather than resign such a privilege.

By methods I should never have dreamed of, but which were wonderfully simple, we—seven poor obscure men—were able to reach and act upon the minds of great rulers, reformers, poets, chemists, inventors, etc., and even to affect, in an appreciable degree, the destinies of mankind. Our best work lay, I think, in strengthening the characters of prominent men of action. One such man had a giant mind, but was indolent; we succeeded in impressing him with the necessity of conquering that defect, and the help we gave him in doing so he devoutly believed came from on high. It was the same with a certain statesman, whose fatal vac-illation was the despair of his party. We acted upon this man's brain daily for some months, until he began to surprise and delight his friends by the display of a salutary and consistent power of decision in a series of difficult political crises.

It was necessary at times to relax our efforts, for the work was of a truly devitalising nature. It was in a literal sense that we gave our lives for others, and the drain could not be long continued. A recess usually lasted three weeks. It was during the first of these periods that I suddenly remembered not having seen Joan for at least a month. I felt vexed rather than grieved. What would she think of me?

I took the first opportunity of calling upon her.

"It is you," she said, holding out her hand with the air of an ordi-nary friend.

"My dear Joan!" I cried, seizing her hand in both my own, "how can I obtain your forgiveness?"

"For what?" she asked, round-eyed with astonishment.

"Why, I haven't been near you for over a month!"

"Indeed? I thought it was longer. However, a month is nothing. I presume you have been busy."

"Yes," I said, chilled by her indifference; "that is my only excuse—a poor one, I know. But," I added, somewhat stiffly, "as it does not seem to matter much to you——"

"We need say no more about it? Quite so . . . Of course, there is no loss of friendship, Gilbert. We were once something more—but—it was not to be, it seems. Life is very strange, is it not?"

I could only look at her. She was very calm, without the slightest trace of agitation or regret.

"You are changed," I muttered at last.

"And you?" she said, with a faint smile.

I was silent. I felt that it was necessary to collect my thoughts. There was something I could not understand. Most certainly a change had come over me as regarded my love for her. My heart sank as I realised that, in some manner, the most unaccountable, we had drifted away from each other . . . Could it be—yes! Swifter than lightning the truth flashed upon me.

I took her hand in mine. Something in my manner arrested her attention, and her face grow very grave.

"I love you, Joan," I said, with a solemnity which surprised me as well as her; "my love has not changed, but it has been tampered with, like yours—oh! not in any ordinary way! It will be difficult, if not impossible, to explain the situation fully to you. But, first of all, tell me, do you view the change with no regret?"

"There is indeed something very peculiar about it all," she said thoughtfully. "I was not conscious of the change at first—in fact, till quite lately . . . But regret?" she pondered a while. "That's the strangest part of it. Regret for a dead love should be a most poignant emotion. It should be unutterably bitter to think that so great a portion of one's innermost self, so to speak, has been lost irrecoverably. Then, why—why has it not even troubled me?"

"Your love for me was real—was no superficial sentiment. It could not die away of itself."

"How could it? True, deep love cannot die unnoticed, and if it be wrenched out of one's being it must leave a wound—a lingering pain. But there has been no wound, and there is no pain. Oh, Gilbert, your looks tell me that there is something—something hideous behind all this! What can it be?"

I reflected a moment, and then said—

"You believe me to be truthful and sensible? I know you do. But you must prepare yourself for things that will try your faith in my veracity, and even my sanity, to the utmost. Fortunately, however, I can offer you proofs."

Then, as briefly, yet as clearly as I could, I related the story of my connection with the Brotherhood of the Seven.

"It seems like a dream," she said. "Can these things really be done?"

I perceived that she doubted, in spite of her faith in me. Then I did a desperate thing, for which I paid dearly afterwards. I confided to her several of those secrets of the Brotherhood by which they held their power, and then I gave a partial demonstration of that power by an experiment somewhat similar to that which Gavrowski had performed with the chessmen.

"Gilbert, this is a monstrous thing," she said at last. "It was surely never intended that men should attain such awful knowledge, even if it be exerted for good. But, with respect to you and me, I begin to see light, though dimly. Please explain further."

"They value my powers. I am necessary to them. It is imperative that a member should have but the one love—his work. There must be no divided duty or affection. They are all disconnected men, and they have willed that I should be so, too."

"And—and—you must give up one or the other?"

"Joan, the work of the Brotherhood is the most fascinating and absorbing—the most glorious you can conceive! Yet, if it is to separate me from you, there is but one course."

"You prefer me, whose love is lost to you?"

"Joan, don't say that! It will return. They—the six—have willed your love away, and have been willing mine away, too; but they shall not conquer—no, by heaven! You are mine, and mine only!"

Her eyes kindled at my words.

"I loved you," she said. "They have robbed me of my love . . . But this cannot be . . . It is so unreal—unnatural. We must fight against them—you and I . . . No, no! My love cannot have flown. I am under an illusion. Yes, that is it. These men cannot destroy such a thing as love. They may delude, but only for a time."

"Think in that strain, Joan. Set your mind and your will resolutely against their influence. Listen, I will show you how best to do it."

I then imparted to her one of the most valued secrets of the Seven—a secret which, in selfish or unscrupulous hands, would work incalculable harm. Only the fierce resentment I felt against my colleagues, and the desire to save our menaced love, could have moved me to disclose such a thing even to a being so good and pure as Joan Westlake.

I had violated the oath—implicit, but not the less real—which bound together the Brotherhood of the Seven.

The same evening I sought Gavrowski, and taxed him with the treachery of which Joan and I were the victims. He looked very grave, but made no attempt at denial.

"You know, my dear friend," he said calmly, "what the work demands. You know the life we must live. You know the necessity for undivided attention if we are to accomplish great things. I have been troubled myself—not with love for woman, but for my unhappy country. You are aware of my desire that we should give our best powers for a time to try and break up the bureaucracy of Russia; but I am overruled. I must be patient; but in the meantime——"

Seeing that I was in no mood to listen to his own grievance, he paused.

"However," he resumed, "you must admit that it is all for the best. The lady no longer cares for you. And what is the love of woman—at best an illusion—compared with the splendour of such powers as we possess?"

"I think otherwise," I said coldly. "And I do not agree that private happiness need interfere with our work. Quite the contrary. It should have a tonic effect upon the faculties."

"As an old member I can assure you that the case is otherwise. It is the constant peril—accident, sickness, and so on—to which such happiness is liable that constitutes the objection. No: members of the Brotherhood must be free."

"I was not told that."

"I am sorry you failed to infer so obvious a condition. We thought you had inferred it; and it was only out of delicacy that we did not ask you to join us in painlessly killing out the lady's regard for you."

Could this be true? I could hardly conceive the possibility of Gavrowski lying to me. Yet—

"You must, however, bring yourself to realise the necessity of alienating your mind from everything but the work—the glorious work—our mission of redemption to mankind!"

"Grand words, Gavrowski," said I, with some bitterness. Then, perceiving that I must dissemble, I added—"Well, as you say, the work must not be imperilled. I suppose I must put the ordinary ideas of happiness out of my mind."

As I spoke, I met his eyes, which seemed to look, not at, but right through me. They were not stern; they seemed mournful and compassionate, yet resolute and unwavering. I bore Gavrowski's scrutiny bravely, and flattered myself that I had deceived him. Nevertheless, his look haunted me for the rest of the night, and returned to me in my dreams.

All that I hoped to gain by delay was the restoration of Joan's love. And this, in the third week of the recess, seemed accomplished, for I was thrilled to find her almost the same lovely and loving girl as I had known heretofore. It was not, however, till the very eve of the reassembling of the Brotherhood that she confessed to me the full return of her love, and, hearing that sweet confession, I found my own as fully restored. But she whispered to me of strange, agonising struggles in the lonely watches of the night, when the secrets I had given her were her only safeguards from the most dreadful and overpowering delusions. But for the last week she had been free, as though her unseen assailants had retreated from the contest. I trembled on hearing this, fearing I knew not what.

I urged her to be careful never to divulge the secrets I had imparted.

"Of course," she said. "But there is really no one I could tell them to who would believe them, except some of your brethren. But you must promise to give up that dreadful Brotherhood. Reflect that we must not do evil that good may come, nor seek to disturb or hasten the operation of natural laws. Promise me, Gilbert."

"There is no need to promise, dear. They are certain to expel me when they know how I have chosen. Fascinating as the work is, I give it up freely. I yield without a struggle to something better and higher still—our love."

"That is well said. But—do you not fear them?"

"No—as long as their secrets are kept. You have my life in your hands, Joan, and it is an added happiness for me to know that."

"Not to me," she said, with a shiver. "But the secrets are safe."

★   ★   ★   ★   ★

Next night I was present at the reassembling of the Seven. By the demeanour of the others I knew that there was serious business on hand. The president was stern and gloomy; Gavrowski's features were darkened by that mournful expression which had puzzled me when I last saw him; the others were very grave.

After some routine business had been transacted, the president rose.

"Brothers," he began, in solemn tones. He paused a moment, and the silence was intense. "We are here to-night," he continued, "chiefly to deal with one of our members who, I grieve to say, has deserted and betrayed us."

He fixed his eyes upon me, and again paused.

"Not so!" I cried, indignantly; but my voice sounded strangely hollow and false.

"I repeat that this member has betrayed us. Knowledge was given to him as the reward of his probation, with the privilege of membership, and he has treacherously imparted a portion of that knowledge to another, and that other a—woman."

Nothing could describe the contempt and loathing with which he uttered that word "woman," and something like a groan came from several of the members.

"The member knows the penalty of such conduct. Before I allow him to speak, I will ask the other members to decide upon the course to be taken."

There was a pause, and then Gavrowski rose.

"I suggest," he said, "that the erring member be pardoned on his undertaking to abandon the woman in question, and allow her to be dealt with by the Brotherhood."

A member briefly supported this.

"An unheard-of indulgence," said the president, harshly. "However, if this is the feeling of the members——"

He looked at them inquiringly, and they nodded assent.

"So be it," he said. "Let the accused member speak."

I arose. "What is meant," I began, in as firm a voice as I could command, "by the words, 'and allow her to be dealt with by the Brotherhood?'"

"She must be destroyed," said the president. "No woman can possess the secrets of the Seven."

"How do you know that she possesses them?"

"We know; let that suffice."

I had long suspected that the oldest members possessed special powers not shared by the rest; this, with the memory of Joan's mysterious nocturnal struggles, confirmed my suspicion, and I grew sick at heart.

"Your answer!"

"Can you think," I said, raising my head and scornfully meeting his eye, "that anyone but an abject cur would comply with such an atrocious demand?"

"You refuse. Then it remains merely to pronounce sentence of death upon you both. We have no formalities. The will of the Brotherhood is that you, having forfeited your life, according to our laws, must die. The woman's death is also a necessity. The sentence will be carried out upon yourself immediately!"

At these terrible words the six settled themselves into an attitude that I beheld with surprise and horror. It was the posture prescribed for the most intense concentration of the will that we could possibly put forth. As yet I was in the dark as to the way in which the awful sentence was to be executed. I fully expected that physical force of some kind would be used, and I had come prepared—desperately and foolishly prepared.

"Murderers!" I cried, drawing a revolver from my pocket; "I——"

Something within me seemed to snap, and I sank back in my seat. The weapon fell on the table before me. Not one of the six had moved a muscle.

I sat, or rather lay, in my seat, helpless and inert, facing my executioners. All power seemed to have gone out of me, physical as well as mental. Yet I well knew that every second lost increased my peril a hundredfold. I tried to rise, but I seemed as if bound to the chair that supported me. I called to my aid that priceless possession which these men themselves had given to me—a will trained along lines unknown to ordinary science, and fashioned to uses unheard of—a weapon more deadly than steel or poison, a power greater than that of armies. But it was opposed to six other wills of equal or superior strength, each bent on its destruction. There could be but one end to such a contest. Two, three, even four might be resisted, but against six there was no hope. Yet I made the effort, though I knew it could only prolong the struggle and increase the agony of my defeat. I felt like a wrestler gradually succumbing under the iron pressure of muscles far stronger than his own. But the anguish was greater by many times than physical torture. Ten thousand hammers seemed to beat upon my brain. The desire to shriek was an agony unspeakable, but my throat refused to utter so much as a sigh. Hours seemed to pass that were but seconds; yet I struggled and resisted.

At last a strange longing for the end began insidiously to take possession of me. I knew this was an illusion conveyed from the minds of my relentless destroyers to my own—perhaps in mercy, but too certainly to hasten my defeat. I tried to expel it, but in vain. Then the strain upon my faculties began to produce effects of their own. A sort of delirium came upon me, so that my brain translated everything into fantastic distortions of the truth. The faces of the six grew larger, their eyes became electric lamps, their necks long, curiously carved stems overwrought with leaves and flowers. Each pair of lamps began to revolve, at first slowly, then rapidly, till I felt sick and giddy at the sight. The ticking of my watch sounded like ringing blows on an anvil, and my heartbeats like the muffled booming of distant guns. Then I heard all the watches in the room and all the hearts—a bewildering, chaotic uproar, which in a little while resolved itself into a grand harmony, like that of a vast orchestra. But through it all pain and fear were never absent; and not for a second did I lose hold upon the idea that I must not yield to the will of the six.

How long this part of the struggle lasted I cannot say, but at length a subtle change seemed to come over me—a change which, I fear, words are inadequate to clearly explain. The whole position appeared to be transformed. I felt that I was no longer present at the scene, yet I was aware of all that was happening. The doomed victim seemed to be some person intimately connected, indeed, with myself, yet not I. I felt a sensation which can only be described as the utter absence of all sensation—unless I except a feeling of extreme lightness. Gradually, however, my thoughts grew more definite; I became conscious, in some degree, of my true position; and then, with a shock, the nature of which I am utterly unable to describe, I realised that my spirit had withdrawn from its tenement of clay, driven out by the united will-power of those six inexorable enemies!

For a moment something like relief filled my consciousness—my deadly agonies, at least, were ended; my enemies had inflicted all they could inflict. But there was my inanimate body, huddled in its chair; and, as I contemplated it, there suddenly came upon me an overmastering impulse to return—a desire for physical life, at whatever cost of mortal agony. This desire was no sooner felt than it was realised. Once more I assumed the burden of life, once more I sat facing those lamp-like eyes; again I struggled with the remnant of my strength against that terrible sixfold power. The eyes had ceased to revolve, though they still glared with dazzling brightness; and the music had died down to a murmur. I knew that this was but a last effort, that if I was driven out of life again there would be no return. I succeeded so far that the lights once more became human eyes. They had not moved, and there was no sign in them of the slightest yielding.

I felt that I must die; why add the sharpness of mortal agony to a death that was inevitable? I was on the point of relinquishing the struggle and allowing myself to drift once more into that world of shadows into which they had thrust me once already. But suddenly there stole into my heart a thought—too slight almost to be called a hope. I had kept my eyes fixed upon those of the president, for in his orbs seemed focussed the power of the six; but now, bitterly regretting that I had not thought of it before, I called up my last reserve of strength to spend them in one despairing effort, and met the eyes of Gavrowski, mutely asking him if he, whose life I had saved, was now to become one of my destroyers. This cost me dear in outraged pride, but the panic fear of death, and the still worse fear of the fate reserved for Joan, if I could not help her to resist their awful power, overcame all other feelings.

That unspoken question seemed to last for ages. Would the answer never come? Was my last hope to perish?

Then suddenly the dreadful spell was broken.

Gavrowski sprang up with a loud cry, and an ejaculation in his own language. He turned and faced the five, and then said—

"No, messieurs, I cannot do it! I cannot render death for life! We must spare him."

The president made a slight signal, and the five continued in their deadly work as if nothing had happened.

Gavrowski rushed towards me and shook my shoulders, but I could not move. Then his eyes fell upon the revolver I had dropped. He grasped it, and, with a terrible oath, fired point blank at the president.

Either the noise of the shot, or the moral effect of Gavrowski's desperate act, broke up the concentration of the five members. But the sudden release from that awful power was too much for me. I fainted. The closing scene I can only report from what was told me afterwards.

The bullet missed the president, who rose, pale but calm.

"You have made your choice," he said to Gavrowski. "You have broken the power of the Seven. We can no longer work together. So be it. The Brotherhood of the Seven is disbanded. The five who remain will seek another country, and endeavour to find two worthier men to replace the traitors. We bear you no hatred, and will not harm you. The sentence on your friend was passed in accordance with our laws. Those laws no longer exist, and he is free. Farewell!"

Some of the members shook hands with Gavrowski, and then the five silently took their leave. I have never seen them since that night.

Gavrowski procured restoratives, and I was soon sufficiently revived to be able to accompany him home. In a few days I had fully recovered; but the first time I looked into a mirror I was grieved, but not greatly surprised, to find that my hair and beard were as white as snow.

This did not make any difference to Joan, except that it increased her love for me, if possible, and has, ever since our marriage, been an excuse to completely spoil me with kindness and solicitude.

Gavrowski left soon after; and recently I learnt by a letter from him that he has made his peace with the five, after much difficulty, and that a great French scientist has joined them; so that the power of the Seven is still a factor, great or small, in the world's affairs.

"With regard to your connection with the Brotherhood," adds Gavrowski, "we all regretted deeply what we regarded as treachery on your part. We now as deeply pity you for the infatuation which led you to betray our secrets to a woman. But we do not grieve that you still live, and are happy in your own way. No; even our inflexible president, I have reason to think, was secretly pleased that you escaped. However, we have taken no risks in the selection of your successor; he is indifferent to all worldly passions and motives, and, we believe, will make an ideal member. You will be pleased to know that our new rules include no provision at all for the punishment of any member who may be so unhappy as to violate the conditions of membership. Our experience with you has left too deep an impression upon us. In future we shall content ourselves with filling any vacancy that may occur with someone upon whom we can utterly depend."

I read this passage with satisfaction and even pleasure, though it was not flattering to myself.

I can never think without a regretful sigh of that glorious though perilous work—perilous, as all abnormal powers must be in this world; but I am more than satisfied with the fate that so violently shattered my connection with the Brotherhood of the Seven.

THE VENGEANCE OF THE DEAD

I.

The disappearance of Martin Calthorpe—"that wonderful man," as his admirers called him, "that arch-impostor," as he was stigmatised by others—was something more than a nine days' wonder, and it has not yet quite faded out of the recollection of those who are attracted or impressed by such mysteries. These will have no difficulty in recalling the circumstances, so far as they were known, of his evanishment. The mystery, however, was so complete that little was left to feed the curiosity of the quidnuncs. When it is stated that he had an appointment with a "client" in his chambers in Brunswick-street on an afternoon of November, 1892, and was waited for in vain, and that he was not seen or heard of afterwards by anyone who could or would admit the fact, the available information (outside of these memoirs) is pretty well exhausted. Some particulars, however, may be added concerning his antecedents preliminary to the well-nigh incredible story of how the mystery was subsequently revealed.

"Professor" Calthorpe was apparently one of those strange beings who, finding themselves possessed of powers outside the cognisance of material science, set about turning them to pecuniary account, without seeking to probe their inner meaning, without realising their legitimate uses. (I say "apparently" for a reason which will be developed later.)

Calthorpe described himself as a hypnotist, a psychometrist, and one or two other "ists"; also as a clairvoyant. In some or all of these capacities he was remarkably successful, to judge by the number of people who were willing to pay him liberally for whatever services he rendered them. Indeed, the house in Brunswick-street was daily besieged by the many who believe in occult phenomena. The professor had a wife, who was a noted spiritualistic medium, and who also drew a handsome income from her "profession."

It was suggestive of the irony of fate that I, who looked upon such people as Professor and Mrs. Calthorpe as little better than criminal impostors, and their clients as mere gulls, should find my destiny involved with theirs. So, at least, I thought then. Later events have changed my opinions considerably, but they have not increased my respect for the crew who seek to tamper with the mysteries of life and death for their personal profit. However, I must not anticipate.

The professor, as I have said, disappeared. He failed to keep his appointment; and the clients waited in vain. The man of mystic powers was not again seen in his usual sphere of life, and all efforts made to trace him failed. His wife could throw no light upon the mystery—or would not. She seemed greatly agitated—overcome by a sort of terror rather than by natural grief. My friend, Detective Mainspray, who was engaged in the matter, gave me these particulars. Mrs. Calthorpe did not long survive her husband. From the day of his disappearance she gave up her "work," if so it might be called, and fell into a kind of lethargy of horror, like one obsessed, making no effort to arouse herself, though by no means resigning herself to the thought of death. Her bodily vigour (which had been great) declined with remarkable rapidity, but as the end approached a frantic rebellion seemed to rise within her. The final scenes were made memorable by circumstances in the highest degree calculated to unnerve those who witnessed them. I, of course, was not present, but I was told that the dying woman's appearance and demeanour were far from being marked by that tranquillity with which those who are at peace with conscience usually approach the solemn portals of death.

The appalling intensity of her despair shocked the few friends who stood around her death-bed. She seemed to be struggling in the toils of an adversary invisible to them, but only too tangibly present to herself. This death-agony was attributed by some of those who witnessed it to an exaggerated horror of the common fate; the more thoughtful, however, accepted this view with extreme reluctance. Later developments, in which I had part, threw a light upon the mystery. The cause of her death was given as heart disease, accelerated by abnormal neurotic conditions connected with the practice of her "profession" as a medium. A circumstance which greatly puzzled not only her friends, but also the physicians who attended her, was her excessive appetite for rich foods during the last few weeks of her life: this appetite, increasing with a rapid loss of flesh, seemed wholly inexplicable. Those who, knowing the quantities of food she had daily assimilated, looked at last upon a body bloodless and emaciated to an incredible degree, were stricken dumb with wonderment and horror.

II.

Neither the disappearance of Martin Calthorpe nor the death of his wife would have interested me to any considerable degree, but for the fact that I knew my parents to have been acquainted with the man. My father, moody, reticent as he had always been within my memory of him, was not likely to divulge any secrets concerning his past life. Through my friend Mainspray, however, I had glimpses of his early career, which taught me that the book of a man's life may contain pages which it is not wise nor well for a son to turn; and, apart from the bald fact that many years earlier a powerful hatred had been engendered between the two men, through some wrong committed by Calthorpe, I knew little, and sought no further knowledge. When the hypnotist disappeared, however, it became plain to me that my father's gloom had sensibly deepened, and I could not help wondering if this had any connection with the matter. My mother had died only a few months before, after a lingering illness, however, and her death would seem to supply a sufficient and more natural cause for the change observable in the bereaved husband.

My father at first neglected, then finally resigned his business affairs into my charge, and thenceforth lived a very secluded life. I saw but little of him, for he seemed hardly aware at times of my existence. Nothing could exceed, however, the moody intensity of the affection he lavished upon his two daughters, Constance and Winifred. Winnie, the younger, was (if he had any preference) his favourite, for her eyes were startlingly like her mother's. We lived in a rather large house near the St. Kilda-road, about two miles from the city. He owned another house in South Yarra, which should have brought in a substantial sum in rent, but it was out of repair, and, for some reason, he would not allow it to be touched.

Not long after the strange death of Mrs. Calthorpe, my father sought medical advice for our Winnie. We all, Winnie included, were rather surprised, for we could see no cause for alarm in her appearance. Winnie herself protested that she felt well enough, except that she found it rather a bore to cycle or play tennis, and much preferred to go out driving with our friends, the Thorntons, in their new motor car. Old Dr. Gair found nothing the matter with her, except that perhaps she was just a trifle less buxom than a girl of her age and build might be. I think he prescribed some sort of tonic. My father received his optimistic verdict with a gloomy contempt, and it was plain that he was by no means satisfied. The incident passed, and for the time we thought no more about it.

Some weeks later, however, I happened to enter the drawing room, where my sisters were talking, and Winnie was saying—

"No; I can't explain it. And I have such strange dreams, too."

"What sort of dreams, sis?" I asked, lightly; but a glance at her serious face told me that she was in no mood for banter.

"Father seems to have been right, after all," said Connie, in her quiet tones; "Win is getting run down."

I looked at the girl more intently. She was paler than I had ever noticed her to be, and her hands had certainly rather a fragile appearance. She was about eighteen at this time, and should have been flushed with exuberant health. Indeed, a few months before she had been full of a somewhat hoydenish energy and vigour. Now all was changed.

Next week my father took her away to the Blue Mountains. They returned towards the fall of the year, but the girl had not improved. In fact, she had barely held her own. My father called in the best specialists, but they were evidently puzzled by the very simplicity of the case. There was no organic disease, either acute or chronic— no disease of any sort; only a growing weakness, an increasing languor; days darkened by a strange weariness, and nights poisoned by dreams which she would not tell.

To me Winnie was a child—"the baby"; and thus I was on more intimate terms with Connie, who was then in her early twenties. We talked the matter over many times, and discussed the expediency of taking the girl away for a more extended trip. "It would do you good also, Con," I said; "you're not looking too well."

I said this without attaching much meaning to the words, but Connie gave something of a start.

"Do you think so?" she said; "perhaps I've been worrying about Win. But, really, I don't feel quite myself lately."

This made me look at her closely, and I saw that there was indeed a noticeable change. But the summer had been very trying, and, as she said, the anxiety about Winnie was enough to account for a certain lowering of physical tone.

My father did not fall in with the proposed trip. He only laughed bitterly when it was mooted, and said, in a harsh voice—

"What's the use? There's no hope."

"No hope." I shall never forget the note of tragic despair in those final words. It was as if a fiat had gone forth—as if in some strange way Irrevocable Fate had spoken with his voice.

III.

In these councils of ours Harry Thornton had borne no part. For some reason or other Connie, who had at this time been engaged to him for nearly a year, was unwilling to take him into her confidence in the matter, and as time went on and her own health did not improve, she became even less inclined to talk about it with him.

Thornton was a strange young fellow in many ways. Whilst he was fond of an outdoor life, excelling in all kinds of athletics, I knew him to be equally inclined to intellectual pursuits; in fact, he took up branches of study quite foreign to ordinary taste. Some years before, he had rather startled his friends by becoming the intimate of one Ravana Dâs, a Hindu pundit of the highest caste (Brahmans), and reputed to possess an extraordinary degree of erudition, both Western and Oriental. Thornton made what we chaffingly called a "pilgrimage" to his Eastern friend, and on his return it was plain that he took his "master", as he called him, with intense seriousness. He continued to correspond with this man, whose portrait had an honoured place on the wall of his study. The face was a remarkable one. It was as clearly and delicately cut as a bronze medallion of a proud, yet gentle, expression, and gave one the idea of a learned ascetic. A certain power, also, seemed to breathe from those features. Anyone studying the portrait (which was done in a sepia by an Indian artist) could readily understand the fascination which the man might exercise over impressionable natures.

The Thorntons were wealthy people, and the young man had license to gratify his fancies. But he lived an extremely simple and blameless life, and I knew of no one more eligible as a husband for Connie, whose tastes, moreover, had much in common with his own.

Harry was not long in perceiving Connie's decline in health; and, connecting it, as I imagined, with that of her sister, grew very anxious. One day, after having taken them for an outing in his motor car, he asked me to accompany him to his rooms in the city.

He said little on the way, but once in his 'den' he spoke abruptly of Winnie's illness, which was at this time rapidly progressing.

"What do you think of it?" he asked.

"The doctors advise a complete change of climate," I said, vaguely.

"Humbug!" he muttered.

"It seems the only chance," I said; "but my father has set his face against it. Says there's no hope; but, of course——"

"The girl will die," he said, in a decisive tone. "The only man who could save her is away in the Himalayas, and could not be reached within I don't know how many months."

"You mean——"

"Ravana Dâs—yes. He might do it . . . or tell us how."

"Is he a physician, then?"

"More than that. But it is not exactly a physician that is needed, Burford. There is nothing, I think, vitally wrong with Winnie. But there are possibilities that medical science knows nothing of. This vague talk about 'going into a decline' is merely a veil for ignorance."

"Well, old man, it you can supply a better hypothesis, one that we can work on, I shall be very grateful," I said, a trifle ironically.

"I can't do that—yet," he said. "I don't know enough; and what I fear is too awfully improbable to spring upon an old sceptic like yourself . . . Tell me," he added abruptly, "did your father know that man Calthorpe, the hypnotist who disappeared about a year ago?"

"Yes—why?" I answered, staring at him in a sort of terror, for which I could not account.

"What was the nature of this acquaintance?" he asked.

"Its nature? Well, I know very little. My father suffered at his hands in some way, and I believe that in a less law abiding country their enmity would have had a tragic ending."

"Burford, your father killed that man!"

"You are mad, my boy—stark, staring mad!"

"Not a bit of it. Oh! if only my master were accessible!"

He stared in a sort of yearning rapture at the portrait on the wall, as if to draw inspiration from it.

"Why do you connect this man Calthorpe with the matter?" I asked. "In the first place, it is not known whether the man is alive or dead."

"Your father's fate is bound up with that man's, Frank," he said, gloomily. "I don't know how. But I can dimly perceive possibilities that horrify me. I did not remark Winnie's extreme weakness till quite lately—unobservant ass that I am! After all, I may be mistaken—the thing seems altogether too hideous—too incredible!"

"This is some beastly superstition your precious master has been filling you up with," I said, impatiently. "Winnie is not the first girl who has gone into a decline. I don't see how Hindu philosophers can help her any more than European physicians."

He made no reply. He was apparently absorbed in the face of the Hindu pundit, and did not seem to hear me. I saw no profit in staying longer, so, with an abrupt "Good-night!" to which I got no reply, I left him.

The next day Winnie did not rise till late in the evening; and, after that, not at all. She declined with an accelerated rapidity, and in ten days passed to her long rest. The close of her life was very peaceful; even the dreams, which had been "too dreadful to tell," left her on the seventh day from her decease. She had long intervals of trance-like sleep, from which she brought back vague memories of an indescribable bliss—as though the spirit, impatient of its fleshly tabernacle, could with difficulty be held to earth by the feeble thread of life.

I need not dwell upon our sorrow. That of my father found some doubtful relief in alcohol and drugs; and only the solicitude and devotion of his surviving daughter saved him, for the time, from utter despair.

"For her sake," he said to me, "I will try and keep up; but she also is doomed—my boy—she also is doomed."

"Why do you talk like this?" I demanded.

His eyes grew wild. "There are devils," he said, thickly; "or men with devilish arts. You may stab them through and through with knives—you may spatter their brains on the wall with bullets—no use! They come back in the night and mock you; they rob you of your dearest ones . . ."

I thought of Thornton's words, and said—

"Had you anything to do with the disappearance of that man Calthorpe?"

He started as if stung, then broke into a harsh laugh.

"The devil should claim his own, one would think," he muttered. "But what are you driving at?" he asked, suddenly raising his head and meeting my eye sternly. "What should I know about Calthorpe's disappearance?"

"I had the idea that in some way—hypnotism or something—the man may have had a hand in——"

"Her death? Nonsense, boy! You rave!"

He would say no more.

IV.

By some process of unconscious reasoning, I had evolved the idea that Calthorpe, dead though he was, was exerting a hypnotic power over my sisters, thus striking at my father through his loved ones. It may seem strange that I, a hard-headed man of the world, should have given any attention to such occult hypotheses. But I had lost one beloved sister through a most mysterious malady, and now that malady threatened the other.

Having questioned orthodox science in vain, however, in my extremity, I lent an ear to the suggestions of an alleged knowledge of forces lying outside the range of ordinary experience—a knowl-

edge I had hitherto denied and ridiculed, as the pretension of pred-
atory quacks and impostors. The drowning man catches at straws,
and every straw seems a plank of safety.

Connie very soon developed all the symptoms which had
marked her sister's decline; and she, too, had mysterious dreams
which no argument or persuasion could induce her to disclose, and
which evidently filled her with a conviction that she was doomed.

One day she came to me from her father's room, in a state of
wild agitation.

"You must watch him," she said. "He is very near madness. I
think he will destroy himself."

"What has he said?"

"Oh, his talk is very wild—I can make little of it. He is possessed
with the idea of some enemy—someone who is dead. 'I must seek
him in his own place,' he keeps on saying; 'I will find him, and drag
him down—down!' Oh, the wildest language! It terrifies me."

I soothed her as best I could; and then, obeying some impulse,
for which I could not account, I went to Thornton's rooms, though
not expecting to see him. I found him there, however, and he
greeted me with an intense earnestness.

"I am glad you have come," he said; "I have received a communication."

"From whom?"

"My master. He came to me last night, in his—but you would
not understand. Let us call it a dream. He knows our trouble, and
will help us. That was impressed upon me beyond all doubt. He
will help us! Isn't that glorious, Burford?"

"He has left it pretty late," I said, grimly; and I spoke of my
father's condition.

"He should be pacified. To pass on to the next plane in his
present state would be extremely perilous, unless he was specially
guarded."

"I can't follow your ideas, Harry," I said, with some impatience.
"But about your friend, Ravana Dâs. You tell me he is away among
the Himalayas. How, then, can he help us?"

"He can easily do so, if he be permitted. Though I have the
honour to call him master, he is himself a pupil—the disciple of a
still higher teacher. Of course, you don't understand these things.

But it was made known to me last night that he will help us, and that he will soon be with us."

"What do you call soon? Unless he travels in some impossible airship, I don't see how— And poor Connie is evidently following her sister. She herself seems to feel it. Only to-day——"

A fixed and startled expression on my friend's face froze the words on my lips. He seemed to see or hear something which I could not. Suddenly the look turned to one of supreme joy and peace, and he sank back in his chair like one relieved of all anxiety.

Involuntarily I turned, and saw that there was a stranger in the room. He was near the door, and must of course have entered thereby, though I had not seen it open. One glance told me that it was the Hindu, the pundit, Ravana Dâs. There were the delicate, finely-carved, ascetic features, with their grave, gentle, yet lofty expression, as of one who knew all that philosophy could teach, and had renounced all that the world could give. To conceive of this man having a single evil thought was impossible. I remembered afterwards that he was dressed in ordinary clothes, such as we wore ourselves; but I did not remark this at the time.

"I am with you, as you see," he said, in a low, musical voice, which seemed just a trifle muffled; "and I will give you what help I can. But time is limited."

"My dear master," said Thornton, with the utmost reverence; "you have saved us all. This is my friend, Mr. Burford."

"Yes. Well? You are troubled about your sister, Mr. Burford; and your father, too? Is it not so?"

His accent was pure enough, but there was a strange intonation or expression difficult to describe. I was completely subdued by the sheer personality of the man, yet I found courage to say—"You have come here all the way from the Himalayas?"

"Yes. But that is not our present business. There was one known to you as Martin Calthorpe, whom you suppose to be in some way connected with the death of your younger sister, and the illness of the one still living. Tell me briefly all you know about this man."

I told him the little that I knew, and also what I guessed. His chiselled face remained impassive during my speech. He was silent for some moments; then he turned to Thornton.

"The man is not unknown to us," he said. "He took the darker path many years ago, and developed some powers. By the unbridled use of those powers he finally wrenched away his lower personality from the higher self, and when the time came he passed from earth suddenly. Doubtless he was what you call killed. Being so utterly evil, he found it necessary—you understand."

Thornton sat bolt upright, deadly pale.

"Of course," he stammered: "I—I should have known; but—but these things are so incredible——"

"You were always of the sceptical ones," said Ravana Dâs, with his gentle smile. "This being is happily one of the last of his kind. We must destroy him."

"Destroy him?" I repeated. "But you say he has already been killed!"

"He has been what you call killed. That is probable. Words are misleading. Our task now is to put it out of his power to do further harm; and I think that can be done."

I was silent, pondering these enigmatical words. When I looked up the Hindu had gone. I turned to Thornton, but he grasped my hand, and said—

"Come again to-night, Frank. I promise you the end of all this horror."

I understood that I had to leave, and went away in a confused and dissatisfied state of mind, yet with a growing hope struggling to rise in my heart.

On my return home, I found the house in a commotion. The cause was soon made known to me. My father had shot himself. Connie was prostrated by the shock and could not be seen. A note was handed to me.

"My Dear Frank" (it read),—"I can bear up no longer. I killed that man's body and now I go to find his black soul. If the wretch's own beliefs are correct, I shall meet him in some sphere of troubled or erring spirits, and there our lifelong war shall be renewed. It is my fate. He and I are bound together. He is striking at me through my loved ones, but the end has not yet come. Farewell!"

A madman's letter? So I should have thought, but for the meeting with the Hindu mystic. Now, to my bewildered mind, all things seemed possible. In some strange realm "out of space, out of time"—I pictured two unhappy, crime-stained, earth-bound spirits, grappling with each other, entangled in an awful conflict for a supremacy that should be eternal.

V.

The requirements of the law having been hastily complied with, I tried to pull myself together for the night's appointment. In a few hours Connie had recovered sufficiently to see me, and I found her, though prostrated in body, calm in mind.

"These are cruel things that have come upon us, Frank," she said, in a tone of gentle resignation, "and I am afraid you will soon be left alone——"

"No, no, Connie!" I said. "It's all unutterably strange, but I have a feeling that something is being done for us even now, when all seems at the blackest. My dearest, you must not lose heart!"

She looked at me strangely. My careless, man-of-the-world attitude in religious matters had often pained her devotional nature, and perhaps she took my words as indicating a reviving trust in the mercy of Providence.

"I feel that I would rather be with dear Winnie," she murmured: "yet I would not like to leave you, Frank."

"Harry wouldn't like to lose you either, sis," I replied, with some faint effort at cheerfulness, at which the ghost of a smile appeared on her pallid lips.

As soon as darkness came I hurried away to Thornton's rooms. He was waiting for me.

"There is work for us to-night, Burford," he said. "My master has traced the whole thing from the beginning."

"An Indian Sherlock Holmes?" I muttered.

"No, nothing of that sort. These men work on different lines—not, perhaps, so very different, though, if the truth were known. He has only to change his centre of consciousness, and read what we call the akashic records—pictures automatically photographed, as it were, upon the ether by all the events that have ever happened—and— But what's the matter? Anything new?"

He had noticed a change in me. I told him of the tragedy at

home. Though greatly shocked, he did not seem very much surprised. He read my father's last words with attention.

"It's a great misfortune, old fellow; but don't let these lines disturb you. The vibrations set up by your father's last thoughts will take him into very unpleasant states of consciousness for a time, no doubt; but he will never meet Calthorpe again—that gentleman goes to his own place to-night. And your father will be helped— there is no doubt of that."

"You seem to know all about it," I said wearily. "But where is your master, as you call him?"

"He is here!" said the young man, gravely.

I turned. The Hindu was seated on a chair beside me. This time I was positive that he had not entered by the door, and a moment before the chair had been empty.

"We must go," said Ravana Dâs, ignoring my amazement. "My time is precious."

"Come!" said Thornton.

We went into the street and boarded a South Yarra tram, just like a trio of ordinary mortals. The Hindu was silent until Domain-road was reached, then he said to me—

"Whatever happens, friend Burford, you must not let your nerve desert you. You have a house in a street called Caroline?"

"Caroline-street—yes. But it is empty."

"Assuredly there are no ordinary tenants there. Yet we shall find someone. I think it will be necessary to destroy your house."

"As you please; but it's rather a fine property."

"Property—wealth—all illusion!" muttered Ravana Dâs, and he spoke a few words to Thornton which I did not catch.

We alighted at Park-street, near the gates of the Botanical Gardens, and walked thence to the street in which the house stood. Together we entered the empty house. Thornton produced an electric torch, and we passed along a passage and reached a store-room or pantry, from which we descended some steps into a cellar, the Hindu guiding us. Except for some lumber, the cellar was quite empty.

"Whatever you see," whispered Thornton, "be silent until he speaks!"

The Hindu stood with folded arms gazing intently at the wall opposite the entrance. Several minutes passed in profound silence. Suddenly a brick fell to the floor. It seemed to come from near the top. It was followed by others in quick succession, till in a few moments an opening was made revealing a small, inner cell, from which came the acrid odour of cement mingled with that of long pent-up air. The Hindu, of whom I now stood in the utmost awe, but in nowise feared, signed us to enter.

Raising aloft his torch, Thornton went first, and I followed. There was but one object in the cell, and that was the dead body of a man; and there needed no ghost from the grave to tell me that it was the mortal remains of Martin Calthorpe. It was stretched upon the earthen floor, and stared with glassy eyes at the low, cemented ceiling.

The body was that of a man in the prime of life—a portly, well-nourished body that might have been merely asleep, but for the staring eyes and a bullet-hole in the centre of the forehead. There was not the least appearance of decay—no more than if the man had just been killed. There was even colour in the cheeks. I thought of another corpse lying at my almost desolated home, and a dull, deadly rage began to swell up within my heart.

Then wonder and horror possessed me. How could this body have been preserved so long? Had Calthorpe met his fate so recently? Or had the walling-up of the cell—

"He has been thus a year or more," said Ravana Dâs, answering my thoughts. "But to your work," he added, taking the torch from Harry.

Signing to me, Thornton took the body by the shoulders, a hand under each; I took the ankles, and we essayed to lift it. Harry is an athlete, and my own strength is above the average, but our utmost efforts quite failed to move the corpse.

"It's no use," said the young man, with a gasp, and we fell back, I in a state of speechless amazement.

"Use your blade, then!" said the Hindu.

Thornton drew from under his coat a heavy Goorkha sword, and approached the body, as though that lifeless clay were a living foe. My feeling of hatred had returned, and I set my teeth.

Thornton bent his knee, and aimed a powerful blow at the dead man's neck. To my unutterable horror the blade stopped within a few inches of its mark and flew from the striker's hand. He retreated, dazed.

The Hindu turned to me.

"Take the weapon," he said, calmly. "After all, it is the son who should avenge his father." He gave the torch to Harry, and stood at the feet of the corpse. One glimpse I caught of his bronze features, and it was no longer a living man I saw. It was incarnate Will!

Nerved with a power not my own, I grasped the sword and aimed a deadly blow. It was stopped as before, and my arm tingled as though I had struck a log of wood.

"Again!" cried the Hindu, raising his two hands, and thrusting them forward over the body.

It was like an order to the soldier in battle. I struck; and this time the heavy blade met with no resistance. The head rolled aside, and there gushed from the trunk torrents of rich, red blood, until the body seemed literally to swim in it.

"It is done!" said the voice of Ravana Dâs. "You know the rest. Farewell!"

He was gone.

The work of carrying the corpse (which was easily lifted now) to one of the upper rooms was accomplished in silence. Fifteen minutes later we stood amongst a rapidly increasing crowd of people, watching a dense mass of flames spurting from all quarters of the wooden house. The roof fell in, and when it became certain that no part of the building could be saved, we left.

It was not yet very late, though it seemed to me that ages passed since I left home. We returned to Harry's rooms, for I was thirsting for some explanation of the things I had seen.

I was feverish with excitement, but Thornton seemed to have acquired something of his master's self-control; and when we were comfortably seated in his little den, with the pictured pale-bronze features of the Indian occultist gazing benignantly down upon us, my friend entered into an explanation which, I must confess, only increased my amazement.

"This Calthorpe," he began, "was a man who had given himself up entirely to evil."

"That much seems to be abundantly evident," I interjected.

"You must try and realise, however, what is meant by the absolute rejection of the good in every shape and form. Ordinarily, evil is relative, not absolute—we seldom meet the aristocrat of crime. The fatal grandeur, the awful eminence of a 'Satan' is rarely revealed to us. Had this man been gifted with intellect in proportion to his wickedness, he could easily have made himself a national—ay, even a world-wide scourge."

"Yet he was not of a low type of intellect?"

"Too low to flee to the grander conceptions of crime. What he has accomplished we shall never know, for he wielded powers that enabled him to laugh at human justice, as your friend Detective Mainspray understands it."

"I have heard you say that the development of these occult powers depends on entire purity of thought and deed?"

"The full development—yes. You have seen how easily my master (who is himself only a disciple as yet) overcame by force of will the etheric resistance which Calthorpe was able to interpose between my sword and his precious neck. Yes, occult powers are, at their highest, united with great loftiness of character and nobility of aim; sometimes they are associated, in a limited form, with a grovelling and sordid nature; and, again, as in Calthorpe's case, they are seen in combination with positive malevolence and tendencies of an altogether evil kind. The so-called 'black magicians' of the Middle Ages were, no doubt, men of the stamp of Calthorpe. Such beings, gifted with powers which, though limited on their own plane, are superior to the workings of physical science as commonly known, must possess, as you will see, potentialities for active evil before which the imagination may well stand appalled."

"And this power—whatever it may be—how could this wretch carry it with him to the next world?"

"The power really belongs to the 'next world,' as you call it, and can be more readily exerted there. But let me explain. This man had literally thrown away the immortal part of himself, since he was all evil, and nothing that is evil can live. He was doomed to a sort of slow disintegration—the gradual conscious decay and death of the animal personality that had wilfully wrenched itself away from its immortal essence."

"You mean the soul? And what becomes of that?"

"It rests on its own plane, so to speak, till the time arrives for its next incarnation on earth."

"Very well. Go on."

"We know that Calthorpe was killed. Having some occult knowledge, he was aware that a soulless entity, deprived of its physical vehicle, was doomed to perish. The ordinary man, after the death of the body, remains for a time in a state the Hindus call 'Pretaloka' until his thoughts are entirely freed from earthly concerns. Pretaloka is the scientific fact behind the dogma of purgatory. While living, Calthorpe could, in trance, visit the lower levels of Pretaloka, and roam about there at will—that is, his thought could vibrate in unison with the vibrations of the spirit-matter of those levels, and thus function there."

"But this was only on condition, I understand, that he had a living body to return to?"

"Exactly. Being without a soul to which he could cling, he needed a body as a sort of point of support. Losing his physical life utterly, he would sink by a natural and inevitable law to a lower state even than Pretaloka, there to suffer, as I have said, the horrors of disintegration and decay, ending in the complete annihilation of the human personality."

"But what use could his body be when he was shot dead?"

"The effect of the bullet would be merely to transfer his consciousness to Pretaloka. By occult arts he could preserve his remains from decomposition as long as they were not disturbed. Evidently your father played into his hands by walling up the body in that cell. If he had only thought of destroying it, as we did, by burning down the house, thus severing the magnetic line of communication, so to speak, depended on by Calthorpe for mere existence, that worthy would have gone to his own place almost immediately."

"And that place is——"

"We will not speak of it," said Thornton, with a shiver. "As it was, in order to remain in the state called Pretaloka (for it is not a place), he was compelled to preserve his late vehicle—his body—in a sort of cataleptic trance, and that he could only do so by stealing vitality from the living and transferring it to the corpse."

I shuddered as I recalled the scene in the cell—the torrents of fresh blood.

"Then," I muttered, "this—this creature was nothing but a vampire?"

"A vampire, indeed—glutting his vengeance and serving his necessity at the same time. Remember how his wife died—she was his first victim; and her fate was the more terrible because she knew what was happening. Calthorpe was a 'black occultist' of inferior powers, or he would probably have been better known to my master, in which case help might have come sooner."

"His powers seem to have been sufficient for his purposes," I said, bitterly.

"Yes. Yet, with a deeper knowledge, he could have dematerialised his body, and removed it to some inaccessible place; and, again with wider powers, he could have kept it alive by extracting the necessary vitality from the physical air, which contains all that is needed for human sustenance. But his fate was decreed, and he himself was the instrument of his own undoing."

"That may be very well, old man, but it doesn't bring back Winnie and the poor, old dad."

"They are far better off where they are, Frank. Religion and occultism agree on that point, as on so many others. The grief of friends for those gone before only harms them, for it attracts their thoughts earthward during their stay in that realm of illusion I have called Pretaloka, and so delays them on their journey heavenward. Thus we should not grieve, but rather, in the words of the poet—

"'Waft the angel on her flight with a paean of old days.'"

"And—and is the creature finally disposed of? Is Connie entirely freed from all further peril?"

"You shall see!" said the young man, his voice vibrating with confidence and joy. "We have slain the cockatrice. Its power for evil is now confined to its own plane. The thing is perishing with its self-created poison. Let us think of it no further."

"One more question," I said. "How did your Indian teacher get here if he were away in the Himalayas only the day before?"

"What we saw was not his physical body at all. The body is the prison of the soul for ordinary mortals. We can see merely what comes before its windows. But the occultist has found the key of his prison, and can emerge from it at pleasure. It is no longer a prison for him—merely a dwelling. In other words, he can project his ego, his soul, his true self—whatever name you choose to give it—out of his body to any place he pleases with the rapidity of thought."

"He seemed a substantial enough body, as far as I could see."

"Doubtless. Thought is creative in a deeper sense than we dream. Science tells us that all the materials that constitute our physical bodies exist in the air we breathe. An advanced occultist can draw thence by the power of will all he needs for a temporary vehicle in which to function; or, if he so prefers he can produce by illusion all that he wishes people to believe they see."

We talked on till daylight, neither of us feeling any desire for sleep. Thornton went deeply into his strange teachings, and I heard for the first time a great deal that was wildly incredible, but I had to confess that, if it was madness, there was no lack of method in it.

Early in the morning, feeling the need of fresh air and action, we set out on foot for my home, still discussing the tremendous questions of man's life and destiny.

Arrived at the house, a servant informed us that Connie was in the morning-room, and that breakfast was served there. Somewhat surprised, and forgetting our unwashed and unkempt condition, we entered. Connie was seated at the table, with a liberal repast before her.

She arose hurriedly, a bright flush suffusing her cheeks.

"I—I felt so hungry," she said; "you really must excuse me——"

I fell into a seat, giving way to a fit of hysterical weeping. And a rush of terrible memories surged up within my heart, and Harry, for all his assumed calmness, incontinently joined in my sudden emotion, and the scene was at once ludicrous and tragic. Two strong young men crying like children, and a delicate girl—whom they had helped in a humble degree to rescue from the clutches of a monster—doing her utmost to soothe them.

It was some time before we could join Connie at her breakfast, but when we did I felt that the meal inaugurated a new period of health and happiness for the dear girl and her devoted lover, and formed a peace and resignation such as I had lately despaired of.

www.ingramcontent.com/pod-product-compliance
Lightning Source LLC
Chambersburg PA
CBHW020841020726
47497CB00005B/1204